INSURRECTION

A Drake Cody Suspense-Thriller Book 4

TOM COMBS

Evoke Publishing

Title: Insurrection

Author: Tom Combs

First Edition: June 2021

Copyright © 2021, Tom Combs

ISBN: Print: 978-0-9903360-8-2

eBook: 978-0-9903360-9-9

Published by Evoke Publishing, 2021

OTHER NOVELS BY TOM COMBS

NERVE DAMAGE (Book 1)

A break-through experimental treatment developed by emergency physician and medical researcher Drake Cody places him and his family in deadly peril. Renegade agents of the trillion-dollar pharmaceutical industry will stop at nothing – including murder – to get possession of the invaluable drug. Mystery, greed, and violence force Drake and his wife to fight for their children, their love, and their lives.

- An Amazon International Bestseller.

- "This book has everything... murder, sex, heroes, villains, 'the good, the bad, and the ugly.' I couldn't put this book down. The action is nonstop. I highly recommend this book."
  – *The Journal of Emergency Medicine*

- "Masterfully written...grabs hold of your jugular right from page one and refuses to let go until the shocking conclusion... a lightning-fast read packed with twists and turns that will keep readers fully engaged and continually guessing. This is the stuff blockbusters are made of!"

HARD TO BREATHE (Book 2)

When an injured woman arrives at the ER with a report of a fall, Drake has her wealthy businessman and hospital board member husband arrested for domestic violence. The sociopathic husband is deeply involved in criminal business dealings, and an abuse trial and conviction will topple his illicit empire.

Within hours, Drake's ugly past is revealed and his medical license threatened. Drake will not yield as a diabolical killer, billion-dollar intrigue, and corruption target him, his victimized patient, and those he loves. Drake fights his way through a legal/criminal/medical maze, where each passing second can take it all away.

- "Nonstop suspense, complex characters, unexpected twists, and 100% authenticity make *Hard to Breathe* a truly great read…"
  – Michael Stanley, Internationally acclaimed mystery author

WRONGFUL DEATHS (Book 3)

- *International Bestselling Medical Thriller*

This fictional but authentic tale puts the reader on the front lines of the opioid epidemic and exposes intrigue, greed, and crime within the medical, legal and business worlds.

- "One of the BEST surprise endings ever penned."
  – TopShelf Magazine

- "Combs writes with formidable expertise…the perfect blend of suspense, action and real-world drama."
  – Laura Childs, New York Times best-selling author

- "Wrongful Deaths starts at a high pitch and never slows down. 'Ripped from the headlines' might be a cliche, but it's a true one for the former ER physician's third thriller in his Drake Cody Suspense series.

    – St. Paul Pioneer Press

John Grisham brought legal suspense and intrigue to the mainstream –
Tom Combs has done the same with
the world of medicine.

DEDICATION

Insurrection is dedicated to two FBI agents with vast anti-terrorism experience, who graciously shared their experiences and knowledge with me as I was writing the novel.

FBI Special Agent Thomas O'Connor, Domestic Extremist Threats expert and veteran of decades on the Joint Terrorism Task Force, also previously worked as a police officer specializing in narcotics and violent gang activity. Thomas is currently the Principle Consultant at FedSquared Consulting, providing instruction and consultation on a variety of counterterrorism topics to both government and private-sector clients.

FBI Special Agent Christopher Langert, former unit chief of Domestic Terrorism and Weapons of Mass Destruction investigations, has also served as Minneapolis FBI Hostage Negotiations Team Leader since 2014. His recent successful resolution of bank robbery and hostage taking in St. Cloud, MN received national coverage.

Like those identified in dedications to my previous books, these guardians of our safety and all their FBI/law enforcement colleagues are exceptional people committed to helping others despite great cost to themselves.

All the best to these agents, their colleagues, and everyone working to keep our country safe. The challenge is great.

CHAPTER ONE

Emergency medicine physician Drake Cody scanned the new pipeline's final section as it carved through the forest and fields to the refinery on the western edge of the Twin Cities. The wooded areas had been gashed, and the bulldozed earth lay as raw and dark as the slash of a knife wound.

The contested oil pipeline project stoked white-hot emotion. Today's event commemorating its completion guaranteed protest, and protest in Minneapolis these days often meant violence. Despite the threat, Drake was pleased to have been selected to be part of the dignitary medical protection team. The autumn colors and fresh air beat the heck out of his regular duty in the emergency room's windowless, high-pressure frenzy.

The petrochemical refinery loomed behind a temporary stage festooned with giant red, white, and blue balloons. Arrowhead Refinery was a massive mechanical jungle of white and chrome structures. The huge tanks holding petroleum and hazardous materials dwarfed the buildings and networks of ladders and metal scaffolding. The refinery grounds themselves were security-fenced and locked down. No one could enter there without armed challenge.

Drake stood next to his hospital's newest ambulance seventy-five yards from the podium of the covered outdoor stage. He estimated the crowd to be about two thousand—ordinary-looking, other than a few holding placards or decked out in gas masks or Halloween-like skeleton garb.

Drake and the two paramedics with him were present to provide medical dignitary protection for the event's main speaker, rocketing-up-the-polls presidential candidate, Minnesota senator Hayden Duren.

The unusual addition of Drake as a hospital ER-based physician to the on-site medical team testified more to the anxiety of those up the ladder than need of his expertise. The paramedics with Drake were ninjas in pre-hospital emergency care. Russell had covered three US presidents' appearances in the past, and Deb had seen everything in her twenty-year career.

"I thought we'd be positioned closer to the senator so we could get to him quicker if needed," Drake said.

"I thought the same at my first one of these, but we need to maintain a buffer zone on these dignitary protection assignments," Russell said. "If an explosion, weapons fire, or anything ugly happens, we can't help the senator or anyone else if we've been blown to shit."

"Makes sense." Drake leaned back, soaking up the blue sky and warm sunshine. If all went well, he could be home with Rachelle and the kids by late afternoon. "It's definitely too nice a day to get blown to shit."

"America the Beautiful" began playing from the public address. A man in a suit walked on stage and approached the podium framed by the huge balloons tethered over and around it.

"Welcome, everyone, to the celebration of the completion of our tremendous new pipeline!" Applause, boos, and shouts arose from the crowd. "This pipeline is not only delivering essential energy to power our country but also an inflow of jobs and money to the citizens of the state of Minnesota!"

More applause and cheers with a few boos. The smiling man on the stage raised his hands.

"As CEO of Fenbridge, I want to thank you and reassure everyone that we always have the environment and your safety in mind." More boos and shouts sounded. "Without further delay, let me introduce

Senator Hayden Duren. The senator was initially not a supporter of this project, but we appreciated and readily accepted the proposals he suggested. His plan reinforces our commitment to environmental safety and guarantees that the state of Minnesota's conservation fund will receive millions of dollars every year the pipeline is in operation." Applause came from both sides of the crowd. "Thank you, Senator Duren. The podium is yours."

Drake and his crew had met the senator a half hour earlier. Apparently, he'd insisted on meeting and thanking everyone involved in his security. The older man's friendly manner, direct gaze, and warm handshake had Drake believing the guy might be as genuine as the campaign hype promised.

The pipeline executive backed away from the podium, applauding as the tall, fair-haired senator entered from stage left in a dark suit. The billionaire businessman-turned-politician crossed to the microphone.

"Thank you." Senator Duren smiled. "We live in contentious times, but the future is bright if we work together. Wisdom and kindness are required to—"

BOOM! Balloons exploded outward from above the podium. Drake flinched. The senator dropped to the stage floor as people screamed. A white cloud descended from the center of the blast, enveloping the senator and stage in a dense fog. A second report sounded from the far side of the crowd and a larger white cloud spewed into the air.

People ran screaming toward the parking area.

"Let's go. Our guy is in the middle of it," Drake said.

Russell keyed the microphone clipped to his uniform as he and Drake jumped in the rig. "Biohazard emergency on site, airborne material. Trigger hazmat and EMS mass-casualty protocol." He flipped a plastic-wrapped bundle at Drake. Deb had the rig moving. "Full protective gear, doc, including respiratory mask."

As Drake ripped open the pack, he caught a whiff of ammonia and a second faint but acrid odor. It was something he'd smelled before.

His memory clicked. Could it be? *Oh man.*

This could be a ticket to hell.

～

SIX MINUTES EARLIER

Tolman Freid held his cellphone to his ear, head bowed. He stood alone in the pipeline event's parking area, but he pictured his wife as if he were standing at her side looking down on her.

She didn't have good days anymore.

"I'm so sorry, sir. Mrs. Freid doesn't respond," the nurse said. "I told her you're on the phone but... Well, you know."

A screech of the public address system intruded. From Tolman's spot next to his black Lincoln, he viewed someone testing the microphone on the balloon-covered stage two hundred yards distant. The petrol scent of the refinery hung fainter than on most days. The sky shone blue and cloudless.

"Mr. Freid, can you hear me?" the nurse said.

"I'm here." His emptiness and hurt never lessened. "Please give me a minute."

It had only been five weeks since he'd had to place Sonya in the memory care unit. She'd still had occasional clear moments back then. No more.

The woman who meant everything to him had become a haunted stranger. Day by day she worsened, and each visit twisted his heart more viciously. Now she spent her days in a wheelchair, clutching a baby doll, muttering nonsense, or crying out in fear of things that existed only in her head.

During this morning's visit, he'd hoped for at least a flicker. Anything. He'd told her he loved her and that he was sorry. No response. He could have been anyone. Or not there at all.

"Thank you for trying. Take good care of her, nurse. Make sure she has everything she needs." His voice broke. "Always." He disconnected.

How could the nurse give his wife what she needed? He hadn't.

Sonya needed to be on the land she loved. She needed her son with her. She needed the home they'd created. Those were the things that had kept her anchored.

Without them she was lost.

He choked down the blackness that filled him.

They'd taken everything from her—and stole her from him.

He looked up as the public address screeched again. The scheduled speakers—the senator and the CEOs of the pipeline and the refinery—stood in the sunshine at the side of the stage.

He'd seen enough.

Music began to play from the public address system. He checked the time, then climbed into his car.

He sighed. It would be soon.

Freedom was never free.

CHAPTER TWO

Drake pulled on his N-95 mask as Deb powered the ambulance toward the chaos around the stage. She braked hard. A clarion beep sounded from the ambulance radio. "Hazmat regional control alert to all responders. All police, fire, and other rescue personnel are to avoid approaching the refinery toxic site unless in full protective gear with a self-contained breathing unit. Repeat. Do not enter the contaminated area without self-contained respirator. No exceptions. Hazmat control out." Through his protective lenses, Drake saw two or three people on their knees at center stage while others were upright and being assisted off the other side. His eyes met Russell's. They did not have self-contained breathing gear, and to get it would take critical minutes the injured might not have.

They exited the rig as if ejected.

The cloud of vapor had settled. Drake raced up the steps and toward the senator who lay propped on one elbow on the stage. He'd been at the center of the cloud. Two men with dark suits and earpieces were crouched near him in defensive postures with guns in hand. They swiped at their eyes intermittently. A third man similar in appearance to the others was on one knee trying to pull the senator to his feet.

Senator Duren, a lean, mid-sixties man with a now-reddened face and bloodshot eyes, looked to be breathing hard.

The agent trying to pull him upright spoke. "Senator, we're going to get you on your feet, load you in a car, and get you out of here." A black Suburban was positioned just off the other end of the stage.

"Whoa. Hold on!" Drake said. "I'm Dr. Cody. The senator is our patient."

"He's your nothing," the agent said. "I've led his personal security detail for fourteen years. He's my responsibility."

"Stop. I'm going to assess him. You and everyone else need to get clear of the stage. Now!"

A second Memorial ambulance pulled into position with lights flashing some distance beyond the Suburban. "Get everyone who was on the stage to the ambulance there." Drake pointed.

Russell slipped an oxygen mask on the senator's face. Drake knelt by the senator, imagining how disturbing his goggles, respirator mask, Tyvek suit, and gloved appearance must be.

"Are you able to breathe, sir?"

"Yes, but it's hard."

The bodyguard leaned forward. "Senator, we'll get you to the car and haul ass out of here."

"Back off, agent." Drake recognized the senator's worsening distress. "We're transporting him by ambulance."

The senator raised a hand and placed it on the bodyguard's arm. "Marcus," he said, meeting the man's eyes. He shook his head.

"Here we go, sir." Drake and Russell picked up the senator in a two-man carry and hustled him toward the ambulance.

Marcus ran alongside. "Anywhere he goes, I go."

"Do what we tell you and don't get in the way," Drake said.

At the back of the ambulance they quickly peeled off the senator's coat and pants while Deb flushed them all with water. They put a paper gown on him and continued the oxygen. Deb jumped to take the wheel while Drake and Russell positioned the senator in the rig with his security man at the foot of the stretcher.

Deb hit the lights and guided the rig through to the parking lot and road, using yips of the siren to move people out of the way. No one in the crowd appeared to have collapsed. Fear showed on faces but no evidence of difficulty.

"How's your breathing, sir?" Drake said.

"Getting worse." His voice was soft and raspy. He coughed. "My face is burning, and it hurts to swallow."

Things were getting ugly fast. Drake's certainty grew—hydrofluoric acid. *Damn.*

Russell slipped an IV into the struggling man's forearm.

"You were exposed to an acid, Senator," Drake said. "You're very sick. We'll be doing a lot of things to you and moving fast, but hang with us. We're going to get you through this. Whatever happens, we've got you."

The senator's color had grayed, and his apprehension grew visibly by the moment. He nodded.

Drake's eyes met Russell's. The senator was crashing and crashing fast. Drake listened to the senator's chest as Russell completed the IV hookup and put on an oximeter.

Drake glanced at the security person.

"You okay? It's Marcus, right?"

"Yes to both. I didn't breathe it. The senator was in the middle of it. Take care of him."

The siren wailed and the big engine powered the ambulance off the refinery road and onto the highway. Seconds ticked by, and despite breathing treatments and maximal support, the senator's color rapidly went from ashen to dusky blue. As the oxygen level plunged, Drake's stethoscope revealed lungs that sounded like a flooding dishwasher.

"We're going to put you to sleep and take over your breathing for you, sir," Drake said with a hand on the struggling man's chest. "I've got you. You'll be okay."

The senator could only gasp and nod, his eyes wild.

Reassuring a crashing patient that things would be okay was not something that could be taught in medical school. It took heart-wrenching experience with dying patients to hide uncertainty so convincingly. Displaying rock-solid confidence and promising survival comforted and helped—even when the final outcome could prove the words false.

His gut told him this was one of those times.

CHAPTER THREE

Tolman guided his Lincoln east on I-94, heading from the refinery toward Minneapolis. He considered calling the memory care unit once more in the hope that Sonya might respond.

Imagine if she were to say his name? He sighed.

It wouldn't happen.

A news report came from the radio.

"WCCU interrupts our scheduled broadcast to report breaking news. A regional hazardous materials emergency has been issued for western Hennepin County. We have reports that a cloud of a currently unknown but hazardous chemical material was released during the public event announcing the opening of the highly controversial Fenbridge pipeline. Hazmat teams and emergency medical system units are responding to the Arrowhead Refinery. We have reports of casualties and an unconfirmed report that Senator Duren, who had been scheduled to speak at the event, may be one of the injured. It is unknown if this was an industrial mishap or a triggered event. Stay tuned for updates and public service announcements."

Tolman checked the time. Memorial Hospital was the nearest trauma center and burn unit. He'd studied the route.

He scrolled to his phone's contact listing for "Citizens" then hit *Send,* launching his pre-written text message.

Disasters triggered fear and panic, but certain people stepped up no matter how catastrophic things got. Their courage and actions could be predicted.

The success of his plan counted on it.

The flashing lights of a police car showed in his rear-view mirror. His stomach plunged.

He hadn't been speeding. *A cop pulling me over for cellphone use when there's a regional emergency?* He snorted and shook his head. Typical illegitimate government-sanctioned activity—police trolling the highway and stealing from free persons by imposing illicit tickets and fines.

He calmed himself as he pulled to the side of the highway. His timeline could not be compromised. Such a waste. He checked his side mirror. It wasn't a highway patrolman but a female suburban cop. The policewoman advanced. Tolman lowered the window and held his sovereign citizen license extended in his left hand. The officer reached for the document as she spoke.

"Good afternoon, sir. Using a cellphone while driving is a violation. I saw that you—"

BLAM! The slug from the .45 in Tolman's right hand entered the officer's body dead center between her collarbones and above her vest. She dropped like a puppet that had its strings cut.

Tolman's ears rang as the metallic and sulfur-tinged scent from the fired round registered. He tucked the weapon away, put the Lincoln in gear, and merged onto the highway. Traffic was not heavy.

He would not allow anything to obstruct his mission.

CHAPTER FOUR

The senator's rapid plunge demanded immediate and total respiratory support. The apprehension in his eyes was enough to signal Drake what needed to be done. Russell had the sedative and neuromuscular paralyzing drugs Drake had ordered ready for injection.

Drake nodded. Russell depressed the syringe's plunger. Seconds later the senator's eyes closed, his body spasmed once, then he went limp. As Drake used the handheld lighted scope to guide the endotracheal tube into Senator Duren's mouth, then down his throat and between the vocal cords into the trachea, he saw blistering and angry redness everywhere.

The acid was eating away the tissues. The scent of chemically digested flesh rose from the tube.

They connected the tube to the ventilator, and the now unconscious and chemically paralyzed senator's chest rose and fell as the machine delivered 100% oxygen and breathed for him.

Drake had once taken care of a worker whose cotton-gloved fingers had become dampened with a dilute hydrofluoric acid cleaning solution. Despite the minor exposure to a low concentration and timely treatment, the man had experienced prolonged pain and almost lost his fingers. Among hydrofluoric acid's horrifying features was that it continued to penetrate deeper into tissues and cause destruction for days. It was one of the most devilish materials in existence.

The senator had been in the center of the chemical cloud. Could he survive the amount of acid he'd inhaled? Drake had never heard of such a case. No definitive treatments existed.

Possible interventions raced through Drake's mind.

Russell updated Memorial ER by radio as Drake tried one last medication—one that, in theory, might help. It did nothing to change their patient's ominous course.

The senator's skin was now the freakish blue of deep cyanosis. His oxygen saturations were critically low, and Drake's stethoscope confirmed that the senator's lungs were drowning in fluid as the damage continued. Senator Duren had a blood pressure and pulse, but there was little doubt what his outcome would be unless Drake could radically change the trajectory.

Drake's protective eyewear were fogged with sweat. He ripped them off and fired them to the side.

"We're fifteen minutes out. What's our status, doc?" Russell held the radio mike in hand.

"We've done everything and it's not enough. His lungs can't deliver oxygen. He's going to arrest any minute." The acid was charring the senator's lungs like meat on a grill. Drake wrung his mind for anything he could do. Something. Anything. *Come on, Drake.*

Russell relayed Drake's grim report to the ER while Deb raced them down the highway with lights flashing and siren screaming. Drake looked into the agonized face of Marcus on his knees at the senator's feet.

"Save him. Please, doctor. He's more than my boss, he's my best friend."

Marcus recognized what Drake had not spoken aloud.

Death was at hand.

CHAPTER FIVE

Memorial Hospital ER

Dr. Michael Rizzini placed the last suture of many in the twenty-six-year-old's chainsaw-injured leg. A significant injury, but one Rizz could put on the path to full recovery. After local anesthetic, Rizz had been able to talk with the patient as he repaired the 4-inch gash to the thigh.

"You don't seem like you'd be a doctor," the young man said.

"Why?" Rizz smiled. "Because I'm too normal?" He backed his wheelchair up a bit.

"Well, uh, er...." The man pointed at the chair. "And you do seem like a normal guy."

"Believe me, I'm anything but normal."

The patient laughed.

"Anyway, thanks—I think," Rizz said. "You're going to get all the instructions written down. The sutures are not magic. If you overdo it, you're going to rip them out. Got that?"

"I got it. Sorry about being weird about the..." Again, the guy indicated the wheelchair.

"No worries. I'll be rid of it soon." Rizz wheeled out.

The emergency department corridor was bustling. Overhead pages, ringing phones, and a jumble of voices sounded. Memorial ER was long overdue for remodeling, but Rizz liked the traditional layout. Individual patient care rooms and larger treatment areas with their old-school curtain dividers were arranged along corridors that met at the open central space where the main desk sat behind a curved counter. A cramped physician radio room and the large glass-walled Crash Room opened onto the central area, completing the layout.

Standing almost anywhere in the department, Rizz could immediately sense the vibe of the place. The sights, sounds, and smells of the ER changed by the moment. In the twenty minutes it had taken him to fix the chainsaw injury, the pulse had quickened.

Rizz had been unable to work the past several months. A bullet to the spine had paralyzed him from the waist down. He was recovering with the help of Drake's experimental drug and marathon physical therapy sessions. Miraculously, he could now stand and take some steps unaided, but to handle work he needed the wheelchair. Today was his second shift since the injury.

He rolled to his computer.

Dr. Trist was at the neighboring console. The short, thin, fill-in doctor wore rainbow scrubs and his hair pulled back in a graying ponytail. The fiftyish *locums tenens* doctor was what some called a hired gun. Short-staffed hospitals hired these fill-in emergency doctors short term for good wages to help cover for their sick or injured regular doctors. The independent temporaries moved about the country working long hours and large numbers of shifts in short-staffed ERs for periods of one to six months. Rizz joked the grueling short-term positions were "take the money and run" jobs.

The state Medical Board required a probationary period during which Rizz's patient care activities were monitored by a physician colleague. Dr. Trist was serving that function for Rizz during this shift.

"Got anything to run by me?" Trist asked.

"Just one for now. A twenty-six-year-old guy in Room 16 with a chainsaw injury."

"Got it. I'll eyeball him," Trist said. "Document well. Use the app I showed you. Helps cover your ass on lawsuits and improves charges."

The temporary doc was older but very plugged in electronically.

Based on what Rizz had seen, the guy probably had an app for scratching his ass.

"We've had a run of new patients," Trist said, frowning. "Looks to me like maybe fifty percent have insurance. Another day of high work and low pay in the country of Emergistan. Does it piss you off to know that at least one in three patients you're sweating bullets to care for won't pay a cent?"

"No worries. Job security is ours." Both of Rizz's shifts found him working with Trist. A solid doc, but Rizz could do without the whining. He found it easy to ignore because he was jazzed being back doing the work he loved.

"Remember to take it easy on these first shifts. I heard about what you went through. It takes time to recover physically, but it's even tougher to get your head on right. It sucks to get screwed over and have your life totally trashed." Trist's eyes clouded and he stared off for a moment. "Been there and done that."

The bleat of the overhead alarm sounded, signaling an immediate need for a doctor to speak with paramedics. It silenced almost immediately. Seconds later, Dr. Amy Vonser hurried down the hall toward Rizz.

"Badness on the way," she said. "An explosion and a cloud of toxic gas at the refinery event. Drake's got a patient intubated, and multiple other casualties will likely be incoming. Burning eyes, trouble breathing. Sounds like chemical burns."

Unreal. Drake's cushy onsite medical standby assignment had gone bad. Disaster tracked Rizz's friend like a bloodhound.

"Burns or blast trauma—either way, they'll all be coming our way," Rizz said. Memorial Hospital was both the level one trauma center and the burn unit for the region. "Lots of wicked substances on the menu out there. We can't let any hazardous materials into the ER. Amy, can you get the decontamination room staffed and ready?"

"Got it." Amy headed for the room near the main ER entry.

Rizz turned to Trist. "Go through the department and clear out all patients who can be taken care of in the waiting room or who are non-urgent. Those headed for admission need to be run up to rooms right now whether staff upstairs are ready or not. There's no way to know how many we'll have incoming."

"Done deal." Trist moved down the corridor.

Despite Rizz being in a wheelchair and on probationary status, Amy had come to him. The locums doc didn't question Rizz as leader. Rizz's wild and reckless behavior outside of work made his personal life a demolition derby, but when it came to the challenges of the ER, he was in his element.

He pivoted his wheelchair and moved toward the central station. Knowing the members of the ER team turned to him when things looked bad pumped him up. He felt more alive than at any time since the bullet had trashed his spine months earlier.

Responding to a potential disaster made him feel good. *How twisted is that?*

He almost felt bad about his reaction...almost.

CHAPTER SIX

Downtown Minneapolis

Tolman pulled into the parking ramp on 10th and Chicago Avenue and found a spot.

He pulled the suitcoat off the hangar hook in the back and put it on. He grabbed the thick, leather-bound, zippered folio from the seat as he slipped his credentials lanyard around his neck:

Tolman Freid

Federal Hazardous Materials Management

Head – Midwest Division

He'd considered entering a false name, but there was no need. Abuses of families, lives, legacies, individual rights, and freedoms were too numerous for the corporate-government machine to track—his name would not stand out. He was just one of many thousands.

He exited the parking ramp stairwell and stopped at the crosswalk light. Two grizzled, homeless men sat on the curb wearing ratty coats despite the warmth, passing a bottle in a brown paper bag. Memorial Hospital and the ER entrance waited a half-block away.

The light changed to green. Tolman headed forward.

The system would not change without sacrifice. Whatever happened in the next hours or days, one thing was certain.

Nothing would ever be the same.

There would be no going back.

RIZZ WHEELED out of the radio room.

The medic had relayed Drake's suspicion of hydrofluoric acid. Brutal stuff. He hoped Drake was wrong, but he rarely was.

His intubated patient was the state senator Hayden Duren. Grim.

No word on how many others had been exposed or their severity. ETA for the senator was fourteen minutes. They had to be prepared for the worst.

Rizz wheeled to the center of the medical instrument and technology-packed Crash Room. The four specialized bays were designed and equipped to treat those with catastrophic illness or injury. Only the most critical, every-second-counts patients were placed here. Unusual and fortunate that it was now empty. If the senator made it to the ER alive, this is where he'd be.

The Life Clock above the bed in Crash Room bay two had been triggered at the time of the initial paramedic call. The red numerals flashed the critical minutes and seconds elapsed. The clock would track the time until the senator was stabilized and admitted to the hospital—or was pronounced dead.

Even when empty, the countless number of lives that had been saved or lost here made the place feel to Rizz as sacred as any church.

As Rizz turned toward the central ER desk, he noted a throng of non-medical people had entered the department. The medical and trauma team alerts had brought the needed additional nurses and others to the ER, but there were many more people than that. Too many.

He spied Stuart Kline, the CEO of the hospital. Kline had Patti, the charge nurse, cornered near the main desk, wagging a finger in her face.

Kline. Even Drake, who followed the "if you can't say something nice" practice, identified the head administrator as the trifecta of "arrogance, ignorance and self-interest." Rizz reckoned Drake had missed a few ingredients in the Kline recipe, including dishonesty and greed.

Rizz wheeled up and *accidentally* caught the back of the CEO's leg with his chair.

"Ow!" Kline whirled, frowning. "What're you doing here, Rizzini? You should still be on leave. The senator is en route and there could be more big-name patients. You're crippled. We need the best. Get specialists down here and have them take care of the senator and any other VIPs. I told her," he flipped a thumb toward Patti, "she needs to get OR and ICU nurses down here now. Nothing but the best. I'm going to—"

"You are going to shut up," Rizz said matter-of-factly. "You'll tell the charge nurse nothing. She knows her job. You don't."

Kline's eyes bulged. "What did you say?"

Kline had been trying to get Rizz and Drake fired for some time. Powerful allies and past actions had deflected Kline's efforts so far. He had no understanding of patient care and was generally detested by nurses and physician staff, yet he somehow remained CEO. His cut-throat management style might be helping the financially struggling hospital's bottom line, but he had no idea what the hospital was really truly about.

Rizz pivoted his wheelchair.

"Patti, Dr. Trist is clearing as many patients as possible out of the department to free up beds, and the decontamination room is ready. Let the hospital nurse manager know we're into our multiple-casualty protocol. We know of one critical patient, but otherwise the number and severity are uncertain."

Patti hustled off, giving directions as she moved.

Rizz turned back.

"I am the CEO of this hospital! You—"

"Save it, Kline." Rizz sighed. "We're facing a potential multiple-casualty disaster, and the emergency medicine doctors and our team will handle it. This is our specialty. We are the experts. You're an accountant who's been promoted a few times too many. Be quiet and stay out of the way."

Kline looked as if his head might explode. "When this is over, I'll have you in front of the hospital board. You're done."

"Whatever. Don't mess with my people and keep out of the way." Rizz turned as Dr. Trist led a group of nonurgent patients and others toward the waiting room. "Good work, amigo. Anyone not essential to patient care should get out of the department and leave the hospital grounds. We've gone to lockdown."

Rizz turned back to where Kline stood.

"You still here?"

"A United States senator is coming to my hospital, and I'm going to make sure—" The doctor-to-the-radio alarm sounded.

Rizz wheeled to the radio room.

"Dr. Rizzini here."

"Ambulance 425 here." It was paramedic Deb. A siren sounded in the background. "Patient is intubated and receiving maximum treatment, but his vitals continue to dive. He had hydrofluoric acid exposure and has profound pulmonary injury. He's deeply cyanotic and his oxygen level is not measurable. ETA is ten to fifteen minutes."

Kline pawed at Rizz's shoulder. "What does that mean?"

Rizz ignored Kline. "425, any idea on number of other victims or their status?"

"A couple of executives from the stage were exposed and are being transported. They didn't look as bad. The crowd around the second eruption was all on their feet and moving away. Didn't see any who looked seriously compromised, but not sure."

"10-4. We'll speed the senator through decontamination and see you in Crash Room bay two. Rizzini out." Hydrofluoric acid. *Damn.*

Kline once more stuck his face in front of Rizz. "What did all that mean?"

Rizz pushed back from the radio and rubbed his eyes. "Drake and the paramedics are doing everything possible, but the senator's lungs are devastated. What it means," Rizz paused, "is that barring a miracle, the senator will be dead before Drake and the crew arrive."

CHAPTER SEVEN

Sweat drenched Drake's face, and the surgical mask fogged with his breath. He'd put on the surgical gown for the procedure over the hazardous materials protective garb underneath.

"Quick prep, please, Russell." The paramedic splashed antiseptic over the senator's exposed left groin and thigh area as Drake pulled on sterile gloves.

"Deb, pull over. We need to be still for a moment." The ambulance slowed, swerved, and stopped. Drake placed fingers at the crease of the senator's thigh and groin, finding the femoral pulse. Using those pulsations as a landmark, he plunged the syringe's four-inch-long needle through the skin and tissues. He advanced it using feel and knowledge of anatomy as his guide while exerting gentle traction on the plunger. The plunger gave as dark-purple blood flashed into the syringe, confirming he'd entered his femoral vein target.

He inserted the guide wire through the needle and then threaded the catheter into the vessel.

He repeated the procedure, entering the adjoining pulsing artery. Blood of purplish hue rushed into the attached syringe. The lack of the normal cherry-red color of the arterial blood confirmed the desperately low oxygen state of their patient.

Senator Duren's lungs could not keep him alive.

Drake quick-stitched the intravascular tubing, securing the lines within the groin vessels of the senator's circulation. Russell purged the lines and connected them to the extracorporeal membrane oxygenation device, rerouting the blood through the cutting-edge technology known by its initials—ECMO. The blood flow of the femoral artery and vein would circulate the senator's entire blood volume through the machine in minutes. The flow now coursed purple out of his body and into the device and returned to the senator a cherry red.

"We're in. Go!" Drake said. The ambulance jumped forward.

The newest of all life-saving technologies had just recently become available in Intensive Care Units and ERs in top hospitals. Memorial Hospital's new tricked-out ambulance was outfitted with the technology as part of a study Drake and Rizz had proposed. The device could potentially save lives if gotten to patients sooner. It had never been initiated in an ambulance.

If the Senator died, Drake would be accused of contributing to his death by delivering reckless and unproven care. Drake knew the truth. Without ECMO, the senator had no chance.

Drake could handle accusations of wrongdoing—he'd faced them before. He couldn't deal with failing to do everything possible to save his patient's life.

The senator's blood circulated through the device. Within sixty seconds, his critically low oxygen saturation level nudged upward. The deathly blue of his skin lessened slightly.

The senator balanced on the razor's edge between alive and dead. He looked ghastly but he was alive.

The radio squawked and a transmission that Drake could not make out came from the cab.

"Jesus, no!" Deb cried out. "Oh my God. Look out the window on the right."

Drake looked up and glimpsed an ambulance and two highway patrol cars with lights flashing on the side of the highway where officers crowded around a suburban police car.

"I just heard the report," Deb said. "It happened right here. An officer shot and killed."

No words. The muted sound of the siren, the soft hum of the ECMO device, and the blow-pause-hiss cadence of the ventilator as the senator's chest rose and fell as his devastated lungs filled and emptied. The acrid tinge of the deadly acid reached Drake's nose through the mask. Sweat trickled down his temples.

There was no question what the sheet-covered form on the ground next to the squad car was. A life stolen. Someone loved who was no more.

"Did they say who?" Russell's voice cracked.

Russell's long years of EMS and SWAT team involvement made him familiar with law enforcement practices. He knew as well as Drake that the victim's identification would not be given over the radio.

"It was a Maple Grove squad car. And they said *she*. They…" Deb's voice trailed off.

Russell's longtime girlfriend was on the Maple Grove police force.

Russell checked the lines, then rechecked the equipment settings. Somehow the medic maintained his focus. For an instant, his eyes met Drake's. The paramedic's pupils were wide and his face pale—he looked as if his heart had stopped.

CHAPTER EIGHT

ER

"I told you to back off," Rizz said.

The smell of Kline's cologne turned Rizz's stomach.

"Declaring him dead now is best for the hospital," the hospital's CEO said. "We can't have media reports saying, 'The senator was admitted to Memorial Hospital, where he died.' We're talking thousands of news reports—perhaps tens of thousands. If he's declared dead in the ambulance or dead on arrival, it avoids the negative press. You could declare him dead on arrival, right?"

"Get away from me," Rizz said. "Whatever happens, it's Drake's call. He'll do the right thing for his patient."

The overhead alarm sounded again. Rizz wheeled to the radio room. He slapped the transmit key.

"Rizzini here. Over."

"Ambulance 425." It was Deb. "The patient is on ECMO. Lines in place and exchange initiated. Oxygen saturations are rising. ETA is five minutes."

"See you in decontamination. Rizzini out." *Wow!* Drake had reached for the only chance the senator had.

Rizz spied Patti, the charge nurse, near the main desk. "Patti, please get an additional nurse to the Crash Room straightaway. Drake put the patient on ECMO."

Patti's jaw dropped, then she spun and grabbed a phone.

"What's happening?" the CEO said.

"Possibly a miracle," Rizz said. Drake trying something never before tried.

"Dr. Rizzini." A security guard approached. "There's a guy says he's with federal hazardous materials management at the security desk looking to talk to whoever is in charge. Says he knows about the refinery and you'll want to hear what he has to say. His ID and documentation look good, but we're on lockdown so I can't let him into the ER core unescorted."

Rizz made a "one second" gesture to the guard as Patti hung up the phone at the desk. The department buzzed in preparation.

"Patti," Rizz said. "Call a Med Team Stat for Crash Room bay two. Drake will run the case. ETA five minutes, but they'll have to go through decontamination. I'll be back in a minute. I may finally be finding out what went on at the refinery."

The guard led the way out the inner ER lockdown doors to the security desk station located between the outer corridor and the doors to the lobby.

The big man standing in the lobby on the other side of the glassed-off security portal looked imposing. Perhaps fiftyish, salt-and-pepper hair, clean-shaven, with the craggy features of an outdoorsman, he wore a business suit and held a zippered leather-bound folio. Rizz guessed the guy to be about six-foot-four. An insignia-marked ID badge hung around his neck. Rizz read:

Tolman Freid
Federal Hazardous Materials Management
Head – Midwest Division

The man spoke through the opening in the reinforced glass barrier.

"Tolman Freid, United States hazardous materials agent." His voice fit his appearance, deep and commanding. "We've learned what the refinery exposures are and I'm here to help. The cloud released from above the stage that exposed the senator was hydrofluoric acid.

Fortunately, it didn't appear to expose anyone beyond the immediate stage area. You're likely familiar with hydrofluoric acid. It's an incredibly bad actor, and this was industrial strength."

"I'm familiar, though I've never treated anyone with an exposure," Rizz said.

"Very few have. I noticed you've limited access to the ER and have a decontamination protocol. Excellent."

"We're in lockdown. No one is allowed into the emergency department core unless cleared by security," Rizz said. "What was the second material?"

"Anhydrous ammonia—we got lucky there. It was released some distance from the stage and near the crowd. It's serious but lightweight compared to hydrofluoric acid. I'd expect eye and respiratory irritation but little damage. The challenge in management is telling who was exposed to hydrofluoric acid and who to ammonia. I can help with that. Prevention and management of hazardous materials exposures is my job. Those who have only ammonia exposure could be observed in your waiting room and you can save the ER for those who need it."

"Absolutely." This was primary in Rizz's mind. "We're freeing up as many rooms as possible, but our capacity is limited." Once again, Rizz hoped the number of patients would be less than feared. "If we can keep low-risk folks in the waiting room, that's huge."

"This was highly concentrated, industrial-use hydrofluoric acid, so it will attack tissues hard and fast. If people aren't showing obvious burns or having significant pain or breathing trouble, it's highly unlikely they were exposed to the hydrofluoric acid."

Rizz had a textbook understanding of hydrofluoric acid exposures but no firsthand experience. He didn't presume to be an authority. "Sounds helpful."

"I'm the federal oversight supervisor for hazardous materials. I'd be glad to join you in the ER and help any way I can. I can also access federal resources as needed."

Coordinating with a sharp, knowledgeable federal resource person made sense. The guy had a striking presence and radiated competence.

"It's Tolman, right?"

"Yes. Tolman Freid."

"Dr. Michael Rizzini. Welcome aboard. Glad for the help." He gave a thumbs-up to the security guard, who activated the heavily reinforced outer ER doors. The man walked through and shook Rizz's hand. Rizz rolled through the outer corridor and into the chaos of the ER core with the big man at his side.

CHAPTER NINE

Refinery, minutes earlier

Due to security concerns, no media had been allowed contact with the speakers or near the stage. Phoenix Halvorsen had been on high ground near the back of the crowd when the gas clouds erupted. People, some screaming, stampeded toward the parking lot. A whiff of ammonia stung her nose. Some of those running were coughing or rubbing their eyes.

She'd watched an ambulance race up to the stage and another approach but stop about seventy-five yards away. They loaded one person and left quickly with lights and siren on. It had to be the senator. Her heart raced. *Front page and beyond!*

The second ambulance loaded two or three people and left with lights flashing but no siren. Probably the refinery and pipeline corporate executives. Of course—the fossil fuel fascists getting special treatment while the common people suffer.

Police strung a yellow tape perimeter about fifty yards from the now-empty stage. All people were kept back beyond that as evacuation continued.

Phoenix texted her editor a bare-bones report of the possible terrorist event with national implications, saying she'd follow with a guaranteed front-page story that would warrant Associated Press pickup and more.

The thought had her flying.

The gas clouds were no longer visible, and it appeared that most people were unharmed. The ammonia smell remained strong. The crowd slowed as the hysteria eased, but all continued to leave. Within minutes, more ambulances appeared. Small groups gathered around them. Phoenix moved closer.

That morning, the Star Tribune editor had initially assigned another reporter to cover the pipeline-refinery event. Phoenix had argued the assignment should be hers. The protest against the pipeline aligned with her passion for calling out greed, corruption, ecological destruction, and the bankrupt morality of present-day America. The Star Tribune editor had pointed out that it was a public event, not a protest. Once more, the paper's editorial staff mouthed the party line, afraid to upset the corporate world. How did they sleep at night?

Phoenix had acted as if she agreed. She'd placed a call to her father, and less than ten minutes later she'd received the assignment.

It was meant to be. She was in the middle of a monster of a story. She'd share her truth and burst onto the national media scene as she always knew she would.

She neared the remaining ambulances where medics were evaluating people. She heard a few coughs and saw several people rubbing their eyes, but none seemed to be seriously ill. *Hmmm.* She frowned. More casualties would ratchet up this rocket of a story even more.

"They're only transporting those with burns or who're having trouble breathing," a mid-twenties guy wearing a skeleton costume said. "This is what the fascist bastards are doing to us—doing to our planet."

Phoenix was pissed off, too. The refinery and the pipelines were outrageous assaults on nature and mankind. But who had triggered the chemical release? It hadn't seemed at all like an industrial accident. Had they targeted the senator and executives? Could environmental warriors be behind the explosion?

Phoenix needed to be there, up close and personal. She wanted to fashion the story in a way that supported her vision. If any activists suffered in the battle to halt environmental evil, she would make them heroes.

Oh hell yes! Her truth shared with the masses and an opportunity for her byline to go national—the ultimate rush. She'd make it happen.

She bent and stumbled toward the nearest ambulance. "Help me!" She produced a hacking cough. "I can't breathe."

An EMT wearing a white suit, gloves, and a mask reached out.

"Where were you?"

"Right up front. I ran. Having trouble breathing." She coughed again.

"We'll take care of you," the medic said. "We'll get you to the hospital, but first I need to wash you off. You were exposed to a strong acid." He had her step behind the opened rear ambulance door and take off her top and jeans. He sprayed her with water from a small hose and gave her a paper gown to put on. He listened to her lungs with a stethoscope, then guided her into the ambulance.

There were four others sitting on the cot and bench seat with oxygen masks on. A heavy, thirty-something white guy with black eyebrows that joined in the middle looked her up and down, lingering on her breasts. *God, what a creep!* She folded her arms across her chest.

The medic spoke to those outside the ambulance.

"You are not in immediate danger. If you are doing well, you can leave by private car and seek medical attention if you have issues. If you had any contact, discard your clothes and shower thoroughly. Do not touch or rub your eyes. More rescue personnel are coming for any who are concerned they aren't doing well."

"Let's roll," he called to his partner as he climbed in and shut the door. He turned to Phoenix and the others as the ambulance began to move. He clipped a monitor on her finger. "We're going to Memorial Hospital and you'll all be checked out there. Depending on how you're doing, you may not need to go into the ER. Fingers crossed."

Phoenix's wish did not match the paramedic's. The heart of the story was now in the ER. She'd do whatever she needed to get inside.

CHAPTER TEN

ER

Drake stripped in the decontamination room. He briefly felt the literally naked vulnerability he knew ER patients regularly experienced. The others in the room were either carrying out decontamination washdown or undergoing it themselves. He toweled off and slipped into clean scrubs and disposable slippers. Russell and Deb had remained at the ambulance, decontaminating and readying it to be back in service.

Marcus, the senator's bodyguard and friend, had been sprayed down and given paper pants and a gown. He was now putting on his holster and weapon, which had also been wiped clean. A state highway patrolman who was also part of the pipeline event's on-site security team had followed them in. Marcus directed him to take up a position just inside the ER's security-controlled entrance in the outer hallway rimming the department.

"The ER is in lockdown," Marcus said. "Hospital security lets no one in until cleared. Coordinate with them. You're backup if anyone tries to force their way in. We have more armed security coming."

There remained the faintest hint of the bitter odor of the hydrofluoric acid, but it was clearing quickly in the negative ventilation room. Marcus had refused further attention, but his reddened eyes and occasional cough had Drake concerned. The man had not let the senator get more than five feet from him.

It had taken time to pull over to the side of the highway to initiate ECMO, but Drake was certain that otherwise the senator would have arrived as a corpse. Other ambulances had already arrived, and patients were already in the ER. Only a few were still awaiting decontamination.

With their decontamination complete, they rolled the senator into the Crash Room. The resuscitation team stood ready to transfer the senator from the gurney to the bed in bay two. The Life Clock above the bed continued to blink the critical minutes and seconds that had elapsed since the senator's collapse.

The blood-filled lines that ran from the senator's femoral artery to the ECMO device and returned to his femoral vein were literally lifelines. Drake bird-dogged the transfer of the senator to the bed. Technological breakthroughs and medical treatments were not immune to the all-too-human mishap of a yanked line or other accident.

With the device working as a heart-lung bypass, the senator's dusky-purplish un-oxygenated venous blood entered the machine and returned through the IV tubing red and oxygen-rich. The machine accomplished what the senator's obliterated lungs could not. It was keeping him alive and, barring complication, might do so for some time.

Rizz wheeled into the crash room, followed by a tall guy in a suit with an ID hanging on his chest and carrying a thick leather-bound folio.

"Looks like fewer critical patients than there could have been," Rizz said to Drake. "Patti is charge nurse and she's been kicking ass. I asked Dr. Trist to free all possible beds and empty the department as much as possible. We're on lockdown, so any people from the scene who need the ER are coming through decontamination. Awesome move on the ECMO, brother."

"I'm virtually certain it's hydrofluoric acid." Drake pointed at Marcus standing on alert near the entry to the Crash Room. He'd put the hospital gown on so it opened in the front, which made his shoulder holster visible. "This is Marcus. He's head of senator Duren's security team and his friend. He may have had some acid exposure. We need to keep an eye on him."

"I'm fine." Marcus nodded, but his eyes never stopped scanning. "Take care of the senator."

"You're right, Drake. Hydrofluoric acid was released." Rizz indicated the impressive-looking man in the suit. "This is Tolman Freid. He's the federal hazardous materials oversight supervisor for the Midwest. His report confirms that there were two different clouds of gas. The one near the stage was hydrofluoric acid and the one near the crowd was ammonia."

"Fits what I saw," Drake said. "Thank God it wasn't all hydrofluoric."

"Roger that," Rizz said. "The senator is by far the worst. The Fenbridge pipeline and refinery executives were off-stage and avoided most contact. They beat you here. They're symptomatic but stable. Dr. Trist is managing them back in the telemetry area. Otherwise, there are a few suspected lesser exposures who just arrived. We're decontaminating them and beginning to assess. Beyond that, it appears most exposures were ammonia. Tolman helped triage, so we've been able to keep those patients in the waiting room. It's an ugly deal, but it could've been a lot worse. I think we're on top of things."

"Thanks for the help, Tolman. This is insanity," Drake said. Tolman was one of those people who had presence. He looked like a leader.

"It may seem insane," Tolman said, "but there must be a reason."

At that moment, a burly, tall, redheaded maintenance guy pushed a four-wheeled cart past the Crash Room. Four other men in work clothes followed.

"I asked to get that worker out of the ER a while ago." Rizz frowned. "And I'm not sure about those other guys, either. They look like nonurgent patients. What are they still doing here?"

"You don't know the worker?" Marcus said, stiffening. "You're not sure about the others?" The senator's bodyguard moved to the sliding glass door of the Crash Room and eagle-eyed them.

"They stopped by the security doors." Marcus pulled out his pistol.

"Jeez. Hold on, man." Rizz moved his wheelchair toward the bodyguard. "What the hell are—"

A deafening blast snapped Drake's head to the side as if he'd been sucker-punched.

The back of Marcus's head exploded. The senator's man dropped like a rock.

Drake turned, ears ringing as his stunned senses returned.

Tolman Freid stood, the leather folio open in his left hand and a blue-black slide-action pistol at the end of his extended right arm just inches from Drake's ear.

CHAPTER ELEVEN

Drake ran to Marcus and knelt at his side. He had no pulse, and a glance confirmed massive destruction and exposed brain matter—the senator's devoted friend and protector was beyond help.

The huge redheaded guy and the men near the main door were pulling weapons from the work cart while moving like a practiced drill team.

The highway patrolman who'd come to the ER as part of the senator's security detail ran in through the inner door. He held his gun outstretched.

"Police. Hands up!" he yelled.

Action unfolded in a blur. The man to the right of the redhead fired a pistol. The highway patrolman recoiled, then snapped off two shots in return. The redhead pivoted with a shotgun in hand. The close-range blast punched a crater in the patrolman's face.

The officer hit the floor, lifeless.

A hand grabbed Drake by the hair, and warm steel pressed against the back of his head.

"Breathe wrong and you're dead," Tolman Freid said.

The invaders bent over their injured man. He moaned and writhed, clutching his abdomen, his blood smearing the white floor.

"Father, Micah's hit bad," said the youngest looking, his voice breaking. "Oh no!"

"Sigurd, you shouldn't be here!" Tolman pushed Drake to the side, keeping his gun trained on him. The big man looked momentarily shaken. His posture quickly straightened. "Everyone ignore Micah. Complete stage one," he ordered. His crew snapped into action.

They quickly pulled more weapons from the cart. The big redhead yanked an axe from the cart, swung it, and cleaved the electrical connection bundle leading to the reinforced ER doors. Another of the now-armed invaders exited into the outer corridor separating the ED from the waiting room and the rest of the hospital.

A third man grabbed a length of chain and secured it around the steel handles of the access doors.

Drake spied Rizz on the floor of the Crash Room. He and his wheelchair had been dumped. He struggled to right it.

"Get excess personnel out of the ER. Lock down and arm all barriers," Tolman said. The redheaded man nodded, and he and two others ran into the corridor, pushing the cart ahead of him.

"Keep everyone covered," Tolman said. The remaining two men held semiautomatic rifles at the ready, though the young one never took his eyes off the wounded man on the floor.

Keeping his pistol aimed at Drake's face, Tolman stepped to the desk, reached over the counter, and grabbed the PA address microphone.

"All ER workers and visitors," his deep voice sounded throughout the department, "step into the hallway and get on your knees with your hands behind your head. Cooperate. You have the opportunity to join us as citizens in reclaiming our sovereign rights from the tyranny of the current illegitimate corporate-government abomination. Do exactly as I say or you will die." He clicked off the mike.

"We need a patient gurney here," Drake said to Patti, then turned toward Tolman. "Get your goons to help her move your injured man. I'll check the officer."

Tolman slammed Drake against the wall. The big man held Drake pinned with the gun jammed under his jaw.

"The cop doesn't need you," Tolman said. "He's dead. Save my nephew or you die."

CHAPTER TWELVE

Senator Duren hung suspended in his near-death state while the ICU nurse Tracy cared for him and monitored the life-saving equipment. As Drake feared, the highway patrolman had been dead before he hit the floor.

Drake bent over the man the officer's dying gunshot had hit. The terrorist leader's nephew now lay ashen and grunting in pain in Crash Room bed one.

His blood pressure was low, his pulse high, and the paleness of his skin, lips, and tongue confirmed significant and ongoing blood loss. Patti had placed IVs in both arms, and fluids raced into him.

Drake reached for the ultrasound transducer. Best known for use in pregnancy, the imaging technology revealed shadowy reflections of internal anatomy. Drake applied gel and placed the transducer on the abdomen. He angled and slid it across a belly covered with a swastika and "Aryan Brotherhood" tattooed in crude prison ink. The screen's display revealed the organs and a localized large, dark shadow that did not belong. The black area represented blood from internal bleeding collecting within the abdominal cavity.

Ultrasound could not reveal the site of the bleeding, but the entry wound was in the right upper quadrant of the abdomen over the liver. Repair of a gunshot injury there could be impossible for even the best of trauma surgeons.

Drake looked beyond the two men with rifles standing guard at the Crash Room door and spied the group's leader with microphone in hand.

It was a ruthless and well-planned takeover. How had they known how to overwhelm the ER security so easily?

"We are in control of the emergency department." Tolman's deep voice came from the recessed ceiling speakers. "All doors have been bolted, and we have placed armed devices that will detonate if the doors are disturbed. As I talk with you now, my texted message is being read by police and those who identify themselves as the authorities. You are completely cut off from the rest of the hospital and everything else. You are the guests of those who are fighting to return freedom to all the sovereign citizens of America. Anyone who fails to obey my commands will be executed without hesitation."

Patti, Drake's friend and the ER charge nurse muttered, "Well, yippee, all to heck. We got ourselves a full-blown terrorist nut job."

It was such a uniquely zero-back-down ER-attitude response that Drake felt a brief lift.

One thing their captors likely didn't know was brought home by Patti's response. If any people anywhere could handle a five-alarm, flaming, scarier-than-crap nightmare without losing their cool, it was the nurses, paramedics, techs, and others who worked in the batshit crazy world of the ER.

From the instant Tolman fired the shot that killed Marcus, Drake knew he was facing madness. However righteous the man may think his cause, nothing could justify these murderous acts. Tolman Freid killed without blinking.

Drake's responsibility was clear. The ER patients and the coworkers he admired and cared for so much needed to be kept alive. This madman and his goons would have to be taken down.

Drake had been locked up with violent criminals and psychopaths before. It had nearly killed him, and what he'd had to do to survive still haunted the shadows of his mind.

He faced that challenge again, but this time he had more to protect than himself.

CHAPTER THIRTEEN

Highway 94

The policewoman's body lay on the highway's shoulder like roadkill. A portable screen shielded her from the gawking eyes of the single lane of traffic passing the cordoned roadway and the phalanx of emergency vehicles.

Detective Aki Yamada stood at the murder site, the bright sunshine and blue sky startling in contrast to the ugliness he viewed. The murdered young woman wore the uniform of the suburban police force. The entry wound below the base of the officer's neck and between her collar bones seemed placed with geometric precision. Her eyes were closed and her face without expression—as if she'd not even had time to register surprise.

A dozen highway patrol and other emergency vehicles were parked with emergency lights flashing. Despite all the officers, investigators, and techs present, there was little talk—just grim faces, clenched jaws, and the sounds and smells of traffic. Sadness and anger hung like a shroud.

"She didn't call it in, but it's on her dashcam," the officer who had been first on the scene said. "Take a look."

The trooper led the way to the slain officer's car, sat in the driver seat, and turned the screen toward Aki. He leaned his head in.

They were silent as the image flickered. It looked like a routine traffic stop. The officer approached the pulled-over car. A silhouetted driver, an arm extended. She'd reached for the license.

Aki's breath caught as the officer collapsed to the pavement.

It had been only seconds. There couldn't have been more than a few words exchanged. Aki slumped against the roof of the car. His legs went weak.

Anger filled him as if it were in the air he breathed. The policewoman had been executed. There was a stone-cold murdering monster on the loose.

"The plates are fake," the trooper said.

"What?" Aki refocused.

"Yeah. We see these homemade plates from the sovereign citizen types. Like Posse Comitatus and the Waco extremist types."

Aki stepped to the front of the car and looked. At first glance they looked like government tax-exempt plates. The small lettering read "sovereign citizen."

The dashcam had shown a silhouette and an extended arm—nothing more.

"I put out a BOLO on the vehicle as soon as I saw the dashcam," the trooper said. "No hits yet."

"Hey, Detective Yamada. You need to see this." An officer trotted over holding a cellphone outstretched. "This text is all over. Someone has taken over the ER at Memorial Hospital."

Aki took the phone and read:

From: Sovereign Citizens

Statement: Senator Duren and everyone in the Memorial Hospital ER are under our control. A few have had to be sacrificed. More deaths are likely. Follow instructions and casualties will be minimized.

The freedom and rights of Americans have been stolen. What untold thousands have fought and died to protect has been taken over by illegitimate and corrupt persons and institutions. This must change.

We are American patriots who recognize freedom has never been free.

We take no pleasure in killing, but lost lives have always been the price of freedom. We will pay any cost to stand up for what is right.

Any effort to breach the Memorial ER will be unsuccessful. All access points have been secured and wired with lethal devices. Our capacity to inflict death and destruction is great—do not make us demonstrate.

I will communicate our demands shortly.

Tolman Freid, free man and sovereign citizen

Aki stared at the screen. What were they dealing with?

Eco-terrorists had been his suspicion upon learning of the refinery attack. Now it looked like a terrorist militia operation. The use of military rank and the license plate nonsense were hallmarks of sovereign citizen extremists.

The deadly acid cloud, the police officer's ruthless highway killing, and now the takeover of the ER, with a US senator and an unknown number of others as hostages? They were all linked. The actions showed planning and organization. Like the Oklahoma bombing, Waco, and the Unabomber, the anti-government rhetoric had escalated to disaster and loss of life.

Aki felt a chill despite the sunshine. Political and religious extremists made other lawbreakers seem tame. Terrorists were more like the criminally insane. There were no limits to what terrorists would do. They convinced themselves their cause supported any actions as just and necessary. The most fanatical could persuade themselves that the slaughter of innocents was noble.

What did they want, and what might they do next? His chest felt hollow, his fear surging.

Aki could envision how easy taking over the ER would have been. Memorial Hospital didn't even have a metal detector at the entry. The overworked, understaffed security guards had access to Tasers but nothing more. The main defense plan was "lockdown," which involved sealing off the ER. When outside threats were identified, the department would lock down. The reinforced doors and locked access points prevented anyone from getting inside to the department's core.

The protective mechanism had been reversed. The terrorist "patriots" were within the core. The ER's intended impenetrable defense mechanism kept them and the hostages beyond reach.

The Feds would have already been storming into town in response to the refinery incident. The FBI would be heading operations at the hospital as well.

What could Aki do? The FBI would grab the reins, but as a senior detective in homicide and major crimes, this was his town. The refinery, the hospital, the roadside slaughter of his colleague—the extremists were attacking the people it was his job to protect.

"Trooper," he said to the highway patrolman. "Crime scene crew is on this. I know where the asshole who shot the officer is. I'm heading out."

"Roger that, detective," the officer said. "Nail the bastard."

Aki jumped in his car, flipped on his flashers, and put the pedal down.

He called dispatch on his cell as he negotiated the traffic on I-94. He wasn't far from the trailer park where the past winter's grisly shootout had occurred.

"Dispatch. Hollins here."

"Aki Yamada. What's the status at Memorial hospital?

"Hold on a second, Detective. Things are going crazy here."

Aki merged onto I-694. The vast metropolitan area sprawled in all directions in the early afternoon light. Nothing looked different, but Aki knew everything had changed.

"Okay, Detective. Sorry for the interruption. All the streets around Memorial are being cordoned off. Operations command is setting up in the lot across from the ER entrance. The FBI is operational lead, and we're support. SWAT has mobilized and the federal hostage rescue team is setting up."

"Thanks." Aki disconnected. His mouth had gone dry. The ER was the heart of the hospital, and Memorial Hospital sat at the center of the metropolitan area.

The extremists didn't have just have the hospital—they held the entire Twin Cities hostage.

CHAPTER FOURTEEN

Decontamination room

Phoenix couldn't breathe. It was for real this time.

She'd maintained her ploy of troubled breathing and fake coughing throughout the ambulance transport. They'd brought her and two others from the ambulance into the ER. As she stood naked, undergoing a spray-down decontamination behind a privacy screen, everything changed. The first deafening gunshot had frozen them all.

Seconds later, three more shots sounded. There was no doubt what they were. Her heart raced and she wanted to flee or hide.

Over the screen, she saw a man with a gun step into the room. There was no way out.

"Everyone, down on your knees. Hand over all cellphones and devices. Any wrong move and you're dead."

No! No! No! Remaining behind the privacy screen, she took off her Apple watch and quickly inserted it like a tampon. Wet and trembling, she put on the ass-backwards gown the nurse had laid out and pulled on the fabric booties.

"Get out here!" yelled a second voice from the other side of the curtain. She stepped out. *Oh, God!* It was the creepy one-eyebrow guy who'd leered at her in the ambulance. Now he had a pistol in his hand and a twisted smile on his face.

Phoenix and two other people who'd shared her ambulance, a pony-tailed young guy with a nose ring and a stocky, mid-fifties Black man, knelt on the floor.

"Cellphones and watches. All your devices. Now!" ordered the creep. The two men handed over phones.

"You, little miss hottie," the creep said. "Phone, now."

She handed hers over.

"You got anything else?" He rifled through her discarded clothes. "Stand still!" He grabbed the hem of the hospital gown and raised it, exposing her. "Put your hands up and spin around."

She had to do as he ordered, sickened by the glint in his eyes. As she turned, he pulled her close and his tongue slathered wet and hot across the side of her neck.

"Oh, hell, yeah." He laughed, a high-pitched staccato, as he pushed her away. She ground the sleeve of her gown against her neck, trying to erase his repulsive wetness. Her stomach heaved.

Voices sounded from beyond the door into the ER. A thin, thirty-something armed man whose face was deeply pockmarked stuck his head in the room.

"The Major blew away a guy. Micah took a bullet to the gut. Red killed a cop. We're in control. Access locked down and wired. Get these people back to the holding area."

Phoenix couldn't breathe. She reported horrible things happening to others—this shouldn't be happening to her.

The hairy creep grabbed her ass and pushed her toward the door.

"Get moving, sweet cheeks." His bizarre laugh repeated.

Her heart was in her throat and she felt as if she might faint.

If I'm going to die, please don't let this disgusting animal touch me again before I do.

ER

Nothing about what was happening matched the righteous goals

Sigurd's father had preached at the militia meetings. Despite having a rifle in his hands and Father in command, everything was out of control. Micah had been shot. Sigurd had been too stunned to even raise his gun.

"Lord almighty, boy." Sigurd's uncle, Red, gripped his arm. Despite Sigurd being man-sized and worker-strong, his uncle still made him feel like a little boy. "Thought you was going to piss yourself. You wanted to be here, boy, so be ready. Hell, you shoot as straight and quick as anyone."

It wasn't true. No one could do much of anything as good as Uncle Red. Some said Red was the best athlete and toughest guy to ever come out of outstate Minnesota. Just now, he'd moved cat-quick as he'd killed the policeman.

Father and Red could handle anything or anyone. He'd never seen either of them afraid. But this was different. *Has everyone gone crazy?*

"It's Micah, Red. He could die." Sigurd felt like he might throw up.

Red looked momentarily thoughtful—a rare thing—then shrugged. "If he does die..., everybody dies sometime. Tolman knows what he's doing."

Red hero-worshiped Father like the younger brother he was. A kid who, as far as Sigurd could see, had never grown up.

"Relax, boy. The doors are locked down and wired. We have fat-cat hostages. Tolman's plan is working."

My God. With Micah shot bad and everything out of control, what was working? It was true Micah was a druggie and a drunk and always messing up, but he was family.

"Lighten up, boy. Grow a pair. We're kicking ass and I'm loving it." Red moved off, smiling.

Sigurd stood open-mouthed. Everyone knew Red wasn't right in the head even before he got messed up in prison, but he thought this was fun? Craziness.

By now the ER had to be surrounded. How could this end up good?

Though he'd had no idea what the plan was, Sigurd had begged Father to let him come. Father refused. He said Sigurd's driving task had been enough. Father had not shared anything more and ordered Sigurd to remain up north.

That was that. No one argued with Father.

But this morning, Sigurd had talked Micah and Red into letting him join them. He'd sneaked into the ER with Micah and the three other militia. They'd all complained of headache and vomiting from a job site where they claimed they'd been exposed to carbon monoxide. They were walked right in.

Getting into the ER had been easy. Sigurd had no idea how they'd ever get out.

Micah might die. Maybe they all would.

CHAPTER FIFTEEN

The nephew of the terrorist leader continued to worsen. The murderer, terrorist, and kidnapper was now Drake's patient. The gunshot criminal needed blood, an operating room, and a skilled surgeon—and he needed them now. Even with the best of care, he could die.

Drake glanced toward the senator lying on the adjoining cart in the Crash Room. Both patients were on ventilators, sedated and critical.

"The senator's vitals are holding, Dr. Cody," Tracy said.

"It's one hundred percent great nursing, obviously," Drake said.

Tracy flushed. While the senator's status was the result of many things, it was true, as always, that nursing was key. Drake had been joking a bit, but Tracy's combination of focus and modesty made it tough for her to accept anything close to a compliment. Her care of Rachelle when she was critically ill had pulled her through.

Additionally, Tracy had cared for his friend and partner Jon in the ICU when he'd been near death.

Drake moved close to her and spoke under his breath. "These people are killers. At some point I'm going to have to try something. Be ready."

She looked up wide-eyed for an instant, then turned away as she reached out to pretend to adjust an IV. She spoke softly but with an edge. "Let me know anything I can do. They can't mess with us and our patients."

She was just over five feet tall and not much over one hundred pounds, but Drake knew how fierce she could be in defense of her patients.

A man with a rifle in hand and pistol in his belt stood at the entry to the Crash Room. He was one of those who'd masqueraded as a patient. Drake had tallied all their captors. Some were related—the huge second-in-command guy called Red was Tolman's brother, Drake's gunshot patient was their nephew, and the young man who seemed out of place was Tolman's son.

The three other men were different. Drake had noted that they and Red, whom they seemed to answer to, all had Nazi and Aryan Brotherhood tattoos. Drake's time behind bars and barbed wire had taught him to recognize predators. These three and the big redhead were ex-cons. These animals had not been rehabilitated.

"Get Tolman. Now," Drake ordered the thin pockmarked one standing guard.

Pockmark gave Drake a hard-eyed glare but moved off down the corridor.

"Have you talked to Rachelle?" Tracy and Rachelle had grown close during the hospitalization. "Uh, oh sorry, I'm sure you haven't. She may not even have heard yet."

"I hope she hasn't." How would Rachelle handle this? Only hours earlier, he'd been thinking they could enjoy part of this day together at their new dream home on the lake. Plans had changed. "Tracy, try and stash anything we might use as a weapon. They already cleared out scalpels and the obvious things. We—"

"What are you talking about?" Tolman's voice startled Drake.

"About saving lives," Drake said, turning to face Tolman as he entered the Crash Room. "About your nephew. He needs blood, a surgeon, and an operating room. I've done everything I can. He's bleeding to death internally. Even with a surgeon and the OR, he might die, but it's his only chance. And the senator should be admitted to an intensive care unit. They both need much more than we have here."

"No one enters or leaves this ER," Tolman said. He looked at his stricken nephew and there might have been a flicker of something. "Give him blood."

"We need the lab to match for transfusion. Blood is not stored in the ER." A lie—they had four units of O-negative blood on hand. Drake wrestled with holding back care—he hadn't done everything he could, but he had to take the long view. There was more than one life at stake.

"You do whatever is necessary to keep my nephew and the senator alive. If you let either of them die, I'm going to kill more people. Understood?"

Tolman turned and began to leave.

"You've got to listen." Drake took a step and put a hand on Tolman's shoulder. Bam! Bone-jarring impact and pain in Drake's back. He pivoted and faced the pockmarked militia man who held his rifle with the butt end raised, threatening another strike. A small prison-ink swastika pulsed at the base of his neck.

"Don't touch any of us, doctor boy. Move wrong and I'll smash your teeth in."

Drake straightened, hiding the pain. He faced his attacker with the eyes of the person he'd been when locked up with such animals. His muscles had gone tripwire tight. A part of him eager to kill.

"Stand down," Tolman ordered. The man backed off, his gaze deflecting from Drake's.

"Your threats won't keep your nephew alive, asshole!" Drake fought to control his anger as he faced Tolman. More than one life hung in the balance. "What I'm telling you is true. I'm doing everything I can for your nephew, the senator, and everyone else."

"My, aren't you the hero," Tolman said.

"Insulting or threatening me doesn't help. Your nephew needs surgery or he's going to die—soon. I do my best to save every patient —no matter what they might have done. Trust me. I'm telling you the truth."

Tolman stroked his chin.

"You want your nephew to be a martyr? Do you want to die?" Drake said. "You've achieved all you're going to. Whatever your deluded power trip is, you've got all you're getting. More deaths just prove you're nothing more than a mad dog. Shut this insanity down, save your nephew, and turn yourself in. You'll get all the headlines, TV, and ass-kissing media attention you want. You can broadcast whatever raving, bullshit manifesto you want."

"This isn't about me!" Tolman's face flushed. "It's about freedom and justice. Lives are always the price that must be paid."

"If you don't end this now, your nephew and the senator and a lot of others, including you, are going to die," Drake said. Did that matter to this man?

"Save my nephew and keep the senator alive. If you fail, I'll kill others. And I'll make sure it's people you care about." Tolman turned and began to walk off.

"Wait!" Drake said. "I have an idea where no one leaves but will give your nephew a chance." Drake held his breath.

Tolman stopped and turned.

Drake's plan dangled by a thread. He hoped it would give more than just the injured man a chance.

CHAPTER SIXTEEN

As Evangeline Duren's driver turned the black limousine onto Summit Avenue, she listened to the fast-paced words coming over the phone from the White House.

"...our people are the best. We'll do everything possible to get the senator home and safe. You have my word."

"Thank you, sir." Her voice held strong, though what had happened to Hayden had broken her into a million pieces. "Hayden means everything to me."

Her insides were twisted in knots. She knew the truth. The President said he'd do everything possible, but there was one thing no President would do. Every US government official and their family understood the grim reality.

The United States government would not negotiate with terrorists.

US policy demanded her husband be allowed to die rather than... She bent and put her face in her hands.

A text message notification beeped. She took a deep, shuddering breath. Time to be strong.

She peered at her phone's screen.

The text message:

If you want him to live, you will pay 5 million dollars within six hours.

Payment will be in cryptocurrency and routed via secure links and dark web portals that will be given to you.

We are aware of your finance/banking background and ability to easily handle this transaction. If you play games—he dies. If payment is not made or is delayed—he dies. If you contact law enforcement or notify anyone of this transaction—he dies.

This will be your last message until transfer is to take place. Mobilize the funds and await instructions.

Next was a photo. A close-up. *Oh, Lord!*

Hayden's swollen, blistered, and discolored face was barely recognizable. His eyes were slits and a breathing tube protruded from his mouth. *No, please!*

What had they done to him? She lightly touched the screen over the image of her kind and gentle husband. Her usually ordered mind pinwheeled. Any hint of resistance disappeared.

Five million dollars. Meaningless compared to the life of her husband and the father of their children—the man she loved. What of the risks and responsibilities of public office he'd accepted? The rules forbidding ransom payments? Should she risk contacting the police?

Before the limousine had traveled ten feet farther, she'd made her decision.

I'll do anything to save him.

THREE MINUTES LATER, the Fenbridge board chairman heard his personal phone text message chime. Since the disaster at the pipeline's opening ceremony, messages had been flying—none of them good. He pulled the phone and accessed the text.

Damn. He'd been expecting this. Five million dollars. The amount was a pittance. Why so little? Either very unsophisticated terrorists or ones placing a premium on the ease and speed of transfer.

Fenbridge had kidnap insurance on all their executives, due to their activities in South America and elsewhere where kidnapping for ransom was common. The money was nothing. At least the actions didn't seem to be that of eco-Nazis. Whoever these terrorists were, at least they weren't bringing attention to the tree-hugger nonsense.

The project had been a headache since day one. Acquiring the pipeline corridor and jumping through the environmental-impact hoops had driven costs to four times projections, but every hick farmer, rube homeowner, and two-bit real estate speculator believed they deserved a fortune. As usual federal, state, and county bodies had all played ball. They'd claimed eminent domain, condemned the needed properties, and transferred the needed property rights to Fenbridge. Even with eminent domain resulting in paying only pennies on the dollar, the costs involved in obtaining nineteen hundred miles of pipeline right of way were staggering. Another five million dollars was a rounding error. It was worth that to minimize any additional bad publicity.

He texted the chief operations officer and instructed him to follow the ransom instructions.

Whatever happened, as long as the oil was flowing the stockholders would be happy. The pipeline would gush with profit for a very long time.

The chairman set down his phone. The kidnapped CEO was likable and a competent fellow—losing him would be bad for business. Fingers crossed the man would make it out okay.

TWO MINUTES LATER, the senior petrochemical plant board member heard the ping. He accessed his phone and viewed the text and photo.

Good God! Kidnapping of executives in South America was a booming industry, but now here at home? In the foreign countries, the personnel generally were released unharmed.

Would the same be true here? It was worth the money to find out. Technically, US laws made ransom payments illegal and could result in an indictment if they paid. The reality was that such a case had never actually been prosecuted.

Five million? It was a no-brainer.

CHAPTER SEVENTEEN

Minneapolis downtown

Three blocks from the hospital, Detective Aki Yamada found streets blocked and additional barricades being put up. Officers waved him away, but he held his badge out the window and snaked past. One block from the hospital, he pulled his unmarked car to the curb near a roadblock where several official vehicles were parked. He flipped his police placard on the dash, got out, and locked the door. The uniformed Minneapolis officer standing by the barricade held a radio in hand.

"Detective Aki Yamada, Homicide and Major Crimes—"

"Sure, I recognize you. I'm Robinson, 4th precinct. Federal, state, metro, Sheriff's Department—everybody has mobilized, but word is it's the FBI's show. We're coordinating the evacuation of the hospital. Gotta get everybody clear without letting anybody in. The whackos used chemical warfare shit at the refinery. Word is they have the ER locked down tight. Where are you heading?"

"I'm looking for the Command Post," Aki said.

"Glad you're here to let the feds know which way is up." He pointed with the radio. "They're set up in the white trailer on the far side of the parking lot across from the ER entrance."

"Thanks, brother. Stay safe."

Aki hurried past three more barricades, flashing his badge. A bomb squad truck, two SWAT tactical vehicles, and two ambulances stood parked some distance from the ER entrance. A drumming sound directed his eyes upward. A police helicopter circled above the towering downtown buildings. Images of 9/11 flashed in his head.

Fire, rescue, police vehicles, and public utility trucks were stationed around the lot and on adjoining streets. A barricade approximately fifty yards from the hospital defined an inner area almost clear of vehicles. Uniformed officers, including some in tactical gear sporting automatic weapons, were positioned around the boundary. The parking lot and area around the operation center were bustling with law enforcement and rescue personnel in the afternoon sunshine. Aki started to break a sweat as he trotted up to the command trailer. Two fit-looking guys in suits stood at the entry. One held up a hand.

"Restricted area. No entry. Sorry, sir."

"Aki Yamada. Senior detective, Minneapolis Homicide and Major Crimes." He held up his badge and ID. "I need to speak with the special agent in charge."

The agent checked the ID. "One moment please." He entered the trailer.

The FBI could be a pain in the ass, especially if an operation's leadership role had not yet been decided. Once jurisdiction was sorted, local police and FBI typically worked well together. This scenario clearly fit as one for the Feds to head up.

The other decisive factor influencing success was the special agent in charge. Most were solid, but some agents were placed in operational leadership roles without having much time in the streets or any history of combat. Aki had one time dealt with an inexperienced agent with an attitude like something out of a bad movie—he saw the FBI as the cavalry coming to the rescue of the inept locals. Nobody had died, but Aki had gotten a headache from the multitude of eyerolls the irritating agent had triggered.

The agent returned and waved Aki in. "Follow me, sir."

Aki followed through the entryway into a brightly lit front room lined with tables, laptops, phones, and radios, leading to a windowless darkened area. Men and women in short sleeves and wearing headsets sat at stations in front of a wall-sized screen where multiple live images of the interior of the hospital as well as blueprints and data were displayed. On the other wall, another large screen showed several additional live feeds indicating police positions and exterior views of the hospital. One screen showed a national news feed covering the story. A lean man with rolled-up shirtsleeves and a loosened tie stood behind one of the seated persons peering at a screen with a phone to his ear.

"Special Agent McGinnis," Aki's guide said. "Detective Yamada of MPD Homicide."

The hawk-nosed man raised a hand and kept his focus on the screen for another moment. "Flag that and send it out," he said to the seated man. He pivoted to Aki with a hand outstretched. Alert blue eyes and a questioning look lit his face. Boyish-looking, though gray showed at his temples. "Special Agent in Charge Dylan McGinnis. Your chief sent you?"

"No. I haven't talked with the chief," Aki said. "I came directly from the scene where a suburban officer was gunned down on a highway stop between here and the refinery. I believe the shooter headed to the hospital. The dead officer's dashcam showed a large male shooter driving a Lincoln with bogus plates. Typical sovereign citizen or militia-type stuff. I saw the text the hostage takers sent. I'm sure the refinery assault, the police officer's murder, and the ER takeover are all tied together. With the pipeline as a target I thought maybe eco-terrorists, but it looks more like anti-government militia freaks."

"Heard about the officer. Sorry." McGinnis sighed. "Because your instincts are on target and I need more local input, I'm going to share privileged information. Strictly confidential."

"I know the turf and all local resources. I can help, and confidentiality is no issue."

"Our primary person of interest parked in that ramp." The agent indicated the parking complex to the east. "His car does have fabricated plates. We ID'd him from the parking ramp's CCTV."

"Who the hell is he?" Aki said. "He killed the officer like she was nothing."

"Tolman Freid is his name," Agent McGinnis said. "An anti-government extremist and now a domestic terrorist. One of a number of sovereign citizen extremist groups. He leads an outstate militia group. These groups attract gun nuts, anti-government whiners, and military wannabes—disaffected losers. But Freid is nothing like the typical militia yahoo. Most are military washouts and general failures playing at being badasses while blaming the government and everyone else for their failures. Freid is a combat veteran who heads up a multi-generation family farming operation. In addition, he started an independent fuel-trucking business decades back that's successful and highly regarded. He's capable and intelligent and has plenty of money. No arrests or convictions, but shares the sovereign citizen ideology that the government is illegitimate and has violated the American people's fundamental and inalienable rights."

"Excuse me, Agent McGinnis." One of the seated persons held a phone with a hand over the mike. "A Dr. Torrins, head of Medical Affairs, calling back from the hospital about the evacuation. They can't get hold of the hospital's CEO."

"Please take his number and tell him I'll call him back in five minutes." The agent turned to Aki. "Up until about six months ago, Freid's militia activities were limited to meetings, rallies, and regular shooting events on his farm, where his followers could fire off a few hundred thousand rounds and make like World War Three. He also filed a flood of 'you have no right to tax me' and 'the government sucks' legal filings. He sees himself as a patriot. His position is that today's US government is illegitimate and incompetent. He believes big business and government are engaged in an illicit partnership. He's magnetic and popular—a natural leader. But up until recently, he had the ideology but never any violence."

"How do you know so much about him already?" Aki asked. "And what changed?"

"The answer to both questions is the pipeline. It went right through his land. The government declared eminent domain, condemned his home, and conveyed rights to the pipeline company.

He filed a defense action in the courts, but in today's world, eminent domain cases result in an immediate summary judgment against the property owner. The courts don't halt the condemnation or confiscation—they hand over the property, pending court judgment. Rulings aren't made for months or years after the fact. That's what happened to him. His case won't be heard for years, but his home is gone."

"That's wrong," Aki said.

"It's what happens. Freid ignored the court's notices to vacate. He said he'd fight to protect his home. He had the skills and weapons to do a lot of damage." McGinnis shook his head. "That's why so much is known about him. He was on everyone's radar. It looked like another Ruby Ridge or Waco disaster ready to happen. The day the demolition and pipeline crews reached his land, a county sheriff was on hand to arrest him if he resisted. The pipeline's private 'Security Assessment' team is more heavily armed than most law enforcement and they're hard core. They were eager to use force. The sheriff was calling for major backup when an ambulance arrived at the farmhouse. Freid's wife had become ill. He thought she was dying and went to the hospital with her."

"She had to be under incredible stress," Aki said.

"In the end, doctors believed it was exhaustion and she had a mental health crisis. By the time Freid returned from the hospital, they'd bulldozed his home, all his buildings, and cut a fifty-yard-wide track through his woods and fields. His house and land sat between two pristine lakes. The pipeline company could have done an alternative go-round route, but it would have been more expensive and involved wetlands protection laws. The eminent domain action claimed it was 'in the public good' to allow the pipeline corporation to destroy Freid's family home and property. It was about tax revenues and corporate profits. I'm glad I had nothing to do with it."

"Ugly stuff. Sounds un-American. Then what happened?" Aki said.

"Nothing—until today. He was on a watch list for a while because they thought he might get violent, but nothing happened. His wife remained hospitalized and went downhill quickly. The medical impression was that she had early dementia, and with the stress, crisis, and loss of her home, her dementia rapidly accelerated. She completely deteriorated. He had to put her in a memory-care facility. He blames the government. Since then, he scaled back his trucking operation and halted any known militia activity."

"Damn. His life was trashed." Aki shook his head.

"Yeah—he worshiped his wife. Her dementia devastated him. Involved law enforcement did a threat assessment and concluded that he was depressed, knew he couldn't defeat the government, and had given up." The special agent in charge scanned the wall-sized panel of video images showing the barricaded hospital and the army of vehicles and personnel mobilizing around it.

"They were wrong."

CHAPTER EIGHTEEN

Predawn, nine hours earlier the same day

Sigurd downshifted, slowed, and turned the Kenworth tanker off Highway 55 onto Glenwood Avenue. His headlights tracked a two-lane blacktop road in the looming predawn. It sure didn't seem like a route suitable for a fuel tanker rig. Sigurd was pretty sure the leased 11,500-gallon-capacity tanker trailer alone weighed over a hundred thousand pounds. Even an empty trailer was over the weight restrictions for a lot of roads and for sure a full one like this. He glanced at Father's map. No mistake.

He rumbled the massive rig through a quiet residential neighborhood of large lots and older homes mixed with million-dollar new construction. The old suburb of Golden Valley sat right next to downtown Minneapolis. He passed a lake and public golf course. He slowed as a dozen Canada geese broke from their waddle and flapped their way across the road in front of the truck. The huge engine rumbled deep and low in the near-dawn stillness.

Last night Father had given him really weird delivery instructions. When Sigurd tried to question them, Father had snapped, "Do what you're told." No one, not even Uncle Red, questioned Father—

especially lately. Father had told Sigurd that after his delivery he was to return to the farm and keep away from the cities.

As Sigurd's cousin Micah had readied to make his delivery of another tanker, he'd bragged that something big would happen later today and he was part of it.

Micah was older than Sigurd, but he was a screw-off.

Why is Micah included and not me? I'm eighteen now and I've proven I can handle family business.

What did Father have planned and why was it secret?

Ever since the pipeline demolished their home, broke Mother's heart, and destroyed her mind, Father was different. He didn't hold any more militia meetings, but his hatred of the government burned more fiercely than ever.

Each day Father returned from the memory care center sadder looking and further away. It was Mother who was close to Sigurd as he grew up. She home-schooled him and taught him how a gentleman behaves. Father had always been distant, but since Mother's mind failed it was as if Sigurd was invisible.

As the truck mounted a rise, Sigurd spied an industrial building a few hundred yards ahead. The building's parking lot was packed with cars—night-shift workers soon to trade off with day-shift crews. Shortly beyond that, the buildings of downtown Minneapolis filled the sky.

Before reaching the industrial building, he slowed on a short concrete bridge that passed over railroad tracks about a hundred feet below. Gray, worn grain elevators rose into the sky above the trees a few hundred yards down the tracks. He downshifted, and the air brakes hissed as he stopped at the start of an overgrown turnoff just beyond the bridge. A rusted chain with battered NO TRESPASSING and RESTRICTED AREA signs blocked the road.

He set the brake, got out, and found the cut chain link Father had told him about. He moved the chain aside, then climbed back into the rig and low-geared down the steep track of crumbled tarmac. He wound down and to the right toward the railbed that passed under the bridge.

He advanced the truck down the crumbling tree- and overgrowth-lined road into the shadow of the towering, deserted grain elevators. A warehouse-sized building with multiple bay doors sat at the base of the towers. He got out and used the key Father had given him to unlock the new padlock on the middle bay door. He swung open each half door, and the loading zones from where the grain had been off-loaded in years past became visible. A musty oatmeal-like odor wafted out, and dust floated in the first shafts of morning light.

He backed the massive, double-hulled tanker trailer into the outbuilding. When in place, he got out and adjusted the trailer supports. He disengaged the air brake hoses, triggering the distinctive pop and blast of air. He completed unhooking the tanker trailer from the truck.

He got in the truck's cab, drove forward fifty feet, and left it idling as he got out and closed the building's bay doors and replaced the lock.

Nothing about this delivery made sense. Father would never leave a tanker trailer at an unattended site—doubly so for a full one. Micah and Red had also rolled out in the dark of night hauling maximum loads, same as Sigurd. Were their deliveries as mysterious as this one?

What was going on?

Back to the road, replace the chain, two hours driving, and he'd be back to their truck yard and what remained of their land. He should stop to see Mother. His gut knotted. The tragic woman in the wheelchair muttering or crying out was not the person his mother had been...and she no longer recognized him.

Even guilt couldn't get him to visit.

He'd been ordered to return to the trailer home at their truck yard, but he was going to do something he never did. Something no one ever did.

He would disobey Father.

CHAPTER NINETEEN

Tolman halted his exit from the Crash Room and eyed Drake with irritation. "An idea?"

"Yes," Drake said. "Without surgery, your nephew is going to die—soon. I'm a doctor. Despite what he's done, I have to do my best to save him. I have an idea that will give him a chance."

"What?"

"Let me try to get a surgeon and OR team to come here. It's far from ideal medically, but it's better than watching your nephew die. I don't know if any surgeon will take the risk, but if you give your word you'll let them leave unharmed after surgery, maybe one will."

"What do you mean 'team'? You said he needed a surgeon. That's one person."

"We also need an anesthesiologist and one surgical nurse at the minimum. They could enter from the flight elevator. You could allow that." Drake paused. "Look at him."

The wounded man lay white as the sheets, his eyes dark and sunken. The ventilator *hiss-pause-blow* triggered the rise and fall of his chest. The odor of blood, dying tissue, and ketones—the sickly stink of a wounded animal—hung in the air.

"Can you smell it?" Drake said. "That's the scent of death approaching. I can't stop it."

Drake had not done everything he could for the man, but he'd wrestle with his ethics later. First, he had to get his people out of the ER alive. The battle with his ideals would not be a tough match. When fighting to keep the vulnerable, the innocent, and those you love alive, he'd learned that ethical arguments and abstract notions of morality could be erased as if on a blackboard.

Tolman paced with his eyes on his nephew.

"No team." Tolman stopped. "If I agree, it's one person—the surgeon. And I'd have to know they're not going to try and slip some kind of doctor-cop in here."

"We can see who's scheduled on call for trauma today," Drake said. "There's an assignment list. And you can confirm the identity of the doctor from their picture in the staff directory. No tricks. If the on-call surgeon won't do it, we can try another one."

Drake worked to hide his desperation. The current situation looked hopeless. A lot of people were going to die—people Drake cared deeply about.

If Tolman agreed and a surgeon accepted, it meant one additional person's life at risk, but it might create an opportunity to save others. Any change gave them better odds than their current situation. Drake held his breath as the terrorist leader pondered.

A brave Minnesotan had recognized his do-or-die situation on a flight on September 11, 2001. He'd led a barehanded charge on the armed terrorists who'd taken over Flight 93. He'd died, but his courage had saved countless others. And he'd died giving it everything he had. At some point, Drake and the ER hostages were going to have to make their own life-or-death charge.

The ventilators hissed, clicked, and maintained their unchanging cadence as the seconds passed.

"Okay," Tolman said. "No tricks and show me the surgeon list."

Drake hid the mix of hope and worry from his face. He already knew the name of the surgeon on call for trauma. He'd had to use the on-call list to reassure Tolman, but the name at the top would have been his last choice.

Could the doctor who was literally and figuratively the biggest jerk in the history of Memorial Hospital improve their odds for survival?

Drake could only hope.

CHAPTER TWENTY

Memorial Hospital, east entrance

Aki and Special Agent in Charge Dylan McGinnis approached the hospital entry on the opposite side of the campus from the ER. Medics rolled three patients on stretchers out the doors toward waiting ambulances. Special Agent McGinnis had asked to get a feel for the hospital and Aki knew it well.

Tactical officers bearing automatic weapons flanked the glass-partitioned automatic doors watching the in-and-out traffic as the evacuation ramped up. They nodded as Aki held up his badge.

"Emptying this place is a major project," Aki said.

"No choice. Eight stories full of patients and healthcare workers sitting on top of an ER held by terrorists who've already used explosives and chemical weapons is a nightmare."

"Let's pray blowing themselves up is not on their agenda."

"We can hope our home-grown terrorist animals are less brutal, but history suggests otherwise. Only the 9/11 atrocity surpasses the death totals of the Oklahoma City federal building. Domestic terrorists and religious terrorists tap into the same rancid pool of evil."

Aki nodded. "As I stood at the side of the highway next to the body of the policewoman who was gunned down, I was thinking of how terrorists are similar to but worse than the criminally insane. Regular murderers kill when intoxicated, in the heat of anger, for revenge, or for gain. What terrorists do is premeditated, planned, and unmitigated evil. Their victims are innocent people who have not harmed them in any way. Like the criminally insane, what terrorists do is senseless, but terrorists do not have mental illness as their basis. They're barbaric. Has anyone ever adopted an extremist religious or political view because terrorists killed people?"

"Never have and never will." McGinnis shook his head. A stretcher bearing an elderly patient with an oxygen mask on was guided past them and out the doors by a medic. "Give me your thirty-second rundown on the hospital layout. I wanted to get a feel of things up close."

Memorial Hospital level one trauma center cared for the victims of violent crime. In addition to the crime victims, the perpetrators of shootings, stabbings, and other crimes also regularly ended up as patients. Aki knew the hospital well. He rubbed his upper arm. Less than a year before, a contract killer had buried an icepick in Aki's shoulder as he protected a patient in the sixth-floor ICU. Aki had chased the killer through the hospital and out the main entrance. A SWAT team sniper's bullet had ended the threat in the same parking lot that now held the FBI's operations center trailer.

"The ER is on the south side of this floor," Aki said. "Radiology, lab, administration, and ORs take up the rest. The basement level has the physical plant, storage, materials, and the main security office. The upper seven floors are patient care. Floors six and seven hold the intensive care units. The helipad is above eight. One dedicated flight elevator links the ER to the helipad. There are multiple other banks of elevators, ten main stairwells, and over 450 hospital beds. Evacuating this place is a huge job."

"Dr. Torrins, president of medical affairs, warned me," McGinnis said. "Suggested it would be like the Brits clearing Dunkirk."

"The ICUs alone seem impossible to me," Aki said. "All the patients are wicked sick. Most are on ventilators and have IV drip machines. Hell, anytime one needs a CT scan on the first floor, it's a multi-person caravan."

The lobby area held multiple patient-occupied stretchers and a flotilla of patients in wheelchairs. All wore hospital gowns. Many had oxygen masks or tubes running to their noses, and all had either IV bags or ports visible on taped arms. Hospital staff wearing scrubs bustled about as transport staff and medics rolled patients to waiting vans or ambulances.

Evacuation would take many hours. Aki wondered if the militia had realized that.

These terrorists showed cunning. They'd chosen their target well. It was impossible to get people to safety quickly. That and using the ER's lockdown mechanism to create an impenetrable boundary suggested a familiarity with the hospital that didn't fit with the militia leader's background.

"This operation shows more hospital knowledge than I'd expect from a farmer and trucking business operator from central Minnesota," Aki said.

"I'm thinking the same thing." McGinnis nodded. "Detective, are you okay with partnering with me on this nightmare? I can use someone like you. I've shared as much as I have with you because if you'll accept, I'm going to get you assigned as my Minneapolis police department liaison."

"They've killed at least one officer and are threatening my city. I'm more than ready to take them down." Aki paused. "There could be an issue with me as liaison—I'm not real popular with the chief. The fact is, he hates my guts." Only an influential anchorwoman's support had prevented the chief from suspending or firing him. Talk about irony, he thought. *The media giveth and the media taketh away.*

"Don't sweat that. I like how you think, and I need someone who knows your department, the city, and this hospital." Special Agent McGinnis took out his phone, hit a key, and raised it to his ear. "Turn investigators loose on all former or current employees of the hospital. Check for any militia or sovereign citizen activity or sympathizers. Go back three years. Focus on disgruntled, fired, or laid-off workers, and also check for any who come from central Minnesota. Track down any who have a link to Tolman Freid, his business, or his family. Get Minneapolis PD on this, too. And have their chief call me —patch him through when he does. Notify all operations personnel that as of now, Detective Aki Yamada is our MPD liaison. Extend all investigative resources to him." He clicked off and pocketed the phone. "Done deal."

McGinnis looked around the bustling lobby. "I've seen enough. Let's get to nailing these bastards."

CHAPTER TWENTY-ONE

ER

After Tolman Freid agreed to the on-call surgeon, Drake watched as the militia leader spoke while the pockmarked ex-con recorded with an iPhone camera. Tolman stood in front of Senator Duren's ravaged ventilator-driven body among the monitors and glistening chrome instruments. The gunshot nephew lay in the adjacent bay, likewise motionless other than the ventilator's effect.

"I'm Tolman Freid, leader of the Sovereign Citizens. The following are my orders: Communication will be of my timing via the mode of my choosing. I will present demands and they will be carried out. Any failure to obey will result in lives lost. I will not engage with FBI or other negotiators, as there will be no negotiations. I repeat—no negotiations.

"The hospital's on-call trauma surgeon will be allowed into the ER. No one else. He will to be dropped off on the helipad as soon as possible. Any attempts to replace the assigned surgeon or interfere with the helipad closed-circuit TV monitors will trigger deadly penalty. Any untoward activity anywhere around the hospital during admission of the surgeon to the ER will trigger deadly penalty. The surgeon is to communicate by phone with Dr. Drake Cody immediately. The call will be monitored."

Drake could not imagine how that phone call would go. On a good day, the surgeon was next to impossible to deal with.

The domestic terrorist continued, "The President, the US Attorney General, and all state governors and attorneys-general must be made available to hear my demands within two hours. Text and video communications from me will be broadcast widely on all media outlets.

"Our actions at the illicit new pipeline-refinery represent a fraction of what we are capable of. Any lack of cooperation will result in a larger-scale, lethal demonstration of our capacity for destruction.

"The current United States' government-corporate power structure is illegitimate, corrupt, and immoral. We are prepared to sacrifice thousands of lives—tens of thousands if necessary—for the cause of justice and freedom.

You have been advised. There will be no further warning."

Tolman nodded and the ex-con stopped filming.

Drake's gut roiled and an icy chill ran down his spine. "Tens of thousands" of lives at stake—this was madness.

"Send that to the media group mailing address and to those who were sent the initial message," Tolman said to his cameraman. "Monitor the news."

A ceiling-mounted TV was on without sound above the desk and behind Tolman at the central station. Red and his prison-ink trio could hardly keep their eyes off the news coverage focusing on their actions. The images Drake glimpsed showed that the refinery explosion and the ER takeover were dominating national broadcasts.

Tolman seemed like a true believer in his cause, but the massive redhead and his ex-con crew didn't strike Drake as devoted types. They acted like the violent sociopaths Drake had been locked up with in the Furnace. Coldblooded humans devoted only to themselves and their degenerate desires. Two differently motivated factions but both deadly.

The medical machines marched on while the odor of the senator's dying tissues and the metallic-fecund tinge of the nephew's draining gunshot wound seemed to intensify.

Drake's mouth was so dry he could not swallow. How would any of those trapped with him survive?

The usual chorus of emergency department phones and overhead pages had ceased since the takeover. Central switchboard must have blocked incoming calls, and of course no ambulances or radio calls were being routed to Memorial ER.

The Crash Room phone rang. Tracy grabbed it.

"Emergency Room," she said. Drake thought he noticed her wince. "Dr. Cody, it's the surgeon."

As Drake took the phone, the barrel of Tolman's gun dug into the back of his head.

"No tricks," Tolman said.

"Brave of you to respond, Bart," Drake said. One thing Drake could say about surgeon Bart Rainey was that he was unique. His private patients and their referring doctors loved him—his patients were well cared for.

Nurses, anesthesiologists, lab personnel, and most other members of the hospital staff did not share the love. There'd been some improvement after recent dramatic events and disciplinary action, but Bart Rainey remained the least popular doctor on staff. His abusive behavior made caring nurses cry, and OR teams dreaded working his cases.

"What kind of train wreck do you have for me this time?" Even under normal circumstances, the huge surgeon's manner suggested every consult from the ER, no matter how righteous, resulted from incompetence on the emergency doctor's part. Every gunshot, knife wound, or accident somehow constituted a personal imposition by the emergency doctor on Bart.

This time the case matched the man's attitude.

"You need to know what you're getting into," Drake said. "These people are killers. Whatever they promise, there's a good chance you could be killed." The barrel of the gun gouged hard into Drake's scalp. As Drake reacted instinctively he knew his actions were dangerous and ill-advised but, as had happened in other deadly situations in the past, he was unable to stop himself. He spun and shoved Tolman, causing him to stumble back a few feet. "Back off!" Drake yelled.

Tolman shot forward, red-faced with veins bulging, and jammed the bore of the gun between Drake's eyes. Their gazes locked.

Drake did not blink. The smart move survival-wise was to look away and back down, but he could not. A trickle of blood ran from the gun's tip down the side of his nose. "This is my ER and my consult, asshole. The surgeon needs to know what he's facing. We tell patients the risks before every procedure. My colleague deserves the same."

Tolman's chest heaved and his face twisted as the gun remained lodged between Drake's eyes. Seconds passed.

Tolman pulled the gun back.

"Bart?" Drake said into the phone.

"I heard most of that. That's the boss man? Sounds like a sweetheart. Hell, you've outdone yourself this time, ER. Give me a report on my patient. We're wasting time."

"You're saying you'll do it?" Drake couldn't believe it.

"Somebody has to save the day, ER. That's what surgeons do."

Drake concisely communicated every significant aspect of the wounded man's condition. He told Bart to bring as much universal donor O-negative blood as he could and identified there would be no anesthesiologist or surgical nurse. Drake and Tracy would assist in the Crash Room.

"No anesthesiologist?" Bart said. "And that damn ICU nurse trying to be a surgical nurse? Ridiculous—this is me essentially solo, and the patient sounds like he's not salvageable. Is the guy who shot him likely to shoot me?"

"The man who shot him is dead."

"That's good."

"No, Bart," Drake said. "It's not. He was a state patrolman trying to stop the takeover."

"A cop shot my patient? What the hell? Are you—"

"Yes, Bart. Your patient is the leader's nephew."

"Son of a bitch, ER. You're asking me to risk my life to save one of the bad guys?"

Drake couldn't bring himself to push the surgeon further. Silence hung. Drake gripped the phone tight. Bart Rainey didn't give a shit what Drake or anyone else thought, but he was also the kind of guy who never backed down from anybody or anything. *It's crazy, but do it, Bart.*

"Tell the jerk leader this and don't forget it yourself. When I operate on a patient, I decide one hundred percent what goes down with them. And remind that know-it-all nurse I'm the doctor—not her."

"Agreed, Bart."

"You're dragging me into a shitstorm, ER. It sounds like we don't have much time. This patient sounds more than half-dead."

"All true. Get here fast." Drake disconnected.

The senator hung on to life with his body internally torched by a hellish acid. The suburban officer had been blown away and left like roadkill on the highway. The highway patrolman who'd tried to stop the takeover was no more. And Marcus, the senator's gallant bodyguard and friend, had his head blown off from behind. Each atrocity battered and bent the bars behind which Drake's primal instincts raged.

The physicians' creed included "First, do no harm," and the first Commandment said "Thou shalt not kill." In the past, Drake had, on more than one occasion, had to reject those rules. When the reality was to either kill predatory humans or allow them to harm or kill innocent others, Drake would not hesitate.

CHAPTER TWENTY-TWO

Telemetry area

"Patti," Dr. Rizzini said, "can you keep an eye on the patient on the ventilator and handle things here while I go to minor trauma?" Both executives, the pipeline CEO and the refinery CEO, had been on the margin of the stage and in contact with an unknown amount of the acid mist. Both were sedated but stable. Judging by their course so far, they'd likely do well medically. The terrorists were the greater danger.

The intubated multiple drug- and alcohol-intoxicated patient who'd been in the department since before the takeover was behind the curtain in the corner bed. Rizz had not seen him as Dr. Trist had cared for him. The patient's ventilator clicked, hissed, and blew in its steady rhythm.

"Take care of patients? I can try. Of course, without a doctor holding my hand it will be scary." Some doctors treated nurses like they were morons and did not appreciate their skills, which was hard to take. Rizz was not that way, so it felt good to give him a jab. Kidding almost made it feel like things were normal rather than freak-out scary.

"Ouch," Rizz said. "Allow me to restate. Nurse Patricia, do I have your permission to leave the telemetry area and go to minor trauma?

Perhaps I can be of service there while you continue your expert management of the patients here?"

"Much better." Even in this nightmare, Michael Rizzini continued to joke.

Rizz winked at her and flashed his smile.

God, that smile.

He turned his wheelchair and rolled away.

Most people struggled with breakups and love lost. Her heart ached for what had never been. Could he really not be afraid?

She moved into and down the corridor and peeked at the device the terrorists had placed across the elevator access doors. Wired to the mechanism was a tank larger than most oxygen units, with an orange light flashing on an electronic module mounted on it. Likely it was filled with more of the nightmarish acid they'd used on the senator.

Insanity!

Domestic terrorists, murder, hydrofluoric acid, explosives, and the very real prospect no one in the ER would survive—*so how's the shift going so far otherwise?*

Trying to be Rizz-like, but nothing felt funny.

Her shoulders were tight. Her fists clenched. She figured it was only because of years in a job that demanded that she never collapse or quit no matter what, that she wasn't curled up in a corner trembling. She took a big breath.

The terrorists had taken over the ER so easily.

Damn! If only administration had listened.

Lockdown didn't do much good when the bad guys were already in the ER.

There were no metal detectors at the entry to the ER, and the security staff did not have guns. Two or three security personnel were asked to do a job that oftentimes couldn't be handled by a dozen. People who were too strong and violent for police to control were brought to the ER. Restraint of wild patients involved hands-on immobilization of drug-crazed, psychotic, or criminal patients with superhuman strength who were capable of and often successful at doing serious harm to staff.

Medications could put out-of-control people down, but they had to hold the patient still before they could inject the medications into them. Sometimes Patti felt like she was trying to inject someone in the middle of a WWE wrestling match, and she'd been battered and tossed around more than once.

There were other risks. Upset "friends" of injured gang members or other patients had rioted in the waiting room. Patti had feared for her safety many times in her career. One deranged person with a gun could kill dozens.

Every medic, nurse and doctor working in frontline healthcare recognized the dangers. Administrators talked about it but did little.

Patti, Rizz, and Drake had represented the ER in a recent meeting with administration demanded by staff.

CEO Kline had chaired the lecture hall gathering, which had been packed with medics, nurses, doctors, and other hospital personnel.

Kline claimed "excessive" security measures scared away "customers." Metal detectors "sent the wrong message." Guards with weapons "didn't appear open and friendly." Calling police to arrest patients who injured staff rarely resulted in prosecution and "sent a negative message."

Kline rejected every concern or suggestion as inconsistent with "customer and community values." Everyone knew it was all about dollars.

Kline specifically identified the lockdown mechanism as a "rock solid" defense against any major threat.

He'd volunteered, as if bestowing a gift, that the hospital employee health plan covered counselors for PTSD or other aftermath issues when employees were victims of work-related violence.

Rizz had called out, "Thank you very little!" and Kline had reddened as everyone in the meeting burst out laughing.

Patti shook her head as she walked back down the corridor to the telemetry unit.

How are your assurances looking now, Kline?

Her evil side wished the weasel were here enduring what was going on. He'd been in the department just before the takeover, trying to tell her how to do her job. Now he was probably sitting in an office somewhere in his two-thousand-dollar suit putting together a marketing plan to reclaim "customers" and lost revenue.

She sighed.

How would he and his marketing gurus work kidnap, murder, assault, and possibly a massacre into their new advertising campaign?

It was too late for them to improve security now. She thought about the patients. Other than the senator and their gunshot captor, the remainder of the few remaining patients in the ER were doing all right.

A thought sent an icy spike to her heart. Did it matter how any of them were doing?

They were being held by terrorist maniacs who'd rigged the ER with explosives and toxic gas.

A lump lodged in her throat. It was all too much. She'd dedicated her life to this ER and its patients—she did not want it to be the site of her death.

CHAPTER TWENTY-THREE

Drake checked the senator. Tracy and modern technology had him hanging on. What invisible destruction was the hydrofluoric acid wreaking inside the man? Drake hoped the senator didn't crash while they were operating on the terrorist.

The guard with the long beard left the Crash Room. He was the third and strangest of the ex-cons who treated Red as their leader. Drake knew from experience that the criminally insane were common among those locked up in US prisons, and he had treated hundreds of actively psychotic patients. The bearded man had not said a word, and his eyes rarely blinked. Drake recognized the distracted manner and wary look of someone hearing voices no one else would. This guy was unpredictable. Dangerous.

"Tracy, there are four units of O-negative blood in the refrigerated storage." Drake pointed. "Please run them in the patient as fast as possible."

"You had blood for transfusion all this time?" Her brow furrowed. "I don't understand how—"

"I can't explain now." Drake had not done everything he could do for the injured man. He'd lied to Tolman about no blood being available. He'd held back essential care to the gun shot patient whose life flickered like a candle in a storm.

Tracy's frown remained, but she moved quickly to retrieve the blood their patient so desperately needed.

With incredible speed, the ICU nurse Drake respected so much had two of the bags of blood hung, and the intravenous tubing looked like maroon threads as the blood ran into the patient. She avoided looking at Drake.

"The reason I—" Drake shut up as the flabby, younger con took his position by the entry to the Crash Room.

"Hey, baby. You miss me?" he said to Tracy. His laugh was jarring and high-pitched. He eyed Tracy in a way that made Drake want to kick his ass. Their guard looked at the wounded man. Drake followed his gaze.

Deathly pale skin. Closed eyes, sunken and dark, and the body motionless other than the chest's rise and fall driven by the ventilator. The man's upper body lay bare, and the blue-black tattooed swastika and script reading *Aryan Nation* stood in contrast on skin as blanched as parchment. The faint but distinctive scent of wounded human, part spoiled meat and part putrefaction, persisted.

"Damn." Another hyena-like laugh sounded. "You sure that boy ain't already dead?"

"Tracy, can you get trays, fluids, meds, drapes, and everything you can anticipate we need to convert this bay into an OR? We'll be assisting Dr. Rainey as he goes in this belly to try and stop the bleeding. He should be here very soon. Are you okay with that?"

"I'm always ready to do whatever will help my patient. Is Dr. Rainey okay with me?"

The Dr. Rainey question identified another issue. He was the surgeon Tracy had challenged when John Malar had been dying in the ICU. Drake and Bart had almost come to blows over the huge man's abusive behavior. For the first time in his career, Drake had initiated a peer review complaint. Some positive things had happened since, but with Bart, problems always remained. He didn't work well with anyone and never forgot.

"There's no one I'd rather have helping than you, Tracy. Bart is a jerk, but he's 100% committed to his patients."

"Every doctor should be," she said.

Ouch again. Drake's withholding the blood for transfusion from the leader's nephew wasn't as it seemed. He caught her eyes and she looked away. No time to explain.

"Trust me. It's life or death." He lowered his voice. "For all of us."

Due to the intensity of what had been going on since Drake brought the senator into the Crash Room, he knew little of the events in the rest of the ER. With Tracy overseeing the senator and preparing their makeshift OR, he walked toward the door of the Crash Room. "I'll be right back."

"You're going nowhere." The flabby guard gave his annoying laugh and stuck his rifle barrel in Drake's face. "Your job is to take care of the Major's nephew." The guy was a slob but big, with a lot of muscle underneath.

Drake pushed the barrel aside.

"We take care of everyone in this ER. I need to see if any patients need me. Piss off, Hyena." Drake walked past while bracing for an incoming rifle butt or worse.

Muttered obscenities sounded but Drake exited with no blow struck.

Take no shit. Show no weakness. Drake had learned to survive among wolves when locked up during his ugly past. Dealing with violent assholes meant pushing normal boundaries, being ready to get hurt, and never showing fear. Drake continually updated his read of their captors. Like the flashing display above the senator's bay, the life clocks for him, his ER coworkers, and their patients were ticking. How much time did they have?

He didn't know when the jumbo jet of an ER would crash, but one thing was certain—they were headed for a collision.

CHAPTER TWENTY-FOUR

The pockmarked ex-con who'd earlier slammed his rifle butt into Drake's back stood on guard outside the minor trauma area. In addition to trying to cripple Drake, the vicious ex-con had carried out Tolman's media and electronics tasks. Drake suspected he was brighter than the others. He sneered as Drake approached. Drake ignored the pain of his contused spine and walked as if uninjured.

"Kiss my ass, punk," Drake said.

The man raised the rifle butt.

"Better not do it," Drake said. "I'm operating on your buddy, the boss man's nephew. Can't save him if I'm hurt."

"That hick ain't my buddy, doctor boy." His sneer remained but he lowered the rifle.

Drake never broke stride.

The minor trauma area, like the rest of the emergency department, had no windows. The open space had fifteen patient beds, each with curtain-like drapes on rings that could be pulled for a semblance of privacy. Most beds were empty and the curtains were open.

Their captors had turned the space into a holding area for some of the few patients remaining in the ER. Besides the leader's nephew, the overall ER patient tally included the senator in the Crash Room, the three patients on monitors in the telemetry area, and those corralled here.

Rizz wheeled his chair up to Drake just inside the door to the oversized room.

"Welcome to the Hospital California, brother," Rizz said. "You can check out—but you can never leave."

Drake smiled. Rizz would crack jokes while being checked in to hell.

"What's our patient situation?" Drake asked.

"We got most patients out when we heard about the refinery. Three patients in the telemetry area. Five patients and one family member in here. Only a few staff left. The bad guys emptied most out at gunpoint as they sealed the doors. Only two nurses and three of us docs. You, me, and the new locums guy, Dr. Trist."

"I met him briefly," Drake said.

"Maybe a touch of job burnout, but he's experienced. He and I have been rotating between here and the telemetry pod while you handle the senator and the gunshot asshole. Patti's covering telemetry and in here and doing the work of four nurses."

"What's happening in telemetry?" The telemetry area was down a short hall from the minor trauma room and typically held chest pain and other at-risk patients who needed cardiac monitoring and close observation.

"No one is crashing," Rizz said. "We're watching the two acid-exposed executives from the refinery closely. Skin burns and pain, so we're keeping them heavily sedated. They're nowhere near as bad as the senator so far, but depending on how much of that shit they breathed in...well, you know." Hydrofluoric acid's ability to continue to penetrate into tissues for hours and days made the executives' outcomes unknowable.

"The third patient?"

"I haven't seen him, but report is he's a recreational drug and alcohol OD. Trist has been handling him. Said the guy's blood alcohol was more than five times legally intoxicated, plus street drugs on board. He's intubated and on a ventilator."

"Okay. Who do we have in here?" Drake asked. In regular use, the minor trauma area held twenty or more patients.

"The terrorists put everyone left in the ER other than the Crash Room and telemetry in here," Rizz said.

Thank God most patients had been cleared out before the takeover and only a handful remained. Drake approached the nearest bed. An elderly African-American woman whose gaunt shoulders poked out skeletally from her gown held the sheet clenched up to her neck.

"Eighty-seven-year-old with dementia," Rizz said softly. "Broke her hip at her nursing home this morning."

"Hi, ma'am. I'm Dr. Cody," Drake bent to her level. She looked at Drake with her eyes wide. "Are you hurting?" She shrank back and shook her head, looking away. Not hurting but definitely scared. "Can I get you anything? Want some water?"

She looked into his face for a moment, eased, then made a come-closer gesture with her hand. He moved so his ear was near her mouth. Her whisper came faint but clear.

"Those bad guys said they'd shoot the niggers first." She clutched her hands to her chest. "You aren't like them, are you?"

Drake remained crouched and placed a hand on her delicate shoulder. "No, Ma'am, I'm not like them. Can you tell me your name?"

"Miss Roberta," she said.

"Miss Roberta, I'm one of your doctors. You're safe. We won't let anyone hurt you. Doctor's orders." He smiled.

"You can order that?" She looked puzzled.

"Absolutely. If anyone disobeys doctor's orders, they'll be in deep trouble." Smiling on the outside, savage thoughts flared in his head.

She smiled. "I would like some water, please."

"I'm on it," Rizz said, wheeling to one of the two sinks within the area.

"Let someone know if you have pain or need anything," Drake said as he straightened.

She caught his hand, clasping it between hers and giving it a squeeze. "Thank you."

Rizz delivered the water and she turned her focus to it.

Several of the privacy curtains were closed. Drake and Rizz moved toward the back of the room. "How're we doing with the other patients in here?" Drake asked.

"An autistic thirteen-year-old kid with a seizure disorder. He's clearing, following a prolonged seizure. He needs IV meds. His mom is with him."

"The boy's name?"

"The kid goes by Newman. Hasn't spoken yet, and Mom says he has some language difficulties. Otherwise, we have a twenty-four-year-old gal, a thirty-four-year-old male protestor, and a fifty-six-year-old working guy. They came from the refinery. They all had respiratory symptoms, but it looks like they were only exposed to the anhydrous ammonia, not the acid. Everyone in here should do well. Most are scared out of their minds."

"Scared makes sense," Drake said. "Tolman blew the agent's head off and didn't bat an eye. You saw the redheaded guy kill the state trooper." Drake glanced toward the door. "Besides being murderers, these prison-ink losers are racist trash—Miss Roberta confirmed that."

"I've picked up that our captors are a wee bit antisocial. Perhaps they're trying to make up for being picked last in dodgeball," Rizz said.

"The big redhead and the three ex-cons, four counting the one who was shot, have Aryan Brotherhood and Nazi tattoos. Hatred and violence is their thing, and I'm sure the one with the long beard is psychotic. None of them are deep thinkers. Tolman is different from them. He's calling the shots. His eyes are empty. He scares me. I don't think he plans on getting away."

"That's not good. He's not looking for money?"

"No hint of that so far. Whatever his mission is, he thinks it's worth his life—and ours. I don't see the others dying for a cause. Could be Tolman is sacrificing them, too. The one who doesn't fit at all is Tolman's son. I get the feeling he was not supposed to be part of this."

"Whether they are all fully committed or not, we could all end up fully dead," Rizz said.

"Agreed. We have to be ready to make a move when we have the best chance. Start thinking of what can be used as a weapon."

"Been doing that from minute one, amigo. The terrorists removed and locked up all the blades and obvious stuff."

"Good luck. One more thing. What do you think about suggesting to everyone that we don't humanize our captors. Don't use their names. Interact as little as possible. We can call the big guy with the weird laugh "Hyena," the wiry pockmarked guy "Pockmark," and the ZZ Top, bearded, crazy-looking guy "Beard guy." Make sense?"

"Trying to avoid Stockholm-syndrome bonding issues?" Rizz said.

"It can't hurt."

"Sure. It makes sense psychologically."

Drake scanned the room. "I'm going to the Crash Room to get ready to handle anesthesia and assist on a laparotomy."

"A surgeon—how'd you make that happen?"

"The truth. Convinced Tolman his nephew definitely dies without surgery. He has a chance if we operate."

Rizz shrugged. "Not sure I care."

"I agree—but getting him to accept a surgeon changes things up. One more person at risk, but I didn't see much chance of us getting out of here alive as things were. Hoping this move provides us, or those on the outside, an opportunity."

"I agree our odds suck. Barricaded in an ER wired with explosives, chemical weapons, a death-wish fanatic in charge, and racist criminals who've already killed cops...where's a life insurance salesman when you need one?" Rizz shook his head. "What saint of a surgeon did you get to step into this nightmare?"

"I had to go with the surgeon scheduled for trauma call today." Drake half-smiled. "I doubt he's ever been called a saint."

Rizz paused for a moment, then his eyebrows arched. "No way."

"I think you got it."

"Is he bigger than a breadbasket?"

"He's bigger than the truck that delivers the bread."

"Holy shit!" Rizz put both hands to his forehead. "Saint Bart, patron saint of zero patience, outrageous outbursts, and staff abuse. Wow, anyone but him."

"I thought the same at first, but consider this," Drake said. "If you were our captors, which doctor on staff would you least want to have to deal with?"

CHAPTER TWENTY-FIVE

Minnesota Twins baseball stadium, six blocks from Memorial Hospital

The glistening Air Care helicopter sat in shallow center field, its powerful engines idling. Aki felt a wave of nausea, thinking about his history with the flying rescue contraptions.

An ambulance drove onto the artificial turf in foul territory down the right field line. Aki and the FBI tech specialist stood near an Escalade with its tailgate open near the dugout. Special Agent McGinnis was on the phone observing on a video link. The vehicle advanced and stopped twenty yards from the Escalade.

Bart Rainey unfolded from the ambulance's rear doors.

"Am I seeing things right?" McGinnis said over the phone. "On my monitor the guy looks to be a giant."

"Yep," Aki said. "He's like six-ten. He's handled a number of the trauma cases my department's been involved with. He's prickly to work with, but the ER docs say he's a good surgeon."

"I've got serious doubts whether letting him go in is the right thing to do," Agent McGinnis said.

"From what I know he's always in charge—or thinks he is. I can't imagine him ever doing anything he doesn't want to."

"Good. Dr. Torrins is second-in-command at the hospital,"

McGinnis said. "He says it's a green light from his angle if the surgeon wants to do it. Dedication to saving lives and all that. Haven't been able to find the CEO. Reports are he might be a hostage in the ER."

"You're better off working with Torrins, believe me," Aki said.

Dr. Bart Rainey's black hair and dark complexion contrasted with his powder-blue scrubs and white doctor's coat. He pulled an oversized toolbox-like plastic case from inside the ambulance. His long strides covered ground quickly. A paramedic trotted alongside, carrying a large reinforced zipped satchel with a shoulder strap. He set it down on the tailgate.

Bart towered over Aki at the back of the SUV.

"I know you," he said to Aki. "Homicide guy. You running this side of things? Let's get moving."

"What's in the case?" Aki asked.

"My instruments. Also brought some anesthesia drugs, as I'm doing this case essentially on my own. One of the gas-passers put together some "white lightning." A mix of ketamine and propofol—should be perfect for this case, and ER guy Cody should be able to handle administering it." He pointed at the large, zippered satchel. "Got a boatload of O-negative blood, some dressings, and other stuff in there. I got what I need. Let's move."

The helicopter engine changed in pitch and increased in volume.

"I have to take a look." The FBI tech grabbed the bag and began to unzip it.

"Hands off." Bart reached out a huge arm, which Aki gently restrained.

"Think about it," Aki said. "We have to check that no one has snuck anything in on you or us."

"Okay, but hurry, dammit." He set the case on the tailgate and signaled the helicopter. The engines revved, and rotor wash reached them.

Aki steered the surgeon to the side but still in front of the camera. He had to yell as the helicopter roared, making ready for takeoff.

"Dr. Rainey, you heard what Dr. Cody said on the phone. You could get killed." Aki looked up into penetrating eyes under massive dark brows. "The odds of a hostage situation like this ending well are not good. I have no idea if they're going to let you fly out after surgery as they promised. Do you truly and completely understand the risk?"

"I'm a surgeon. I don't back down. You wouldn't understand, and you've wasted enough of my time. Get me onto that helipad—now. Even I can't save a guy who's already dead."

CHAPTER TWENTY-SIX

ER – telemetry unit

Tolman moved to the nurses' counter in the area the medical people called telemetry. Red and two of his ex-con gang stood nearby. Tolman stood tall. He'd always maintained a soldier's pride in staying fit. Red shared Tolman's height, but his arms and chest were massively muscled. Always big and freakishly strong, his prison time had turned Red into a beast—in many ways.

The telemetry area had ten beds, each with a ceiling-mounted module from which a horsetail of cables hung below. From his time as a patient in a field hospital in Iraq, Tolman knew the modules displayed vital signs and other information. Only three of the beds were occupied.

A gag and harsh coughing came from the curtained patient bay in the corner. Dr. Trist and the nurse named Patti were taking care of the Black overdose patient.

"Take a big breath," the nurse said from behind the curtain. Another cough. "Good. Big breaths."

Tolman figured they must be getting the patient off the breathing machine. The medical people's focus on patients made them easier to manage. The job they did keeping the senator and Micah alive was impressive. The government official was his blue-chip hostage. The pipeline and refinery fat-cat executives were prime as well. The government always lied, pretending to value all people's lives equally, but the rich and powerful were many times more "equal" than others.

Red's two followers stood next to him, unkempt and slouched. The racist tattoos on their necks and arms confirming their lack of class. Their weapons handling skills were the only features Tolman respected. The bearded one he'd left on guard with the prisoners in the big room was different but no better. He was clearly not right in the head.

More wet-sounding coughs sounded from behind the curtain, then stopped.

"They should let the nigger die," the pockmarked ex-con said.

Tolman worked to keep disgust from his face.

Red's white trash Aryan Brotherhood ex-cons sickened him. Nothing about them approached the courage and discipline of the many Black men Tolman trained and fought beside as a Marine. And besides vouching for these rejects, Red's judgment in accomplishing the ER takeover had failed in a much more significant way. An unforgiveable way.

Red had allowed Sigurd to join with Micah and the ex-cons as they infiltrated the ER. Phony complaints of headaches and nausea while working in a poorly ventilated space with gas engine powered equipment guaranteed admission to the ER to rule out carbon monoxide poisoning.

The plan had worked as he'd been told it would, except that Sigurd should have been at their home base far from the cities. His son was to have no part of the deadly hospital-based portion of the mission. He was too young and too good for his life to end.

Sigurd was, and always had been, like his gentle and loving mother. He should not be here.

Red understood nothing more than his animal urges. He'd caused a lifetime of trouble, and endangering Sigurd was his worst. *Damn him!*

"I'll surveil the helipad from the security video so there'll be no surprises," Tolman said. "They'll land, drop off the surgeon with no more equipment than he can carry, then take off. Anything other than that, and I light up our first remote target. We don't disarm the barrier or access the elevator shaft until I say. Red, you set up a crossfire at the elevator door and search the surgeon and whatever equipment he brings in immediately. Don't miss anything. I don't trust the government or their FBI lackeys."

"This is bullshit," the overweight young ex-con said. "That Micah-dude knew the score going in. Even if he lives, he'll be worthless. Screw him. More money for the rest of us."

"Shut up." Red raised a hand as if to backhand the man. "We do what Tolman says."

The man cowered, his eyes wide. "Sorry, Red."

Tolman's stomach roiled. He should have known better. Despite claiming commitment to freedom and the principles involved, the three losers Red had met while in prison cared only about money and their white supremacy delusions.

Tolman had laid out an operation that involved big money and escape. He'd known the odds were long against it. He understood and accepted that their mission would likely end in death or prison.

He didn't feel a thing about deceiving and sacrificing Red's losers.

"Big breaths and cough," the nurse's voice came from behind the curtain again. "Can you swallow?"

Tolman envied the professionalism and dedication of the healthcare workers. The animals Red had recruited were dedicated to nothing beyond themselves. Historically, most anti-government revolutionary actions were stopped before they started due to loose talk, informants, or undercover law enforcement. Red had assured his crew were zero risk. That had tipped the balance for Tolman. He acknowledged they'd kept the plan quiet and executed as ordered.

The flabby ex-con was right in what he'd said about Micah. Breaking lockdown and allowing the surgeon into the ER posed a serious threat. By now an army of law enforcement personnel surrounded them and were ready to exploit any crack in their defense. Micah on his best day wasn't worth risking the mission. He was a drug-addicted, criminal disgrace to the family. His death in a noble cause would elevate him.

Putting Red at risk had come harder.

His brother was a man-child. His impulses and appetites drove him, and he had no awareness of anything deeper. He could no more recognize the corruption and illegitimacy of the government's theft of Tolman's home and the destruction of his wife's mind and health than understand Chinese.

Tolman needed Red for the plan to succeed. Dog-loyal and physically worth any three men, Red participated because he trusted Tolman totally. The manipulation had bothered him, though after Red's failure to keep Sigurd clear, the sacrifice became easier.

Freedom was never free. Fighting for justice was worth their lives, those of their captives, and many beyond that.

One man counted on getting out of this untouched. Tolman did not begrudge him that ambition. His strategic contributions had proved invaluable. His knowledge essential.

"The copter is coming," said one of Red's stooges.

Tolman made for the security console to monitor the closed-circuit image.

Tolman needed to fulfill the pledge he'd made to his wife in the last days before her mind slipped. Red's lack of judgement had created the problem. The ER doctor's suggestion had opened a door. Tolman could see no other way.

If there was any hint of FBI deception, they'd suffer his destructive power.

They'd been warned.

CHAPTER TWENTY-SEVEN

Operations Control trailer

Dylan McGinnis disconnected with the SWAT team leader. Personnel for four different entry and hostage rescue actions were in position and ready to execute at any time. All of the actions would involve losses, likely extensive losses. The terrorists' position left open two types of options—bad and worse.

His phone buzzed.

"Agent McGinnis here."

"Echo placed and gifts delivered."

"Roger that." McGinnis disconnected. The control center's video screens showed multiple views of inside and outside the hospital. The helipad's red windsock hung limp atop the building after the delivery of the surgeon. The late afternoon's sunshine and expanse of blue sky contrasted with the subdued light and closed-in feel of the operations center.

The team of headset-wearing technicians and the computer consoles, instruments, and video screens reminded Dylan of TV images of NASA control during historic space launches he'd watched as a child. In this instance, a different kind of countdown was underway. and no one knew when "blast-off" might occur.

While risky and the result uncertain, the surgeon's entry presented the first potential chink in the otherwise impenetrable lockdown of the ER. If the surgeon died, he'd die a hero. And despite blowback, the Bureau would be legally clear. Dr. Rainey's recorded exchanges with the ER doctor and Detective Yamada confirmed he knew what he was getting into, though he'd not been informed about the bug. Keeping that secret had been Dylan's decision.

If the high-tech bug were discovered it meant a risk of retaliation, but without more intelligence they were helpless. It could improve what by every assessment were horrendous odds. It could also cost the surgeon his life and the lives of others. Dylan stretched his neck. When would this end?

A communications tech extended a phone to Dylan. "It's the Director."

"Special Agent McGinnis. Yes, Boss?"

"Are resources deployed?"

"10-4. Ready to execute entry and attempted hostage recovery at any moment." Dylan did not need to spell out the status of the huge team of agents and support staff beneath him. Minneapolis SWAT was in position now, but the FBI Hostage Rescue Team had scrambled from Quantico at the first report of suspect terrorist action. They'd be arriving soon and were the tactical team preferred to execute any possible entry of the ER. Most recently, the Special Agent Bomb Coordinator and the Special Agent Weapons of Mass Destruction Coordinator and their teams had arrived on-site.

"Damn, Mr. McGinnis, this is a grim one," the head of the FBI said. "The state governors and attorneys-general have been network-linked as the terrorist demanded. Most of them are career politicians and attorneys—from both sides of the aisle. They usually can't agree on whether it's day or night—and can't make a decision without the input of research staffs and opinion polls. The President is following this minute-to-minute. I know you don't need any more pressure, but I want you to understand that what you recommend will likely be the call. You're the man on the ground at the front, and I've told everyone, including the President, that I trust you completely. What's your take at this point, Dylan?"

Dylan took a deep breath. "Tolman Freid is a unique threat. His combat background, intelligence, and abilities make him unlike any militia or sovereign citizen leader I'm aware of. Everything has been well-planned. He and his crew are formidable—extremely so." How credible were the terrorist leader's threats of massive destruction? The sophistication of his actions to this point and Dylan's gut told him the domestic terrorist wasn't bluffing.

His history, proven leadership, intelligence, and basis for righteous rage made Dylan's throat tighten. How many lives would Tolman Freid be willing to sacrifice?

"What's your best assessment of what he wants?" the director asked.

"There's been no mention of money. He claims he's a patriot, and his extremist views on the government-corporate power structure are long-standing. He suffered devastating injustice in the loss of his home and, in his mind, his wife. I believe rage and revenge are primary factors," Dylan said. "I suspect in the end he wants what all extremists want—revolution."

"I was briefed on what happened to him and his family," the head of the FBI said. "Unfortunately, sometimes things that are technically legal are flat-out wrong. What's your assessment of worst-case?"

"He's a fanatic—as deadly or worse than any foreign terrorist. The lockdown mechanism of the ER has been turned inside-out. They've wired all access points with explosive devices, and chemical weapons are likely. The acid they used at the refinery is brutal stuff. Without a change in status, the likelihood of recovering hostages is extremely low, and our tactical team casualties will be high. They may blow the entire building. We don't know."

"Not what I'd hoped to hear," the director said.

"There's an even more worrisome possibility," Dylan said. "The explosions and chemical weapon release at the refinery were limited, but it confirmed they have engineering skills, as well as hazardous materials access and explosives knowledge. Volume and delivery mechanism are the only things limiting the creation and placement of a much larger and deadlier device. They've shown they have the ability to create a weapon of mass destruction. I hope they haven't done it."

"My God, that would be our worst nightmare," the director said.

"Apologies, sir, but no. The worst is if they've created more than one."

CHAPTER TWENTY-EIGHT

Minor trauma area

Rizz wheeled to the counter next to where Patti prepared an IV solution.

"For the seizure kid?" he asked.

"Yes," she said. "Other than him, no one else needs anything IV. No one is very sick back here. Between our earlier clearing out for possible mass casualties and our captives driving others out, we don't have many patients at all. If you need to go anywhere to help out," she switched to speaking under her breath, "and kill these creeps," she returned to normal volume "I can handle everyone back here."

"Thanks." He lowered his voice. "Look for and gather anything that can be used as a weapon. At some point we're going to have to make a move. By the way, you're cute when you talk about killing creeps."

She rolled her eyes, but he saw the hint of a smile as she took the IV solution and headed toward one of the curtained sites.

Damn, he had to watch himself. The comment about 'cute' he'd just made could cost him his job if overheard or said to the wrong person. Patti and the majority of ER people knew him well enough to not take offense at his politically incorrect comments.

He'd worked with Patti for years and everything about her was special to him.

He'd never told her how he felt. He avoided admitting it to himself. With her he used jokes to keep his distance. He did it with everyone. It kept him safe.

He loved most of the people he worked with. Working shoulder-to-shoulder in the intense world of the ER forged bonds as close as family.

He wondered if what he felt was reciprocated, or if he was looked at like a drunken uncle. Most people knew that outside of work he specialized in partying, one-night stands, and shallow relationships. Did they tolerate him at work because he made them laugh and kicked ass as a physician?

What did they think of him a person?

Yikes, Rizzini! What's with the self-analysis and feelings crap?

His personal philosophy included avoidance of serious self-contemplation. He tried to stay focused on what he needed or wanted to do and doing it. Right now, he didn't need to worry about who liked him or about keeping his job—the challenge was how to keep himself and everyone else alive.

Three patients sat on adjoining cots with the curtains open. Rizz had scanned their info and mentioned them to Drake, but only Trist had examined them. They were from the refinery, and it appeared they'd been exposed to anhydrous ammonia and not the hydrofluoric acid: a stocky fifty-six-year-old Black man, a thirty-four-year-old man with long hair and a nose ring, and a twenty-four-year-old blonde woman whom he unprofessionally identified as a babe. They all wore hospital gowns, the young woman wearing three of them overlapped, with a sheet over her shoulders as well.

Rizz rolled to them.

"I'm Dr. Rizzini. How are you all doing?"

"I'm Antoine. Physically doing good," the sturdy-looking fifty-six-year-old said. "Cough about gone and eyes aren't burning anymore."

"I'm Cecil," the thirty-four-year-old interrupted. "When are you going to get us out of here? This is outrageous. I insist—"

"Damn, can you be quiet, boy?" Antoine said. "The doctor is trapped as much as any of us. Always got to be griping."

"I understand," Rizz said. "This is scary stuff."

"Excuse me, doctor, but you don't understand this one. He hasn't shut up since he climbed into the ambulance." Antoine shook his head. "He's a professional whiner. Came from Illinois to protest our pipeline—"

"I'm an activist!" Cecil's voice climbed. "I'm dedicated to engaging for the social good. As a man of color, you should appreciate what I—"

"What I *appreciate* is that you are working to lose me my job. I'm a union pipefitter and I'm proud to work at the refinery. I bet you probably live in your momma's basement and don't know a thing about taking care of a family."

"Okay, easy, guys. We've got more immediate problems." Rizz said.

The young lady spoke, her voice breaking. "I'm Phoenix Halvorsen. I'm okay physically, but I'm scared. Never been so scared. I need to be protected. It's very important I stay safe."

"We'll all watch out for one another, Phoenix." Rizz said. *Feels fairly important that I stay safe too, pretty lady.*

"Doctor, one of those racist pigs has been abusive toward her person," Antoine said. "The fat younger one who laughs like a lunatic. I call him Hyena. He's acting like he might...you know...do bad stuff to the young lady." He shook his head. "He needs his ass kicked."

Phoenix put her face in her hands. Antoine shifted from his seat and sat next to her, putting a protective arm around her.

"Do any of you have a military background or know how to fight?" Rizz said.

"I support civil disobedience, but I don't believe in violence toward my fellow humans," Cecil said.

Antoine huffed. "Those are your fellow humans? Damn." He turned to Rizz and held up a fist. "Semper Fi. Two tours in the Sandbox."

"Thank you, sir. Glad you're with us," Rizz said.

"No offense, doctor," he grimaced, "but can't say I feel the same."

Rizz smiled.

"I'm not tough," Phoenix said, her eyes tear-filled. "I need to be kept safe."

"You'll do fine, young lady," Antoine said. "You got a plan, doctor?"

"Dr. Cody was just here. You saw him, right?"

"He told the pock-scarred Nazi to kiss his ass. I'm a fan," Antoine said.

"Drake is heading things up, but it's going to take all of us. When it's go-time it's full out. We give it everything we've got." Rizz scanned their faces. Antoine and Phoenix nodded. Cecil did not meet his eyes.

"Protesting won't help, Cecil," Rizz said. "We fight or we die."

PHOENIX CLOSED the door to the minor trauma bathroom. She adjusted her gown, put a leg on the commode, and retrieved the iWatch.

She felt like she was starring in a disaster movie, but she could no longer tell what her role was. She ping-ponged between being the so-scared-she-felt-sick girl who needed the others to protect her and the gifted reporter who'd be the one to break the biggest stories ever. The one who, despite her fear, had been internally crafting the words to capture the drama. Only she was capable of deciphering for the American people what was happening and why.

The scared girl in her would do anything to be safe. She was too young and too important to die. Her parents, her nannies, and her instructors had all told her she was special. She knew it was true. It would be such a waste if she did not realize her dreams. The world would be a lesser place.

In the moment she knew her role. The one she'd been destined for.

Her byline would be on front pages and television worldwide.

It was a newspaper fact that bad news was great for business. An exclusive report involving a high death-count disaster would make her a media star—as long as she were not one of those killed. She held in her hand the means to share the story that would make her ambitions reality.

Should she do it? Dare she?

She opened the notes function and dictated in a voice just above a whisper. She used her imagination and creative skills to craft a story that would engage readers and highlight the underlying social injustice she believed gave rise to it. As she finished, she was on the verge of tears. The story had come to life in minutes. Never had a story flowed as readily. She'd exercised creative license, but she was entitled. If she did not survive, this submission could be her legacy. It would color her as selfless, heroic, and committed to others. It was her due.

She entered her editor's email address and stared at it with her thumb over the "send" button.

The article would ignite the first stage booster of her rocket to fame.

She pressed the key.

Immediately, she gasped and clutched at the device with both hands as if to catch the electronic message in flight.

Her stomach clenched. The scared girl in her recognized what might happen. *My God!*

What had she done?

CHAPTER TWENTY-NINE

ER corridor

The flight elevator indicator flashed the declining floor numbers. Drake knew the sensation Bart Rainey was experiencing as the elevator plunged from the helipad to the ER. Weightlessness followed by the gravity multiplier of deceleration. Drake managed critically ill patients during his descents, but he'd never had to face armed extremists when he arrived.

The elevator pinged and the doors slid open. Dr. Bart Rainey ducked his head as he stepped out. A satchel hung over one shoulder and he gripped a plastic suitcase in the other hand.

"Son of a bitch!" The pockmarked con regripped his rifle as he took in Bart's nearly seven-foot towering mass.

Bart Rainey, MD—the largest person Drake had ever met. Despite having seen him many times, his size still stunned.

"On your knees, nigger," Red said. Shorter by four or five inches, the heavily muscled ex-con held his rifle aimed at Bart's head.

Bart caught Drake's eyes. He shook his head. "Damn. Greeted by a moronic racist, though that's redundant. You've outdone yourself this time, ER."

"I said, on your knees, boy!" Red stepped forward, his jaw clenched. He stuck the gun barrel in Bart's face.

"Lighten up, sunshine." Bart raised a hand and moved to push the gun barrel aside. "Where's my patient—"

Blink-quick, Red pivoted and slammed the rifle butt into Bart's gut. The blow sounded like a bat striking a side of beef. Bart's breath left in an explosive *huhh*. He collapsed to the floor, the case he held dropping from his hand. He lay on his side, doubled-up, gripping his stomach and fighting for breath. Red stepped forward, eyes wild, and raised his boot above Bart's head.

"No!" Tolman yelled.

Red's foot froze over Bart's head.

"We need him."

Red drove his foot down. The sole of his boot impacted the floor like a piledriver an inch from Bart's face.

Drake advanced to check Bart.

"Get back!" Red's attention turned to Drake.

"He's hurt," Drake said. "He's the only chance Micah has."

Red stood gasping, his muscles flexed, his lip curled, looking as if he might snap his rifle in two.

Even when Red had gunned down the state trooper, he'd shown little emotion. Now he looked more animal than human. Bart had a dark complexion. He could be of mixed race, though Drake had never given it a thought. Is that what triggered Red? Or was it the threat of Bart's size or the surgeon's apparent lack of fear? Drake as a juvenile violent offender had seen similar savagery when a gang member stomped a rival's face to pulp.

"The doc is right, Red. Search him and his gear. Don't miss anything," Tolman said.

"And you," Tolman said to Drake. "You didn't think to mention the surgeon is a damn giant?"

"It's a doctor's skills that matter, not what he or she looks like," Drake said.

Red's eyes still burned as his crew began to search Bart and his gear. "Whether he saves Micah or not, if this mud person gets uppity again I'll kill him. Count on that."

Drake swallowed. Bart had barely survived the first minute. Had Drake's plan improved their odds or ignited disaster?

CHAPTER THIRTY

Crash Room

The blow Red landed would keep most men out of action for hours. Once able to breathe, and after being searched, Bart stood as if unhurt and stared at Red.

"Try more roughage in your diet, little guy. You won't be as cranky," Bart said.

The flabby ex-con's hyena cackle started but died instantly with Red's look.

Drake picked up the satchel and case and helped Bart into the Crash Room. Once out of sight of the others, the surgeon doubled over.

"Let me examine you." Drake put a hand on Bart's shoulder. "He could have ruptured your spleen."

Bart straightened and pushed Drake's hand away. "Punkass racist bitch. Been hit harder playing hoops. Get scrubbed, ER."

Bart began to prepare for surgery with winces and sharp inhalations as he moved.

Drake gowned, then did an assessment of the senator, who looked terrible but unchanged. ECMO continued to do the job his lungs could not. The senator's ventilator didn't accomplish gas exchange but helped maintain the airways. The rhythmic sound and rise and fall of his chest somehow reassured. The fetid odor of his devastated lungs circulated—faint and unsettling.

Tracy stood gowned and gloved next to Bart. Drake readied himself to assist from the other side of their patient. Three surgical stands were in position with sterile trays of instruments, sutures, and packing.

"You sure you're okay, Bart?" Drake said.

"I'm light-years beyond okay. It's time for me to do my thing. You two try not to mess up my work." Bart in full surgical garb with mask and cap looked even more massive and imposing than usual. "My rule number one—do what I tell you, when I tell you." He paused a beat. "And if you have any questions, refer to rule number one."

Tracy had done a great job turning Bay three of the Crash Room into a functional OR. Sterile sheets hung on the clips of the curtains that slid to enclose the treatment bay. Two large surgical suction setups and an autotransfuser were in place to manage and collect the blood during the procedure. The monitor module hung above the bed, beeping at the pace of their patient's struggling heart. The man's abdomen showed through the blue surgical drapes with a portion of his swastika evident. The surgical lights centered around the ugly, gaping defect where the bullet had entered. Six units of the blood Bart had brought had been run into the patient and two additional were infusing.

"Keep blood running wide open at all times," Bart said. "Okay, inject the lightning, ER. He's as close to dead as can be. Even with a real anesthesiologist and surgical nurse, saving him would be a miracle. If I pull it off with you clowns, I'm a magician."

"Thanks for the pep talk." Drake fit the syringe to the IV port. "Tracy's doing the work of three people and kicking ass. Give me shit if you want, but disrespect her and you and I are going to have an issue. That's my rule number one, amigo."

Drake pushed the plunger, and fifty milliliters of white lightning—a milk-white combination of ketamine and propofol—surged through the IV into the patient. The anesthetic mixture combined the properties of propofol and ketamine—the patient would feel nothing, be unaware, and the drugs would not blunt the function of his heart.

The neuromuscular blocker drug Drake had injected two minutes earlier would maintain the patient's paralysis. The ventilator marched on, driving the deeply anesthetized man's lungs to deliver oxygen and expel carbon dioxide.

"He's good to go, Bart."

"Be ready. When I open this mutt's belly, it will decompress the vessels like undoing a tourniquet." Bart held the scalpel poised above the midline of the abdomen. "Every bleeding site will become a gusher. Visibility will be shit and he'll bleed out in minutes if you mess me up. Keep those lights centered and suction aggressively, but keep the hell out of my way."

He nodded his head toward the surgical stand and open tray of instruments he'd positioned nearest him. "If I ask you to hand me something, do it fast and do not cut me."

"Understood," Drake said.

"Observe and marvel, children." Bart's scalpel carved a deep track down the midline, the skin opening and the deep glistening tissues bursting into view as if the belly were being unzipped. The peritoneal membrane enclosing the abdominal cavity bulged dark and threatening. Bart incised it and blood surged out like a burst pipe. The metallic, fecund smells of blood and gut penetrated Drake's mask.

Bart plunged one suction device deep into the abdominal cavity while Drake directed the other. Twin columns of blood raced through one-half-inch suction tubes and into the collection chambers of the auto-transfuser for re-infusion.

The blood level in the abdominal cavity descended like water in a full kitchen sink with the drain unplugged. As the blood retreated, the bowel, liver, and spleen rose into view.

"Shit, shit, shit," Bart said. "Bullet trashed the liver, and most of the bleeding is coming from retrohepatic."

Drake marveled that Bart could discern any details in the intra-abdominal mess, much less tell where the blood was coming from. Drake's experience in the OR while training had included assisting on a patient whose bullet wound involved a retrohepatic or "behind the liver" bleeding site. The vessels located there can't be reached surgically to repair or tie off. The patient had died on the table.

"Suction, ER, damn it." Bart's huge hands flew. "I need to see. Pull your head out of your ass."

Using large, curved needles and heavy suture, Bart repaired the gaping irregular defect the bullet had exploded in the liver. Bart's huge fingers danced as he tied off multiple bleeding vessels.

Drake's ears noted a change. The beeping of the pulse monitor had accelerated.

"Blood pressure has dropped to eighty over sixty, Dr. Cody," Tracy said. "Pulse has climbed to one twenty-five."

Despite Bart's speed in handling the bleeders, they couldn't keep up with the blood loss. With many bleeding sites controlled, Drake could now recognize the site of the major flow Bart had somehow seen in the first instant. Dark blood welled from the surgical no-man's-land behind the liver as if from a faucet.

"How much fluid and blood in so far, Tracy?" Drake asked.

"I'll tell you, damn it." Bart said. "Not enough! You're not keeping up. You're killing this guy." His brow glistened with sweat. His hands continued to race.

"Two liters of lactated ringers and the fourth and fifth units of blood are almost in. Everything is running in wide open." Tracy's voice was calm. "Transfusion record is the four units we had, the six from Dr. Rainey we raced in pre-op, and now finishing the fourth and fifth additional units. Total of fifteen units. We only have four units left. We're collecting and recirculating all we can with the autotransfuser as well."

Drake looked at the vitals monitor. Blood pressure seventy-five over thirty. Pulse one-hundred-thirty.

"Bart, blood pressure is dropping and pulse rising. Even with autotransfusion, we're not able to keep up."

"I'm not deaf, ER. I heard her." Bart had virtually all the bleeding stopped except that from behind the liver.

"Retrohepatic, damn," Drake said.

Bart shot a raised-eyebrows glance at Drake. "Surprised you comprehend what I'm dealing with, ER. Impossible to get at surgically. Interventional radiology could embolize but not an option in your cuckoo's nest today. It's like I'm operating in a third world country. Only chance is to pack him tight and buy him some time."

Drake grabbed a stack of the surgical sponges. The aim was to pack enough of the sterile gauze-like material into the abdomen to put pressure on the bleeding sites and stop the bleeding.

Bart began wedging the sterile packing strategically within the abdomen. They coordinated almost instantly. Drake began to take initiative and hand Bart what was needed before he had to ask. Tracy kept blood and fluids flowing. They worked quickly without words while the monitor's beeping and the ventilator's sounds marked time. The high-intensity lights, surgical garb, and pressure had all their brows sweating.

The bleeding slowed to an ooze. Tracy called out vital signs that stabilized and then began to improve.

"We put a finger in the dike," Bart said.

Drake winked at Tracy. Bart had slipped up. He'd said "we."

"It's up to you now, ER. Can you get crazy-ass boss man to have this nearly dead Nazi flown out?" Bart continued his skilled work, his hands seemingly on autopilot as he placed large sutures to close the abdomen wall. "If he gets flown to another hospital, interventional radiologists can access the bleeding sites from within the blood vessels and inject them with foam gel to block the flow. With all that I did to slow the bleeding, that might be enough to save this terrorist asshole. Far from a sure thing but his only chance."

"I can try. At times he seems reasonable, the next instant he's a lunatic."

"Sell him on it, ER. We can't do it here because he and his gang of losers have shut this hospital down. And see who else you can get to ride out on the bird. For starters, get Tracy safe."

What? Tracy's head raised and Drake felt sure that under her mask her jaw had dropped.

"I'm with you on that, Bart. We also need to get you out of here. Tolman's brother is looking to take you out. He's an animal."

"He can kiss my ass. I pissed the racist bastard off real good, and I liked it. I'm Greek, Italian, and Cherokee and proud of it, but he obviously hates whatever he thinks I am. I'd like to keep it that way. I'm not backing down from that jerk-wad. Get Tracy, the patient, and whomever else you can safely out of here. With the number of guns around here and the goons who have them, I'd say the possibility of someone needing my skills looks pretty high." He pulled a suture snug. "I'm hoping I'm not needed, but I prefer saving citizens rather than racist cretins like this guy."

"You know what giving up your flight out of here means?" Drake lowered his voice. "I believe our only chance of getting out of this alive is to attack at some point. Feels like we're on one of the jets headed for the World Trade Center on 9/11 and we need to make a move before we crash and burn. They're dug in, heavily armed, locked down, and booby-trapped. Any law enforcement action is probably going to end up with most or all of us dead and who knows how many others."

"Damn, ER. Try and control your optimism and don't ever go into sales," Bart shook his head. "Whenever you call me, it's a train wreck, but this is the consult from hell."

"Guilty as charged," Drake said. "So you won't take your ride out on the copter?"

Bart pulled another suture snug.

"I'm staying," the big man said. "But I insist on one thing."

"What?" Drake said.

"When it's go-time, I got dibs on that carrot-topped douchebag."

CHAPTER THIRTY-ONE

Drake, Bart, and Tracy stepped out from the curtains surrounding their makeshift OR.

They stripped off the gloves, surgical caps, masks, eye shields, and gowns. The layers of protective gear always acted like a self-contained sauna for Drake. His head was sweaty and his scrubs were dark over his chest and armpits. Bart looked as if a bucket of water had been dumped over his head. The surgeon ducked back through the curtains. Tracy, also subject to the heat lamps, high-intensity lights, and stress, had a damp brow and temples but somehow was otherwise sweat-free.

"I'll recheck the senator now," Tracy said. "And Drake, I'm not climbing on a helicopter. The senator needs me. Patti and I are the only nurses. I'm not leaving."

Her eyes left no doubt.

Who could Drake get to safety? First, he had to convince Tolman to let his nephew be flown out. And if not Bart or Tracy on board, whom? Who best to get a ticket to live? Those left behind, staff and patients alike, stood a good chance of dying. The choice of who stayed also affected the chances for survival of those left behind when they made the do-or-die attack Drake anticipated they must.

Clacking curtain rings sounded as Bart pulled the OR barrier open a couple of feet. His shaggy, black-haired head craned down toward Drake.

"My patient may be a racist-creep, but he's a racist-creep with improved vital signs." He shrugged. "Damn, I'm good. Gonna be a shame to have to turn his care over to lesser doctors, but I'm used to that. I'll get him packaged and handwrite a surgical report and instructions on how to carry on. Get the boss dickhead to let him get flown out of here. It'd be a shame to let my brilliant work go to waste." He ducked back behind the curtain.

Often a jerk but a dedicated jerk. Single and a loner, Bart proved to be someone very different than his words and history suggested. He would be a great ally in any fight.

Drake thought about Rachelle and the kids. What had they heard? He looked at the Life Clock ticking above the senator's bay. It seemed impossible that only a couple of hours had passed since the explosion and acid release. The senator was hanging on, and he was not alone. Everyone's life clock was ticking now.

RIZZ ROLLED into the Crash Room as Drake toweled off his sweat-soaked hair near the sink in the far corner.

"You just finished surgery with Bart. Was it the ego-boosting experience I'd expect?" Rizz said softly enough that Bart could not hear.

"Nothing a few years of intensive counseling can't fix." Drake smiled. "But Bart did strong work. Brutal injuries. Great work keeping the guy alive."

"Speaking of brutal, I'm sorry, Drake. I blew it. This shitstorm is my fault." Rizz shook his head. "Security told me Tolman's documentation checked out, and the guy looks like he stepped off an executive recruitment poster. I let the leader of a domestic terrorist group into our emergency department and watched him take over. Damn me!" He hammered his fist on the arm of his wheelchair.

"Easy, Rizz. Anyone would have," Drake said. "His whole damn goon squad was already in the ER with a cache of weapons. They checked in as patients or posed as workers. Tolman could have done the same but probably got off on the ego trip of posing as a government official. As far as the documentation goes, that's a specialty of these sovereign-citizen types."

"I feel like I let everyone down."

"The hospital's commitment to security has been half-ass. We all knew that this or some other badness was coming. This could have been most any hospital or ER in the country. Don't beat yourself up."

"I wish I could turn back the clock."

"When you figure out that trick, let me know," Drake said.

"Thanks for trying to make me feel better," Rizz said. "But this is ripping me—"

Muffled yelling sounded from the corridor outside the Crash Room.

Drake moved into the hall. The voices came from the emergency department auxiliary X-ray suite adjacent to the flight elevator.

Their captors had emptied that room. They'd closed that door, but now it was the origin of the disturbance.

The yelling stopped and bizarre laughter accompanied what was now the voice of a man pleading. As Drake looked, the door swung open. Drake's jaw dropped.

CEO Stuart Kline staggered through the door and then lurched ahead as the flabby, hyena-laugh ex-con landed a fierce kick to his ass. Kline sprawled forward, landing with his hands outstretched on the floor.

"Don't hurt me!" Kline's custom suit, coiffed hair, and cufflinks appeared even more out of place now than they did all the other times he appeared in areas of patient care.

He flipped to his seat and backed up against the wall, holding his hands raised in front of him. "Don't hurt me. I can help you. This is my hospital."

Tolman Freid and the other captors approached from both ends of the corridor.

"Who's this pretty boy?" Red said, staring.

"*Your* hospital?" Tolman Freid said with a frown.

"I'm Stuart Kline. I'm the CEO of Memorial Hospital. I can help.

Just don't hurt me." He looked around and flushed as he saw Drake and Rizz. "Er, uh...and don't hurt them either."

"Where'd you find this guy?" Tolman asked the cackling, fleshy con.

"I went in the X-ray room there. You know, being alert and checking on stuff. I heard a noise and found him hiding in a cabinet."

Drake pictured Kline curled up in the tiny X-ray cabinet since the takeover.

"Who checked that room before?" Tolman asked.

"Well, er, it was me," the Nazi-tattooed terrorist said. "He wasn't in there then."

Tolman went to the door to the room.

"And you just checked again because you're so alert, huh?"

"Er, yes. Yes, sir."

Tolman pushed open the door. The cloying scent of marijuana reached Drake's nose.

"Come here," Tolman said.

The ex-con moved toward him.

"Stick your head in here."

The man did.

"You smell anything?"

"Er, uh, no."

"That's surprising," Tolman said. "Especially for an alert guy like you." He half-turned away, then pivoted back, burying his fist in the fleshy man's gut.

"Ufff." Air exploded out of the ex-con as he dropped to the floor, doubled over.

"No more screw-ups, and do not ever lie to me. This isn't your Aryan prison gang dealing with a bunch of fellow imbeciles. We're facing SWAT and tactical ops teams, likely including military personnel. Get your act together. That goes for all of you."

He scanned the eyes of the other armed men. All but Red failed to hold his gaze.

"You vouched for these losers, Red. Keep them in line. And lock Mr. 'This is my hospital' in that room by the main desk. He could be useful." Tolman wrinkled his nose. "The cowardly little shit sure is willing."

CHAPTER THIRTY-TWO

Senator Duren's residence

Evangeline Duren stood with a fist to her mouth while their home office printer spit out a copy of the newest ransom payment instructions. Her mind was going a hundred miles an hour, but her thoughts ran into dead ends everywhere.

The ransom demands had posed no challenge. Evangeline had retired from a career at the highest levels of finance, and Hayden donated more money to charity each year than she'd made at her peak. They had so much money it was, in some ways, a political liability. If not for Hayden being a self-made man who was genuinely kind and likable, his wealth could trigger resentment among voters. She shuddered thinking of losing him. Fear gripped her chest as if she were being squeezed in a giant fist. He was even a better man than claimed in the most flowery of his campaign materials.

She'd gathered the five million dollars the kidnapper demanded quickly without the need to engage in attention-attracting transactions. The conversion to cryptocurrency and transfer instructions likewise posed no difficulty for her. The terrorists' demands and payment strategy showed sophistication in money and electronic transfer processes.

They must have researched her background. Most people would not have had the knowledge needed to follow the payment orders. It was not an accident that the demands were quick and easy for her to follow. Though she knew it was a group of terrorists, the communications made her feel as if she were dealing with one person. That person wanted the payment to be quick and untraceable. Did that mean this would all be over soon and Hayden would be back safe in her arms? *God in heaven, please!*

"What can I do, ma'am?" her assistant Harley Aften asked. "Can you give me the phone numbers from the texts you received? I can check call origins without it being known."

Harley Aften's job label was driver and executive assistant. His brother Marcus held the same title. They were much more. The former Army Rangers and police officers were two of the five individuals who provided round-the-clock security for the Durens. Marcus had been the first, and the bond he and Hayden shared went beyond work. Knowing Marcus was with Hayden gave Evangeline hope, despite the horrifying images she'd seen of what had been done to Hayden. As long as Marcus lived, she knew he would do everything possible to keep Hayden alive.

"I'll give you the numbers, but I'll remind you that you must not say anything about the ransom to anyone," Evangeline said. "I return-messaged that I needed proof of life, and I included Marcus, too."

"I won't say a word, ma'am. Thanks for doing that for Marcus. We'll get them home."

"Whoever is doing this to us is sophisticated. They're intelligent and knowledgeable. I don't know if that's good or more reason to be scared." Her voice cracked. "I keep thinking about movies and TV where they don't leave witnesses and...and..." She put her face in her hands and her shoulders quaked as she cried silently. *Please come home, Hayden!*

Harley stepped forward and put an arm around her. "They'll be okay, Ma'am," he said. "Marcus will make sure of it."

STAR TRIBUNE EXECUTIVE OFFICE

"What do you mean, *should we* run this?" circulation manager Ron Dill said. "You can't be serious. If it bleeds, it leads. We run it just as it is—raw, emotional, and totally exclusive! We break this every way to Sunday. We string this, with prominent Star Tribune attribution, out to every national and international media market—AP, UPI, and everywhere. And we need a spokesperson—how about Tricia Camino, the crime reporter? We can get her interviewed on Fox, MSNBC, CNN—everywhere—as a breaking story exclusive from the Star Tribune."

"Hold on, Ron. There are deeper considerations." Senior editor Stan Troback took his glasses off and looked at Ron and fifty-four-year-old Margaret Spikehan, who was the newspaper's majority owner and the main decision-maker in the room. "What about safety?"

"Safety! Are you shitting me?" Ron flapped his hand toward Marv and turned to Margaret. "Let's use Tricia for sure. She's smart as hell and it won't hurt that she's a babe." He hesitated. "Appearance is important only from a demographic analysis perspective, of course."

"Has legal looked at this?" Stan turned to Margaret. Ron was a lost cause when it came to appealing to notions of journalistic integrity or responsibility. As in many meetings, Stan felt like the dinosaur in the room. Margaret would sit and say little, but in the end she would decide. Stan had to persuade her. Ron never thought beyond revenues and profit.

"Legal? God, Stan," Ron said. "What are you worried about? That our reporter has slandered a gang of domestic terrorists who released a chemical weapon, took over a hospital ER, and are holding a US senator and others hostage?"

"Ron, please," Stan said. "Can you think past circulation and revenues for one second? This young reporter is in danger."

"It's Phoenix, Phoenix Halvorsen. Besides her father being part owner of the paper and on the board, the girl is ambitious. She's the one who ran the story on possible racist care at Memorial Hospital. Almost broke big," Ron said. "She wants us to run this."

"Yes, I know who her father is. She makes it impossible not to— she uses his influence to get her the assignments she wants. And need I remind you her claims in that hospital story were baseless and almost got the paper sued. If not for her father, we all know she would have been fired." Stan shook his head. "Ambitious young reporters take journalistic and personal risks. Some will do anything to see their bylines on front-page stories and climb the media ladder to fame and fortune. I wonder if she thought this through? We need to be careful."

"Damn, Stan. Half the time you're afraid our slant will upset the board or stockholders. Other times you're worried about the police or others being offended. Now you're afraid this story isn't 'safe.' She's a big girl. Come on, man. This is a gift. It's huge."

"The issue of 'slant' is a broader discussion, Ron. In this new age, ambition and politics trump journalistic responsibility and commitment to the truth. You've read her draft—it's inflammatory, plus it makes her sound like a cross between Ruth Bader Ginsburg and Wonder Woman. If these criminals see it—and they likely will if we do what you recommend— how do you think they'll react? They're terrorists, Ron."

"Are we a news organization or what? Have some courage."

"Putting others in increased danger is not courage, Ron. And concern for the safety of others is not cowardice."

"Hey, we don't make the news, we report it."

"Sometimes I wonder," Stan said. He was ready to give up and retire. Much of what passed for journalism these days had degenerated into something he did not want to be associated with anymore. "At a minimum, we need to discuss this with legal and law enforcement. It's not just about ratings and ad revenues. We could get Phoenix and others killed."

Stan and Ron looked to Margaret at the head of the table.

Her brow furrowed. She sipped from a glass of water, set it aside, and folded her hands in front of her.

"I agree we have a responsibility to protect our reporter, even if she were not Edwin Halvorsen's daughter. We also need to inform the public. That's the business we are in. We will edit any fanciful, dangerous, or biased content from her draft and run the abridged version past legal and law enforcement just before we publish. We're not conceding editing authority to legal or law enforcement but are open to hearing major objections or concerns for public safety. I agree with wide distribution and making Tricia available to the major networks."

She picked up her small notepad and stood up.

"This is a horrible, terrible story, but one that will make our paper the focus of world news. We will take advantage of that opportunity fully. Pray that our young reporter returns to us intact."

CHAPTER THIRTY-THREE

The Cody family's new home

Rachelle's cellphone trilled, causing her to jump as if a firecracker had gone off behind her. She grabbed her phone from the table near the picture window overlooking the lake. The caller ID read *Jon Molnar*.

Jon and Rizz were not only Drake's emergency physician partners but his closest friends. Shared tragedy had made them special people to Rachelle, too. Rizz had taken a bullet to protect Rachelle, Drake, and their children. Jon had been shot and near death and was recovering in isolation at his parents' home in Duluth. Drake had shared reports that Jon's physical recovery was on track, but his mental and emotional health were a worry.

"Jon?"

"Rachelle, this is terrible. What have you heard? I'm driving down from Duluth now."

"Dr. Torrins called me. I'd been outside without my phone. Just after he reached me, an FBI agent came to the house. She just left."

"Are you okay?"

"It's terrorists, Jon." Her voice broke. "They're holding Drake and others hostage. They killed a policewoman on the highway and at least one other person in the ER."

"As soon as I heard I jumped in my car and am headed for the cities. I talked with Torrins. He said they have Rizz, another doctor, Tracy, and at least one other nurse hostage, plus patients," Jon said. "Drake isn't alone. They'll help each other."

"But you know he'll be in the middle of it. He thinks the whole damn ER and everybody in it is his responsibility." She'd held together so far, but any moment she might crack. Her heart lodged in her throat. "I'm praying, Jon. I'm so scared."

"Me, too," Jon said.

"The FBI agent who came to the house said they're doing everything they can, but—" She swallowed. "I worry he'll get himself killed trying to protect the others."

"Is anyone with you?" Jon said.

"The kids are with Kaye. She had them today, and we agreed it made sense for them to stay with her until this is over. They're safe, and if they're around me they'll feel my fear. I'm hanging on but it's hard."

"Is it a good idea to be home alone?"

"The FBI offered, but I didn't feel comfortable with a stranger around. Our new place locks down tight and is fully wired with alarms. The FBI said they'll have police watching the place, and we're on a cul-de-sac."

"I don't know, Rachelle, maybe—"

"Believe me, I'm not taking any chances, Jon." Having survived the nightmare of being held hostage with the kids made caution like breathing. She rubbed the scar tissue on her hands and wrists. "I'm safe inside looking out over the lake with a shotgun lying on the table and a remote trigger to our security alarm within reach." The lake was calm, the sky clear, and the birch and oak of their shoreline framed the view in fall colors. How was it possible something so ugly could be happening less than a twenty-minute drive away?

"I just learned no one is allowed near the hospital," Jon said. "I don't know what to do with myself, and I'd feel better if you weren't alone. How about I come to your place?"

"You don't have to—" She paused. "What am I saying? Yes, that would be nice."

"Great. Please text me the address. This is not the way I wanted to visit your new home. I should be in the cities before long. I'll call when I get close. Call me if you need anything, and stay safe."

"I will. Thanks." Rachelle disconnected, then texted the address to him.

She could tell Jon was plenty scared. Such a kind and caring man— it made the horrendous things that had happened to him even crueler. Hearing his voice helped. She was glad he hadn't tried to minimize her fears or falsely reassure her.

She picked up the shotgun and checked the safety once again. The weapon both comforted and scared her.

She was safe, but how must Drake be feeling? Even though he never seemed afraid of anything and he handled disasters for a living, this was another order of magnitude beyond bad.

How was it possible that they once again faced such horrible danger? Was she still being paid back for the terrible mistakes of her past?

She loved him and knew he believed he loved her. She wasn't confident it was true—would he love her if he knew the truth? She might lose him without her ever having had the decency to confess the terrible lie at the heart of their time together. *God, if you bring Drake back to me, I'll tell him everything. No more living with the lie.*

Perhaps Drake didn't feel fear, but she did. And she'd failed many times before. Now her fear was beyond measure, but she was not that person anymore. No hyperventilating. No panic. She'd do her best for Drake and for the children.

She must.

CHAPTER THIRTY-FOUR

"Where'd they put Kline?" Drake asked Rizz as he rolled into the Crash Room. They moved to a back corner. The sounds of the monitors, ventilators, and the ECMO machine provided cover.

"They locked him in one of the Psych rooms," Rizz said. "More fitting than they know, but I wonder why."

"What was he doing in the department today? He usually avoids anyplace where there are patients."

"Think about it. Imagine Kline hearing that a US senator and potential presidential candidate is on the way to the ER for care."

"Oh, man. He ran his clueless butt down here to tell everyone how to take care of the VIP," Drake said.

"Hassling Patti and got on me like a flea on a dog."

"Did you tell him to take off?"

"Multiple times and in no uncertain terms," Rizz said.

"So you weren't subtle."

"Am I ever?"

Drake smiled.

"I thought he'd left or been driven out before the terrorists pulled their reverse lockdown," Rizz said.

"He must have been crammed in that tiny dark radiology booth all that time," Drake said. "Did you hear what he said to Freid? This is 'my hospital' and offering to help. How does that guy look at himself in the mirror?"

"He's a real piece of work." Rizz shook his head.

"Why do you think they're keeping him separate from everyone? Because they don't want us hostages dying of annoyance before they get whatever they're after?" Drake said.

"They're not that kindhearted."

"I feel bad ripping on the guy. He's facing death, same as we are," Drake said.

"But he is Kline, Drake. And we need some laughs. Remember he's the one who shot down all our requests for better security."

"That's undeniable."

"Besides, him being here might be a good sign. We should stick close to him. He's like a cockroach. He survives."

"I hope you're right, but it's hard to imagine any situation that's improved with the addition of Stuart Kline."

TOLMAN FREID UNLOCKED and opened the door to patient room 15. The brightly illuminated, all-white, windowless room smelled of body odor and a hint of cologne.

CEO Kline, who was sitting on the cot, flinched and drew back as Tolman entered.

"So, Mr. 'This is my hospital,' you said you can help me. How? All I see is a corporate coward who hid like a rat."

The stylishly dressed CEO looked from side to side as if concerned someone might overhear. "If you get me out of here safely, I'll do anything. I have influence."

"Anything?" Tolman said.

"I'm sure you have good reasons for what you're doing. Nothing to do with me. It makes no sense for me to get hurt or die."

Wow. No loyalty, not even pretense—it's all about him. Tolman felt like he needed to be decontaminated just for being in the same room.

"I'm not hearing how you can help me," Tolman said.

"This isn't my battle. I have a hospital to keep profitable and a life to live. Hopefully a long and comfortable life with plenty of money."

"It's all about money to you?" Tolman said.

"Everything is about money," Kline said with total certainty.

Tolman stroked his chin. Good men died for principle and the good of others. Individuals like the Gucci-camouflaged rat in front of him were all about greed and themselves.

"Are you looking to get paid?"

"Payment wouldn't work. The money would be tracked to me in no time," Kline said.

"Some know how to move money in ways that can't be traced." As the words left his mouth, Tolman did a mental about-face. *Pay him?* He held the coward's life in his hands. The corporate toady would do what Tolman needed.

"There's a chance I could let you go," Tolman said. "You'd need to follow my orders exactly. If you agree, there'd be no going back."

"I'm open to negotiation."

Tolman fired out his hand and slapped Kline, the sound like the snap of a trap. "Shut up!" The man sickened him. A corporate bloodsucker for whom only dollars mattered—an example of the sickness destroying the country. "Negotiate? With you? You're a pathetic weakling."

Kline's held his cheek, his eyes wide and tear-filled.

Tolman had been treating the CEO with respect the man did not deserve. "You'll do what I tell you. Fail and I'll broadcast this conversation." Tolman took the phone out of his top pocket and showed the recording indicator.

"No need for that. Just tell me what you want me to do." Kline straightened and dropped his hand, his slapped cheek blazing as if burned. "I can be very effective."

"We have a helicopter flying in to take a patient and possibly the surgeon who operated on him out. I could let you on that flight—"

"Yes, I'll be glad to do it. Whatever it is, just tell me."

"Dr. Cody asked that I send out others as well. He wants to send as many as the copter can handle. That won't be happening."

"I understand. No nurses or patients. I agree. You need to send me. I'm the one who can help you. I'm the one who needs to go."

The man caused Tolman's skin to crawl, but the CEO could help take care of the only thing Tolman cared about besides his mission.

"Can I ask why you keep me locked up, separated from the others?"

"No. Just shut up. You're being spared in spite of how much you disgust me. If I had not had an issue arise that you can help with, I'd kill you right now."

The CEO shut up. Beads of sweat glistened on his brow.

Tolman kept the corporate worm isolated because the man couldn't share what he didn't know. The less he knew, the better.

The cowardly snake would help solve the problem Red and his nephew's lack of judgment and failure to follow orders had created.

CHAPTER THIRTY-FIVE

"Major! Hey, Major. You should see this." Drake recognized the pockmarked con's voice coming from just outside the Crash Room.

Drake slid the Crash Room's glass doors open. Pockmark stood, gun in hand with his attention on the ceiling-mounted TV behind the main desk. The screen showed the Memorial Hospital ER entrance and parking lot in the warm light of late afternoon. In the foreground caption, the words "Fox Breaking News" showed.

"Turn that up," Tolman ordered as he entered from the corridor and stood at the counter with his crew all within sight. The volume swelled.

A talking head appeared in front of an aerial shot of the hospital, the parking lot, and the activity there. The scene switched to a close-up shot of the anchorperson. "...while you were looking at live images, I've been handed a breaking news exclusive from the Minneapolis Star Tribune. This is reported to have come from *inside* the captive emergency department.

"Earlier reports speculated eco-terrorists had been responsible for the refinery explosion and subsequent ER takeover. A communication from the group suggested a political agenda, but the Star Tribune now identifies that the domestic terrorists are racist ex-convicts, many of whom have tattoos of swastikas and other Nazi and Aryan Brotherhood symbols. Aryan Brotherhood is a white supremacist gang with its origins in United States prisons."

Tolman slammed his hand down on the counter, eyes bulging and face red.

The commentator continued, "Two law enforcement members are reported to have been executed inside the ER. All captives are in fear for their lives. Stay with us for more updates about the domestic terrorist takeover in Minneapolis by suspected white supremacists or a group with ties to them."

"Damn you!" Tolman whirled to face his crew. Pockmark and the hyena were closest, and they shrank back. "You losers and your racist garbage have perverted my mission."

He stomped to his spot behind the main counter and as he passed, all except the huge redhead cowered.

"That report was sent from the ER somehow. You idiots missed a phone or computer. Find it now!"

Drake watched as Tolman took deep breaths, then picked up the ER overhead page microphone.

"This is Tolman Freid, militia leader and patriot." His words reached every corner of the department. "One of you violated my commands. Turn in your phone or device and I'll have mercy. If the device is not turned over within ten minutes, I will kill one or more of you. This is not a threat, it's a guarantee. Ten minutes."

Drake's throat tightened. He had no doubt the maniacal leader would do what he said.

CHAPTER THIRTY-SIX

Minor trauma area

No one came forward with a phone or device. Tolman's stooges roughed up people and searched but found nothing.

Drake had no idea how the information had gotten to the media or who had leaked it. It looked like that person would not confess.

The terrorist leader, the man who believed his actions were that of a patriot, the fanatic who believed his *cause* meant more than all of their lives, had changed since the news broadcast. His command had been violated, and the motivation behind his mission had been publicly perverted on national media. His fuse was burning fast. Someone would die soon.

What could Drake do?

Their captors moved everyone into the minor trauma area except for Bart, who was caring for his post-surgical patient in the Crash Room, and Patti, who was watching over the acid-exposed executives and the overdose patient in the telemetry area.

Red stood with the pockmarked Aryan and the hyena, the big fleshy younger guy with the sick laugh. They stood near the door with rifles in hand and pistols at their belt. The spaced-out, bearded con and Tolman's son were to the right of them. The boy held a rifle, but he fidgeted and his eyes darted back and forth.

Rizz and Dr. Trist were near the front of the room. Drake stood at the back.

Tolman paced among the patients on their cots, all the privacy curtains open. He waved the blue-black .45 he'd use to kill Marcus, the senator's bodyguard and friend. He looked at the wall clock.

"Time is almost up. Turn in the phone or device or someone dies. Do it now and I'll have mercy." He stood silent, his jaw clenched, a fearsome energy radiating from him.

The air grew heavier. The faint buzz of the fluorescent lights hummed. Drake's mouth went dry.

"There's no need to kill anyone," Rizz said from his wheelchair. "No one here is a threat to you. We're helpless."

"Dr. Rizzini is right," Dr. Trist said, squinting through his wire-rimmed glasses. "Killing accomplishes nothing."

Tolman swung the gun toward them, shifting his aim from doctor to doctor. "Anyone who questions me jumps to the front of the line. Either of you want to die?"

Rizz and Trist stared at him unflinching.

"I need doctors to keep my prize hostages alive. But not all of you," Tolman said. "You're expendable." He held the weapon with his arm extended, alternating between their faces.

Seconds ticked by with the possibility of death pressing like gravity.

"Nope." He lowered the gun. "Neither of you will die right now, but don't push me." He turned toward the others in the room. "Less than two minutes left. Unless I get that phone, it's *bang*. Final countdown. Who is it going to be?"

Tight faces, some looking side to side. No one spoke. Phoenix, the pretty young woman who'd been exposed to ammonia gas, sat bent over, her hands covering her face.

Tolman held the pistol to Miss Roberta's temple. "Should I shoot the helpless old lady?" He shrugged. "No, not her. How about the kid?"

He approached Newman, the thirteen-year-old autistic boy getting medication via IV for his seizure disorder. The teen now sat awake and alert, making repetitive hand gestures. His mother sat in a chair at his bedside with a rosary in her hands. She choked back sobs as Tolman held the pistol against his temple. The boy showed no expression. He cocked his head as if the gun were not there but did not make eye contact with the terrorist leader.

"Nice not are you. Mom my scared make," the boy said, not interrupting his hand gestures.

"No," Tolman said pulling the weapon back. "He's not the one."

"Shoot the nigger," Pockmark said, pointing at Antoine, the stocky fifty-six-year-old refinery worker. "Or let me. I don't like the way that coon looks at me."

"Does he look at you like you're a white trash loser?" Tolman said. "He should, because you are. You and your Aryan Bastard brothers with your Nazi tattoos and racist babble convinced one of these people," he waved his gun, "to spread a false and disgusting idea about me and my noble mission."

Pockmark's lip curled but he made no other move.

Tolman was physically superior to all but his massive brother, but the Aryan ex-cons held weapons in their hands. Tolman insulted them, yet they laid back like submissive wolves confronted by the pack leader. Drake had seen a similar dynamic when behind bars—deadly gang members submitting to a ruthless leader.

"Thirty seconds and one of you dies." Tolman said loudly. He swung the gun around. "This is real. I do not bluff."

The autistic boy's mother sat with eyes closed tight, her fingers advancing beads on the rosary.

Rizz in his wheelchair met Drake's eyes and shook his head in an almost imperceptible "no." Not the time to go for it—no chance—they'd be slaughtered.

"Twenty seconds," Tolman called out.

Drake's throat tightened. His body went numb. Despite Rizz's "no," if one of the ER team were selected, Drake would attack despite the overwhelming odds. If it were one of the others, would he do nothing?

Tolman stopped his pacing behind the thirty-four-year-old Cecil.

He grabbed Cecil's ponytail and jammed the pistol against the back of his head.

"How about you, nose-ring, virtue-signaling protestor? Did you try and impress your left-wing lemmings by publicly smearing me and my cause without even knowing what my mission is really about?" Tolman's voice and intensity rose. "I'm not a racist, and these Aryan wannabes are just mercenaries. They don't represent me or my cause. My mission is about freedom and fighting corrupt government-corporate injustice." The muscles in Tolman's forearm stood out like steel bands as he twisted Cecil's head.

Cecil blanched and his lips trembled. Tears streaked his cheeks.

"Don't kill me! Please! It wasn't me." He sobbed.

"Damn," Tolman said. "You're making this easier, you sniveling worm. FIVE, FOUR, THREE..."

"Kill the Black guy," Cecil wailed.

"TWO..."

"Wait!" Bart Rainey's voice boomed as he filled the doorway, ducking his head as he entered the room in one stride.

Everyone froze. Tolman turned, still holding Cecil's head, looking like an image from a mythologic beheading.

"I found the source," Bart said. "It wasn't a phone." He held the large, empty zippered satchel out in front of him. "I took the Doppler amplifier out to check a pulse. I turned it on near the satchel and it squealed." From the pocket of his scrubs, he pulled out the audio Doppler pulse device, about the size of a cigarette pack. Its probe was connected by an eighteen-inch coiled electrical cable.

"That's an electronic bug?" Tolman asked.

"Not the Doppler," Bart said. "Watch." He turned on the device and bent, moving the probe until it reached the pea-sized black plastic fob attached to the satchel's zipper. A high-pitched squeal sounded from the device.

"It's this little fob that looks like nothing," Bart said. "Electronic feedback. Looks like someone has been listening in. I have an idea who."

"You snuck that in here," Tolman said.

"If I'd known I could get word to the outside, I wouldn't have been talking about these cretins and their lame tattoos." He inclined his shaggy head toward the armed crew. Red's jaw clenched. "I'd be sharing tactical information."

Tolman paused. "How do I know you didn't?"

"You don't, but I didn't. I didn't know it was there until a minute ago." Bart responded with the same *I don't give a shit what you think— I'm right* arrogance that drove those who worked with him nuts.

"So you have all the answers, huh, big man?" Tolman let go of Cecil's hair and removed the barrel from against his head. Cecil collapsed on the bed, hiding his face. "What did the FBI hear?"

"The FBI or whoever heard us talk as I operated," Bart said. "Someone somewhere heard audio of my surgical brilliance while ER guy and Miss Nursey Know-It-All gossiped about your racist, ex-con losers. The stuff in that news report is what they gabbed about while pretending they were capable of helping me during surgery. My patient is still alive thanks to me, but he needs to fly out of here now. Has ER guy talked to you about that? If my patient doesn't get someplace with interventional radiology ASAP, all my magic will be for nothing."

CHAPTER THIRTY-SEVEN

Tactical Operations mobile

Special Agent in Charge Dylan McGinnis faced the two lean, muscular, hard-eyed veterans of military special forces. The smell of gun oil, body odor, and leather hung faint but distinct in the enclosed space of the tactical unit's mobile operations vehicle.

The Minneapolis SWAT commander and the recently arrived FBI hostage rescue team leader could be brothers. Other than the SWAT leader's long O's and irregular cadence as a "Minnesootan" and the FBI hostage-rescue commander's brusque Boston chop, they spoke the same language.

"We take the lead. Minneapolis SWAT is backup on the perimeter. I recommend immediate forced entry and insertion," the FBI hostage-rescue veteran said. "We do what needs to be done. Hitting them now is the best chance of eliminating the threat of a mass casualty event. We have the men. We have the weapons. We have the commitment. This is what we do. These bastards need to be exterminated. Casualties are unavoidable. Some or all of the innocent souls in there will likely be collateral damage. There are no zero casualty options."

"Roger that," the Minneapolis SWAT team leader said. "Whoever goes in will lose people, but each minute that goes by gives the terrorists and their collaborators more time to plan and execute destruction."

Dylan had just finished listening to the recording from the bug from the ER. Everything pointed to disaster. *Damn!*

Tolman Freid had threatened devastating retaliation for any tricks, and he'd caught them red-handed. Dylan had thought the technologically advanced bug so tiny and innocuous it would not be found. It had taken the smarts of the huge surgeon and damn bad luck for it to be discovered.

The surgeon had come forward and revealed what he'd found in order to save a hostage's life. He'd had no choice.

Bad luck or not, Dylan would be held responsible for whatever came next, but blame wasn't what had his stomach in knots.

The terrorists had used explosives and chemical weapons, then barricaded themselves with a state senator and an entire ER as hostage in the heart of the fourteenth-largest metropolitan area in the country. An unstable, murderous leader who'd been victimized by government actions and threatened to inflict widespread death and destruction if not obeyed had just had his orders defied.

How many thousands were at risk?

What about the lives of those in the ER? Was there now even the remotest chance the terrorists would allow the surgeon or anyone else to fly out?

On the recording, the nurse Tracy had refused the possibility for freedom, due to her commitment to the senator and other patients. Likewise, the surgeon declined the offer, despite a direct murder threat from Freid's brother on top of the general risk.

Law enforcement had a file on "Red" Freid. A sociopath embraced as a hero during his teen years because of athletic ability that had brought glory to the rural Minnesota town. All of that despite his brutal nature and violent acts. Who knew how many girls he'd sexually assaulted or men he'd brutally beaten before his crimes couldn't be ignored any longer? After two stints in a county detention center for assault, he'd beat a man to death. A manslaughter conviction had sent him to Stillwater penitentiary.

In that jungle, he'd become an enforcer for the Aryan Brotherhood.

After years of incarceration, a gang of Black inmates took him down and left him near dead. Hospitalized with a brain injury, he'd recovered but with more issues. Tolman's promise of employment and semi-guardianship had influenced the parole board. Red Freid had been out for six months. Prison had made him an even greater threat to all those around him. He belonged in a cage but instead now held innocent people captive.

Three other ex-cons had been identified from CCTV images, and each had files documenting similarly vicious histories. The terrorists had lifetimes of training in murder and brutality. How were any of them loose in society?

Dylan sighed. A ride on the helicopter might be the last chance anyone in the ER had to escape the lockdown alive.

"Sir?" the hostage rescue team commander said.

"Hold on," Dylan said.

Was there anything he could do to stop what Tolman Freid had put in motion?

Would sacrificing those in the ER in the hopes of *possibly* protecting the lives of many others make tactical team assault and entry the right decision? If so, when?

As always, history would, after the events unfolded, judge what *should have* been done. If they waited and mass destruction occurred, he'd have blown it. Turn the tactical squads loose now, and similar destruction would be proof he should have waited. Even if the tactical forces killed all the terrorists quickly, they could have time to trigger a fail-safe mechanism to detonate devices. His gut knotted. *Damn!*

The two tactical leaders waited, watching him.

Each held a cellphone in hand, ready to pass on the "go" order. Weapons and armaments glistened in racks along the walls of the tactical unit's vehicle. Dylan breathed in the scent of gun oil. The tactical command center's crackling radio transmissions, the flickering of its wall of live images, and the static-charged air surrounded the strike commanders as their stares pushed Dylan to attack.

"Freid thinks he's on a patriotic mission," Dylan said. "His deadline for the politicians and government officials to be assembled must be for him to make his demands. I don't think he'll trigger his worst until he's done that. Unless I'm ordered from above, we're going to wait before turning your teams loose. None of our options are good. Perhaps time will improve our choices."

The tactical commanders frowned as one.

"Respectfully, sir, you're wrong," the FBI tactical team leader said, not sounding respectful. "A decision delayed is a decision made. Death and destruction can't be undone. Terrorist threats and weapons of mass destruction do not allow us the luxury of hoping for things to improve."

CHAPTER THIRTY-EIGHT

Drake and Bart stood just outside the Crash Room facing Tolman behind the counter.

"The medical details are beyond you," Bart said to Tolman. "He is flown out or he dies. I'll call the accepting hospital and tell the doctors there what he needs."

"If I agree, you can go with him as I promised," Tolman said.

"I'm staying," Bart said. "My skills are likely going to be needed here again sooner or later. I might even have to save you."

"I gave my word you could fly out. It's your decision if you stay," Tolman said. "Red wants to kill you. If you stay, I expect he will. My brother is loyal to me, but no one can control him."

"Your brother can kiss my ass," Bart said. "I've done what can be done for your nephew surgically. The rest can be handled by someone else. Ask ER guy, he knows enough to back me on that."

"He needs to be transferred as soon as possible," Drake said. "I'd like to send at least one nurse and three others."

"I never agreed to that," Tolman said.

"It can't hurt and—"

"No," Tolman said. "The FBI lied. No new deals."

"A nurse and at least one other person," Drake said. "Your nephew needs them."

"Have the FBI send whoever is needed to transfer Micah," Tolman said. "We load Micah into the elevator and leave him on the helipad to be picked up with two others. We then bring the elevator down and secure access. When the shaft is secure, we allow the helicopter to make the pickup."

Two others? Better than he hoped. After the deceit of the FBI's bug, Drake expected none.

"We need a minute to discuss who to choose," Drake said. "It's—"

"It's been decided," Tolman said. "One will be my son, Sigurd. He had no idea of my plans and had nothing to do with today's actions. He ended up here due to the idiocy of my brother and my nephew. He has harmed no one, is completely innocent, and deserves release with no charges."

Drake's jaw dropped. *His son!* Things that had not made sense suddenly did.

Tolman seemed to share the same disdain for his injured nephew that he did for the other ex-cons. Drake had not sensed the concern he was accustomed to with critically injured patients and their loved ones.

Had allowing the helicopter and surgeon been all about getting his son to safety?

From the start, the kid did not fit with the rest of the crew. He showed none of the bigotry or viciousness of Red and the ex-cons, nor the passion or coldhearted fanaticism of his father. He'd been wide-eyed in the midst of the deaths and injury. He'd held weapons but looked not at all inclined to use them. He might truly be innocent.

"You said two, so we need to pick the other," Drake said. It might literally be a lottery ticket with life as the prize. "We—"

"I've decided. Your CEO Kline is the other. No discussion. The coward convinced me he was the best choice."

Drake choked back the rush of bile that surged to the back of his throat.

CHAPTER THIRTY-NINE

Drake checked the terrorist's vitals. Bart's intra-abdominal packing continued to keep the bleeding at bay. Bart and Tracy had the patient on a stretcher cart for transport. The wheel locks clunked as they were released, and Drake rolled him to the elevator. None of the other doctors, nurses, or patients were allowed in the corridor. The militia members held their weapons ready.

Tolman stood with his son at his side near the elevator doors. The eighteen-year-old shifted from foot to foot, avoiding Drake's gaze.

"Father—"

"Quiet, Sigurd. I've made my decision," Tolman said.

The young man stopped short and hung his head.

Red dissembled the elevator's booby-trapped barricade. He removed a device that looked something like an oxygen tank, though it appeared to be made of plastic. Almost certainly, it held hydrofluoric acid, which Drake knew from his drug research background could not be stored in steel as it ate through metal. No valve control was evident, and wires ran to an attached small, rectangular module with a tiny red light visible.

Tolman hit the elevator call button and the doors pinged and slid open. Sigurd flinched.

"Bring him," Tolman called out. Pockmark marched a hooded Stuart Kline around the corner and to the elevator. He placed him inside. No one spoke.

They then rolled the nephew's stretcher with its IV pole into the elevator.

Tolman faced Sigurd and put his hands on his shoulders.

"Son," Tolman said, "don't believe the lies the government will tell you about me or anything else. They stole our home and destroyed your mother. Never forget that."

"I won't, Father. I know what they did." Tolman gripped Sigurd in an awkward hug, then guided his son into the elevator.

"Keep Father safe, Uncle Red." Sigurd's voice cracked as the elevator doors slid shut.

Red secured the elevator access and rewired the tank-like device. The elevator light showed arrival at the helipad.

Tolman moved to the console behind the central desk and checked the closed-circuit TV image.

Watching Tolman and his men, Drake wondered once more how they knew so much about the ER layout and security features.

"They're on the helipad now," Tolman said to Red. He picked up the phone and spoke to the operator. "FBI, now." He put the phone on speaker.

"Dylan McGinnis, FBI special agent in charge. I'd like—"

"I'm in charge," Tolman said. "No games and no negotiating. The patient is on the helipad, and the surgeon communicated care orders to the hospital he is being transferred to." Tolman paused. "Also on the helipad is an innocent victim—my son, Sigurd Freid. He is eighteen years old. He has not been a willing part of this action. His presence was the result of a gross lapse in judgment and miscommunication by other members of the militia. I demand he be released without charges."

"Maybe we can work something out. Perhaps—"

"No!" Tolman yelled. "You will do this and do it directly. You've already lied and tried to trick me. I've exercised restraint. Failure to free my son or any other defiance will end that."

"I can't guarantee your son's release on my own. He's been part of—"

"He has not!"

"It is not realistic for you to expect that I can—"

"I don't expect, I demand," Tolman said. "If I do not get a call from him confirming he is free, I will trigger one of the multiple devices we have placed about the city. In the meantime, I'm emailing a video to all major media, to be shared with the President, state governors, attorneys-general, and others I instructed you to contact earlier. They will agree to the demands on the video or—"

"Government doesn't work that way. It takes—"

"They will respond or suffer the consequences. Also, it is essential the media correct their errant communications regarding me and my mission. I have to acknowledge the racist attitudes of some members of the militia, but that is not part of my mission. My objective is pure. It addresses some of the ongoing abuses of power by the corrupt government-corporate cabal and their infringement on the rights of citizens."

"You have to be reasonable. It's not—"

"I've tried *reasonable*. The government does not respond to reasonable."

"Please. Tell me—"

"I've told you all you need to know. Any attempt at a tactical operation or takedown of the ER will result in death and destruction far beyond what any American city has ever suffered. The video will be distributed shortly. It reveals the truth about the US government. I'm a man of my word. Any further deceit, and the blood of thousands will be on your hands."

CHAPTER FORTY

Hospital lot, auxiliary command trailer

"Somehow, I was able to stay calm. I knew the others were looking to me for leadership." Kline adjusted his lapels. Aki noted the suit had a wrinkle or two, but the CEO's appearance did not suggest he'd been roughed up. Perhaps his one cheek was reddened?

Aki, Dylan McGinnis, and Dr. Torrins, the hospital's second-in-command and chief of medical affairs, sat across from Kline. Two male and one female FBI agents sat at the end of the table with notepads. A voice recorder sat in front of them with its tiny red light glowing.

"When the terrorists said they wanted to send me out on the helicopter, I said no. I told them I wanted to stick it out in the ER with my team and suggested they send a patient or nurse in my place. They insisted. I hope the others are holding together without me."

Dr. Torrins rolled his eyes.

"Why do you think they insisted?" Aki asked.

Dylan had said they'd present this meeting to Kline as a debriefing, although it was more an interrogation. The agent had not ruled anything out.

"Somehow they learned I was the hospital's CEO. Maybe they think letting me go showed good faith. Actually, their leader seemed reasonable. Well, er...under the circumstances." Kline brushed something off his suit and straightened his tie. "Maybe they felt the hospital staff would be easier to control without their leader."

Dr. Torrins gagged as if he'd choked on something. He cleared his throat.

"The young man, Sigurd, who flew out with you," Dylan said, "claims he did not know his father's plan and did not knowingly participate in any criminal acts. Does that fit with what you saw?"

"I didn't see him do anything criminal. His father said the boy was not supposed to be in the ER. He had ordered the boy to stay home. I believed him."

"Did you see him with weapons or engaged in threatening or guarding any of the kidnap victims?" Dylan asked.

"No. Nothing like that. I didn't see him do anything," Kline said. "I spent most of my time trying to get the leader to set the others free." He shrugged. "It might be I was so much trouble that's why they put me on the helicopter."

Aki looked at Dr. Torrins. Aki had interfaced with him during previous challenging times. The man was rock-solid. The CEO's words had the doctor shaking his head.

"What can you tell us about the number of captors, their weapons, their positions, and the presence of explosives or any booby traps? What did you see for barriers to access?" Dylan said.

"Again, when I wasn't confronting the leader, I was trying to oversee the senator's and executives' care, while trying to keep the staff and patients from panicking. Because of all that, I wasn't able to get a full view of things. The staff and patients were terrified. I did my best to keep their spirits up. I'll let you know what I saw."

"Other agents will discuss what you saw in a moment," Dylan said. "The leader had agreed to let the surgeon fly out after operating on his nephew. He claimed the surgeon turned that option down. Is that what happened?"

"Exactly. I tried to make Dr. Rainey take my place, but he wouldn't budge. It was either me or no one. I figured the information I could share would be even more valuable than what I was doing supporting the other captives."

"Thank you, Mr. Kline. I'm going to have you stay here, and these agents," Dylan indicated the three at the end of the table, "will continue your, uh, debriefing."

"Sure, and excuse me, but I want to remind you all it's *CEO* Kline. Happy to answer questions. I was also wondering when I'll be speaking to the press. I know the community, and Memorial Hospital customers would want to hear from me."

"We'll let you know. Share everything you remember, no matter how small, with the agents." McGinnis turned. "Detective Yamada, Dr. Torrins, please come with me." Dylan led the way out of the auxiliary trailer.

Aki could not wait to leave.

Kline's BS had gotten so deep he feared he'd drown if he'd had to stay longer.

DYLAN LED the way down the ramp from the auxiliary trailer into the hospital parking lot that glowed in the low-angled sunlight.

There was less activity and fewer personnel evident. A continuous concrete barricade had been positioned 75 yards from the brick and concrete of Memorial Hospital.

As they neared the command post trailer, Dylan stopped and faced them.

"You know and work with the CEO, right?" Dylan asked Dr. Torrins.

"That is my personal and professional burden," Torrins said.

"And you've dealt with him before?" he asked Aki.

"The hospital has been the site of major crimes in the past few years. Kline has been involved in a couple of investigations—both as a witness and a conspirator. His actions were shady, but he dodged prosecution."

"Do either of you think he could he be involved in this?" Dylan asked.

"Off the record," Torrins said, "I can't stand him. He's a narcissist, a liar, and a manipulator. He knows nothing about medical care. What he cares about is himself and money. All that said, I don't see him involved in this."

"I agree with Dr. Torrins. Kline is a greed-driven guy," Aki said. "So far, this is all about extremist militia and their cause. If a money angle becomes evident, I'd look at Kline, but otherwise I don't see him as a part of this."

"My impression is that he was lying," Dylan said.

"Agreed," Aki said.

"Can either of you help me understand what's going on?" Dylan said. "Do you think he's talking straight about Freid's son Sigurd?"

"Those answers were the only ones that sounded remotely believable," Aki said.

"I felt the same," Torrins said. "The story of Kline as a brave, selfless leader rallying his team is outrageous. The medical staff universally detest him. I'm not sure what he's playing at. One thing I'm sure of is that he's looking out for himself."

"The agents will get everything they can out of him. Hopefully something useful. If I find that he's lied to us I'll have him prosecuted," Dylan said.

"Good luck with that," Torrins said. "It's wrong that he was released instead of someone else. How are my colleagues and patients in the ER going to be rescued? It looks impossible."

"It doesn't look good," Dylan said. "The terrorists are dug in and the odds are against us."

Aki didn't like hearing Dylan say those words, despite their truth. "On the recording from your bug, Drake Cody said the hostages would have to make a go for it on their own at some point," he said. "It will be Drake and a few other captives without weapons battling a heavily armed team of militia-trained ex-cons and killers. Their odds are remote, but there's one thing that gives me hope."

"What's that?" Dylan asked.

"I've seen Drake Cody survive impossible odds before."

CHAPTER FORTY-ONE

Drake looked into the Crash Room through the open glass panels to the empty bay where Tolman's nephew had undergone surgery. In and around that space lay pools and spatters of blood, stained bandages, and the crumpled packaging from which sterile instruments had been torn. The three surgical stands sat at awkward angles, their trays covered with the used instruments and soiled blue surgical drapes abandoned there.

In the next bay, Tracy tended to Senator Duren. Instruments packaged in clear plastic hung glistening and ready along the walls behind them. The clicks of the Life Clock were just audible among the rhythms of the resuscitation equipment.

Tolman sat behind the counter at the main desk. Drake faced him from the other side of the counter. The pockmarked ex-con stood at the end of the counter, keying a laptop in front of him. His rifle lay on the counter at the ready.

Tolman, his massive brother Red, and the three Aryan Brotherhood ex-cons—Pockmark, Hyena, and the bearded one Drake was certain was actively psychotic—all handled their firearms with practiced ease. *How can they be taken down?*

"I've seen how you look at me," Tolman said to Drake. "You're wrong to judge me."

"You gunned down Marcus, an honorable man committed to protecting his friend the senator. The senator, likewise a good man, is struggling for life with his lungs destroyed because you exposed him to one of the most devilish substances known to man. And you've done much more."

"I've been forced to do distasteful things," Tolman said. "I've been chosen to change the course of history."

"Multiple murders, chemical weapons, kidnapping, and terrorism. Your actions aren't distasteful. They are cowardly and barbaric."

"I protested within the system for over twenty years trying to stop the injustice and accomplished nothing. What my family and I suffered in violation of our rights as free people and sovereign citizens left me no choice. The unlawful and illicit alliance of the corporate, military, and political systems of the United States must be resisted."

"Excuse me all to hell for not cheering the bullshit notion of you as a hero." Drake shook his head. "You're a terrorist. Like all terrorists, you're subhuman and disgusting. Your justifications are intellectual and moral rubbish."

"You are ignorant. Your misguided insults are not worth response. I'll be sharing my story soon," Tolman said. "Do not judge me before you know my truth. Walk a mile in my shoes."

"If it means I don't have to listen to any more of your clichés and extremist crap, share it now."

Tolman glanced at the clock behind the desk. He did not react to Drake's insults. His condescending, self-righteous manner confirmed the depth of his fantasy.

"It's time for the traitors to freedom to listen." He turned to the pockmarked ex-con. "Prepare to broadcast."

"The main video, right?" Pockmark bent over the laptop. "I'm embedding it with instructions for recipients to share on Facebook, YouTube, and more. It's uploaded, and I've compressed it for rapid transfer. It will be all over the world in no time."

"Yes," Tolman said. "Release it to all media outlets, the government address list, social media, the entire distribution."

"I'm doing it now." His fingers flew across the keyboard.

Tolman indicated the ceiling-mounted TV behind him. "In a matter of minutes, though they are nothing more than greedy, celebrity-driven shills, the media jackals will broadcast my truth everywhere."

"I'm dealing with some of your 'truth' right here," Drake said, nodding toward the Crash Room. "A skilled nurse and technology are keeping the senator alive. You're responsible for his suffering and much more. You're a traitor to humanity. I've been waiting for you to roll out the ultimate in self-serving rationalizations—that the end justifies the means."

Drake turned his back and moved toward the Crash Room.

Tolman's laughter made Drake stop and look back. He'd not seen the fanatic as much as smile and now the big man laughed hard. "What?" Drake said.

"The end justifies the means." Tolman huffed and shook his head. "In five words, you just laid out the foundation for every act of government tyranny and abuse in US history."

CHAPTER FORTY-TWO

"It's coming on!" Pockmark pointed his weapon toward the TV.

Drake and Bart moved to the Crash Room door.

Their captors gathered and focused on the TV, though they maintained weapon-ready positions.

A TV anchorwoman appeared. The backdrop showed a live shot of the emergency room entrance of Memorial Hospital and the busy barricaded parking lot. The early evening sun cast long shadows of the personnel and vehicles there.

"We at CNN and other media outlets across the country received the following video within the past few minutes. It is identified to be from the leader of the extremist group that has claimed responsibility for the oil refinery explosion and toxic gas release, followed by the takeover and lockdown of the emergency room of Memorial Hospital in downtown Minneapolis.

"Multiple hostages, including billionaire Senator Hayden Duren and two oil industry executives are being held along with an unknown number of hospital staff and patient hostages. At least two law enforcement personnel are known to be dead, and more casualties are suspected. Our network and other media have made the decision to share the video in order to keep the population informed. This does not in any way condone or support the lawless actions and criminal behavior of the extremists holding the Twin Cities and the entire country hostage. Given the nature of the content, we will give you a moment to screen for suitable aged viewers while we take a short commercial break."

PHOENIX TREMBLED when the hyena entered the room. Every time he looked at her, she felt violated.

"The Major is going to be on the news again," he said. One of the doctors had labelled the disgusting creep "Hyena" and it fit.

The nurse Patti had gone to help in another area. None of the doctors were around.

The small ceiling-mounted TV showed CNN news. The lead-in promised breaking news on the Minneapolis domestic terrorist story. The events were no longer "news" but her life—and possibly her death. *I don't want to die!*

The disgusting creep extended his tongue at her. She relived the gross sensation of it on her neck in the decontamination room—the memory so vivid she rubbed the spot as if to wipe it clean.

Her heart pounded. Her newspaper's reporting of her story had enraged the terrorist leader and made her impossible situation worse. The words coming from the TV were meaningless noise to her. Her head was filled with static. She held on to one thought—somehow she must survive.

When the leader had placed the barrel of his pistol on Cecil's head and counted down the seconds, she'd known what others would think she should have done.

She hadn't confessed that she was the one who'd had a phone.

Anyone who condemned her would be wrong. Her decision wasn't selfish. She *had* to be ready to let others die. Hers was a special role and she had to live. Her responsibility demanded it.

"You," the brute said to Antoine. "Come here, boy."

"I'm not your boy," the stocky workingman said. "I was George and

Kayla Whitlock's firstborn son and proud of it. I'm fifty-six years old. I'm nobody's boy."

"Well, *boy*, I need you to shut up and come with me right now or I'm gonna have to hurt Miss Roberta here." He jabbed the elderly sleeping woman's chest with two fingers. Her eyes burst open and she cried out, her hands clasped over the spot he'd struck.

"You gutless punk." Antoine bristled. "Don't be harming the lady."

Phoenix admired Antoine's courage. The look on his face left no doubt what he'd do to the vicious brute if the ex-con didn't have weapons.

"Don't give me no trouble, boy. I'm going to put you in another room so you don't cause no trouble," the disgusting creep said. "You ain't nothing but a big-mouth spook, but I want you out of here. Head out the door and to the right." He indicated with the pistol.

"Leave him alone, please," Phoenix said.

"He'll be fine, sweet cheeks. Don't you worry." A vulgar expression and his bizarre laugh.

As the hyena followed Antoine out, he removed a few large plastic zip ties from his pocket. He returned a minute later without Antoine. He moved toward her with a sick smile.

Her worst fear came closer.

Strength left her. She could not breathe.

Oh God. He was coming for her.

Her hands were ice. No air. strength gone. Gravity in the room had doubled.

He neared. The hateful symbols on his arms peeked out beneath his shirt. A pistol and an ivory-handled knife hung sheathed at his belt. His close-set piggy eyes defiled her.

"Only the old lady, mumble-boy with his mommy, and the ponytail faggot protest-coward left with us, babe." He pointed at Cecil. "I know you won't be bothering us. You showed earlier you got your mind right."

Cecil sat blank and sunken-eyed. He'd not said a word since his humiliation.

Her abuser strutted toward her. Each step ratcheted her fear beyond imagination. *Oh God.*

The news report droned, but Phoenix could not register anything beyond her terror.

He grabbed her arm and pulled her to feet. Somehow her legs supported her. She moaned. "No. Please."

"No worries, wench. It'll all be good. Real good." He pulled the huge knife from the sheath on his belt. He held the tip to her throat. "Scream or fight and I drive the blade home."

The sound in her head was now a continuous shriek. He pushed her, and her feet moved as if of their own accord to the solid wood door to the bathroom. *Someone save me!*

He opened the door and pushed her in, then closed the door behind them.

Alone in the bathroom. The place where she had retrieved her iWatch and sent her story. Her effort to claim glory in the profession she cared so much about meant nothing. Her story, her responsibility, the fame and recognition—none of it meant anything now.

The hyena's eager leer triggered a dread immeasurably worse than anything in her experience.

He grabbed the sheet she had over her shoulders and yanked it off. He reached to the back of the hospital gowns. He touched her while holding the blade against her throat. He squeezed her breasts through the fabric, then snapped the tie to the first gown and ripped it from her.

"Oh baby, you're going to love this." He grabbed the hair on the back of her head and pressed his lips to hers. The shrieking in her head drowned out everything. He pinned her against the wall. The tip of the blade burned as it penetrated the skin of her neck. *God, please let me die.*

A wave of pressure and the room became brighter. She craned her head past her attacker. Cecil stood in the open doorway holding a metal pole. He raised it and as he did her abuser reacted.

"Jesus!" he said as Cecil swung the IV pole.

Her attacker raised a blocking arm, and the pole smashed into it with a meaty *thud.* He cried out.

"Don't touch her!" Cecil raised the pole again.

The hyena moved quickly, crouching, spinning, then springing forward and driving a fist into Cecil.

A deep *huh* came from Cecil's mouth and his eyes went wide. He clasped his hands over his upper stomach where he'd been struck.

The hyena straightened, giving his horrid laugh. "You messed up, faggot. Hero ain't your style."

Cecil dropped to one knee, his mouth gaping. His hands fell limp to his sides. The ivory handle of the knife protruded from his stomach, the blade buried to the hilt.

He tried to stand, then collapsed onto his back.

Phoenix knelt by him, her mind wailing. All the color left Cecil's face and his eyes went blank, directed to the ceiling. His mouth moved in guppy-like gasps. He was trying to speak. She couldn't make it out. She moved her ear closer to his lips. She heard, "Tell them..."

And then he was still.

CHAPTER FORTY-THREE

Minutes earlier

All eyes around the main desk and Crash Room were fixed on the TV. Even with this distraction, their captors handled their weapons and positioned themselves effectively. Drake kept looking for weak spots to take the militants down, but they left no openings.

The commercial ended, the anchor spoke, and the screen filled with a video of Tolman standing next to a bench in a landscaped alcove in front of a building. No traffic or other sounds registered.

Tolman stood rugged and tall. He wore a cowboy hat and looked quintessentially American. The Marlboro man characters from ads long past came to mind.

"I am Tolman Freid." His voice was deep and commanding. "I am a free man. My rights are sovereign, as natural law guarantees me and every free person. All of you watching are sovereign citizens, which means you have rights of unquestionable ascendancy that no man or government can override."

Drake noted Tolman interacted with the camera like a pro. How many millions might be watching?

"I have more than met my responsibilities as a citizen. I fought, killed, and was wounded in a war I now recognize as having been illegal and corrupt. I have paid taxes for which there is no legitimate basis. I have engaged in legal commerce and honest work and in so doing provided for my wife, family, and many others. I am guilty of no crime. This video is part of a painful but necessary mission.

"The inequity and suffering that my loved ones and I have suffered at the hands of the United States government demanded response. These events and my place in history have obligated me to correct fundamental wrongs. The actions that I and fellow patriots have undertaken are not criminal. They are the actions of freedom-loving patriots.

"I will present one example of how the United States government, collaborating with billion-dollar corporations, has colluded, conspired, and executed injustice and the blatant abuse of personal freedoms and inalienable rights. This and other abuses are occurring to thousands of free persons each day. I'm enlisting you as fellow free-born sovereign citizens to reclaim justice and your rights as free people. To do so, first let me share with you the beauty and wonder of the Freid family farm and home. My home."

The screen image changed, revealing a large white clapboard farmhouse with a huge front porch. The camera then panned back to show an orchard and a large red barn and silo. All were bathed in the warm light of near sunset. Tolman continued in voice-over.

"The land and farm have been in my family for three generations. My grandfather cleared this land. My father died in World War II, fighting for this land and the freedom it represents. There has never at any point been failure to pay taxes, no matter how corrupt, nor any other violation or claims against this home or property."

The camera panned left and revealed the house to be on the slope of a gentle ridge. Two hundred yards distant, a lake with cattails rimming its margin shimmered. Wooded lakeshore separated the water from fields of corn.

The camera swung back to the right, past the iconic homestead and barn. The ridge sloped gently down through a vegetable and flower garden. A few hundred yards away on this side, a second lake of several hundred acres sparkled in the fiery glow of the setting sun. A tree-covered island and a point extending from the southern shore lay covered with white pine backlit by the orange glow.

Drake glanced at Tolman as he viewed the video. The big man's eyes glistened.

The video continued.

A fit woman riding a high-stepping black horse approached the camera. She came close enough for her salt-and-pepper hair, high cheekbones, and striking smile to be visible. She brought the horse to a halt. Then with a slight twitch of the reins, the animal rose on his hind legs and pawed the air like something Drake had seen in a western movie.

She stuck out her tongue. "You can't catch me, old man!" She laughed and the steed pivoted and began to gallop away, its hooves thudding.

The image lurched, and the ears and mane of the horse the camera operator rode came into view as a chase began. As the bouncing camera neared the woman, his laugh joined hers. The image went black for a moment. A head and shoulders shot of Tolman as in the opening scene appeared.

"What you saw was our world not many months ago. The beautiful woman you saw is the most special person in my life."

He bent his head, and when he raised it the rugged features were drawn and his eyes were full.

"Here is our homestead today."

The image changed, revealing Tolman standing in a field of overturned and deeply rutted earth. An oil pipeline tracked along the ridge, with fifty yards of carved earth on either side. Uprooted trees showed the margins of the destroyed orchard. No vegetable or flower garden was identifiable. The house, barn, and silo were gone. The pipeline's path lay gouged along the ridge like a grievous wound.

"The government stole and destroyed our home, using a law as their weapon. *Eminent Domain* is the name of the government tool used by those in power to steal. Under the guise of 'for the betterment of all,' the government steals the property of free men and their families.

No due process. No legal recourse. Our home and family were destroyed so corporations could increase their income. The government illegally condemned and destroyed our home to increase tax revenues from their illicit corporate partners."

The image returned to the bench near the nondescript building. It came in for a close-up and Tolman's intensity grabbed Drake.

"The destruction you have seen is only part of the damage." He began to walk, and automatic doors and an entry to the building appeared.

The video image transitioned to the laughing woman on the high-spirited horse.

"You're looking at my wife as she was only months ago," His voice narrated the shot. "Since then, her home was stolen and demolished. Her family uprooted. The injustice, pain, and cruelty were more than her free and gentle soul could withstand."

The image returned with Tolman now in a carpeted open room with elderly people in wheelchairs and nursing staff moving about.

"Here is my beautiful wife Sonya today."

The camera panned to a gaunt woman, clutching a child's doll while curled in a wheelchair. She looked up, lost and fearful, her cheekbones and distinctive features making her recognizable but just barely.

Oh my God, thought Drake.

"Hello, my love. It's me, Tolman."

Her face remained blank. No reaction.

"This started the day they destroyed our farm," Tolman said. "They stole our home and destroyed the love of my life. They ruined our world for their money and power. Weeping does no good. I can't file complaints or legal action within their rigged system. It does no good. I've taken the action I was forced to take. It is not just for me. It is for all free and sovereign people."

He placed a hand on his wife's twisted shoulder. No reaction from her. His pain radiated like heat from a furnace. He let his hand trail from her and stepped to the side. His head and shoulders filled the screen.

"The guidelines for what I demand the government do will be distributed now through traditional media and the internet. The site is shown on the screen. I ask you all to join me in starting, at long last, to regain our freedom and root out the cancer that has sickened our country. If the government does not respond to my demands, blood will flow in the streets. Freedom and justice have never come cheap. I am prepared to pay any price."

CHAPTER FORTY-FOUR

As his video ended, Tolman locked eyes with Drake as if to say, "Judge me now."

Drake looked away. His fears had been confirmed.

He knew the rancid taste of injustice, having been unfairly arrested, charged, and convicted of a crime he did not commit. The time he'd endured imprisoned with violent offenders had forged, twisted, and scarred his soul. Scioto Juvenile, known as "The Furnace," had four times the violence of the maximum-security adult penitentiary. Drake had been a dog among wolves.

He'd been forced to become something else.

Since that ugliness and all that had followed, he'd fought to control his anger and experience-honed instinct for violence. His conscience had visited dark and anguished places—but it had not died.

Drake understood Tolman's anger. When Rachelle and the kids had been harmed, his rage had been like the molten steel he'd poured when working a job in the foundry. He'd kill to protect them—and he had.

What would he do if he'd faced what Tolman had?

He knew what he wouldn't do.

He wouldn't release a deadly chemical weapon causing unimaginable pain and lethal injury to the senator and possible others.

He wouldn't have killed an innocent policewoman or put a bullet through the brain of Marcus, the honorable friend and bodyguard of Senator Duren.

He wouldn't have gathered a militia of racist and criminal brutes to kidnap, terrorize, and kill innocent people.

Bad things happened. The government and legal system were hugely flawed, and miscarriages of justice and violations of individual rights and freedoms occurred too often.

Despite those failings and the heartbreaking abuses and losses Tolman and his family had suffered, nothing remotely justified what he had done.

As hypnotic and effective as Tolman's powerful video was, Drake knew the truth.

The video was a sales job aimed at persuading people Tolman was noble and heroic.

He was neither.

Tolman's history, his manner, and his militia followers showed he could sell himself and his hatred in a winning way. He was a leader. But he lacked something essential.

He had no conscience. The lives of others meant nothing to him.

And his persuasive words belied the madness of his actions.

Tolman still looked at Drake, his expression smug. Only a sociopath could believe his atrocities were justified.

A woman's piercing scream sounded from down the corridor. Drake flinched and looked toward the minor trauma area.

Tolman barked orders as the bearded ex-con and Pockmark leveled their rifles on Tracy, Bart, Rizz, and Trist.

"Get them in there." Tolman pointed into the Crash Room.

He pulled his pistol and led the way down the corridor. Drake ran behind Red and Tolman toward the minor trauma area. The screams did not relent.

Drake entered the minor trauma room behind his captors with their weapons.

The seizure patient and his mother stood backed against the sidewall with eyes wide and staring. Miss Roberta lay on her cot with her arms covering her head.

Phoenix knelt on the floor next to the sprawled body of Cecil. The hyena stood at his feet. Phoenix stopped screaming as Drake neared, then stood trembling with her hands to her mouth.

The ivory handle of a knife protruded from Cecil's abdomen just below the ribcage—the huge blade buried in a kill zone. Blood saturated his shirt around the knife. Cecil's eyes were open, blank and unseeing, his expression strangely composed. Drake knelt by his side and confirmed he was gone.

Hyena was trying to wrestle his pants and belt around his gut.

A rumpled sheet and two patient gowns were visible on the floor of the bathroom through the open door. Phoenix knelt partially exposed, draped in one torn gown on her shoulders.

Tolman took two strides forward and drove an overhand punch into the hyena's face, knocking him onto his back on the bathroom floor. Blood spouted from his nose and mouth. Tolman pivoted, took two more steps, and slapped Red with a blow that would have knocked most men to the ground. Red barely flinched. Tolman yelled, his face red, veins bulging, "Your disgusting goons are not patriots. They are not men. They are animals who are dishonoring my cause!"

He stood, panting, shaking his head.

"Have that white-trash loser," Tolman pointed at the hyena on the floor trying to stop the bleeding from his face, "put this body with the others."

He stood in front of Red, still breathing hard. "We're coming to the end. If you can't get your scum to soldier up, my mission will fail."

Drake grabbed a sheet from a nearby cot and moved to Phoenix. He wrapped the sheet and his arms around her. She trembled as if she were freezing.

She put her head on his shoulder. He knew things he could say to comfort her. He'd many times been in the position of helping victims of tragedy and horrendous abuse.

But today his priorities were different. He hoped he was right because what he needed to do went against his nature.

He leaned his head by her ear and whispered, "I know you're the one who has a phone." Her trembling body stiffened. "We need it, Phoenix. It might save us all."

If she were the one, she'd withheld her secret throughout the nightmare of Tolman's threats. If he were wrong, his treatment of her was cruel.

She looked at him, her expression unreadable.

CHAPTER FORTY-FIVE

Drake and Phoenix stood next to Cecil's corpse. The coppery smell of blood hung. Phoenix pushed free of his arms.

What must she be feeling after the horrible assault, Cecil's murder, and then Drake's confronting her about the phone? Had he been wrong?

His gut said no. *Damn, Phoenix, just admit you have it. No one is judging you.*

The hyena got to his feet, trying to cinch his belt one-handed while holding a torn hospital gown against his bleeding face. Tolman stared at the man, his lip curled and eyes cold.

"An honorable military leader would execute him straightaway," Drake said.

Tolman looked up, and for the first time a flicker of doubt passed over his face.

Were his terrorist fantasies of honor and patriotism fading?

Red re-entered the room, pushing Antoine and holding cut plastic zip ties in his hand. Antoine rubbed his wrists, no doubt sore from trying to rip himself free when Phoenix had screamed. Red shoved Antoine toward his cot. "Sit your ass down and mind your place, boy."

Seconds later, Rizz rolled into the room. He saw Cecil's body, Phoenix, and the rest. He paled.

His eyes locked on the hyena. "You murdering bastard."

"Go back to the senator," Tolman said. "Who let you leave?"

"Go to hell, grand wazoo," Rizz said.

Drake's eyebrows rose. Was there any situation where Rizz would back down?

"Dr. Rainey has the senator. I came to get Drake," Rizz said. "The pipeline executive's breathing is worsening. Drake is the only one who has seen how the acid advances."

Tolman nodded. "Whatever."

Drake guided Phoenix to Antoine. She flashed reddened eyes at Drake as she sat next to Antoine and accepted the arm the sturdy man put around her. She whispered to Drake without looking up, "You're wrong."

Drake hoped he was being lied to. If she hadn't communicated with the outside, who had?

Drake followed Rizz as he wheeled into the corridor toward the telemetry pod. When out of sight of minor trauma, Rizz stopped. He looked up and his eyes were moist.

"God damn it, Drake. Cecil dead. Marcus and the cop—who's next? It's ripping me up. I keep thinking of how I walked that son of a bitch Tolman into the ER like he was my prom date." He showed his teeth and sucked air. "Damn me." His head drooped.

Drake crouched in front of the wheelchair, grabbed his friend by the shoulders, and shook him. "Stop! Right now. You hear me?"

Rizz looked up, his eyes wide. Drake held a finger in his face.

"I'm not screwing around. It's up to us to save the people in this ER and maybe many more. We already dealt with this. End your worthless guilt-and-shame trip right now. Pull your head out of your ass and get pissed. We need to stop these shitheads and make them pay."

Rizz took in a deep breath and blew it out hard.

"We've beaten the odds before," Drake said. "I need you, brother."

"Sorry. Just a temporary mental meltdown." He rubbed his face with both hands and took another big breath. "I'm back."

"Glad to hear it, amigo." Drake knew no one more courageous or resilient. Even with legs that barely functioned, there wasn't anybody Drake would rather have with him when facing things at their worst.

"I am pissed," Rizz said. "It's open season on these murdering scum." The fire had returned to his eyes.

"You got that right," Drake said. "There's no way to know how long law enforcement can let this string out. SWAT teams could attack in force anytime. Tolman sees himself as a martyr. I don't think he has an exit plan. He wants to go out in a blaze of glory."

"I get the same vibe," Rizz said. "A full-blown fanatic who thinks he's a hero."

"When the government refuses his demands, I'm afraid of what he'll do. I believe him that he has destructive devices planted in the city. Even if we don't make it out alive, if we can stop him from triggering them, it's a success," Drake said.

"Whoa! Hold on. Any plan that leaves me worm-food is not a success." Rizz said. "Half my body, including my favorite part, is just coming back after being AWOL. Heroic is cool, but I'm not into dying. Besides missing all sorts of fun, I've got serious doubts about me and the hereafter."

Drake's always-joking buddy wasn't joking.

"You and me both," Drake said. "The plan is to get everyone out alive but, like always, a lot is out of our hands. We do what we can." Drake thought of Rachelle, seven-year-old Shane, and five-year-old Kristin. How many more innocent people might Tolman's terrorist madness kill?

"It's about more than us, Rizz."

CHAPTER FORTY-SIX

Drake and Rizz remained in the corridor. Rizz's shame trip had ended —or had at least been pushed aside. Drake's greatest friend and proven against-all-odds partner was back. They remained uninterrupted just outside the telemetry area.

"Strategy?" Rizz said. "There are five of them, all heavily armed, and every one of them handle their weapons like pros. Damn extremist militias might fire more training rounds than police or military. And Tolman and Red are huge guys, and all of them are vicious. We attack?"

"No choice. At some point we have to," Drake said. "We're like the passengers on the flights on 9/11. Doing nothing assures death. As you've bragged a number of times, it was a Minnesota guy who led passengers in an unarmed attack of the terrorists. They kicked ass and were breaking into the cockpit when the terrorists recognized they were beaten and crashed the jet into an empty field. Think about the lives saved."

"Ultimate courage and smarts. Tom Burnett was the man. His voice on the cockpit recorder was captured at exactly 9:57 saying 'Let's roll.' It's grim but makes me proud. He's a Minnesota hero."

"We're like those passengers. We go into do-or-die mode if there's a sign that law enforcement is making their move or if an opportunity arises before then."

"Any specifics?" Rizz said.

"If we can take down one or more and get our hands on their guns, our odds skyrocket. Can you operate the weapons they're carrying?"

"Not sure, but Antoine is a former Marine, and Trist talked gun stuff to me before. His long hair and rainbow scrubs suggest otherwise, but he's a gun guy."

"Antoine has guts," Drake said. "I really don't know anything about Trist, but if he knows guns, that's good."

"Roger that," Rizz said.

"And Bart has shown he's more than a massive, egomaniacal son of a bitch. He's fearless."

"He's a force of nature. And I've seen your savage side." Rizz went silent and looked away. "You have issues, brother."

Drake swallowed. Violence had been recurrent in his life. He'd lost control and almost killed a gangbanger who'd struck a nurse. It had felt like twigs snapping as he'd crushed the throat of the person whose bullet had put Rizz in a wheelchair. And his time behind bars had started with him nearly killing people who had abused his now-gone younger brother.

He'd suffered consequences each time, but they were among the most singularly gratifying moments of his life. At an instinctive and primitive level, there was no uncertainty—what he'd done was right.

"We're not lightweights, but still..." Rizz frowned. "Proven killers with mega-firearms who also have a decided physical edge. Any one of them could take us all out in less than a minute."

"We have the mental edge."

"And we're better looking, especially me, but that won't stop bullets."

"If we can time our attack with that of law enforcement, our odds will improve big time. Increased distraction and more," Drake said. "We strike from the inside at the same time the cavalry charges from the outside."

"Agreed, but unless you have ESP, there's no way," Rizz said.

"I think someone has a phone," Drake said. "The newspaper info did not come from the FBI bug." If Phoenix wouldn't hand over her hidden phone or didn't have one, what were his options? "If we can find it, we can contact law enforcement."

Rizz's eyebrows went up. "That would be huge."

"It's far from a sure thing, but we need to choose an attack time and communicate it if we can." Drake thought about Tolman's promise to allow him to talk with Rachelle soon. "Tom Burnett and the Flight 93 passengers attacked at 9:57 a.m. Let's plan on 9:57 p.m.. Spread the word, devise weapons, and be ready to get it on anytime. If a SWAT team attacks beforehand or we see an opportunity to move, we attack. Otherwise, we plan on 9:57 p.m. as go time. With me?"

"Understood. If an opportunity arises before 9:57, we grab it. Otherwise, that's our time to get medieval on these bastards. I'll spread the word, brother."

They had a time—an appointment with death—who would die was the question. Drake clenched his teeth as a chill ran through him.

Rizz sighed. "There should be a bounty on these bastards. I hope justice counts for something."

"I believe it counts, Michael. Now lead the way to the executives. I hope they aren't heading down the acid path the senator is on," Drake said. Without ECMO, the senator would be long dead. His chances of long-term survival and recovery were something Drake didn't want to think about.

"They're fine, Drake. I made that up so we could talk. But follow me. I want you to see someone."

Rizz rolled into the tele unit. The two executives lay sleeping with oxygen masks on their faces and IVs in place. Heavily medicated for the superficial but painful skin burns, the pipeline and refinery executives were out of it.

Rizz rolled toward the corner bay, which still had its curtains drawn. "You heard about our intubated guy found down on the street, right? Trist took care of him." Rizz said. "Minutes ago, I stuck my head in."

"He's the one patient I haven't laid eyes on. Suspected recreational alcohol and drug overdose, right? A blood alcohol level a third of what his was would kill most people. I heard he got off the ventilator already."

"Yep. Miraculous."

Rizz spoke through the curtain.

"Sir, I've got that doctor you wanted to see. You can ask him your question now." Rizz pulled back the curtain, the ringlets clacking.

In front of Drake was the prematurely grizzled head, gaunt body, and ready smile of the Captain.

The Captain had been admitted to Memorial Hospital more times than could be counted. In the days before electronic health records, his charts had occupied over three feet of shelf space. He'd survived more critical illnesses, devastating trauma, and recreational substance misadventures than the entire populations of some small cities.

A thin scar showed white against his weathered blue-black skin as it traced from his ear to the corner of his mouth.

"Greetings, Bones," said the Captain. "I sensed your projection earlier."

Warmth surged through Drake. The Captain, a schizophrenic and substance-abusing ER regular, had a special place in Drake's heart. As he moved closer Drake picked up the scent of wood smoke and alcohol that revealed the Captain's consumption and homeless in-the-rough living.

"Hi, Captain." True to form, the Captain's recuperative powers had him alert and looking "normal," despite being on a ventilator less than an hour earlier. Incredible.

"You wanted to ask me something?" Drake said. At times, the Captain shared thoughts and observations that stunned.

"Yes, Bones. My question is—do you think you could find me a sandwich? I would most appreciate it."

Most might not be alert or eat or drink for more than a day, but the Captain had rebounded from near dead to hungry and talking as if on time-lapse photography. The homeless man had a fixed psychotic delusion. He believed he was an intergalactic scout. His mission was to evaluate earth, its people, and its products for possible benefit to those of his home planet. He particularly took to sampling mind-altering "earth products."

Drake's favorite ER regular could drink more alcohol, take more drugs, withstand more trauma, and survive more devastating illnesses than anyone on the planet. Despite, or perhaps because of the Captain's mental illness, he was a caring soul who'd shared premonitions so on target it had seemed mystical.

Beyond that, the ER regular had saved both Drake and Rachelle's lives.

"Yes, Captain, I'll find you a sandwich. Meanwhile, we're all in serious trouble. Deadly. Do you understand what's going on?"

"I have detected the presence of people who have not evolved. Cruel and ugly—remarkably backward even for your primitive species."

"You're right. We will have to take drastic action to protect ourselves and others," Drake said.

"My kind function on a much higher plane than those of your planet. We do not embrace violence. We do, however, recognize predators. They exist throughout the galaxies in many different forms. I will help if able."

Drake stared into the rheumy brown eyes of the man who was in his 50s but looked much older. One nurse said he looked like Morgan Freeman after a ten-year bender. He called Drake and all doctors "Bones," which Drake suspected was of Star Trek origin. As fond of the man as Drake was, he remained uncertain if anything resembling traditional friendship was within the Captain's capacity.

"I have a related inquiry, Bones."

"Yes. What is it, Captain?" Drake leaned in close, hoping for the type of astounding, seemingly psychic insight that had averted disaster in previous dire circumstances. He could use it.

"Do you have any orange juice in the little plastic cups? If I could have two of those, I would be most thankful. I'm very thirsty."

CHAPTER FORTY-SEVEN

Dylan removed his headset in the operations trailer's soundproof communication booth.

The meeting Dylan had participated in was currently triggering thousands of messages and calls throughout the country. The decision-making and consequences were as high-level as anything imaginable.

The terrorist militia leader had separated himself from typical sovereign-citizen zealots. His demands were extreme but reasoned and well-stated.

Dylan scanned the document again. There was a fair amount of technical legalese, but the main aspects boiled down to two demands:

Federal and state injunctions were to be immediately enacted to halt the "quick seizure" of any citizen's property before due process.

A referendum to strike down current eminent domain actions would be placed on all ballots. A US citizens' vote would sustain the law or trigger development of a new and just process.

The domestic terrorist's demands had raced through the internet and all US media outlets. Tolman Freid had manipulated the media like no criminal ever and had the entire nation as his audience.

The ugly truth was that Tolman's claims of injustice had merit. As a citizen and attorney, Dylan agreed that the terrorist and his family had been victims, and the legal system had offered no protection.

Examination of the current eminent domain law was reasonable. Demanding action by using murder, kidnapping, and extortion was not. A governmental miscarriage of justice did not excuse killing and wanton criminality of the worst kind. The US government would not and could not respond to terrorism. Dylan sighed as he opened the door of the communication booth.

Aki Yamada stood facing one of the control trailer's walls of video screens. Multiple agents and technicians in headsets sat at consoles with laptops in front of them. Dylan flashed on memories of NASA space launches and images of mission control. The murmur of voices and the smell of new carpet and coffee vied with the musky tinge of stress-triggered body odor. Dylan's team knew what was at stake. The dry mouths, sweaty palms, and furrowed brows were at "Houston, we have a problem" levels.

Dylan stepped next to Aki as the silent CNN News feed scrolled "Breaking news—domestic terrorist's demands trigger upswell of positive public response" along the bottom of the screen.

Dylan took a deep breath. The news would stoke the terrorist leader's ego. Would that affect his reaction to the government's response to his demands? How could Dylan placate the rabid terrorist?

Aki moved next to Dylan. "Having fun yet?" The detective was not smiling.

"It's grim. I just got off a conference call with more higher-ups than Mt. Olympus. Let's talk in the communication room."

Dylan led Aki into the small, shielded room where he'd just communicated with the leaders of the US government, including the President. Dylan leaned against the counter edge and indicated one of the two chairs to Aki.

"There's agreement among the government leaders," Dylan said.

"Reject Tolman's demands?"

"Totally and completely. The United States does not negotiate with terrorists. Done deal."

"Do they think Freid is bluffing?"

"I think most believe that not only are the threats real, but he wants to follow through with them. That's the assessment I shared. Tolman Freid wants to make a statement that will never be forgotten. Like Timothy McVeigh in Oklahoma in 1995 and Osama Bin Laden on 9/11 in 2001. Bin Laden didn't kill for his religion. McVeigh had no higher ideal. Terrorists convince themselves it's about their cause. Despite what the extremists claim, in the end what's often said in counterterrorism is true—"the *it* is never the *it*." Virtually all terrorists kill because they are pathetic narcissists who seek recognition. They're twisted sociopaths who care nothing about human life. They confuse infamy with admiration. Terrorist leaders are all megalomaniacs—it's about power, conceit, hate, and delusions of grandeur."

"I believe that," Aki said. "Where's Tolman's son?"

"Being questioned nearby. Freid had an attorney on retainer. So far we've kept them from getting together. We're pushing the kid hard."

"Had an attorney on standby, huh?"

"Yes. Freid considered every contingency. It's hard to imagine he believes the government is going to respond to his demands."

"Maybe he thinks he's so special they will," Aki said. "Is it time to turn the tactical teams loose?"

"If we knew a SWAT team entry would stop him from unleashing further destruction, the go signal would have been given a while ago. The powers that be are ready to write off the ER and those in it if it stops a greater disaster."

"That's grim."

"The explosion and acid release at the refinery show the terrorists' potential. Their initial action was purposefully small. We have to believe him when he says they can do much worse." Thoughts of mass destruction and thousands of casualties filled Dylan's head. "I've been instructed to agree to anything to buy time, though in reality he'll get nothing." He shook his head. "He'll see through it."

"The guy is clever. He's using the media as if he were a movie director," Aki said. "Millions watched his broadcast and read his statement. He presented a story people sympathize with, and the media eats it up. The reality is, he's a multiple murderer and terrorist who is holding Memorial Hospital and one of the biggest metropolitan areas in the country hostage."

"We requested a media blackout but met flat refusal," Dylan said. "In effect, the media outlets are actively partnering with a terrorist. He had this figured in advance—how to get all-world ratings on his made-for-TV video and history's biggest soapbox for his manifesto. The narrative is he's a hero. I'm afraid in the end he's ready to be a martyr."

"What's the latest projection if the tactical teams go in?"

"It'll be rough." Dylan grimaced. "Few, if any, hostages are projected to survive, and high casualties for the tactical personnel—lots of death. And we have no knowledge of what kind of or how many remote destruction devices he has in place. That's what worries me most."

"So what's next?'

"I talk to him and lie a lot. Hope something rolls loose. Last chance before we go tactical."

"Can I talk to his kid?" Aki said. "I checked his record and it's clean. If he really didn't know what was going down, he's got to be scared and confused. Maybe he can help?"

"Do it," Dylan said. "We're still running Freid's attorney around while the kid is being interrogated by our best. See what you can get from the son while I talk to his father. Somehow we need to change our trajectory." He scanned the CCTV images of the hospital and widespread emergency efforts. "Right now we're riding a bullet train to disaster."

CHAPTER FORTY-EIGHT

TOR account, Dark Web

Access step 134. Encrypted. Key double encryption. Transmit off echo site.

Ghost entry. Enter username...complete.

Enter password...complete.

Second username. Triple encrypt identification access complete x 3.

Access complete. Click Open:

Bitcoin cryptocurrency access account.

Show history...

Enter.

The screen flashed. Three transactions appeared.

Deposit one: five million dollars.

Deposit two: five million dollars.

Deposit three: five million dollars.

Account total: fifteen million dollars.

The origin of each deposit was identified only by a long string of numbers and symbols. But there was no doubt. The deposits had originated from Senator Duren's funds, the Fenbridge Pipeline corporate account, and the coffers of the petrochemical refinery.

The money was his. He'd expected a lottery-winner rush, but this was better. A warm surge and a relaxation of his muscles. Not exhilaration but a bone-deep sense of satisfaction.

He could convert the cryptocurrency to standard currency and initiate redistribution whenever he chose. It was easy to use untraceable routes to transfer funds to the international accounts he'd opened. These offshore banks' existence depended on protecting the anonymity of their depositors. *And the US government and its corrupt IRS tax thieves would get nothing!*

He could have gotten more, but the amounts he'd chosen allowed speed and ease of transfer. These millions were small change for fat-cat Duren and the giant fossil fuel corporate maggots. The transactions had taken only hours.

Fifteen million dollars.

He would focus on the future and put the past behind him.

He had one final challenge. It was no small thing.

He had to remain alive and out of jail.

CHAPTER FORTY-NINE

Tolman sat at the main desk staring at an iPhone screen as Drake passed him on the way into the Crash Room. A second smartphone sat on the desk.

"I have a question for you," Tolman said.

Drake stopped.

"Do you like your wife?"

Drake frowned. "What did you say?"

"I asked if you like your wife?"

"Of course, I like my wife," Drake said.

"It's not a dumb question," Tolman said, staring at a phone screen Drake could not see. "You treat people who are abused by their partners. You have friends and coworkers who have grown apart from their spouses. More than fifty percent of marriages end in divorce. Don't scoff when I ask if you like your wife."

The terrorist leader had from the start zeroed in on Drake as his primary contact person among the hostages in the ER. It seemed Tolman Freid wanted to convince Drake that his motivation and terrorist actions were noble. While there was little doubt Tolman wouldn't hesitate to kill Drake, it seemed his opinion mattered to him.

"I care deeply about my wife. She's a kind and loving person. She's the amazing mother of our two children. She's a person who has faced challenges that dwarf those you claim as justification for the evil you have done."

Tolman shook his head and chuckled. "You doctors are interesting. You and your friend in the wheelchair are not normal. You do not show appropriate fear. You dare to insult me. Likewise, the surgeon who smarted off to Red. The nurses are much the same. I find myself both intrigued and annoyed by you people."

"Believe me, we're thrilled we intrigue you," Drake said loading as much sarcasm as he could into his words. "As far as you being annoyed —feel free to get your terrorist ass out of our ER anytime. We won't miss you."

"Ha! You are funny. You may not miss me, but I bet you're missing your wife." Tolman held up the cellphone. "I worked long hours and was away from the farm a lot, but since cellphones, I could call my wife anytime. It was as if we were together no matter how far apart we were. Now, I can be right there with her, but she's still scared and alone in a different universe." He paused and his eyes lost focus for a moment. "If you could speak with your wife, what would you say to her?"

"I'd tell Rachelle to take the kids and notify all those she can to leave the city. I'd tell her the whack-job terrorist doesn't care whether he or others live or die. I'd tell her I believe you have destructive devices planted throughout the cities and that your ego, self-delusion, and cowardice threaten death and destruction."

"Cowardice? I've proven I'm willing to risk death for my cause," Tolman said.

"Not fearing death is not courage—not in someone who has nothing to live for," Drake said. "You pretend it's about your cause, but it's all about you. Your anger, your powerlessness, your insignificance. You want recognition. You're a megalomaniac."

"I don't know why I let you talk to me like that." Tolman shook his head. "Doctors are arrogant. You believe only you know the truth."

"I know terrorism and killing innocent people is abhorrent," Drake said.

"Freedom and justice always come at a cost. That cost is lives. Those in power respond only to force."

"You accuse me and others of arrogance?" Drake said. "Killing innocent others to support your opinion is the ultimate arrogance. A man who kills women and children is not a man. You want people to think you're special. There's nothing special about cruelty and murder."

"You treat me unfairly, Dr. Drake Cody." His eyebrow twitched. "But because I know what it is like to lose a wife and I'm feeling generous, I'm going to do you a favor." He held one of the smartphones up. "I'm going to let you talk to your wife. It is the last and only kindness you can expect from me. It's more than you deserve."

Drake's throat clenched, his breathing tightened. He read Tolman's message as clear as if printed in bold letters.

This would be the last time Drake would speak with Rachelle.

CHAPTER FIFTY

Tolman's preparation for Drake's contact with Rachelle had only taken a few minutes. Drake's mind was in hyperdrive. His desperation was at odds with the complex task he needed to accomplish. He needed more time to figure how to—

"Now." Tolman held the phone out. "You get fifteen seconds to speak, then I take the phone and play what you recorded. Understood?"

"What if she doesn't answer?" Drake stalled, using each second in a near-panicked drive to find the right words.

"We'll leave it on her messages." He extended a phone to Drake while he held a second smartphone where Drake had dictated his brief message. "Call her and keep it on speaker. Try anything and I'll cut you off. Remember, this is a gift."

He entered the numbers, and the ringing began.

"H-hello?" Rachelle said.

Drake's heart went to this throat. Hearing her voice triggered a tidal wave of emotion.

"Rachelle, it's Drake." This was a last chance. He had to make it work. "I only have a few seconds, then there'll be a recording—"

"Oh, Drake!" Her voice broke. "Are you okay? I'm—"

"Rachelle, we only have seconds. The terrorist is monitoring me. Listen to what I say now and on the recording he's going to play. Believe every word. It's life or death."

"A recording? Life or death?"

"No time to explain. I love you. Tell the kids how much I love them. Take care of them as best you can, and don't be afraid to move on with your life if—"

"Don't talk like that, Drake. I'm going to see you soon—"

Tolman gave the cut signal.

"He's going to play the recording now. I love you."

Tolman took the second smartphone and held the iPhone to it. The message Drake had recorded and Tolman reviewed started:

"Rachelle, I love you. Everyone in the cities is in great danger. Get Meryl and the kids and leave town. Tell Aki and Jon. Roll out tonight. Go to the Burnett resort. I'm sure he'll let you do a p.m. check-in instead of a.m. like before. Things are going to be okay but if not..." Drake's voice cracked and wavered. "All my love to you and the kids forever."

The recorded message ended and Tolman ended the connection.

Will I ever see Rachelle or the children again? Drake turned and rubbed the tears from his eyes.

Tolman sat with his hands open at shoulder height and a smile on his face.

The smug bastard!

"Quite touching, doctor. After gifting you that call, you can't say I don't have a heart."

A spark in the shadows of Drake's mind flared. Could he dive over the counter and crush Tolman's throat before he or the pockmarked militia man on guard could shoot?

"If you have a heart," Drake said, "it's twisted, black, and dead."

CHAPTER FIFTY-ONE

Underground parking ramp, Hennepin County Government Center

"Where's Sigurd's attorney now?" Aki stood just outside the converted supply room being used for interrogation. The parking basement of the Hyatt Hotel was one of multiple downtown sites law enforcement had taken over. The low light, concrete walls, and windowless construction of the near-empty subterranean structure felt dungeon-like.

"Somebody told the lawyer his client had been moved from downtown to the uptown precinct." The agent smiled. "No idea how that could've happened."

"What have you got out of him?" Aki said.

"Got some details on the players and the general layout, which we shared with the tactical guys. Otherwise, he pretty much follows the storyline. Says he tagged along with his uncle and cousin, despite his father having ordered him not to. Claims he didn't know what was going on, but knew it involved family and felt he should do his part. When his uncle broke out the guns and he saw his cousin shot and two law enforcement killed, he freaked. He had tears in his eyes when he told me. He doesn't seem anything like what I'd expect for a terrorist's son."

"You saying you believe him?" Aki said.

"If he's a liar, he's a damn good one. He's been around the sovereign citizen and militia stuff all his life but doesn't seem like he's a true believer. He's more into the family farming and trucking operations. He's scared and confused, but he's as polite as anybody I've ever interviewed. I find myself almost liking him."

"I'll give it a go. We need to learn something that can help."

"Have at him." The agent indicated the door.

Aki realized this interrogation could be the most important of his life. The stakes were beyond measure. He opened the metal door. It closed behind him with a loud clunk.

The terrorist leader's son sat at a small table. He didn't have handcuffs on and there was a can of Coke in front of him. An empty chair sat on the other side of the table. The layout was very much like the interrogation rooms of the Minneapolis Police Department.

"I'm Detective Aki Yamada. I'm with Minneapolis Police."

"Yes, sir." The tall, lean young man stood up and extended his hand over the table. "I'm Sigurd Freid."

Aki shook Sigurd's hand, the kid's palm sweaty. They both sat. The young man didn't seem to know what to do with his hands, wringing them, then putting them on the table, and finally shifting them to his lap. Other than the display of nerves, the clean-cut young man looked like he'd fit going door-to-door with a Christian youth organization.

"I need you to help me stop more people from getting hurt or killed. That includes people very close to you."

"I'd like to help, but I don't think I can," Sigurd said.

Aki fixed the young man in his gaze. Sigurd bit his lip but did not flinch or look away.

"Your father is an angry, grieving man. His home was taken from him, and he believes that harmed your mother."

"It did." Sigurd leaned forward. "They destroyed our home and my mother. My mother..." His voice broke.

Aki had seen her on the video.

"I'm sorry," Aki said. "That was tragic and shouldn't have happened, but it did. We can't change that. Going forward, there's only one question that matters." Aki laid his hands flat on the table and looked into the young man's eyes. "Do you know what the question is?"

Sigurd cocked his head. "What?"

"Do you want your father to live?"

The young man didn't move but his face blanched. Tears welled in his eyes. The soft whisper of the room's ventilation hissed.

"He's my father."

"If we don't stop him," Aki said, "he will die." The words hung in the vault-like room.

Sigurd pursed his lips and swallowed, his eyes wide. He clasped his hands as if in prayer.

"When we attack the ER, it will be with extreme force and he'll be killed. If he somehow survives that, he'll be arrested. Unless we can stop him from killing more people, he'll be tried and executed as a terrorist mass murderer. If you want him to live, he needs to be stopped now."

The room hung silent but for the faint sigh of the ventilation.

The young man breathed deep. He held both hands flat on the table with fingers outstretched as if trying to brace himself.

"Will you help save him? Tell us all you know." Aki reached out and put a hand on the young man's forearm. "You're his only chance," Aki said. He sensed Sigurd bending. *Come on, kid.*

Sigurd abruptly looked away and pushed back in his chair. "Father said—" He stopped talking. He held both hands to his temples and rocked forward and back. "I need some time to think."

"Aren't you listening? There is no time!" Aki's words had fired out like rockets.

Sigurd flinched and backed away.

"I'm sorry, Sigurd. I didn't mean to yell." *Damn.* He'd lost his cool. "We're talking about people's lives, Sigurd. Please."

Sigurd did not look at him.

"Father said we have a lawyer," the terrorist's son said. "Can I talk with him?"

It was as if Aki had been trying to hook a fish and startled it with a clumsy yank of the pole. His gut went hollow. This boy's help could mean life or death for thousands.

I blew it big time.

CHAPTER FIFTY-TWO

The door closed behind the Japanese-American detective as he left. The solid *clunk* and pressure wave in the windowless room made Sigurd's ears pop.

He stared at the detective's card and the number handwritten on the back.

"This is where I can be reached. Have them call me immediately with anything. As soon as you can, Sigurd. There's no time," the policeman had said.

Aki Yamada. The detective had pronounced his first name "ah-key." He was the first Japanese American Sigurd had ever met.

Growing up on the farm and having been homeschooled by his mother, Sigurd hadn't met many people from different backgrounds. In central Minnesota farm country, diversity meant which Scandinavian country had people's family originally come from. Father didn't allow most TV, and they mainly used the computer for farm and trucking business. Most of what Sigurd learned had come from his mother. Before she got sick, Mother had made learning interesting and fun for him. And she was good at it, too. When he'd taken his GED and tried one standardized college entry test, he'd scored in the top five percent.

Father said Mother had "babied" Sigurd. He knew his mother loved him—it was different with Father. Sigurd didn't know if Father even liked him.

During his homeschooling, Mother had taught him about different people and said all people are more alike than different. She told him that most Americans, whatever their background, were law-abiding, hard-working, and good people.

What Sigurd heard from many of the militia was the opposite. Uncle Red and his friends spoke ugly of foreigners and minorities. Red would have called the detective a Jap or something else mean. He used the N-word and others for Black people and said horrible things.

Father would shut them up. He'd told Sigurd the color of a man's skin didn't make him good or bad. He didn't allow "white trash nonsense" talk to be part of his organization.

Mother said Red had "mental" troubles that had worsened while he was in prison, especially after he got badly beaten by a bunch of Black prisoners.

Red had been locked up for most of Sigurd's life. He remembered his uncle being fun before those years. Since Red's beating and release from prison, Sigurd was afraid of him.

Father had said, "Things were done to Red in prison that shouldn't happen to any man. Be careful around him."

And yet Sigurd had begged Red and Micah to let him join them. No one would tell him what was going on, and Sigurd had no idea when they entered the ER about the craziness that was planned. *How could I be so stupid?*

The metal door opened, and the FBI agent who'd talked with Sigurd earlier stuck his head in. "Your attorney is on his way. Do you have anything you want to say to me? Or we can call Detective Yamada if you're ready to talk."

"I'm thinking about what he said. I don't know how I can help. Is the lawyer going to be here soon, sir?"

"The lawyer is coming but time is running out. Any minute could be your father's last. Knock on the door when you're ready to do the right thing." The agent shut the door.

It felt like there were no air in the room. Sigurd's heart raced. Even if he wanted to, could he change anything? How? Might the lawyer help?

Time is running out.

Would Father and the others surrender and go to jail?

Sigurd's stomach dropped. Could anyone escape from the barricaded ER?

Would Red and his scary convict friends allow themselves to go back to prison?

He got to his feet and began pacing. His thoughts jumped and clawed like an animal being driven into a cage. There was no way out.

Red and his crew would never give up, and if the FBI tried to take the ER, it would be a bloodbath. In that fight, Father wouldn't have a chance—there was no way out.

The detective was a straight-shooter and believed what he'd said. Unless Sigurd could somehow help, Father would die. Would Father really kill innocent people to accomplish what he thought was right? Sigurd didn't understand what he hoped to prove.

He ran a trembling hand through his hair. Loyalty to his father, uncertainty, and fear wrenched his mind and heart. Father had given him strict orders. Was it betrayal to try and help the detective?

A last thought struck—if Mother's mind were whole, what would she want him to do?

CHAPTER FIFTY-THREE

Phoenix watched Dr. Trist tend to her attacker's smashed and bleeding face. The short, thin doctor with the long hair and wire-rimmed glasses said nothing as he worked. She did not see him as someone who could protect her.

Cecil's murderer whined and swore as the doctor worked on him. The pockmarked con looked on. When the doctor finished, small rolls of gauze protruded from each nostril. The swelling of his nose and face had turned his piggy eyes to slits. They called him Hyena for his sick laugh. Now he looked like a warthog. He was the ugliest creature ever.

She hoped his pain would never end.

Hyena got up and stepped over to Cecil's body. He bent and gripped the pearl handle of the knife lodged in Cecil's chest. He yanked but it remained stuck. He put his boot on Cecil's chest and pulled again. The blade ripped free as if it were a nail pulled from a board.

"All-world kill shot. Drilled the faggot right through the heart." Hyena cackled, now seeming unfazed by his injuries.

"Bull's-eye." Pockmark nodded.

The murderer wiped his bloody blade on Cecil's shirt and placed it in its sheath.

He looked at Phoenix, pursed his lips, made *kiss-kiss* sounds, and winked a blackened eye at her.

Her stomach heaved.

Hyena and the pockmarked man picked up Cecil's body and dumped it onto one of the wheeled cots as if it were garbage. They rolled past her and into the corridor. The smell of blood and a fouler odor wafted in their wake.

"Are you okay? Can I do anything for you?" the long-haired doctor asked.

She shook her head.

"There are meds we can give as a precaution. Did he—"

"He did not penetrate me." She couldn't imagine how things could be more horrible, but at least Cecil had stopped that. None of it should have happened. She should have been protected better. Her anger grew.

"Let me know if I can help." The doctor left the room.

She rested her head in her hands. She didn't deserve any of what had happened. She was the ultimate victim. This nightmare had started with her commitment to educating the public on the immorality of the pipeline and refinery. Her dedication had led to this —held hostage by racist domestic terrorists and assaulted by a repulsive creature. The memory of his touch sickened her.

And it was not over.

She could end up dead, killed by a terrorist whose views on government corruption and corporate greed were, ironically, similar to her own. The system did need to be torn apart.

It had taken wisdom and resolve for her to stay quiet when the maniac held the gun to the heads of others. A reporter must protect their source at all costs—even if that source is themselves. This story and all of its meaning must be shared with the public. Only she had the knowledge, abilities, and moral wisdom to tell it.

Phoenix's responsibility transcended herself. Only someone as enlightened as her was suited to inform and educate the ignorant populace—her calling was every bit as sacred as that of any of the doctors. To have sacrificed herself would have been a disservice to her profession and the world.

Drake entered the minor trauma area.

The elderly Roberta lay with eyes closed. The boy with autism and a seizure disorder sat focused on his repetitive hand gestures. His mother was seated on a chair next to his cot with eyes closed and a rosary clasped in her hands. Her lips were moving.

Antoine had a cart to himself, as did the person Drake had come to see.

Phoenix lay under sheets with her forearm across her brow.

Drake approached close and spoke softly. "Phoenix, we need to talk. Please come out in the hall."

Without looking at him she sat up, got to her feet, and walked toward the hall. Drake followed.

In the empty space near the cast room, she stopped and leaned against a cart parked there.

She looked at him. "What?"

"Unless we coordinate with those on the outside trying to save us, we will likely die. If we can communicate with them, our odds will be vastly better. I felt you react when I mentioned your phone after Cecil was killed."

"That doesn't mean anything. I heard what the surgeon said. The FBI had a bug." She sounded like a petulant teen.

"Phoenix, there was a bug. But I know what we said during surgery and at all times around it. It wasn't what was in the newspaper's report. Dr. Rainey made that up to keep the terrorist from shooting Cecil, or anyone else. I know it was you who communicated what appeared in the news." He didn't know for sure but...

"No!" She shook her head. "You can't know that."

"Please, Phoenix. I'm not judging you. No one will blame you. No one else needs to know—"

"There's nothing to know." She jutted her jaw forward and her eyes challenged.

Pressuring her after all she'd gone through felt harsh, but he sensed a hostility toward him that made no sense. Why? She had to be lying.

"I'm so sorry for all you've gone through." Drake shook his head. "I wish it was over, but it's not." *C'mon damn it, where is your phone?* "If we can find a phone, perhaps if you were to happen upon one, it could be the difference between living and dying—for all of us."

She shook her head. "I won't be finding the phone." Her eyes would not meet his. "I wish there was a phone. I want to live. It's essential that I live. Believe me, even if there was a phone before, there isn't one now."

No longer a phone.

God in heaven, help us!

～

PHOENIX RETURNED to her cart and laid down, then pulled the sheets over herself.

"You okay?" Antoine asked. "Anything I can do?"

"Just scared. Please keep me safe."

"Will do my best, young lady."

She put her arm across her brow once more. Antoine didn't make demands. He didn't question.

Dr. Drake Cody wanted her to believe he wasn't judging her—she knew better.

She hadn't confessed to having a phone when the terrorist leader held the gun to Cecil's head and was two seconds from pulling the trigger. Anyone who knew the truth might condemn her. They might claim she was selfish or cowardly. People were ignorant—they had no idea.

It was obvious Dr. Cody had judged her.

She wondered if he suspected what her profession was. Like so many others, he likely didn't acknowledge or resented the vital role of her and her profession. Journalists' interpretation of world events informed the uninformed masses and were the foundation of social and political conscience.

Whatever unfolded in this current nightmare, her recounting would shape and define its basis and meaning. It was her special calling, and she must survive to fulfill it.

Of course, recognizing she was special in no way meant others were lesser. No one should be deemed inferior because of their race, background, or socioeconomic circumstances. That's not what she was talking about. No way.

She and brave others like her in the media had the courage to share their informed opinion, social awareness, and unique understanding. It was a heavy burden, but one she'd been born to fulfill and prepared for her whole life. She'd been told from her earliest memories that she was special. She had no doubt.

Dr. Cody said that without the phone, their chances of escaping alive had dimmed. He said he knew she had the phone. Said it could be the difference between life or death—for all of them. Her throat tightened and a chill gripped her. She curled up on her side and pulled the sheets tighter around her.

When she told Dr. Cody there was no phone, she had not lied. She didn't have it anymore.

As soon as she could, after the terrorist leader's near-execution of Cecil, she'd escaped to the restroom, and, trembling and nauseous, retrieved the iWatch device and flushed it down the toilet. In her panic she'd believed she'd be killed if it was found. The possibility of the phone helping her survive had not occurred to her.

Thoughts of her life flashed through her head like the riffling of a deck of cards. Always safe, secure, and provided for—her background, support, education, and opportunities had made her the incredibly special person she was.

The terrorists had killed a policewoman. They'd gunned down the senator's security man and a state trooper. Her attacker had plunged a knife into Cecil's heart.

More would likely die, but she must not be among them. She needed to survive to tell her story and ascend to her proper place in journalism and life. Fear weighed on her like a two-ton weight. She'd take no chances and do everything possible to keep herself protected and out of harm's way.

Phoenix Halvorson—reporter, educator of the public, and moral compass for society.

She must survive.

Her truth must be told.

CHAPTER FIFTY-FOUR

Home of Senator and Evangeline Duren

Evangeline sat at the desk in Hayden's home office. She gripped the armrests of his chair and closed her eyes. Hoping to somehow sense him, all she could register was fear. She'd never met a kinder or more caring person than Hayden. Her heart ached.

Why had he been targeted? He saw being a senator as an honor and a way to help people. He'd never hurt anyone. Her eyes blurred with tears. On the desk under her hand was an invitation to an upcoming state function. She read: "To the right honorable Senator Hayden Duren and Madame Evangeline Duren." Her mind flashed to the image of Hayden battered and connected to the breathing tube. The words blurred through tear-filled eyes.

Please save him, Lord. Bring him back to me.

Her phone pinged. A text appeared. It was to "Wife of the corporate thief/executive collaborator of the corrupt US power structure." Evangeline's hands trembled as she read.

The tiny portion of the ill-gotten funds you and your husband have amassed arrived in the site I designated. Congratulations.

Further requirements for his release remain. You will continue to tell no one about these communications or the steps you've taken. Any disobedience or deceit and your husband will be killed.

You will not be contacted again. Your husband is seriously injured but is receiving expert medical care. All of my interactions have been in good faith. I am an honest man.

In a previous response, you asked that the security person Marcus be included in this negotiation and exchange. You requested proof of life.

His inclusion in the ransom exchange cannot be added after the fact. My contract is with you alone and involved only your husband's life.

The security person is not and was not part of any agreement.

As a demonstration of my integrity and the stark consequences of any disobedience or deception, I'm informing you that you will not receive proof of the security person's life. Marcus is dead. He died honorably. His loss is another stain on the record of the corrupt and illegitimate corporate-government complex that has defiled our land and violated common law and the rights of free persons.

Tears ran down her cheeks as she finished reading. Marcus, dead? *Please, no!*

Knowing that Marcus was with Hayden had buoyed her hope.

Marcus "died honorably," the text said. What could someone who did such terrible things know about honor?

Her heart went out to Marcus's brother, Harley. How could she tell him?

And the animal responsible for Marcus's death and Hayden's suffering sat in judgment, claiming the moral high ground. Rage, fear, and sadness swirled within her.

She'd never been so helpless, yet she dare not tell anyone. More tears coursed down her cheeks. Some way, somehow, the man she loved must return to her. Her sobs broke loose, and she collapsed to her knees.

Hayden, oh God, my Hayden.

CHAPTER FIFTY-FIVE

When horrible things had happened to Rachelle, especially in the years before meeting Drake, she'd taken drugs, suffered panic attacks, and curled up in a ball.

Not now. She had changed. Drake needed her and she would not let fear stop her.

Her throat tightened. Would the brief phone call be the last time she'd hear Drake's voice? He seemed to be saying good-bye forever.

His message to take care of the kids and not be afraid to "move on with your life" had plunged an icy knife into her heart. *God, no.*

No whining. No panic. She had to concentrate. Drake did not give up. And neither would she.

He would do everything possible to be there for her and the children. He'd done so in the past. She imagined herself in his arms, his strength, his passion—he would return to them. She bit her lip and trailed her hand to the thickened tissue of the burn scar overlying her neck. *He had to...*

She took pen and paper and began to write down everything she could remember from the call. First, he'd instructed her to contact friends and included Meryl. Just thinking about that evil woman made her shudder. Meryl had been their friend like a hungry wolf was a friend to a newborn fawn. Clearly it was a signal.

The bizarre parts of Drake's spoken and recorded message held hidden meaning. But could she decipher it?

Burnett resort? She'd never heard of it. *Do a p.m. check-in instead of a.m. like before?* She knew they'd never been there. Tell Aki and Jon to *roll out tonight?*

What did it mean? Nothing clicked into place.

The greasy fingers of fear trailed down her spine. There was not enough air in the room. Panic pressed her like gravity.

A loon cried, its plaintive wail resonating deep within her. She took a deep breath and focused out the window as the sun neared the horizon. The lake lay like a mirror reflecting the fire-orange sun and sky.

Drake needed her. She would not surrender to her old ways.

She plumbed her memory again, reviewing every word. Her ability to recall had not scattered despite her fear.

But the meaning of the words escaped her.

She was failing the test.

Drake's voice sounded in her head—*take care of the children, move on with your life.* Her breathing tightened.

She held her clenched fist to her mouth, reading his words, straining to find meaning. Drake wouldn't give her something impossible for her to solve.

But wait. He would.

He'd had to. He hadn't been able to craft the necessary message in a way that Rachelle could decipher *on her own* while keeping the real meaning hidden from the terrorist. He'd sent a message she could not understand because he'd had to.

She ran her eyes across Drake's mysterious riddle once again.

She needed help, but the terrorist had threatened to kill Drake if she shared news of his call with anyone. Would the murderer who held Drake know? The first hint of pins and needles tingling in her fingers and a hunger for air signaled the start of panic. *No!*

Drake had said to *move on with her life* if he were killed. *Hell no!* She would not let fear or weakness cost her the man she loved. She would not be moving on. The terrorist animal and his threat could rot in hell.

She knew where to find the help she needed.

She'd take the life-or-death gamble.

CHAPTER FIFTY-SIX

The extremist leader sat at the ER's main desk holding the phone. "This is Tolman Freid. Connect me with the agent in charge." He had the phone on speaker. Bart and Tracy stood next to Drake at the entry to the Crash Room. Drake was trying to keep his head clear. He couldn't let the emotional battering ram of his just-completed call to Rachelle let him lose focus. He needed to be alert to any advantage, no matter how small.

Tolman Freid liked an audience. Drake increasingly felt the twisted extremist sought recognition and respect. He seemed to want to impress Drake most of all.

All their captors were within earshot. This was show time. The time Tolman had scheduled for the government authorities to respond to his demands.

The connection clicked.

"Hello. I'm Dylan McGinnis, special agent in—"

"What is the government response?" Tolman said.

"I will answer, but there has not been time to—"

"Enough!" Tolman said. "I'm fluent in the lies and delaying tactics of the US government and its agencies. Tell me that the government has agreed to my demands. That and confirmation of my son's freedom are all I need to hear from you."

"Yes, I will have an answer, but—"

"You violated our agreement with the surgeon's transport by planting your electronic bug," he said, his face reddening. "You engaged in deceit then, and now you pretend there is no governmental response. Another lie. I warned you—any further treachery or defiance will force me to give a demonstration of the devastating price you will pay."

"No! Please. I apologize. It takes time," Dylan said. "Your son has not had any charges filed. The other requests you—"

"Not requests—demands. This is not a negotiation." Tolman's jaw clenched and the timbre of his voice thickened.

He held the phone out, staring at it as the muscles in his forearm stood out like steel cables. He let out a long exhalation before repositioning the phone.

"The government will lie, cheat, and kill to maintain business as usual." The volume of his voice had lessened but not the intensity. "The thievery and cruelty of eminent domain is not justice. The US government always believes the ends justify the means. And the ends for those in power is maintaining the system that feeds it money and power. You violate the basic rights of free persons and trample the lives and liberty of the individual. I won't tolerate more lies. There will be deadly consequences. This is your final chance. Have my demands been accepted? Answer yes or no."

Drake held his breath. The sounds of the life-supporting equipment marched in offset cadence from the Crash Room. The air around the main desk hung heavy. The senator's heart monitor beeped as if a countdown. The seconds stretched.

"I will answer." The agent paused. Drake imagined the speaker's frantic scramble to somehow placate the terrorist leader. "I understand your frustration—"

"You understand nothing!" The veins in Tolman's neck stood out. "Answer now or face hell's fire."

Legal injustice had irrevocably damaged Drake's life and the lives of those he loved. The bitterness in the extremist's words resonated with a part deep inside of him, but Tolman's actions had erased any possible sympathy.

"Please don't do anything rash," the FBI agent said. "We can—"

"Your time is up. I've been left no choice." Tolman shook his head and sighed. He closed his eyes and his shoulders slumped as if he'd just heard tragic news. "As a merciful man, I will share one caution. Rescue personnel should use maximum respiratory protection. Death and destruction are on the way."

The hyena licked his swollen lips and shifted from foot to foot. The pockmarked con's face slid to a sick smile.

"After the display their defiance triggered, the attorney general, the speakers of the house and senate, and the President are to release a joint statement agreeing to my ultimatum. This is not negotiable. You have until ten p.m. to provide confirmation my demands have been met."

"Mr. Freid, please wait—"

"Freedom comes with a price. It always has, it always will." Tolman paused. "Prepare for the first installment. Recognize this is just a taste of what I can and will deliver."

He hit disconnect and the line went dead.

CHAPTER FIFTY-SEVEN

Tolman's threat left the air charged like the moment before a lightning strike that had once nearly killed Drake. Bart and Tracy stood frozen next to him. Tolman remained seated at the desk with his crew of armed misfit killers positioned throughout the room awaiting his next move. No one spoke.

Drake tensed. Could he stop Tolman from delivering the destruction he threatened?

Tolman eyed the red iPhone in his hand.

The rhythmic actions of the machines and the beeping of the heart monitor continued from the Crash Room. The sounds of one man clinging to life while the lives of unknown innocent others hung on the actions of a madman. The Life Clock above the senator's bed flashed, clicking the seconds away.

Bart leaned close and the big surgeon's heat and breath registered as he whispered, "No bueno, ER."

Drake's heart pounded as the sense of menace crested. Thoughts of desperate, sure-to-fail actions careened through his mind.

Tolman scanned the room, his gaze stopping briefly on others then linking with Drake.

"You've seen it. I've acted in good faith and have been met with deceit and lies. They've left me no alternative."

Liar! Drake screamed in his mind. *You knew all along what their answer would be. You planned from the start to deliver the destruction you've threatened.*

Tolman raised the red iPhone. Drake's throat locked. No one moved. The certainty of impending disaster loomed.

"I did not want to have to do this." The madman hit keys as he spoke.

"Don't!" Drake sprinted toward the counter and launched himself at Tolman. Before he cleared the counter, Drake was yanked to a halt as something locked around his ankles. He ended stopped short, outstretched on the counter.

Drake turned his head. All the terrorists had their weapons trained on him. His ankles were clasped in the grip of Bart Rainey's massive hands.

"You had no chance, ER. Bad time to get dead. You're needed," the big surgeon said.

Tolman sat with the phone in hand as if Drake's charge had not happened.

He locked eyes with Drake from just beyond arm's length. "They left me no choice." He depressed a final key.

All were still. Drake held his breath. The machines and red digits of the Life Clock marched on, though somehow seemingly slowed.

The rumble started low and faint like distant thunder. It increased like a frenzied crescendo of kettle drums. The ER trembled. Lights flickered.

Drake had experienced similar noise and power with major storms, but this was not thunder.

"Yee-ha." The hyena cackled. "Light 'em up, Major. Smoke 'em if you got 'em."

Tolman said something and at first it did not register. In the echo in Drake's mind the maniac's words came clear.

"Freedom comes with a price."

CHAPTER FIFTY-EIGHT

Minutes earlier, Golden Valley suburb on edge of downtown

"Be real quiet," Jeff Berglund said as he slipped through the brush on the hillside.

Chad crouched and answered in a whisper, "How much farther?"

Jeff pointed a finger at the small rise about forty yards ahead.

The hillside glowed in the late afternoon light. This was the time that Jeff had seen them before.

He glanced to the west. The low sun was copper, and the undersides of the scattered clouds blazed red as sunset neared.

Jeff moved forward, watching where he placed each of his Nike-clad feet. He wore the long-sleeved camo T-shirt he often wore to school.

Despite the mild temperature, Chad wore the fire-engine-red letter jacket that he was rarely without.

"Stay down," Jeff whispered. "No noise and move slow." He slipped sideways around the crest of the hill, crouching to keep bushes between him and the opening he knew was just beyond the rise. His heart hammered and the excitement of the stalk made his chest tight.

Chad had often ignored Jeff or been a jerk, but he was one of the cool guys. Jeff hoped it wasn't a mistake to share his special place with him.

Jeff got on all fours and crawled closer to the crest. He turned and signaled with a finger in front of his mouth to Chad who was likewise on all fours. As he neared the top, Jeff belly-crawled the last few feet through the wild grass. He used his hand to spread an opening in the grass.

They were there!

A smile stretched his cheeks. Awe and wonder gripped him each time he saw them. Only a couple of miles from downtown and a few hundred yards from the nearest road, it was a special wild place.

He glanced at Chad, who stared wide-eyed.

There were three of them. The kit foxes frolicked around the packed dirt at the mouth of a den opening into the hillside. There were scattered feathers and the remnants of mice and other small creatures Jeff had watched the red bushy-tailed mother fox bring to the den.

They were without their mother now. They growled, yipped, and wrestled with each other in an attempt at being tough guys that made Jeff want to laugh.

Since he'd first discovered them, he came every day and watched for as long as he could.

He bragged at school that he'd seen something amazing.

And Chad, one of the popular kids who never paid attention to him, had been interested.

Jeff didn't want to be selfish and couldn't see what harm could be done by sharing.

He turned toward Chad, expecting to see his new friend's smile and excitement.

What?

Chad was on his knees with his arm cocked and a rock in hand.

God, no! Jeff rolled to his back, raised his legs, and drove both feet into Chad's stomach. Chad grunted as he flew back into brambles.

Jeff swung his head toward the den and saw the kits disappear into safety.

Chad scrambled to his feet, blood coming from a scratched ear and cheek.

"I'm going to kick your ass, loser."

"You were going to hurt them." *Why?* Nothing made sense.

"They're vermin," Chad said. "It's better to kill them before they do damage. Everyone said you were a weirdo or some kind of faggot. You're dead meat." He bent down and picked up a rock, taking a step forward and drawing back his rock-held fist.

Jeff reacted as his uncle had taught him. He fired a side kick into Chad's knee. The blow landed cleanly.

Chad screamed and went down.

Jeff turned and ran. Racing down the steep bank, he jumped bushes and fallen trees. Branches scratched his face. He reached the bottom of the hill, broke out of the woods, and turned toward the abandoned road. As he crossed the railroad tracks, time crashed. In a blink the world exploded. A deafening sound filled his head as his body was picked up and hurled. A blast of heat, sound and power propelled him through the air.

He landed on his belly, face under the water of a swampy culvert beside the tracks.

Heat seared his back, his clothes igniting. He raised his head and was struck blind. He was within a fireball—a continuous roar, pain beyond any he'd imagined possible, and the smell of burned hair and cooking flesh.

As consciousness faded, a lone thought flickered. *Will the foxes be okay?*

CHAPTER FIFTY-NINE

"What the hell?" Police officer Robinson lurched and looked toward the origin of the deafening blast. Windows on nearby buildings shattered as the wave of wind rocked him. The hospital's asphalt parking lot rolled wave-like beneath his feet.

"Oh my Lord!" A National Guardsman in full gear stood staring, open-mouthed.

Against the backdrop of sunset, a massive cloud of black and gray smoke towered into the air. Personnel in the hospital parking lot stood frozen for a moment. Giant flames flickered within the growing mountain of smoke that dwarfed the buildings of the western edge of Minneapolis.

"It's not far. Couple of miles, maybe three. Got to be this side of Highway 55," Robinson said.

He spoke into his radio. "Huge explosion and fire west edge of Minneapolis, possibly Golden Valley. It is not the hospital. Repeat, not the hospital. Appears to be south of Highway 55 and east of 169. It's huge."

A lone siren sounded from south of the hospital. Others joined in as if recruited like dogs by the original. The Doppler-shifting directional yowl of a Civil Defense siren began to wail.

Robinson's radio screeched. He held the radio to his ear for a moment.

"Roger that," He clicked off, then spoke loudly, so all those near him in the lot could hear. "Fire-rescue and hazmat notified. Anticipated hazardous materials and toxicity. Divert all traffic systemwide. No one to approach the blast area. Repeat, no one to approach." His volume lessened. "Heaven help us."

SECURE COMMUNICATIONS TRAFFIC AND EXCHANGES, Hennepin County Incident Command System

ICS reception: "Suspected terrorist action. Fire and explosion. Epicenter is Golden Valley. Origin appears near railhead and abandoned grain elevators. Reports of toxic gas and hazardous materials. Suspect hydrofluoric acid. Full hazmat protocols. Self-contained breathing essential."

ICS reception update: "Industrial site with large number of employees just east of blast epicenter. Multiple fatalities and casualties a certainty."

ICS reception update: "Establish initial boundary two miles out. MPD to divert all traffic. Current wind eight mph from the Northwest. Initiate evacuation of Golden Valley, Hopkins, Kenwood, and southwest Minneapolis. More anticipated."

ICS reception update: "Hazmat assessment ongoing. We have windows shattered more than 800 yards out. Full mobilization. Advise all that Memorial Hospital remains unable to accept patients. Advise alternative trauma centers, burn units, and community hospitals to anticipate large influx. Total emergency systems activation."

EMERGENCY OPERATIONS CENTER

"Jesus, we're talking historically ugly," Hennepin County Incident Command leader, Fire Battalion Commander Rondo said.

"Unbelievable, Chief. One small positive—from a quick look at the grids, it looks like the epicenter of the blast is in a low-density area. Woods, marsh, and a generally undeveloped valley along railroad tracks. God help us. I know there's a big industrial operation and ball field nearby. Please, God, I hope no kids' games were going on."

The radio buzzed.

"Hazmat rescue squad Zero-Bravo-Tango. Over."

"Reading you, Chief Rondo here."

"On the ground in full gear at eastern edge of blast zone. Can't get nearer due to flames. Registering high concentrations of hydrofluoric acid. We're dealing with at least a several-acre immediate kill zone. Sustained towering flames and black-gray smoke. Suspect hydrocarbon and other components. Based on our entry route, population appears panicked. Local traffic snarled. Rescue vehicles are blocked. Appreciate any help with traffic control. Need to maintain wide perimeter and monitor winds. Toxic substance assessment ongoing. Will do our best."

"Roger that. Incident Command out."

The chief turned to his second-in-command. "You're right on the location. This is going to be heartbreak deadly, but imagine if this had been downtown..."

CHAPTER SIXTY

Drake's gut burned hollow, his mind staggered. "What have you done?"

Tolman raised an eyebrow from his seat behind the counter.

"What I warned I'd do. I'm a man of my word."

The ceiling-mounted TV flashed to a remote shot showing what looked like a volcanic plume rising above the western edge of the city. The sun had disappeared below the horizon, and in the diminishing light, huge flames twisted and flashed within an ascending mountain of black smoke.

"You murdering bastard!" Drake said. "You killed women, children, families—innocent people." Could this be real? His consciousness could not accept the heartless slaughter and destruction.

"They chose to defy me." Tolman shrugged. "I could have hit them much harder. I exercised restraint. I've behaved honorably."

As disbelief waned and Drake's mind exploded with rage, Dr. Trist ran into the main area from the corridor, white coat flying.

"What the hell was that?" he said.

His eyes went to the TV and his mouth opened. The fire and tower of black smoke looked like orange lightning dancing within a massive thunder cloud.

"God, no!" Trist's arms went limp. He turned toward Tolman Freid. "Please tell me you're not responsible for that."

"They were warned," Freid said.

"Warned?" Trist shook his head. "You're an idiot. A moron."

Trist held his hands wide and looked about the room, focusing on their captors. "Don't you see what he's done? He's given the authorities no choice."

Tolman Freid ignored Trist's outburst as he had Drake's.

"What are you talking about, asshole?" Red frowned, looking at the others as if to find the answer.

"He's given the government no choice," Trist said. "They'll be coming. If not now, soon. They have to stop you."

"If they attack, we'll blow them away," Red said, gripping his weapon.

"You'll die." Trist nodded toward the TV and the grim images there. He raised a skinny arm and pointed a knobby finger at Tolman Freid. "You're insane. You just signed our death warrants." His head dropped and his shoulders slumped.

"We'll all die."

CHAPTER SIXTY-ONE

The FBI hostage rescue team commander's fist slammed on the console in the operations trailer's shielded communication room. "We have to move—now!"

Dylan did not flinch. Even as a child, when others became agitated, he became calm.

"Full assault right now?" Dylan said.

"Hell yes!" The tactical commander's face reddened. Sirens wailed in the background. "If we'd gone in earlier like I said, we might have stopped what we're dealing with now."

Dylan sighed as the screen in the communications booth showed huge flames and billowing black smoke in the twilight. The adjacent screen showed countless sets of headlights moving like sludge along highways. He considered all the angles.

"I don't share your certainty. If we'd tried an entry action into the ER, a similar or worse detonation could have occurred with the hospital as the epicenter. But perhaps hindsight will show we should have gone in."

"It sure as hell will," the tactical commander said. His jaw clenched.

Dylan shared the molten rage and desire to immediately attack the terrorists. He also understood the most effective responses would come from the deliberations of an ice-cold head and heart. He could crush the hot-headed commander in a pissing match, but how many lives would that save?

"I'm dealing with the here and now, not what might have been," Dylan said. "Do you know the status of the evacuation efforts for the hospital and downtown? Any idea of the number of non-tactical law enforcement, support personnel, and citizens in proximity to the hospital right now?" He paused. "Evacuation is nowhere complete, and there are still thousands in blast range of the hospital. Those people are being moved out as fast as we are able. When we make our move, we have to do everything possible to minimize death and injury. We need to have support available for dealing with the consequences."

"Excess caution gets people killed. There are no sure things," the commander said.

"Have you considered the impact of a second explosive or chemical weapons release if we breach the ER now? What is the city's capacity to respond while already overwhelmed handling the casualties from the Golden Valley explosion, fire, and hazardous materials emergency?"

"Damn it, man, sometimes you just have to take action." The commander shook a clenched fist.

"I hear you. The evacuation is going at full speed. We're linked into the Incident Command System and will be updated continuously on fire and rescue, hazmat, police and EMS capabilities, response times, and overall status. All those forces are currently more than maxed out."

Dylan paused and locked eyes with the commander.

"And just between you and me in our little shielded room here," Dylan said. "Drop the pissed-off, tough-guy crap. We're on the same team. If you want to second-guess and trash me later, have at it. I know what's at stake and accept responsibility for my decisions. You will communicate and behave as the professional you are. Get your act together. Understood?"

Dylan paused, anticipating a possible blow-up.

The commander put a hand to his brow and sighed. "You're right. This mission has got me jacked up like no other. This is my city, my home, my neighbors. I'm always worried about my team, but this one..." He rubbed his forehead. "Apologies. I got emotional. My bad. You can count on me and my team."

"I know we can." Dylan put a hand on the man's shoulder. "We're all on edge, and no one can know for sure what is the best path. I'm considering everything, especially your input. When it's time to take them down, I know you and your team will give their all."

"Yes, sir. One team, one mission."

"Thank you, commander." Dylan's phone trilled.

"Special Agent McGinnis here."

"Special Agent, this is Hennepin County Incident Commander, Fire Chief Rondo. Calling with a situation report—"

"Hold one second," Dylan said. "I'm putting you on speaker so my hostage rescue team leader can hear. Okay, go ahead."

"This is info as of two minutes ago. Initial blast kill zone estimated at seventeen acres, with minimal expected survivors within that radius. The origin appears to have been in an abandoned grain storage complex in a low-lying area, something of a valley. Fire is ongoing, including a number of residences and one industrial building where second-shift workers were present. That looks to be our known major source of casualties. Fortunately, most of the blast area is undeveloped and low utilization. The epicenter was near railroad tracks, marsh, and woodland."

"Any idea of the nature of the device?" Dylan asked.

"We won't get any forensics out of there for a while and don't expect much. There won't be anything left of the grain elevators, buildings, or anything else. Everything in and around the blast site has been incinerated—they'll be nothing but dirt and ash. As noted, no one within the kill zone will be alive, so there will be no immediate witnesses. The break we got with the epicenter's location is that much of the lateral blast force was reduced. The valley walls blunted the explosive forces and limited pressure waves laterally."

"Hazardous materials? Toxins?" Dylan asked.

"We've gotten one hazmat team to the outer perimeter of the blast, but they're limited by ongoing flames. They've confirmed hydrofluoric acid in high concentrations. It hangs and spreads with the wind—it's brutal stuff. We've evacuated local neighborhoods and downwind areas

—so far winds are quiet, but secondary injuries and casualties from the acid are expected. Water neutralizes the acid immediately so rain would be ideal, but the forecast says that's not going to happen."

"What are your overall expectations?" Dylan marveled at the efficiency of the Incident Command network and emergency response community. So many complex and interrelated elements to consider and coordinate. And each aspect involved the highest stakes.

"It's too soon to even guess on the number of dead and injured. The fire, smoke, acid, and traffic delays are severely limiting access. We can't be definitive about the presence or absence of other toxins but none detected so far. No personnel can access the area without self-contained breathing apparatus and full hazmat protective gear. We set the boundaries for the central hot zone and established a remote satellite warm zone where we can initiate decontamination and EMS personnel can assess, triage, treat, and then transport the injured.

"Strong work," Dylan said.

"Fire and rescue, hazmat, police, and EMS are fully mobilized, but resources are overextended, and traffic is bad and getting worse. Many citizens will panic. Metro community hospitals and St. Paul's trauma center and burn unit are doing all they can, but they'll be swamped. Overall status is changing by the minute. We'll keep you informed."

"Roger that, Chief," Dylan said. The incident commander's updates were essential info for Dylan. The terrorists were going to need to be rooted out of their locked-down and booby-trapped fortress and it wouldn't go easy. An additional explosion, fire, and multiple casualty event would overwhelm the region's human and physical support capabilities. Managing the community's emergency response resources was a giant, ever-changing Rubik's cube. "Please let me know the moment you feel we have the resources available to address a second critical event." Dylan disconnected.

The tactical team commander met Dylan's gaze and nodded. They were in agreement on the "if" of a tactical entry to the ER—it had to happen.

It was the critical "when" that no one could know with certainty. That's what would decide if any in the ER would survive and if tens of thousands of innocent people would perish horribly.

CHAPTER SIXTY-TWO

Red and his trio of Aryan Brothers stood in the corridor near the cast room. Tolman remained out of hearing in the main ER at the desk he'd established as his base.

"The explosion was righteous, but when is your brother going to let us know about the big money?" the battered hyena said, his broken nose making his voice nasal.

Pockmark put his smartphone in its holster. "For sure. I want to hear more about the money and our escape status. Your brother is sounding a little fanatical. I'm okay with helping his cause, but that isn't the reason I'm here."

"Tolman's not fantastical or whatever you said," Red said jutting his chin toward the pockmarked con. "You may be smart, but you're not near as smart as him."

"What about us having some fun?" the hyena whined. "I didn't do anything wrong and he busted my face. I'm still definitely going to finish boning that young babe. We ain't doing—"

"Shut up!" Red said. "We do what Tolman says. We'll have enough time and money for pussy and partying forever."

"But damn, Red. Your brother is an uptight asshole. I gotta do that bitch soon—"

Red snatched him by the neck and pinned him against the wall with his feet off the ground. Red's teeth showed and his muscles strained his shirt.

The hyena's blackened eyes bulged.

Pockmark put his hands on Red's arm. "Red, no."

Red opened his hands as if releasing a bag of garbage, and the hyena dropped to his ass on the floor, coughing and gagging.

The bearded con had watched Red's explosion with no reaction. "Red?"

"What?" Red was breathing hard.

"I need to kill some people." The bearded man rarely spoke. When he did, the things he said made even the toughest cons freak. He was a normal sized guy who didn't stand out other than his long beard—and eyes that made you look away. He was what the inmates called a wobblehead or a Manson—the kind of violent, bizarre nut-job nobody messed with. The ones who had meds given to them during the pill run each morning. The bearded wobblehead had been convicted of hacking an elderly sleeping man to death with a machete in a homeless shelter. The Aryan Brotherhood had allowed him to join as even the fiercest Black inmates stayed clear of him.

Red scared most everyone because of his savagery and strength. The machete Manson-man freaked everyone out because he truly was criminally insane. In the rare moments he talked, the content was bat-shit crazy and horrific.

"You'll be able to kill soon enough," Red said. "Before we take off, we kill them all, but the big smartass surgeon is mine."

"I'll wait if I can," the bearded man said, his voice flat. "There are ones here who want to hurt me. I can't let anyone hurt me."

The others looked at each other and even Red fidgeted. The wobblehead was on a wavelength all his own.

THE BEARDED MAN had seen some of the newspaper articles back when he'd been arrested for using the machete to do what he'd needed to do. The police said the investigation had taken so long because there were no known witnesses, and they could find no motive. The paper and the courts said the killing of the old man was brutal and senseless.

They were wrong. He had the best of all motives. What the police and the courts thought didn't matter. Listening, not talking, mattered. It meant life or death, and the Voice had never been wrong.

It told him before they could act. Each of those he executed had planned to harm him. The Voice warned him. And let him know exactly what needed to be done to them.

He'd eliminated the threats—he wouldn't be alive if he hadn't.

After his arrest, they brought in psychiatrists. Earlier in his life, he'd spent time in places that were not prisons but were in ways worse. Places that tried to take over his mind. They'd forced drugs on him. Medications that silenced the Voice and left him unprotected.

But the Voice eventually broke through. And it had always warned him in time.

He didn't care what others thought. His being alive proved he'd needed to do what he'd done. Heeding the Voice's warnings was what mattered.

He didn't care about the Aryan Brotherhood ideas. He'd joined them in prison after he'd learned some Black prisoners could hear the Voice.

When the Voice warned him about the Black people who wanted to harm him, they could also hear. They knew he was aware of their plans. He'd almost been killed by those in prison who heard the Voice. The Aryan Brotherhood had helped keep him safe.

When the hospital mission was over, he planned to stay near Red. There would be money, but that was not important. Red helped protect him from the Black people who heard the Voice's warnings. He could kill the others without help. With Red he was safe from all threats.

He did not understand why so many people wanted to harm him. There were many things he did not understand, but he knew what was important. The attorneys had tried to keep him out of jail by asking him to plead insanity.

He was not insane. It would be insane to make others aware of the Voice and how it warned and protected him.

He unlocked the closet-like room in the farthest back corner of the ER. It looked like storage and cleaning but also had a small clean counter with measuring tubes and small bottles containing plastic strips. After taking the ER, they'd locked this room and a couple others. He checked out the first bottle. *Benzene.*

He'd had to kill thirteen people, though only the man in the homeless shelter had ever been tied to him. He'd kept quiet about the Voice and after years got parole and placed in a halfway house. He'd hooked up with Red within days. Red had asked him to be a part of this mission because he knew he wouldn't say anything. It's easy to keep a secret if you don't talk.

He sniffed the bottle. Nice. Like paint thinner or glue but better. The label said flammable. The smell had told him that—he could pretty much always tell which liquids would burn by the smell. He opened the cap and stuck his nose over the bottle and sniffed deeply. He could feel it in his brain. *Nice!* He took another deep sniff then screwed the cap back on.

Earlier the Voice had shared a warning of new threats. Shortly after the big boom, the Voice spoke. Two of the hostages meant him harm. They were of the kind that could hear the Voice warn him. They were old and pretended to be harmless but that was the way most of the others who'd sought to harm him had been.

The Voice knew better.

He had to make himself safe.

CHAPTER SIXTY-THREE

Tolman sat behind the counter watching the medical team through the glass-paneled wall of what they called their "Crash Room." Dr. Cody, the quiet blonde nurse, and the big surgeon continued to keep the senator alive. The way they worked reminded him of his military days. Everyone knew their job and did it. Competent and professional. When problems arose they didn't whine—they overcame them.

The counter and desk he sat at was at the center of the ER. He found the spot to be a natural command post.

Two new burner cellphones lay on the desk he'd chosen as his command post. One was red, the other black. The red phone was his primary trigger and the black his back-up.

A matching phone had been hardwired into each of the destructive devices he'd strategically positioned about the city. When he entered their numbers and then connected, immediate detonation would occur.

No one but him knew all of the locations. No one but him knew the phone numbers.

He picked up the first phone to enter the trigger numbers into its memory. His brow furrowed as he entered the first four digits of the ten-digit exchange to the first remaining device.

Red approached the counter. "Tolman, my guys are bitching—"

"Quiet, Red. Don't bother me now." He took a deep breath and focused on each digit as if it were under a microscope. Mistakenly completing any connection prematurely would touch off destruction many times greater than any US city had ever faced.

Tolman frowned. *Red's guys are bitching.* His lip curled as he pictured the disgusting Nazi-tattooed slob trying to pull up his pants after assaulting the young woman. The nose-ring hippie he'd knifed was no loss, but abusing a woman was something Tolman could not abide.

The ex-cons were white trash filth. Tolman's noble and patriotic mission had already been tainted by the "from inside the ER" news report focused on their moronic white supremacist garbage. A bitter taste in his mouth gave him the urge to spit.

If he didn't need him, the pig who'd assaulted the girl would already have received a bullet to the head. The acne-scarred one was solid with electronics and media communications. The crazy one with the beard and zombie eyes had not been a problem. He followed orders and said nothing, but Tolman knew he couldn't trust him.

Though they'd sworn otherwise, none of them truly believed in the mission—they were unworthy of him or his cause.

He'd used them based on their weapons skills and Red's promise they could be trusted to not give away the mission beforehand. Informants or undercover penetration by law enforcement was the overwhelming number-one cause of failed antigovernment militia actions. The convicts' Aryan Brotherhood "blood-in, blood-out" loyalty and ability to keep their mouths closed had been prison-proven. They had kept quiet about the mission and executed the takeover well, but it had not changed what they were.

Tolman completed the trigger entries into the memory of the red phone. He knew that if and when he completed the connection, it would change the course of history.

Red sat eating a sandwich. Even the muscles of his jaws and face were exaggerated and rippled as he chewed. Red had never learned about boundaries, consideration of others, or how to stay out of trouble. Their father had worn himself out beating Red, but it had made little impression and no difference.

Once when they were children, Red had forgotten and left a paddock gate open. Father's prize bull had got out and torn down a barbed wire fence, freeing horses and getting cut. Father had made Red put his hand on the paddock latch and slammed the gate. Red's staggered but he did not cry out. Father put Red's hand in the gate again. Red's face had no color, his child eyes had blazed as he stared up at Father. Father slammed the gate again.

Red never submitted. Anger always at a simmer ready to boil over. Defying authority fueled him yet somehow he'd always been totally loyal to Tolman

Tolman knew the bitching Red's guys had directed at him was likely already gone from his mind. For this mission, Red was an attack dog supporting Tolman in accomplishing his mission.

He didn't think of Red with emotion. Tolman also recognized he didn't feel about his son like he believed other fathers did theirs. Before the government completely destroyed her mind, his wife had made him promise to keep Sigurd safe. It was a relief to have engineered his removal from the hospital. Other than his wife, those around Tolman had either been a responsibility or useful tool—feelings were not a factor. That hadn't been his choice. It was just the way things were.

Sonya was the only one who'd touched his heart.

History called upon special people to rise above emotion and see the big picture—to make history-changing decisions and harsh sacrifices untainted by weakness or sentiment.

Tolman recognized he was one who had been so chosen.

Red would be sacrificed for the mission, as would the others.

Red's "team" were not worth a thought. They did not deserve to be part of this mission, and their lives meant nothing. Red's passing gave him pause, but it was a much nobler ending than his brother could ever achieve otherwise.

Tolman entered the digits on the back-up phone. His chest tightened, knowing that each of the detonations would dwarf the destruction in Oklahoma City and kill more people than the 9/11 collapse of the Twin Towers.

He'd had significant and strategic help putting the mission

together, but it was his vison, his leadership, and his courage that were making it happen.

Yet Drake Cody had called him a coward.

Fate had put him and Drake Cody together as opponents, but Tolman admired the doctor. He wished the man were on his side. Principled, intelligent, and brave—unlike any of the crew Tolman was saddled with.

And yet Drake Cody maligned him.

The doctor did not understand. Many transcendent historical figures were denounced in their time, but the passage of years honed perspective.

Tolman might be called an extremist or a domestic terrorist now, but history would see him differently.

Timothy McVeigh had executed a crude blast, killed 168 people, injured over six hundred more, and done millions in damages in Oklahoma City. But McVeigh had not effectively harnessed the media to explain why.

Tolman's actions would make McVeigh's and others' efforts look like a backyard barbecue. Through the years, Tolman had watched the media abandon all journalistic responsibility and integrity. They were now "entertainment" whose bias and content chased ratings, political favor, and advertising dollars. He'd crafted his strategy and used the media's flaws to ensure his message would reach everyone.

His actions would force the US government-corporate conspirators back towards service of the people, by the people, and for the people —and begin the job of tearing the corrupt system down.

Success was at hand. His actions and exposure dominated the media in a way no other patriot ever had. The deaths, spectacle, and destruction of his mission would be covered like none other in history.

As he entered the last device's trigger number into the phone's memory, his thoughts wandered.

He realized the impending deaths of the ER people weighed on him more than he'd anticipated. He admired Dr. Drake Cody. He respected the crippled, smart-mouthed Dr. Rizzini in his wheelchair, and the huge surgeon who'd refused to be intimidated by Red. The nurses were dedicated and courageous.

Imagine if he'd been banded with people like these ER professionals? Independent of his mission, his wife would have admired them. He'd never involved her in his militia activities, and the thought of her even being in the same building as any of Red's crew turned his stomach.

Tolman entered the last digit of the last number into the phone memory.

Two phones—a primary and a back-up—each with the trigger numbers programmed in their memory. Connection with any of them would detonate and set new records for lives sacrificed in the cause of freedom.

Energy pulsed through his arms and shoulders.

He would never again be pushed aside or humiliated by the government or their corporate accomplices. They could not declare eminent domain over him and plow him under as they had his home. He'd be front-page news and the top story on every media outlet throughout the world. He'd be in history books and studied in universities for years to come.

The government had destroyed his wife's mind and her ability to recognize him, but the rest of the world would know him.

The name Tolman Freid would never be forgotten.

CHAPTER SIXTY-FOUR

Antoine coughed, the throat irritation almost gone. The damn anhydrous ammonia was what got him into this mess, and turns out he was fine. Working the refinery, he knew many of the materials there could kill you. He exercised care on the job every minute of every shift for more years. And then he gets exposed by crazy, racist terrorists when he wasn't even working. *Damn!*

He'd been at the event on his day off to support the pipeline. All he'd wanted was to keep his job. And it was a respectable and damn good job—it had allowed him to provide for his family.

His two boys were gone. The oldest was off in New York, doing some kind of art thing Antoine didn't understand. Good for him, though. The second boy, Mikal, had started his second tour with the Marines.

Mikal did the military thing smarter than Antoine had. He had a plan in place the whole way—advance radar technology and remote explosives sensing. He was one of the guys who used technology to keep grunts like Antoine had been from getting blown to bits.

He wished there'd been more of that kind of smarts around when he'd been in Afghanistan. Too many of his USMC brothers had been killed or torn up by IEDs, booby traps, and other wickedness.

The assholes who'd taken over the ER were every bit as bad as the Muslim terrorists in that godforsaken sandbox where he'd lost friends.

Their terrorist leader, the big guy Tolman, hadn't been down to this room other than when he'd been swinging his .45 cal around threatening to kill.

He carried himself like a former leatherneck, but he was an evil SOB and a different breed than any Marine Antoine was familiar with.

The ex-cons and their Aryan Brotherhood racist poison were a concentrated version of the ugliness Antoine had known from his earliest days as a kid growing up in his backwoods hometown.

The hyena who'd assaulted Miss Phoenix was bigoted, classless scum.

White supremacist losers were always those who weren't superior to anyone.

Poor Cecil. Antoine hadn't learned much about him, but he'd bet the guy was living in his parents' basement in suburbia somewhere. Probably had spent untold hours in some mega-dollar private college getting a degree in something for which there were no jobs. His plan to save the world included the standard mantra against fossil fuel, law enforcement, and free enterprise, and he saw the USA as fundamentally evil.

High up on Cecil's list would be his ideas on what people of color needed in order to be saved, though he'd probably known few, if any, Black or minority people. Wearing a Black Lives Matter t-shirt and prancing around seeking attention in demonstrations did not make this kid or any other protestor a voice for Antoine. The presumption that Antoine needed others to speak for or rescue him left a taste like milk gone bad.

Cecil had never supported himself or a family, and he'd certainly never served in the military. It didn't make him a bad guy, but the snowflake had no clue on how to solve his own problems, much less Antoine's or the country's.

Cecil had traveled here to oppose the pipeline. But how was shutting down good-paying jobs at the refinery going to help things? If Antoine lost his job as a pipefitter, who'd pay the bills for his wife's MS treatments? How could he put money away to help give his daughter the wedding she dreamed of?

Antoine liked his job. He loved his country, even though he couldn't stand a number of the bigoted knuckleheads in it. He honored those he'd fought with and who'd died to protect it.

The young doctors were right. They were going to have to fight. He sized up the lumpy Hyena and his Nazi tattoos. Dangerous but undisciplined.

The skinny pockmarked dude was smart and vicious—a bully.

The guy with the beard gave off a crazy vibe. The kind of nutjob who could mess you up.

Tolman, the leader, was disciplined and deadly. All were heavily armed and comfortable with their weapons.

The heavily muscled, big redheaded guy looked at Antoine with something ugly in his eyes. He wasn't right. He was a beast always on the lookout for someone to dominate and destroy. He was the kind of guy who got off on proving he was the baddest of the bad.

Antoine wasn't into that game. Let the man think anything he wanted. Antoine needed to keep a low profile around that one.

He'd keep his head down until it was time to attack.

Antoine's thoughts kept returning to Cecil. When Tolman held the gun to his head and Cecil said, "Kill the Black guy," Antoine knew the white liberal's words had shriveled up his virtue-signaling insides. The regret and humiliation of his moment of weakness had left Cecil devastated. Before Antoine had a chance to try and buck him up, Cecil had been killed by the hyena while trying to do the right thing.

Antoine forgave Cecil his words when the gun had been pressed against his head. He understood. He wished he'd had the chance to let the young man know that sometimes a guy has to cut himself some slack.

When it came time to fight, Antoine would be fighting for the woman he loved and their children. Fighting to keep others in the city from being harmed. He would imagine Cecil was with them—a well-intentioned guy who'd made a mistake but proved himself in the end.

That was more than many men were ever able to do.

CHAPTER SIXTY-FIVE

As Drake made his way to minor trauma, Dr. Trist approached from telemetry, pushing the Captain on a wheeled bed.

"This guy has recovered so much he doesn't need the monitors. Incredible," Trist said. "The nurse tells me he's done this before. Indestructible as a cockroach." He paused. "How's the senator doing?"

Drake winced at the cockroach reference. "ECMO is keeping him alive. His lungs are toast. He's tough, but I'm afraid the damage is too great."

"And look at this guy." Trist indicated the Captain, who looked to be sleeping comfortably. "The senator probably won't make it, while this crazy piece of shit survives his umpteenth self-induced, near-fatal event. He'll be looking to get high again within the hour. It doesn't pay to be a solid citizen, working, and prod—"

Drake had Trist's bicep in his hand and gripped it hard. His thoughts flamed. He thrust the wincing Trist against the wall in the empty hallway. He came within a hair of throwing a punch before he let go of the wide-eyed doctor.

"Shit, man. What's your deal?" Trist frowned, rubbing his arm.

"You know nothing." Drake struggled for cool. "If you ever talk about or treat a patient in this ER like that again, I will kick your ass."

"What the hell? You're threatening me?" Trist said.

The animal part of Drake showed, the part that had made the predators in the Furnace back away from him. "You have no idea how close I am to losing my temper."

"Whoa." Trist did not back up. "Lighten up. I didn't realize you were a specialist on humor and morality. I've worked in a lot of ERs, each has a different culture."

"That shit isn't funny anywhere, and this man means a lot to me." The fire that had flared in Drake's head began to recede. *Damn, Drake. You need this guy. Get a grip.*

"Screw your lecture. I'm done taking shit from people." Trist shook his head. "I've spent most of my life taking care of drunks, abusers, criminals, and losers who don't give a damn, and many of whom never pay one cent for their care. I sweat bullets trying to do the right thing. My payback? Between a corrupt malpractice system, weaselly lawyers, a divorce, and being ripped off by the IRS, my reputation was ruined and I went bankrupt. I had to pay my own lawyers to fight the false claims of malpractice. I won but went broke fighting them. Now I'm humping shifts in understaffed ERs in hick towns and inner cities at an age everyone else in the specialty has retired. Talk to me in a few decades, kid."

"Sounds like you've had a bad road, but that doesn't okay you being an asshole," Drake said. "Even so, I shouldn't have lost my temper."

Trist looked at him with a pinched expression. He folded his arms across his chest.

"You're new to our ER," Drake said, "but we're all on the same team and soon we'll be fighting for our lives. We need to pull together. I've heard you're a gun guy."

"I'm familiar with every weapon they have. I own a few of them."

"It looks like we are going to have to attack sometime. If you can get your hands on one, you know what to do. The plan is we make our move all together. If you hear it start, join in. When I know more you'll get word."

"I'll do all I can. Tolman needs to be taken out," Trist said. "He triggered the explosion in the city and is the main threat of more. I don't think he'd trust any of the lowlifes around him with that power.

When the battle starts, we need to make sure he dies—he can't be allowed to live."

"We're on the same page." Drake took the head of the Captain's cart. "I'll deliver the Captain to minor trauma. Why don't you get back to telemetry and be ready to go primal? Find anything you can use as a weapon. We good?"

"I'm ready." Trist moved down the hall.

Drake guided the cart and the sleeping Captain forward.

Drake was not a Pollyanna. He understood and lived the frustrations of caring for the self-destructive, the unappreciative, and the downright nasty. But not being sucked into the bitterness Trist felt was part of what made people in emergency care special.

Trist was as burned out as black toast, but despite his sour attitude, he saw one thing with the same clarity as Drake—Tolman Freid was the critical target.

CHAPTER SIXTY-SIX

Drake approached the minor trauma area, rolling the Captain asleep on the cart.

Phoenix's attacker sat on a chair, leaning back just outside the door. Purple discoloration showed under his eyes and across his swollen nose and face. Gauze rolls protruded from his nostrils. He held his gun in ready position but barely glanced as Drake walked past.

"What's with the hyena? Did getting his face smashed settle him down?" Drake said as he positioned the Captain's cart along the wall next to Roberta's.

Rizz responded in a whisper. "Asked him if he wanted pain medicine. He's got a couple of Percocet on board. Offered him more, but that's all I could get him to take."

"An emergency doc trying to talk a patient into taking narcotics. That's a switch."

"No limit to the weirdness lately," Rizz said.

Drake moved back to the doorway. "Hey, Hyena. You'd better get down to the main desk. I think they're looking for you."

"Hyena?" He frowned. "Think you're a comedian, huh? What's going to be funny is when I blow your head off later." Cecil's murderer got to his feet, keeping his rifle at the ready as he left.

Drake looked at the wall clock, then Rizz. "Ready to go?"

"I've told everyone. Let's check on them," Rizz said.

He rolled to Roberta, the elderly Black woman with the hip fracture.

"I did a nerve block and she's been doing well," he said to Drake. "How's your pain, Miss Roberta?" Rizz put a hand on her arm.

"I don't hurt at all anymore." She patted Rizz's hand. "Thank you."

"Things are going to get loud and crazy soon," Drake said. "We may have to move you quickly. It will be scary but we'll keep you safe."

She nodded, looking more clear-eyed than earlier. "I'm scared, but I have faith. Jesus is with us."

Rizz moved to Newman, the autistic teen. His mother sat in a chair next to his cart. She fingered her rosary beads, reminding Drake of his mother. She'd been silent other than when Tolman had placed a gun to her son's head.

"How're you two doing?" Rizz said. The mother nodded without looking up.

"Ready you roll and rock to?" Rizz asked the thirteen-year-old, who continued his repetitive hand gestures.

The teen looked up, his hands paused, and he smiled. "Yes, hell. Rizz doctor. Ass kick jerks we to going."

Rizz held up a fist and the teen gave him a bump.

Drake marveled. Rizz was a socially inappropriate smartass who broke all the rules and would likely be deemed an alcoholic and sex addict by many. Despite all that, he was the most beloved emergency doc Drake had ever met. Paramedics, cops, and patients ranging from drunken brawling bikers to sweet little old ladies with dementia like Roberta connected with him instantly.

Antoine stood as they approached—chin up, shoulders square, and hands held behind his back.

"Ready, Antoine?" Drake asked.

"Whenever, Doc. Eager. The murdering bastards."

"Proud to have met you." Drake shook his hand. "At 9:57 we kick ass."

"Semper fi. Flight 93. Let's roll."

Drake smiled. A quiet, tough man of selfless character—having

Antoine in the fight boosted Drake's hope immeasurably. One man like him could make the difference between life and death for them all. He helped Drake believe they had a chance.

Rizz tilted his head toward Phoenix and gave a shrug. She lay curled on the cot facing the wall.

Drake stepped near. As far as he knew, she'd not spoken to anyone since revealing the loss of the phone to him. Where was her head at?

"We have a chance, Phoenix. Don't give up. We need you."

She turned. Her hair was tangled, and she had bags under her eyes. "You and the others need to keep me safe." She turned back to the wall.

Drake and Rizz moved to the corner alone.

"I'm not counting on her for anything," Rizz said. "Here's the rest of our lineup, amigo. You and Bart are badass, and Antoine is a former Marine. You three are formidable physically, but you aren't armed. Dr. Trist knows guns, but barehanded he's a flyweight. Patti and Tracy, like all ER and intensive care nurses, are tougher than steel, but hand-to-hand combat is not their thing."

"Don't forget the others," Drake said.

"Oh yeah," Rizz said. "I forgot the Captain. Every combat operation needs an intergalactic scout who, two hours ago, was comatose on a ventilator. And rounding out our team is a thirteen-year-old kid with autism who recently had a seizure, his scared-to-death mom, and an 88-year-old lady with a broken hip and dementia."

"So you're saying you like our odds?"

"If I were a betting man—and, along with my other vices, I am—my guess is we'd be worse than a thirty-to-one shot."

"We've had more than our share of against-the-odds wins. Plenty of people are alive who wouldn't be if we hadn't," Drake said.

"The smart money is on the jerks, but I'm betting with my heart. I'm putting everything I've got on the lovable, long-shot underdogs."

"I know we always joke, but I may not have a chance to say this later." Drake put a hand on Rizz's shoulder.

"Oh no, you're not going to go all Hallmark on me?" Rizz said.

"Just telling it straight. I love you, brother. And about the God stuff and your worries about the hereafter, I think you judge yourself pretty hard. If nothing else, we should score some points for years of working our asses off trying to help others."

"I hope so," Rizz said. "And love you too, Drake. Sincerely. Never met anyone I admire more."

"We do all we can. If we can stop the terrorists from triggering any more explosions, we'll have done good, no matter what else happens.

"I'm on board with saving others, but as I said earlier, the dying thing—not so much," Rizz said.

"We'll do what we need to. No choice." Drake swallowed. "I admit I'm scared—real scared. But no one I'd rather have at my side."

"Likewise," Rizz said.

Rizz extended his hand up to Drake, who clasped and shook it, feeling the thick callouses the months in rehab and the wheelchair had formed.

Drake, Rizz, and their friend Jon had trained and worked together for years, facing the worst that happened in their city. Men, women, and children literally died in their hands. The pain, self-doubt, and emotional scars had forged a closeness for Drake that rivaled the special bond he'd had with his long-dead younger brother, whose palsied limbs and ravaged-from-birth body had housed a mind and spirit stronger and more courageous than any Drake had ever known.

"Will you be able to stand?" Drake asked.

"I did forty-three feet unaided at my last therapy session. Ready for the Olympics."

"You're the best." Drake smiled inside. Rizz's report under any other circumstances would be cause for joy and high-fives. "Some bad news I haven't told you—there is no phone."

"Damn. So we're flying solo, huh?" Rizz said.

"I have one possibility in play that's such a long shot long it's not even worth mentioning." Did Rachelle reach out after his call? *Jon—she needs Jon.*

"So we get 'er done or ball game's over, right?" Rizz said.

Drake felt he'd contributed to his brother's death and it haunted him. The thought of allowing Rizz to be killed turned his gut to a block of ice.

"What the hell. We're probably overreacting," Rizz said. "Who's afraid of incredible firepower, explosives, and chemical weapons wielded by a gang of criminally insane murderers led by a ruthless egomaniac with a death wish?"

CHAPTER SIXTY-SEVEN

Rachelle's phone trilled. She flinched but relaxed when she saw the caller ID.

"Jon. How much longer?" she said.

"I'm headed down your street," Jon answered. "Sorry I couldn't be faster. Traffic is snarled."

"I'll watch at the front door."

She kept her shotgun in hand and stood looking out the plate glass section of the door. The twin beams of headlights traced the cul-de-sac in the twilight, and the vehicle pulled into the driveway. *Thank God!*

Jon Malar. He and Rizz and Drake had met at the start of their emergency medicine training and formed a special trio. Some people talked about the intensity of military boot camp, which lasted three months. But Drake and his friends had survived the emergency medicine residency training for four long years, dealing with life-and-death pressure up to a hundred hours a week.

They didn't complain, but she knew they'd paid a price. And the challenges did not let up when their training ended.

Rachelle saw their recently troubled, recovering friend through the glass.

She opened the door and he stepped in. She secured the multiple locks and reset the alarm. They hugged, Jon's embrace hesitant and characteristically shy.

"I'm ready to do whatever I can," he said.

"Thank goodness. It was meant to be. I need your help."

"I've been holding my breath the whole drive down. When I heard about the explosion, I thought..." He rubbed his forehead. "I was afraid the hospital—"

"I could hear it and feel it, Jon. I thought it was the hospital, too." She put a hand on his arm. "I've been trying to decipher Drake's phone call. You need to help me figure out what it means."

"Of course. Tell me from the start."

"He said it might be the last time we ever talk..." She swallowed, then took a deep breath. "We only got to speak live for a few seconds, and the rest was a short recording. The terrorist monitored it all." She waved Jon up the few short stairs to the main level and led him to the table where her notes were. "I've been working on it since the call, but it makes no sense. At least it makes no sense to me. If anyone can figure it out, I know it's you."

"Do you remember exactly what he said?"

"Sit here." She pulled back a chair at the table. "I wrote down everything I remembered. I think I have all of it. I've been trying so hard to figure it out that my head hurts." She slid the two handwritten pages of notes in front of him.

Jon's brow furrowed as he bent over the pages. "Part of it is obviously real, talking about you and the kids, but the rest? I'm sure you're right. He's sending a message."

"Drake wouldn't send me something that couldn't be deciphered," Rachelle said. "But with the terrorist monitoring, I don't think he could say what he needed to in a way I could understand on my own. Drake's words pointed to you. You being on the way here was more than happenstance. It's fate."

"I've not been doing well with fate lately." He met her eyes just long enough for her to see the pain there. "I've caused death, not prevented it."

Rachelle believed she understood. Perhaps she was the only one who did. The burden she suspected he carried was heavy—but this was not about him.

"Now is not the time to wrestle with your conscience."

He winced and avoided her eyes. She'd heard he had been avoiding everyone and not doing well. There was no time for sympathy. He was needed now.

"Snap out of it, Jon. Get in gear. Figure out the message and help save Drake, Rizz, and the others. You know they'd die trying to help you."

He straightened, his jaw clenched. "You know I'd trade places in a second if it would get them safe." His eyes blazed as he bent over the pages. "I'll give it all I have."

"Fast, Jon. Do it fast. Drake's time is running out."

CHAPTER SIXTY-EIGHT

Many of Tracy's nurse friends believed ICU nurses were all control freaks.

Whatever she was, intensive care nursing was the best fit for her.

Tracy disconnected the senator's endotracheal tube and suctioned his trachea and bronchi. The fetid, char-like scent had grown stronger. The suction tube returned grisly tissue unlike anything she had seen come out of a patient before.

Believing ICU nursing meant being in control was just plain wrong. Just as with the desperate care they were delivering to Senator Duren, they were anything but in control.

Would the acid continue to penetrate even deeper? Might the anticoagulant required for ECMO combined with the ongoing acid destruction erode into a major blood vessel and cause disastrous bleeding?

Or perhaps the opposite? The procedure involved the risk of clots that could block blood flow to a leg, lung, or worst of all, the brain.

They could anticipate problems and do their best to prevent them, but control was impossible. All people die eventually.

She checked pulses in the senator's feet, ankles, and arms. Almost without effort, she processed the senator's color, the rise and fall of his chest, the sound of the ventilator, and the rhythm of the beeps tracking each beat of her patient's heart.

What ICU and the ER nurses shared was managing patients so vulnerable that anything less than flawless care meant catastrophe or death. The patient numbers and pace were different, the responsibility and commitment the same.

Dr. Bart Rainey entered the room. Tracy didn't know what to think of the giant surgeon. He was Memorial Hospital's worst abuser of nursing and other staff. Drake Cody and Bart had almost come to blows in the ICU when Bart's mistreatment of Tracy had been so bad he faced peer review and hospital discipline. Since that ugly event, there'd been no grossly offensive behavior, but his interactions with her were distant and passive-aggressive.

As she checked the senator, she pondered the conflicting feelings her work with the surgeon these past hours had generated.

"All good?" Bart asked. "Anything you're concerned about?"

Oh my God! He was communicating like Drake Cody. The usual exchange involved grunts and condescension, typically followed by a list of complaints or insults.

"Dr. Rainey, it's possible we might not survive this. I wanted to say it's been surprisingly gratifying working with Dr. Cody and you today."

"Well, it shouldn't be surprising," he said. "I'm the best, and Drake Cody is not bad for an ER doc."

"See, that's the part I don't get." She was done holding back. "Why the insult? He's an all-around great doctor, and everyone in the hospital knows it. I believe you're committed to your patients, but your problem is that you're rude and abusive. You treat nurses and others with disrespect and act as if they're a threat to your patients rather than their essential caregivers. What makes you behave like that? It doesn't help your patients and it makes it miserable to work with you." She braced herself.

"So now that we're in deep shit, you decide it's time to bust my balls?" Bart frowned down at her.

"I'm curious, and at this point social or professional niceties don't mean much," she said. "Why do you behave like such an ass?"

"Well, sorry, nursey. I don't need to explain myself to you or anyone else, but I'll tell you two things. First, I'm the one responsible for my patients, and I decide what they need. If they do badly, it's going to be because of what I believed was the correct thing to do, not some course of action I've been badgered into. If I start letting anesthesiologists, nurses, and goddamn administrators influence my patients' care decisions, they'll be in trouble. I know best what my patients need.

"Second, nurses need to execute my orders—period. That's what's best for my patients. Doctors who are buddy-buddy with nurses don't get the same response as doctors they're afraid of. Nurses know if they don't complete my orders quickly and correctly, they'll pay a price. That's in my patients' best interest."

There might be a sliver of truth in what the man said but overall, she felt sad for him. She'd learned a number of things about Bart Rainey on this day of disaster.

He did care about his patients. He was skilled and decisive and courageous. Those were good traits for any doctor but particularly for a surgeon. His refusal of the helicopter ride to freedom revealed selflessness and character she would not have guessed was present.

His reaction to the gorilla-brute Red showed he would not back down—no matter the risk. Anytime the two huge men were in sight of one another the air became charged, as if two dominant animals met in the wilderness and were facing off.

"I may not have a chance to say anything later, so I'm telling tell you now, Bart." She used his first name consciously, something no nurse ever did. "I respect many things about you, but you're messed up. Dr. Cody says medicine is a team sport and no one does it alone. He's right. If we survive this, please recognize that the people you work with care just as deeply as you do. We're on the same team, so stop being a jerk."

The machines and monitors created a chorus revealing the senator's struggle for life. Bart towered over her, his eyes focused on her, and his face did not reveal his usual irritation. He took a step back.

"Been a hell of a day," he said. "You did a decent job setting up our makeshift OR and helping with the case. Everything was half-ass, but you couldn't help that. You've done solid work. You're a good nurse."

Tracy tried not to show her surprise. A compliment from Blackheart Bart! No nurse would believe it.

"Thank you."

"I heard what you said. I'll think about it. I wish all the people I work with were as solid as you—they sure as hell aren't." He paused. "You just used up as much teachable moment as I got, nursey." He stood tall. "Our next case—kicking terrorist ass. Let's crush these freaks."

CHAPTER SIXTY-NINE

"Yes, Reverend," Roberta said to the Captain. "The nice young doctor gave me a shot by my leg, and it doesn't hurt at all anymore. It's a miracle. Praise Jesus." She smiled.

"I'm not a Reverend, Miss Roberta," the Captain said. "I am an intergalactic scout."

"That sounds like a good job," Roberta said. "Where is your home? Does your family live here? Maybe they attend my church."

"It's a galaxy many light-years from here. We on my planet are much more highly evolved than those of you on earth."

"That's nice. Do they play bingo there? I like bingo."

Antoine chuckled from where he was seated on the neighboring cot. "It's true, brother. Some on this planet are not highly evolved."

The Captain rubbed his grizzled chin. "Earth people have limited capacity, but some on your planet, like the docs and nurses of this ER, have reached levels that approach the least developed of those in my world. They have heart and believe in doing what is right. This impresses me greatly."

"Are you familiar with churches such as Miss Roberta mentioned?" Antoine said.

"I like the message they share," the Captain said, "but it seems too few on your planet live accordingly."

"You are diplomatic," Antoine said. "What about the people holding us captive? They have murdered people, including stabbing to death a harmless man less than one hour ago."

"They are among the ugliest and least evolved I have been exposed to."

"Any ideas on how we can beat them?" Antoine stood and moved closer to the Captain, his back now to the door to minor trauma. He spoke softly. "They have high-powered weapons and we have none. How can we stop them? How can we—"

"How can you what?" The hulking menace of Red filled the doorway. "What are you talking about?"

"You have good ears for one of your planet," the Captain said. "We were talking about earthly troubles."

Red looked at the Captain who lay on the cot, IV line still in place, his features worn and haggard. He turned to Antoine.

"You saying it was troubles, too? You think I'm stupid?"

Antoine moved away from Red and sat back on his cot. "It was nothing. Just two men talking."

"Wrong," Red said. "Two damn monkeys. And like all your kind, you talk too much and don't show white men the respect you should."

"Excuse me," the Captain said. "Your aura is projecting anger and hatred. It is unhealthy."

Red ignored the Captain. He had Antoine locked in his gaze. Red moved within a foot of him, his massive chest above Antoine's face, the power and tension in his body a visible thing.

"Please," the Captain said sitting forward. "You have not evolved enough to know how wrong your thinking is. If you—

Red reached over and slapped the Captain with a backhand, knocking him flat on his bed. He snapped his attention back to Antoine, his eyes burning.

"You smarting off to your superior, boy? The massive enforcer was a coiled spring.

"There's no need to be hitting that sick old man. You got an issue with me, deal with it." Antoine leaned his head back so he was looking into the huge man's eyes. He spoke softly and clearly. "And I sure as hell don't see anything superior."

Blink-fast, Red's massive arm fired forward like the piston of some brutal engine. His knuckles drove deep into Antoine's throat. The blow smashed flesh and shattered bone and cartilage—sounding like a pile driver impacting an animal's carcass.

Antoine was driven onto his back, then rolled off the cot to the floor. His hands clutched at his throat. He made horrible wet, gasping sounds.

The Captain reached out and clawed at Red's heavily muscled arm.

Red ignored the Captain's efforts. A twisted smile grew on his face as he watched Antoine writhing on the floor. Miss Roberta moaned.

The Captain turned to Phoenix and the teenage boy who with his mom stared silent and wide-eyed.

"Scream for Bones. Now!" the Captain said. "Get Dr. Cody. Antoine is dying!"

CHAPTER SEVENTY

Drake glanced at the Life Clock. He'd reset it in countdown mode so the red numerals would hit all zeros at 9:57. There were only minutes left until their Armageddon.

Bart Rainey stood gowned, gloved, and masked at the bedside of Senator Duren.

The senator's arm vein IVs were flowing, but Drake anticipated the upcoming need for drugs that couldn't be given through those lines. That and Drake's long-range hope for the senator meant he needed a central intravenous line placed in one of the major veins of his neck and chest.

Central lines were routine but required skill. A five-inch-long introducer needle penetrated the skin and was advanced deep into the neck or upper chest guided only by the physician's use of external anatomical landmarks. The landmarks varied with each patient's body type.

Complications included piercing a lung and collapsing it or penetrating the major artery that ran alongside the target vein—either result could kill someone as ill as Senator Duren.

Drake as an emergency specialist and Bart as a surgeon had both performed the procedure many times. Common but with significant risk.

As Bart passed the five-inch-long needle under the senator's collarbone and angled it into his chest toward the base of the neck, panicked screams erupted from the corridor.

Drake scrambled out of the Crash Room and into the corridor toward the screams. He ran into Newman. The frantic teenager clutched at Drake, pulling on him and pointing toward the minor trauma area.

"Dying Antoine!" the teen yelled.

Drake sprinted ahead and collided with Red as he exited minor trauma. It was as if he'd run into a side of beef.

Red grabbed Drake by the neck with one hand and held his pistol against Drake's chest with the other.

"Watch where you're going." He glanced back into the room. "Don't bother with that back-talking boy. He's done." Red shoved Drake to the side and swaggered down the corridor.

Drake scrambled into the room. Antoine writhed on the floor, eyes bulging, color gray. his hands clawing at his throat, his neck muscles stretched like piano wire.

Drake dropped to his knees at the distressed man's side.

"Save him, Bones!" The Captain extended his arm over the railing of the bed, his hand reaching for Antoine.

Newman's mother sat with hands over her mouth and eyes wide. Phoenix remained curled on her cot, her arms wrapped over her head.

Patti ran into the room, followed by the swollen-faced and weapon-at-the-ready hyena. The con looked down on the struggling Antoine.

"Ooo-wee. The boy must have smart-mouthed Red. He won't be doing that again." His sick laugh trilled as he stepped back. "When Red does his thing, they don't never cause trouble ever again."

Controlling his fury, Drake assessed Antoine. His abdominal and chest muscles were rigid as he struggled to breathe but could not. His mouth and tongue were clear. Drake palpated the sturdy man's throat, a crackling sensation like Rice Krispies under his fingers. The structures within Antoine's neck had been pulverized as if hit by a sledgehammer.

Drake bent and tried to deliver a breath mouth-to-mouth. No air would pass. The vocal cords, tissue, hyoid bone, and cartilage structures that formed the passage to the lower trachea and lungs had been destroyed. The cartilage rings of the upper trachea and allied structures forming Antoine's airway had been crushed as if by a vise.

Antoine's eyes begged as his movements weakened. He'd been without oxygen for too long.

His gaze clouded and his color worsened. No route existed for air to enter.

Every second mattered. How long had it been? Brain injury or death could occur at any time.

Drake's gaze raced around the room. The terrorists had stripped all instruments from the area.

Patti crouched on the other side of Antoine.

"Patti, run to the Crash Room and grab a handful of endotracheal tubes and the scalpel we stashed."

She was up and moving before he finished speaking.

The hyena stood five feet away with his rifle at the ready and a sick grin on his face.

Antoine's eyes flickered then closed. His hands dropped from his throat and stilled.

"Give me your knife." Drake pointed at the brutal weapon that had killed Cecil.

"You crazy?"

"Give it to me now, you sick bastard. You'll like it. You'll like what I have to do."

With some airway problems, cutting a small passage or inserting a large hollow needle into the neck and through a membrane just beneath the Adam's apple is enough to allow air passage. Red's devastating punch had obliterated all those structures and eliminated that remedy.

Lifesaving rule number one—the "A" of the lifesaving ABCs—is airway. If no airway, secure an airway—by whatever means necessary. Drake's course was brutal but obvious.

No sedation, no anesthetic, no nothing... Antoine's fading

consciousness warned of impending death, but he would still feel everything acutely.

"Now, asshole!" Drake held his hand out. The con pulled the knife from his belt, flipped it, caught it by the blade, and slapped the handle into Drake's hand. He then stepped back holding his rifle trained on Drake.

"Give me a good show, Doc."

Patti raced back into the room with her hands full of equipment as Drake positioned himself on one knee, bent over Antoine, who was now as still as death.

"Antoine, you'll feel pain and sensation unlike anything ever. You must not move."

If the blade passed one centimeter too deep or to the side, Drake would slice critical structures and assure Antoine's death.

Drake nodded toward Patti, who got on the floor and held Antoine's head between her knees while she gripped his forehead.

Newman appeared at Drake's side.

"Yes, we need you," Drake said. "Hold his arms. Lay across his chest."

The boy did so without hesitation.

Drake gripped the knife mid-blade, almost as if holding a giant dart. The size and shape of the brutal blade fit the task. He took a breath and drove the steel deep into Antoine.

The tip of the blade penetrated the skin at the lowest portion of the neck, drove through the underlying tissues, and entered the trachea. Antoine's eyes exploded open. Drake felt the man's body go rigid.

The blade yielded a gritty snap as it penetrated the trachea's bonelike cartilage. A short, violent inflow of air whined like a jet turbine as Antoine's chest expanded. Air then blasted out, making a whistling sound as an aerosolized mist of hot blood sprayed on Drake's face.

He twisted the knife blade, separating the tough fibrous tracheal rings, which made a sound like a cracking walnut as he enlarged the vital pathway. The pupils of Antoine's bulging eyes expanded, and the black depths fell away.

Another big breath, and a mist of air and life-warm blood bathed Drake's hands and forearms. Without needing to ask, Drake found a stainless-steel clamp slapped into his palm by Patti.

Creating an airway meant nothing if it could not be maintained. Any slip or loss of control, and the opening would retract and disappear as the layers of bloody flesh shifted and made the passage unfindable. They'd immediately be back to the dire place they'd begun.

Drake inserted the instrument—similar to needle-nosed pliers—through the surgical opening he'd cut and then opened it widely, expanding the passage. Antoine's legs thrashed, but Patti and Newman held. A glimpse of the white cartilage of the inner trachea flashed in the keyhole of life he'd created. Once more, without having to be asked, Patti held the needed instrument out to him—a stainless-steel tracheal hook.

"You're brilliant," Drake said without shifting his laser-locked gaze.

He inserted the slim instrument into the surgical passageway he'd cut, then pulled up, seating the tool's hooked end in the hard, unyielding inner portion of the trachea as if catching a fish.

Antoine's desperate breaths whistled fast and deep, and the coppery smell of blood grew. His chest heaved as if he'd just completed a sprint.

His pupils were huge. His muscles and jaw clenched. Unimaginable pain for Antoine, yet Drake felt a near-joyous rush—the injured man's reactions were those of someone whose brain had escaped damage.

"4-o tube please," he said, his eyes locked on the airway he'd created. The ET tube hit his palm.

He slipped the end of the airway tube and its small inflatable balloon cuff into the hole in the trachea he had created and which he now controlled, protected with the tracheal hook. He advanced the tube the appropriate distance though the surgical entry and down the trachea.

"Inflate the balloon and we'll tie it down." Antoine was not safe until the lifesaving tube was anchored.

Drake held the tube in position while Patti used the strong, ribbon-like material to tie around the tube and then around Antoine's neck. She tied it snug enough to secure the tube without it being too tight around his neck.

They did not need to connect the tube to a ventilator. With the tube in place and oxygen reviving his brain, Antoine breathed on his own.

"Let's get him on a cart and to the Crash Room," Drake said.

Drake looked into Antoine's eyes. "Sorry, Antoine. There was no time for anesthesia. I'll get things numbed up straightaway. Hang in there, sir."

Antoine, stunned and gray with pain, gave a slight nod.

Drake saw the knife in his peripheral vision and reached for the handle. Something hard jammed into his back.

"Back off," Hyena said. "That was cool, but ain't no way you're touching that blade again."

Drake turned. The battered hyena held his rifle and wore an expression like Red's as he'd left the room, leaving Antoine writhing on the floor, struggling for life. The bastards enjoyed the suffering of others.

The muscles of Drake's neck and shoulders went tight. How did anyone degenerate to this level?

The murder of the policewoman on the highway, Tolman executing Marcus in the Crash Room, the death of the state trooper, the murder of Cecil with the blade Drake had just used—all this and the explosion in the city that had killed and injured countless more—none of it mattered to the terrorists.

Tolman claimed they were supporters of justice and freedom. Patriots? Heroes? Far from it.

Drake knew what they were and what needed to be done.

He would not hold his instincts for savagery in check. He would fan them and pump them up like a fighter before the bell, a football player before the snap, a soldier before battle. He would free the primal animal in him that he kept caged, pacing and shrieking, within the shadows of his mind.

The terrorists must die.

CHAPTER SEVENTY-ONE

Drake guided the head of Antoine's bed into the Crash Room bay next to the senator. The same bay they'd used to operate on the gunshot terrorist earlier. The beeps of the cardiac monitor and the mechanized sounds of the equipment marched on. Bart was in the minor trauma area with Rizz, checking on the Captain and the others.

As soon as they'd placed Antoine on a cart in minor trauma, Drake had injected a long-acting local anesthetic into the tissues around the airway he'd carved into the trachea. Now Antoine's eyes were open and his face was no longer contorted with pain.

He moved air easily through the tube. There was no active bleeding. He couldn't speak because his upper airway had been bypassed, but even if he were able to get air to his voice box, it would make no sound. If Antoine survived, he would need surgery to reconstruct his larynx and crushed airway anatomy.

Patti slipped an IV into one of his arms. Drake listened with his stethoscope to Antoine's lung sounds and assessed the status of the sturdy workingman and former Marine:

Airway—the surgical airway and lifesaving tube were open and functioning.

Breathing—he had no difficulty moving air.

Circulation—despite a throat injury the likes of which Drake had seen only in high-speed car accidents or snowmobile or motorcycle accidents, there was no ongoing bleeding. Blood pressure and pulse were good.

Other than a future with reconstructive surgery and a voice that would never be normal, Antoine was in no danger.

No danger? Drake checked the clock. They were all in a place beyond danger.

Antoine had been near death, and if the tube became dislodged, he would die in minutes. Drake had recognized with certainty that the combat veteran was the kind of courageous, quiet, "ordinary" man whose character couldn't be overestimated. Like the barehanded, brave Americans who'd kicked terrorist ass on Flight 93, he was the kind of man who made a difference. He'd been a source of hope as a warrior. Now they'd lost him.

First no phone, now no Antoine. Drake's stomach knotted. Besides the fear of death, the thought of having his life ended by cowardly, bigoted bastards profoundly pissed him off.

Tracy moved from the senator's bedside and began assisting Patti with Antoine. The coordination between critical care nurses was a wonder of modern medicine. Drake stepped next to the senator.

"How is he?" Drake asked Tracy.

"His pulse and blood pressure jumped a few minutes ago. I'm afraid he had increased pain. I gave him more meds, but please look him over when you can."

The ECMO device continued its soft hum. The ventilator's hiss-pause-blow pace was smooth and rhythmic.

The oximeter confirmed oxygen was being introduced by the heart-lung device.

Among the smells of disinfectant and blood hung a faint but fouler scent. Drake put his nose near the senator's mouth, nose, and the endotracheal tube. The rank odor was stronger.

Drake envisioned the hydrofluoric acid continuing its slow but relentless penetration and destruction of the senator's tissues. There was no way to know when it would cease.

"It's as if a flamethrower had been fired down his airway and into his lungs," Drake said.

"So much damage you can smell it," she said.

"Like nothing I've ever smelled before," Drake said.

"Everything I've read or heard says he's a wonderful man." Her eyes were downcast, her face drawn.

Drake wasn't giving up, but things looked dismal for the senator. Sometimes in Drake's work, he had to question if what he was doing was lifesaving effort or hopeless torture. This good man would not have survived to reach the ER without the miraculous new technology. By all accounts, he shouldn't be alive now. The senator was in an agonizing battle. Was there a path to survival for him, or had Drake just delayed the inevitable?

He moved back to Antoine's bedside. He was confident about the former Marine's injuries. With care, he'd survive and recover. The senator's status was different.

Despite the other deaths, the terrorists' explosion in the city, and the potential of what was likely in store for them all, the thought of losing the battle for the senator's life hit Drake hard.

If they somehow made it out of the ER alive, what could be done for Senator Duren? Drake's mind raced as he plumbed his knowledge and imagination for a miraculous route to recovery.

A thought came to him. It was flat-out audacious. Could it possibly—

A shadow fell over Drake as if a thunderhead had passed in front of the sun. He looked up.

Red stood at the foot of Antoine's bed, blocking light.

"I put that boy down. Told you not to bother," the massive, Nazi-tattooed brute said.

Antoine had received pain medicine, but he was fully conscious. His eyes were locked on Red with death-ray intensity.

No one spoke. The ECMO device, ventilator, and beeping of the cardiac monitors seemed to have shifted in tone. The faint but foul odor of the senator's destroyed lungs tainted the air. Drake's mouth went dry.

"Can he talk? Can he feel pain?" the menacing freak asked.

Red hadn't spoken much near the start of this nightmare but that was changing. The physically scariest of the terrorists had become more active as the ordeal lengthened.

"He's conscious and he can feel pain. And he's had more than enough of it," Drake said. "He can't talk because you destroyed his throat."

"If he'd learned not to talk back, he might have lived."

"He's alive. He can see and hear you."

Red moved closer to the bed and peered at Antoine's face.

"You're right. The boy is looking at me." Red pivoted and grabbed Tracy, locking her against his chest with her back against him. He held his pistol against her head.

"You two move over on the other side of the senator," Red said to Drake and Patti. "Either of you steps from around that bed and I blow this bitch's head off."

Drake's heart hammered. He tried to swallow and couldn't. The brute was not bluffing. He and Patti moved as directed.

"So he can hear and understand, huh?" Red said. He looked at Antoine and moved close, his one-arm grip on Tracy controlling her as if she were a small child.

"Remember what I told you, boy?" Red said looking down into Antoine's eyes. "I said you'd pay."

He shifted his pistol to his left hand and grabbed the endotracheal tube that gave Antoine life with the right. "It's payment time." He ripped the tube out with one massive yank and hurled the blood-and-gore-covered lifesaving device across the room.

Antoine bolted upright, reaching for Red. Red pushed Tracy to the floor in the middle of the room and stepped out of reach of Antoine's hands. Antoine fell back, clutching at his bleeding throat, his chest and neck muscles once more locked in the desperate fight for breath.

Drake ran to Antoine's side, hoping to drive his finger into the wound and reclaim the lost airway. Massive arms locked around him from behind. He fought for what seemed like forever against an arm-bar chokehold that held him off the ground. Head bursting, vision going red, he threw elbows and kicked backward at the man's legs. His blows landed but the grip did not yield.

A glimpse of Antoine. The man he so admired now limp, his eyes unseeing, his color deathly.

Drake struggled, fighting, fading. Helpless. *No!*

His vision went to black.

CHAPTER SEVENTY-TWO

Minor trauma room

Her son was doing okay, but when would he be safe?

She hadn't screamed. Not when the young man had been stabbed or when the huge brute had nearly killed Mr. Antoine. While her boy was usually lost in his own world, if she cried or became upset in front of him, he would often become uncontrollably agitated. The autism therapists called them meltdowns. His meltdowns were almost as scary to her as his seizures.

It was one more thing she had to look out for. They'd taken Mr. Antoine to another room, and now Dr. Rizz and the giant surgeon were helping the old Black man. She felt safer with them in the room.

Newman did not watch them but focused on his hand movements and rocked back and forth like he so often did.

He never cried—not even as an infant. At first she'd thought that was a good thing.

She'd gradually learned things weren't right for him. Her boy was not like other children.

She hadn't known anything about autism.

Her only child required close care and patience. Her husband had left them. He blamed her for their son's troubles.

Newman's first seizure happened when he was five. She'd never been more scared in her life. She was sure he was dying.

The doctors said the seizures were dangerous and could cause harm but were unlikely to kill him. "Unlikely to kill him..." How could she deal with that? Sometimes the doctors and their explanations left her more scared than before. With medicines, the seizures lessened but did not disappear.

Each one paralyzed her.

Children with special needs need special parents. No one in her life had ever told her she was special.

As he'd reached school age, kids called him retard, spaz, crazy, psycho, and more. They made fun of his speech trouble and riding the short bus. He rarely spoke and when he did, the words were mixed up and usually directed only to her.

His name was Ronald but when still a little boy, he decided he would be called Newman. It was from a character on the Seinfeld show. She didn't understand why.

Before her husband left he'd believed their boy was stupid—"even dumber than you," he'd said. An early teacher said he had a "bad attitude."

She knew better.

Newman was smart, very smart. So much smarter than her that it brought her joy. His unusual speech and strange hand gestures were things the autism clinic people said were common but made others uncomfortable. People stayed away from him.

He played computer games and watched TV all the time, probably too much. She tried to do everything the therapists recommended, but she believed she was failing him.

She imagined how amazing it would feel to hug him, or even more wonderful, to be hugged by him. Those were dreams. His condition made human touch too much for him. If he understood how much she loved him and how special he was, perhaps things would change for him. It had not happened yet.

The man had held a gun to Newman's head and threatened to blow his brains out. The criminals who had taken over the ER had killed a man in front of them and hurt Mr. Antoine.

Her boy had not had a meltdown. He'd twice spoken with the doctor called Rizz and had helped with Mr. Antoine. She'd been stunned. Her son never interacted like that.

It was a breakthrough. If the things happening weren't so scary, she would've cried with happiness.

She took a shuddering breath and clenched her rosary beads.

She was forty-six years old, small, and not strong. People called her slow. She'd never been in a fight in her life—unless being beaten by her husband counted.

The men who threatened them were evil. She believed in God and he had given her a job. A job she would not trade for any in the world. She was mother to her special boy.

She would fight to the death to protect him.

CHAPTER SEVENTY-THREE

Jon scoured Rachelle's notes again.

Had she missed anything obvious? Not likely.

Had *he* missed anything, was the better question.

The wind had died. Not a ripple showed on the lake's surface. The twilight glow in the west made the lake's surface shine like stainless steel.

"One of the first things he said was 'get Meryl and the kids and leave town.' At first I thought I'd misheard, but that's what he said. It tipped me off right away."

Burn scars covered parts of Rachelle's wrists and hands. Meryl had been responsible for those injuries and more. She'd been the farthest thing from a friend to Rachelle, Drake, or any of them.

"Much of what he said makes no sense to me," she said. "Burnett resort? A p.m. check-in instead of a.m. like before? We never went to a resort. I googled Burnett and Burnett resort and there are pages of hits, but nothing I saw clicked. I'm sure he pointed me to you for help."

"That makes sense. With the terrorist listening, he couldn't be direct. Our work together gives us a lot in common he could reference."

"It hurts to admit it, but sometimes it feels like you, Rizz, and that damn ER are a bigger part of his life than I am."

Jon felt awkward. What she'd confided seemed intimate. Rizz and Drake used to make fun of Jon's Eagle Scout and choir boy outlook—his innocence. His wife's death and the public revelation of her sordid hidden life had ended his always seeing the best in people. Faith had betrayed and humiliated him. He was haunted by that and what had followed.

Rachelle put a hand on his shoulder.

"Focus, Jon. I think Drake provided you the answers."

"I didn't have answers before, and it almost cost us our lives. Rizz is in a wheelchair because of me." He couldn't get past what he'd done. Did Rachelle know? *The medications and counseling can't erase it. Maybe nothing can. I—*

"Damn it, Jon." Rachelle slapped her hand on the table. "Don't drift off feeling sorry for yourself. Look at the words, Jon. What do they mean?"

He flinched. He was so messed up. He focused on her notes, his brow furrowed. Finding the answer could be the difference between his closest friends and coworkers living or dying. *Roll out, check-in, Burnett resort?*

Rachelle had ruled out it relating to her and Drake.

Jon google searched *Burnett* like Rachelle had. The first few dozen listings were meaningless among more than sixty million results—

He entered *Burnett Resort.* Eight million results. Nothing looked like a fit. He was failing his friends as he had before. He fought the urge to throw the phone across the room. *Let Aki and Jon know. Roll out.* Nothing seemed to—*wait!* The answer flared like a struck match.

Jon knew this story. Rizz had shared it. Burnett—a Minnesota guy.

He entered Burnett and 9/11. Tom Burnett was the first entry. Captive passengers on a jet aimed for Washington, DC, Tom Burnett with others launching an attack on the terrorists, the "let's roll" message captured on the flight recorder identifying when they went into action. Of course. That was Drake's message—not *roll out* but *Let's roll.*

He read faster. There—the time of the passengers' attack was 9:57

a.m. on that fateful morning. Drake was saying attack tonight at 9:57—p.m., not a.m.

Of course, Drake was going to fight. He would lead the attack tonight.

Jon looked at the clock. His gut sank. *Oh my God!*

"I've got it. I understand Drake's message." *Was there a chance?* "Call Dr. Torrins! I'll try Aki."

He pulled up Detective Yamada's number. Rachelle already had her phone to her ear.

"Oh, no! It went straight to message." Rachelle looked pale.

Jon held his phone to his ear. One ring. Two rings. *Please, God!* The bulldog of a detective had to answer. The third and fourth ring.

Jon looked at the time again.

"Answer, Aki, answer!" The phone rang a fifth and sixth time...

CHAPTER SEVENTY-FOUR

Aki just made out the sound of his phone in the bustle of the command trailer. Techs spoke on headphones, phones rang, and bodies surged as preparations for tactical entry continued.

"Detective Yamada here."

"Jon Malar, Memorial Hospital emergency physician. I—"

"Yes, doc?" As the detective who'd saved Jon from a hired killer and also investigated the murder of his wife, Aki would never forget the soft-spoken, brutally betrayed physician.

"I need to talk to whoever is dealing with the crisis in the ER," Jon said. "You, FBI, or whoever. I need them now."

"I'm in the FBI command trailer. Things are critical right now. Can it—"

"No. There's no time. It's a message from Drake."

"Hold on. The FBI agent in charge is standing right next to me." Aki signaled Dylan and pointed at the phone. "A message from Drake."

Dylan took Aki by the shoulder and they entered the communications booth. Aki activated the speaker as Dylan closed the door. "A message from Drake?" Aki said. "How? When? We need to—"

"It was a one-time, very brief phone call to Rachelle." Jon said. "His message is all we have. You have to act now."

"What did he say?" Aki said.

"Drake and the captives inside the ER are going to attack at 9:57 p.m.. They're going after the terrorists like the passengers on Flight 93 on 9/11. You've got to help them. You need to coordinate your assault with theirs."

Aki looked at the clock. His heart jumped to his throat. Dylan stood with brow furrowed. A matter of minutes.

"Are you sure?" Aki said. Dylan stood expressionless, his eyes steely. Inside, Aki knew he had to be going a million miles an hour.

"I'd bet my life on it," Jon said. "Rachelle wrote down everything. The message was in code that we had to figure out. Drake will be leading an attack on the terrorists in the ER like Burnett and the passengers did on Flight 93. Rolling at the same time—9:57—but p.m. not a.m."

Dylan spoke. "Special Agent in Charge McGinnis here. Thank you. Your message has been received."

"They're running out of time," Jon said. "You have to help them."

"We understand. Hang on and other agents will talk with you." He opened the door and signaled an agent, then turned to Aki.

"We roll at 9:57. Hit them fast and hard—inside and out."

CHAPTER SEVENTY-FIVE

Aki tracked the wide-angle CCTV views of the parking lot, the operations trailer, and the after-dark cityscape as Special Agent McGinnis gave instructions and responded to phone calls. Streetlights and banks of spotlights lit up the parking lot and all eight stories of the Minneapolis hospital. The view to the west centered on the towering plume of smoke that pulsed with orange-red flames within, like a mountain of volcanic magma rising into the sky.

Other screens showed tactical team members strategically positioned inside the hospital, staging for ER insertion. The assault team members' terse radio exchanges with the command center increased Aki's already coiled-spring urge for action.

Only a few fire, rescue, and tactical vehicles and personnel remained out in the open in the lot. Dylan had ordered the perimeter pulled back, and the individuals outside it were positioned behind blast barricades.

Aki worried that the terrorists inside the ER could be viewing the parking lot and hospital exterior on TV. The media jackals were broadcasting indiscriminately, despite requests from the FBI to refrain. If the extremists were watching, they might recognize that the decks were being cleared for battle. Aki itched to be on the move as the tension in the command center pressed down on him. The multiple murmuring voices, the flashing images, the scent of stressed bodies—the cost of failure unimaginable.

The central command activity did not fit Aki. He wanted to be in the first wave to enter the ER and leave the excruciating command decisions to the cool head of the man standing next to him. He clenched his fists. What could he do?

There was a brief pause with Dylan not addressing techs or agents as he disconnected from a call.

"Any progress in the search for explosives or destructive devices?" Aki's jaw clenched. *Domestic terrorists using explosives and chemical warfare against fellow Americans—the disgusting bastards!*

"We're spread thin because of the Golden Valley blast, but every spare first responder, hazmat, explosives team, sniffer dog, and citizen volunteer is looking." He bit his lip. "The Twin Cities metro area is more than eight thousand square miles. We have no idea exactly what we're looking for, how many, or where."

Aki said nothing. There was nothing to say. His commitment—what his ex-wife called his obsession—to solving and preventing murders had triggered his divorce, almost got him killed more than once, and often left him questioning his sanity. The potential for disaster hung like towering purple-black thunderclouds over his city. Tornadoes of fire and destruction could touch down at any time. Aki, Dylan, and countless others were doing all they could to stop that from happening.

"Damn, Dylan. This is messed up. There are no good options."

"We can't count on finding the planted explosives, chemicals, or whatever weapon of mass destruction they've planted. Staging for assault of the ER will be complete within minutes. The tactical units are in position, awaiting our 9:57 entry action. We're going to pull back the command center five minutes before incursion. This trailer will be moved back, and everyone but the tactical ops people staged inside the hospital will fall back. We have no idea how large the kill zone of any hospital-based explosion might be."

"If it's massive, there's no way the terrorists could escape," Aki said.

"Don't you think the ER devices are more likely strategic-scale to give them an opportunity to get free?"

"Hopefully, we never find out, but it looks like their leader wants to go out in the proverbial blaze of glory. Our objective is to take them out fast—before they can trigger anything in the ER or elsewhere. Our intel suggests there may be an ER entry route that can be breached without a massive explosion, though it's a gamble."

The agent looked calm, his voice measured.

Imagining the pressure made Aki's mouth go dry and his gut ache.

"Special Agent." A bespectacled tech with headphones on stood up from the communications console. "Call routed from the interrogations site. The terrorist leader's son wants to speak with Detective Yamada. We had instructions to patch him thorough immediately."

"Put him on speaker with a one-way video link," Dylan said.

The agent hit some keys and the console screen lit up. A ceiling-mounted camera angle showed Sigurd pacing in the interrogation room. The young man rubbed his neck and put both hands on his head without stopping his pacing.

"Sigurd? This is Detective Yamada."

Sigurd stopped and looked up into the camera, speaking immediately.

"Detective Yamada. I heard about the explosion. Oh, my God." He shook his head, his face pale. "I didn't know. I—"

"Sigurd. We have no time," Aki said. "Tell me what you can. It may already be too late."

"Was it Golden Valley, near grain elevators?" Sigurd's voice cracked.

Dylan nodded and signaled Aki to respond.

"Yes. Golden Valley, and the explosion was centered near grain elevators. Are there more?"

"Oh, God." His voice broke and he sobbed. "Father told me to leave the trailer there. I had no idea."

Dylan scratched out a note and held it up to Aki. *We checked. All Freid trucks are accounted for. None in the city—??*

"All your father's trucks are accounted for," Aki said. "Are there more truck bombs or other devices, Sigurd?"

"What? More bombs?" Sigurd stopped and his mouth gaped. "No! Oh my God. Please no!"

"Sigurd. Get it together." Aki spoke sharp and stern. "Are there other trucks?"

"Yes. He leased trucks. Three twelve-thousand-gallon super tanker-trailers and the eight-thousand-gallon rig I delivered." He clutched his temples. "How many people got hurt? This can't be real."

"It's real, Sigurd. Where are the other trucks? Where? More lives are at risk."

"I don't know. Believe me, I'd tell you if I knew." The young man wrung his hands. "Red and Micah each drove one last night before I delivered mine. I think Father had already delivered the other one."

"He's going to kill thousands. Think, Sigurd, think. The trucks. How can we find them?"

Sigurd bent, holding his head in his hands and moaned.

"God in heaven, help me. I don't know." He dropped his hands, closed his eyes, his arms hung limp. He took rasping breaths, his chest heaving.

"Only you can stop it, Sigurd. Think. How can we find the trucks?" Aki said.

Sigurd stiffened, then cocked his head as if he'd heard a faint sound.

"Update!" He straightened, looked up, and stepped toward the camera. "That's where he got them. Update Leasing. I saw our invoice. Our firm is Freidom Trucking—spelled like our name. The leased tankers should have GPS beacons like ours do. Insurance companies demand it. Call Update Leasing and try to track them."

"Good, Sigurd. Very good." Aki said.

Dylan was already snapping off orders for phone, computer, and local law enforcement contact with Update Leasing. Several personnel jumped into action.

On the screen, the terrorist's son looked like a wet rag that had been wrung dry. He shook his head.

"Find them," Sigurd said. "Please find them. I'm so sorry." He slumped to the floor, ending seated with his back against the wall.

Aki covered the mouthpiece and looked at the clock and then Dylan.

"It's only minutes until you said we'd attack," Aki said.

"I can't green-light entry now." Dylan shook his head. "No way. We have to hold tactical back until we find and disarm those trucks. They're not just explosives—they're weapons of mass destruction. Thousands of lives are at risk."

"But there might not be enough time," Aki said. "Drake and the hostages will attack at 9:57, no matter what." As he spoke his thoughts aloud, he recognized no one was more aware of the consequences than the FBI agent in charge.

"We have to find and disarm those devices crazy fast. Otherwise, we'll have to count on what you told me earlier."

"What's that?" Aki held his breath. Anything remotely hopeful he'd said, he'd forgotten.

"That your friend Drake Cody has survived impossible odds before."

CHAPTER SEVENTY-SIX

The agent at the console stood and waved his hand. Dylan and Aki rushed to him. He covered his headset mike with his hand.

"I've got Update Leasing. Biggest truck leasing outfit in the country. Based in Dallas."

"Put them on speaker," Dylan said.

The agent nodded and spoke into his headset. "Check under Freidom Trucking. F-r-e-i-d -o-m spelling. We're looking for the lease of four tanker trucks. We need them tracked immediately as a matter of national security."

Dylan held his breath. Everything had to go right, starting with this call. His mind flashed a gestalt of what it would be like to have the greatest terrorist destruction in US history occurring on his watch. The thoughts pushed to the side as a voice sounded from the speaker.

"National security! I'm pulling it up straightaway, honey," a woman's husky voice. "My name's Lola. I'll get you whatever you need. Heard about the bad business going on up your way. What happened to *Minnesota nice* anyhow?" Clacking keys were audible. "Lord almighty! Darn computer froze on me."

A couple of the agents cursed. Dylan echoed the expletives in his mind but kept his outside cool. The electronic clicks, beeps, and hum of the command center's equipment continued, but all voices went silent. The entire command team hung as one. The seconds stretched.

"Thank you, Jesus. It's back." More keys sounded. "Nothing under Freidom spelled with ei or Freedom with ee Trucking. No history of any transaction ever. Sorry, honey."

"Check Freid. First name, Tolman," the agent said.

"Lordy, first name Told-man? Must be a Minnesota thing. Can you spell that for me?"

The agent spelled Tolman and Freid. Key clicks sounded.

"Oh darn. Nothing under Tolman Freid either," she said. More clicks were audible.

Dylan's chest clenched. *No!*

"Check under—"

"Hold on, sweetie. Yes. Wait. Here's a Sonya. Sonya Freid. Hmmm. Minnesota. Yessiree. Four supertankers. Lease originated three weeks ago. I just made you happy, right?"

"Yes. We need immediate GPS transponder tracking information. Do you have that?"

"Absolutely, honey." More clicks. "What's your email?"

The agent responded.

"They're on the way. But I can tell you in a jiffy where the rigs are at if you'd like."

A second agent at the console gave a thumbs-up, then dropped his hands and his fingers flew over the computer's keys.

"We've received the coordinates, but please share what you have."

Dylan felt as if he were floating. He glanced at Aki, who shook a clenched fist.

Something going right!

"Hmmm. Something's wrong," the honey-smooth voice continued. "I'm only showing three trucks. But yes, Mr. Minnesota. I'm seeing three in the Twin Cities. None of them are moving. Not registering the fourth anywhere. That shouldn't be."

"Thank you, Lola. Please stay on the line."

"My pleasure, Mr. FBI, and we're praying for y'all up there in Minnesota."

Dylan turned to the agent at the console to his right.

"We're up," the agent at the screen announced. "We've got them on display."

"Broadcast coordinates via phone and secure modes to all first responders and rescue personnel as well as citizen sites," Dylan said. "Have explosives and demolition team members on standby to link by phone with people on scene when they get to the trucks. Our tech people will have to talk responders through disarming. Initiate evacuation efforts around any sites discovered. No radio traffic— terrorists may be monitoring. Inform regional incident command that finding these trucks is the top priority. Everything needs to be done flawless and fast."

Dylan looked at the clock. Not much time to find and disarm before Drake Cody and those in the ER would launch their desperate attack on the terrorists holding them captive. They were going to roll at 9:57. Dylan had planned to green-light the tactical team ER entry at that time.

Though Dylan hadn't spoken with Dr. Cody, he felt he'd given his word.

He may have lied.

The consequences might haunt him forever.

CHAPTER SEVENTY-SEVEN

The operations trailer gave a lurch, and Dylan sensed movement as the diesel rig pulled the command center farther from the hospital. The agents remained in their seats, monitoring the displays and working their jobs without a hitch. Images of masked and Kevlar-clad tactical agents wearing self-contained breathing masks with full weapons packages showed from each of several floors of the hospital.

"How long from when you give the order until tactical can breech the ER?" Aki asked.

"A minute or two. Three at most." Dylan looked at the flashing clock. "No word on the trucks or their being disarmed yet. You understand what that means?"

"Maybe. I hope I'm wrong."

"We have to find and disarm the trucks before I can give the green light."

"No alternative?" Aki asked.

"None. As soon as Tolman Freid realizes we're making a forced entry, he'll detonate the trucks. He sees death and destruction as his glory. He's not going to allow his mission to be crashed into an abandoned field."

Dylan's chest tightened as if gripped by steel bands.

Those in the ER might die. The SWAT team members staging in the hospital might die. If the truck bombs were not disarmed in time, thousands—or tens of thousands—of innocent men, women, and children might die.

"You'd do that?" Aki said. "Let Drake and those in the ER attack without support?"

"I have no choice. I understand you have friends in—"

"They'll be annihilated," Aki said.

Dylan tried for calm, but heat flashed to his face. His jaw clenched. He turned and thrust his nose to within an inch of the detective's.

"Shut up, for God's sake, Aki. You think I don't know?" His ugliest decision ever. All options were a roll of the dice, with horrific loss of life a virtual certainty. *Damn!*

He pulled back and regained control. The detective stood wide-eyed.

"I'll share an even uglier thought." Dylan sighed and looked at Aki without blinking. "If we haven't found and disarmed the terrorist truck bombs before 9:57, I have to hope your friends' attack is crushed easily. If Tolman Freid believes they're going to take him down, he'll ravage this city in death and destruction like our country has never seen before."

RED'S GRIP had caused Drake to black out for only a few seconds. He'd recovered almost as soon as he'd hit the floor. He wasn't injured.

He and Tracy took Antoine's body back to the cast room where the bodies of Cecil, the state trooper, and the senator's friend and security man Marcus lay wrapped in sheets. Rizz, Patti, Bart, the Captain, and the others in the minor trauma room bowed their heads or held their hands over their hearts as the good man's body passed. Drake felt respect and resolve in the air.

When Drake returned to the Crash Room, he passed within a few feet of Red, who sat eating a sandwich and drinking apple juice as if killing Antoine was an insignificance already forgotten. Drake's core seethed and spit like molten lava. He wanted to rip the animal's heart out.

He couldn't allow himself to indulge his rage. But he had plans. From the start he, Rizz, and the other captives had sought out weapons. The terrorists had removed the obviously dangerous instruments and equipment, though they'd missed some, and the ER team had hidden other items away.

Drake opened the plastic wrapper of a four-inch-long spinal needle —the type he used for doing spinal taps on adults. He used the senator's body and bed as a screen as he worked.

He picked up one of the oversized vaginal swabs he'd taken earlier from the supply room. About an eighteen-inch-long thin shaft with three inches of cotton puff attached to one end, it was very much like a giant Q-tip. Drake used his trauma scissors to cut the shaft, leaving an eight-inch shaft and the affixed cotton puff.

Drake inserted the cut end of the swab's shaft into the hub of one of his two spinal needles. The spinal needle's shaft and laser-sharpened tip glistened in the light. His finished product looked like a small arrow or an overgrown dart with the cotton puff as its feathers.

Keeping it shielded from sight, he loaded his creation into the opening of a three-quarter-inch-diameter, two-and-a-half-foot-long cardboard cylinder that had been packaging for a chest tube. The lightweight arrow-dart fit into the tube like a twelve-gauge shell into the breech of a shotgun—it was a blowgun.

Drake checked that he was unobserved. He ducked down behind the senator's bed, raised the weapon to his mouth, aimed, and blasted a launching blast of air. The dart whistled across the Crash Room and buried itself in his target with a crisp *thwack*. It had rocketed the thirty feet in a blink and buried to the needle's hub in the rubberized mattress of bay four. The weapon exceeded his hopes. It had nothing near a gun's stopping power, but its potential for significant injury or distraction from a distance might give Drake a chance. He'd take anything.

Two blowguns versus multiple firearms. Was this suicide? *Damn.*

The confidence he'd manufactured to convince Rizz, Bart, and the others to join him in attacking was fiction.

The terrorists had multiple high-power, large-capacity weapons and were practiced fanatics at using them. Drake had sold his friends and the patients on joining him in this do-or die-attack. His stomach twisted.

As the Life Clock ticked off the last minutes, his fear and self-doubt bubbled in a stew so toxic he could taste it.

CHAPTER SEVENTY-EIGHT

Aki Yamada strapped on a Kevlar vest, then a flak jacket with "police" emblazoned on the front and back. His pistol was holstered, though it and his protective gear should not be needed. The wall of closed-circuit videos showed groups of tactical officers with strapped-on gear staged at several different spots within the hospital. Aki would join them in minutes.

His role was not what he wanted. The FBI Hostage Rescue Team refused to let any outsiders join in their operations. Minneapolis SWAT had the same practice, and for good reason. The officers involved in these actions had shared hundreds of hours of practice, simulation, and frontline experience. When a takedown operation's plans went out the window, as they almost always did, the team members' familiarity with one another could mean the difference between success or failure. The involvement of outsiders increased the chance of miscommunication or mishap, or the tragedy of deaths due to "friendly" fire.

Aki would not be involved in the initial incursion. He'd only been cleared for entry in the second wave—after the hoped-for successful entry and live-fire ended. Waiting would be excruciating. He longed to be with the entry team and do all he could to save the ER people he

admired so much from the vermin that threatened his city. It might be
unhealthy, but the job and his duty were his life. He could be blown to
pieces, but the fact had no impact on his desire to be a part of the
attempted rescue.

He checked the time as he'd done every minute since Dylan made
the decision to hold off assault until the truck bombs were found and
disarmed. The sick feeling in his gut grew stronger.

If 9:57 arrived before the truck-based weapons of mass destruction
were neutralized, Drake Cody and the others trapped inside the ER
would make their desperate attack alone. *Goddammit!* He felt so
helpless.

Aki's phone trilled, the displayed number unfamiliar. He debated
ignoring it, then answered.

"Yamada. Homicide, Major Crimes. Who's this?"

"Harley Aften. You know me. My brother and I were on the force
but have been working security for Senator Duren the last several
years."

"Of course, Harley." Solid guys. Harley's brother was chief of
Duren's security and one of the hostages. Aki hoped Harley wasn't
calling for an update. "Pressed for time, partner. Anything I can help
with real quick?"

"The deal is—" Harley's voice broke. "It's very likely..." A pause and
a big breath was audible. "...Marcus is dead."

Aki felt like he'd been punched. "What? Wait, Harley. I haven't
heard that. How—"

"Just listen," Harley said. "The senator's wife was contacted by text
message hours ago. A ransom demand. Five million dollars. She paid it.
Included the typical threat to kill the senator immediately if she
contacted the police. She wouldn't show me the text messages, but I
saw the photo of the senator they sent from the ER. It was authentic
as hell."

"What about Marcus? You said—"

"Later she got a second text from the kidnapper acknowledging
that the ransom transfer had been received. It repeated the threat to
keep quiet but admitted straight-up they'd killed Marcus."

"Damn, Harley. I'm sorry." It sounded like the style of the

terrorists' heartless leader. "But maybe there's still hope. Any other info? Things are happening and I have no time."

"I should've called sooner. Mrs. Duren insisted no authorities. I was torn but—shit, I blew it, Aki. They killed Marcus, and then the explosion in Golden Valley—there's no way they're letting the senator go. He could be dead already. I had to let you know. I have the numbers that the texts were sent from."

"Text them to me and I'll get the FBI team on it immediately. Damn, Harley, I'm afraid it may be too late to help. Bad shit is about to go down."

"I understand. My mistake and I have to live with it. I'm texting the numbers to you now. The Durens are Marcus and my best friends. If the senator is killed and Mrs. Duren believes my talking with you contributed to it, I don't think I could take it. Please keep my name out of it if you can."

"I'll try, Harley."

"And Aki," Harley's voice thickened, "I can feel in my heart that Marcus is gone. Find the cowards who killed my brother. Find them and take them out."

AKI SHARED Harley's info with Dylan, then ran to the medical office building adjoining the hospital. He entered the basement link being used by law enforcement to access the hospital out of sight. He breathed hard as he stopped short of one of the assembled entry teams on the hospital's second floor.

The tactical operatives were in ready position near the elevator shaft access. Aki noted clenched jaws and intense eyes, the sounds of weapons being checked, body odor, and the smell of gun oil as they waited for the signal that would start the battle that might mean their death and the death of thousands if they failed.

Aki's phone vibrated.

"Anything on the trucks, Dylan?" Aki asked.

"Truck news, but first I want to share we got your ransom messages tracked and evaluated," Dylan said. "Generally consistent with Freid's other communications, but our profiler says the money element and wording suggest a second source or influence."

"Freid believes he's a patriot. A money grab doesn't feel like him." Aki said.

"Agreed," Dylan said. "Both the pipeline and refinery businesses now admit they received ransom demands as well. We're on it, but it's too late to change what we need to do."

"Someone is cashing in on this. Money is what winds Stuart Kline's clock. It seems heavy duty for him, but the CEO needs to be turned inside out."

"Someone provided insider hospital knowledge to make this plan happen, and Kline fits that way as well. That said, I think he's too lightweight for this," Dylan said. "We needed this ransom info sooner. Who's your source? Are they potentially involved?"

"Definitely not involved and it would be a kindness to keep them anonymous. Nothing more to be learned there. What about the trucks?" *They've got to be disarmed—now!*

"We located all three of them easily with GPS. Police arrived at two of them in the last couple of minutes. No time to get our explosives experts there. No one on scene at the third one yet, due to traffic and a hard-to-reach location. Power lines, darkness, and obstacles keeping the copter from putting down close. We expect a first responder there any minute. Officers from your force are on the scene of the first two trucks. They're just now linking by live cellphone video with our bomb and weapons of mass destruction technicians so they can see what devices we're dealing with. Everything hangs on the techs being able to figure out how to disarm the trigger mechanism and talking the officers on scene through shutting them down in time." Dylan paused, then answered as if he'd read Aki's mind. "I'll launch the ER entry action the very second the damn things are neutralized."

Aki checked his watch. His gut plunged.

Not enough time. In minutes, in the ER one floor beneath him, Drake Cody would lead his desperate charge.

Valiant people were going to be slaughtered and hell could break loose in Aki's city.

CHAPTER SEVENTY-NINE

Each second moved Drake closer to the ultimate confrontation of his life. The life support machines marched on, and the fetid smell of the senator's charred lungs tinged the air of the Crash Room.

Tolman sat on the other side of the glass wall at the main desk of the ER behind the counter, presiding there like a judge in court. One red and one black cellphone sat on the desk. The nickel-plated .45-caliber pistol that had killed Marcus lay next to the phones.

The Life Clock clicked closer to 9:57.

Drake prayed as he felt the menace of death approach so near he could taste, feel, and smell it. *Prayer?* Did he deserve divine help? Praying showed more faith than he sometimes felt.

He hoped for God's or law enforcement's help but knew he couldn't count on anything beyond himself and his fellow doctors and nurses. The Captain had just come off being on a ventilator, Miss Roberta battled dementia and a newly fractured hip, and the thirteen-year-old autistic boy and his fear-shocked mother were not warriors. The self-focused Phoenix and her "you need to protect me" attitude proved she thought herself too precious to join in their fight.

It would be up to Drake, Bart, Rizz, and Trist. Bart was a giant and had proven today that his longstanding maltreatment of coworkers masked courage and character. Rizz's bravery was beyond doubt, but his spinal cord injury left him barely able to stand. Trist was an unknown. He was burnt-out and mad at the world, but he'd gotten in Tolman's face and called him out after the detonation in the city. He knew guns but was small and scrawny. The odds of him overpowering any of the terrorists were not good. Patti and Tracy were nurse-tough and brilliant, but physical combat was not their thing.

They faced a gang of terrorists, most large and physically imposing, and all heavily armed. Any one of them could potentially kill Drake and his entire rag-tag collection of fighters in one sustained blast of weapons-fire.

A lump lodged in Drake's throat. Would he ever see Rachelle and the kids again?

It was time to ignore the doubt and second-guessing. Time to silence the nagging voice that questioned his every move and thought. Time to unleash the part of him that had reveled in brutally injuring or killing those who'd hurt or threatened the people he loved.

The light shifted as Bart Rainey moved next to him.

"I'm changing my surgical approach, ER." The massive surgeon said under his breath. "No anesthesia, operating with my fists, and creating as much uncontrolled bleeding as possible."

Bart wore a white coat over his scrubs and had his surgical cap in place—a fitting battle uniform for this hard-to-understand man whom Drake had started to think of as a friend.

Leaning against the counter just a few feet from Tolman stood Red —the opponent Drake least wanted to see near the extremist leader.

The enforcer was huge and brutal. A pistol was jammed in his belt and his rifle lay on the counter next to him. Thoughts of what Red had done to Antoine stoked a scream for blood that challenged Drake's focus on his critical target.

Drake checked the flashing Life Clock. One minute and counting. Now was their time.

Images of Rachelle and the children flickered through his head.

Thoughts of his younger brother Kevin, struggling with flailing arms and crutches to propel his palsied body. He never complained. He never quit. Drake had turned from him, and it had led to his death—he would never again fail others as he'd failed Kevin.

Drake thought of the policewoman killed at the side of the highway, and Marcus, the senator's murdered friend and bodyguard. And the tens of thousands that the madman was ready to sacrifice in his deluded quest for revenge and glory. Drake saw the terrorists for what they were. They fueled within him a rage that roared with blast-furnace intensity. It fired his muscles, trip-wired his reflexes, and slammed the door on any thoughts of hesitation or mercy. He'd killed before. He'd crushed the life out of others who'd posed a mad-dog threat to others as the terrorists did now.

Drake could be defeated only one way—by his death. He would never give up.

He used the senator's body as a screen and pulled back the sheet uncovering the two cardboard blowguns he'd chambered with his spinal needle darts.

He looked at Bart and nodded toward the clock. Bart waggled his eyebrows. The surgeon stood as fearless as he had when he'd stepped out of the flight elevator and faced Red for the first time.

"Remember I got dibs on the creature who killed Antoine," Bart said. "That bastard is mine."

～

Minor trauma area

Rizz had a towel over his lap on the wheelchair. He'd put on a white coat to give him more cover. He smiled inside, thinking that it also made him look like the doctor his mother was so proud of him being.

He looked at the clock. "Let's roll" time approached.

He scanned the room. His crew was ready.

Patti, the nurse and woman too good to be true. Funny, smart, courageous, and someone who stirred in him the kind of feelings he shouldn't have for her. She was too nice. Too lovely. Too genuine, deep, and vulnerable for someone like him.

He sighed. Minutes from potentially being killed and facing a battle that would cost or save countless lives, and he was obsessing about a woman.

But of course—the wonders of women dominated his world, and one or more of them always had.

In this face-reality moment, he had to acknowledge the truth about his feelings for Patti. He was a coward. He feared rejection, as would almost certainly be the outcome if he made his feelings known. And if somehow he did get close to her, when she inevitably dumped him, it would deliver the kind of hurt he'd vowed to never risk experiencing again.

The seizure kid caught Rizz's eye. The teen interrupted his hand movements and riffed a few seconds of air guitar, then smiled.

"Right on, Newman," Rizz said with a thumbs-up.

The boy's mother sat with rosary in hand, eyes closed, and her lips moving. Rizz hoped her prayers would help.

The cart that had been Antoine's lay empty. Someone had drawn a cross and a flag on the bare sheet there. *Semper Fi!* He'd been so much more a man than any of the terrorist lowlifes.

Phoenix—he'd given up on her. Perhaps her self-absorption was from the shock. Rizz felt guilty judging, but something about her wasn't right, and he believed it had started long before today. She'd retreated into herself...or was solely *into herself* where she'd been from the start?

The creature who'd assaulted her and killed Cecil was disgusting even by the subhuman standards of the Aryan white supremacists. Seated at the door with blackened eyes, a swollen face, and a gauze-packed nose, the hyena held his weapons at the ready.

Pockmark approached the hyena from the corridor. Rizz would never forget the ex-con's laugh at the rumble of the remotely detonated bomb and the tremors it sent through the ER. The thought of men, women, and children burned, maimed, or killed provided the creature amusement.

He and those party to such barbarism deserved to die.

The terrorists seemed increasingly alert. Perhaps the giant

redheaded ape's barbaric attack and murder of Antoine had excited them.

Maybe they sensed time was running out and their illicit reign would soon end. Rizz checked the clock. He hoped they were right.

He'd do all he could to make them corpses within the next several minutes.

CHAPTER EIGHTY

Juanito Morales directed the spray of water at the rear of his truck. He'd pulled into the driveway well after dark. He'd started the tree work and stump removal job just after sunup and hadn't finished until twenty minutes ago. His muscles ached, but the dollars he'd earned made it the kind of job he'd take every day.

His mother was eager for him to start at the U of Minnesota in a week, but Juanito was having second thoughts. He squinted in the brightness of the single flood light illuminating the driveway of their St. Paul home as he finished hosing the mud off the new paint job he'd done to the old Ford F-250. He had an interest in engineering, but the money he was making as a landscaper and general contractor was big time.

His skills and the graduation present of the truck that had been his father's had opened the door to big money working this summer. He had so much business, he was bidding jobs on the high side and all anyone said was "When can you start?" He'd been thinking about getting a plow and hiring a couple of good workers for snow removal during the upcoming winter. Nineteen years old and being able to bring home real money year-round would really help the family. Maybe college could—

His phone sounded. He reached in his pocket and opened his outdated flip phone.

"Juanito, it's Uncle Tomas. Listen to what I say and then move faster than you ever have. Get your mother and little brothers and sister out of the neighborhood right now. I'm at the station and just received a report that there's a truck bomb within several hundred yards of the house."

"A bomb?"

His uncle Tomas, a St. Paul police officer, sounded scared, and he was never scared.

He said the truck bomb could blow like the one in the Minneapolis suburb. Juanito had heard about that craziness minutes earlier on the radio when driving home. Terrorists had taken over the hospital ER in downtown Minneapolis and set off a huge bomb. Juanito had seen black smoke and he'd been miles away. If not for his chain saw, he likely would have heard the blast.

Juanito raced inside and told his mother. She bossed, her voice shrill, as she loaded Angel, Miguel, and Maria into her car under the driveway light. She squeezed him hard, kissed him, then jumped behind the wheel.

"Tio Tomas said traffic is bad, but it is safest to head for the highway and go east," Juanito said.

Looking pale, she slammed the door and started the car.

Juanito yelled through his window as he climbed in his big pickup. "I'll be right behind you."

She pulled out and took a right. He followed.

His uncle said trees, traffic, and wires had kept first responders and a helicopter from getting to the truck. If triggered, they expected an explosion, fire, and poison gas that would take out a large area. An east wind had picked up and would spread the airborne poison.

Up ahead, he saw the brake lights of his mother's car stopped behind a line of cars jammed up trying to get onto Shepard Road. Oh no! Which way could they—? His breath froze. In that instant the realization hit him. Based on his uncle's description, Juanito recognized where the truck bomb must be.

He slammed on his brakes and stopped, his hands clenching the wheel so strongly they hurt. His chest tightened as if in an icy grip. His heart drummed.

Before his father had finally passed from the cancer, he'd said, "A man takes care of his family and neighbors. Anyone who fails to do that is not a man." He'd heard Tio Tomas say, "Police, fire, and medics do not run from trouble—they run toward it." Juanito swallowed and made the sign of the cross. He cranked the wheel, reversed, and made a T-turn, pointing his truck in the opposite direction. He slammed the gas pedal to the floor. As he hurtled past their home and toward the river, he saw the taillights of cars backed up and blocking the road ahead. Word of the truck bomb must have spread. No wonder responders had been unable to get to the site.

Without hesitation, he powered the big pickup over the curb, and his headlights swung over houses, gardens, and lawns as he drove through the front yards toward the end of the block.

He blared his horn, launching left over the curb onto the cross street that paralleled the river. After less than a block he jumped the curb on the right and went off-road into the brush, bushes, and unkempt grass of the undeveloped land adjoining the river. His headlights bucked as he smashed into, over, and beyond a wire fence blocking the support of the Smith Avenue high bridge and the electrical power station. He winced as the paint job and body work on the truck he'd done was demolished.

His headlights lit up a huge tanker trailer parked under the base of the bridge adjacent to the power plant. He slammed on the brakes, dust rising in the beams of his headlights.

Juanito swallowed, his mouth dry. An explosion here could collapse the high-traffic bridge, take out the power plant, and spread airborne poison throughout the crowded neighborhoods where most of Juanito's friends lived.

He dialed 911 as he jumped out of his truck and approached the huge tanker that crouched like a mechanical beast in the beams of his truck.

"I'm Juanito Morales. My uncle is Tomas Morales of St. Paul Police.

I'm here at the truck-bomb site by the power plant and Smith Avenue High Bridge. I'm for real. Get me the bomb people." *Please believe me!*

The 911 operator did not hesitate. Seconds later, a calm voice came on. "FBI explosive technician here. You're on the scene? What do you see? Can you send video?"

"No video." Juanito told him what he saw.

"We have no time," the bomb specialist said. "Do you see a metal box-like housing near the front right tires of the trailer?"

He stepped forward and looked. "Yes. It's got a huge lock on it. The steel of the box is thick." It looked like the metal box had been spot-welded onto the trailer frame.

"On the other trucks, the trigger phone and detonation load was inside that box."

"I get it, but what can I do?' Juanito heard his voice climb. His temples were wet with sweat, despite the coolness of the night. His heart pounded as if he'd run a mile.

"You need to get inside the box. The police used Jaws of Life devices to open the others."

"I don't have anything like that," Juanito said as he raced back to his truck. "If I can get in, then what?"

"Cut the wires or disable the phone any way you can. Be careful getting in, there's a detonation explosive in the box."

"Detonation explosive?" Juanito powered his truck up to beside the steel box.

"The phone triggers the explosive in the box, which then detonates the entire trailer. The box bomb triggers the weapon of mass destruction."

Weapon of mass destruction? How far away had Mama, Angel, Miguel, and Maria gotten?

The FBI man's voice returned, speaking rapid-fire. "Reports of gunshots in the ER. It's going down." The voice was no longer calm. "All I can say is, get that box open and destroy that phone immediately, or you and a lot of other people are going to die."

Juanito jumped out and grabbed a pickaxe from the bed of his truck. He raised it above his head and smashed the huge lock. The hardened steel padlock didn't even have a scratch.

No way could he pound it free. His stomach dropped, his throat clenched.

He screamed into the night sky. "Madre de Dio, help me!"

CHAPTER EIGHTY-ONE

Telemetry area

Trist stood alone behind the nurses' counter in the telemetry area. The two executives remained sedated and stable, the beeps of the cardiac monitors steady. His years as a locums temporary doc made him always an outsider. Whether working in level one trauma center ERs in big cities or in the ERs of small hospitals in towns in the middle of nowhere, he kept to himself.

Screwed over by asshole patients and their greedy lawyers, his life ruined and pushed to bankruptcy by false malpractice claims, the thieving of the IRS, and divorce from a greedy bitch of a wife, he knew without doubt that people were overrated.

Trist held one of the two-foot-long sections he'd unscrewed from an IV support and checked the stainless-steel bar's heft. He'd stashed one other under the sheet of one of the executives' beds. Everything would depend on whether he could take down one of Tolman's scum and get his gun. He slipped his fabricated weapon under a pile of lab printouts on the desk behind the counter of the nurses' station.

Rizzini, Drake Cody, and the nurse Patti had all taken shifts caring for the acid-exposed executives. Getting the VIP patients to the hospital had been essential. The case reports in medical journals described that hydrofluoric acid typically did not kill quickly—but it could have happened. He didn't want to think about the execs and the senator all having died at the scene.

Drake Cody starting ECMO in the ambulance to keep the senator alive was incredible. Trist could not have imagined making that intervention. Drake Cody was a sanctimonious prick, but a damn good doctor.

His lecturing Trist on how every dirtball who chose to abuse the ER deserved to be treated like a prince had been tough to stomach. Cody would change his view after more years taking abuse from non-paying and ungrateful patients—no matter if they were rich or poor.

How would the hotshot young doctor feel after a couple of decades of being screwed over by asshole patients and their lawyers, being ripped off by both an ex-wife and the IRS, and working to exhaustion round-the-clock trying to get out of debt? *Welcome to my life.*

Somehow everything had come together to put Trist in this ER at this moment. After all that had unfolded, his future—his entire life—came down to what happened in the next few minutes.

He'd worked too hard for too long to end up a fatal statistic or a sidebar to a terrorist atrocity carried out by a maniac leading a team of degenerates.

It was as Drake Cody said—in order for Trist to live, Tolman Freid and his crew needed to die. Trist had mixed feelings about Cody, but right now anyone who kept Trist alive and helped make Tolman and his goons deader than dead was okay.

The pockmarked con entered Trist's area.

Trist eyed the man's weapons. The Glock 9-millimeter on Pockmark's belt was the 14-shot magazine model. His long-arm was a Remington semiautomatic 12-gauge shotgun. Not good for precision work, but loaded with double-aught it could cut down a lethal swathe among an attacking group. These militia were maladjusted cretins, but they knew their tools.

Chest tight, mouth dry, Trist didn't know if he was more excited or scared. His future came down to what happened now. He glanced at the clock.

Only moments until "let's roll."

This moment was such a rush. It was his life's ultimate win-or-lose moment, and some things were going his way. Pockmark was the least physically imposing of the crew though smarter than the others. He was the crew's electronics and communications man. But Trist had recognized the man as a druggie. He'd engaged him in conversations about weapons several times. He'd noted the man's large-caliber handgun preference. With them both being small men and gun-lovers, Trist had shared, "It's not the size of the man with the gun but the size of the gun with the man."

Pockmark had laughed and given a thumbs-up. The idiot likely thought Trist admired him.

Trist's heart hammered out the time. *Fifteen seconds!*

"Hey, big gunner," he said. "I have some pain pills here these patients don't need." He indicated the sleeping men. "Percocets. Interested?"

"Percs—no shit?"

"Sure. Help yourself." He set the small white cup on the desk next to him. He turned his back and bent over the desk, shuffling the printouts. His body coiled and his senses amplified. *Do it, loser.*

Footsteps on the stone floor and a slight shadowing of light confirmed the ex-con had drawn near. Behind his white coat, Trist grasped the jumbo spray can of alcohol disinfectant. His heart thundered. He sensed the tiny scuff sound of the medicine cup being picked up, followed by a swallow. *Now!*

Trist pivoted, depressed the spray button, and thrust the can in Pockmark's face, blasting a geyser of chemical sanitizer into his face.

Pockmark screamed and pawed at his eyes.

Trist grabbed the steel rod from under the papers and swung it like a riot policeman's baton. The impact of steel on skull sounded like an aluminum bat hitting a baseball. Pockmark went down.

Trist jumped on him, ripping the gun from his belt. He jammed the barrel under the man's chin and squeezed the trigger twice. Pockmark's face and head exploded in the deafening blasts.

Adrenaline stoked him. Pure energy pulsed through his veins. The smell of blood, the sulfur-tinged bite of the fired rounds. *Hell yes!*

Screw guilt or remorse—he'd never killed before and he dug it. A gun in his hand and live targets ahead.

Tolman Freid had big plans. Trist's were bigger. Like a hard-on dream, he'd shoot his way to security and come out a winner on the other side.

He'd survive and live free while Freid and his scum died.

CHAPTER EIGHTY-TWO

The minute hand of the wall clock twitched. The final sixty seconds swept forward. *This is everything!*

Rizz took deep breaths and visualized success like when he'd been a college sprinter waiting for the starter's gun.

Pockmark had left the minor trauma room a minute earlier, leaving only the hyena. Their captor sat in a chair with his back to the wall, his automatic rifle in hand, pistol at his belt. His deformed, swollen face and the gauze rolls protruding from his nose made him look more like a hog than a hyena. His head was tilted back and his lids half-closed.

Fifteen feet separated Rizz from the man he must kill.

The Captain lay on the bed nearest Rizz's target, his body covered by a sheet and blanket. The grayish cast to his black features had lessened. His eyes were closed and his breathing easy—had the Captain forgot? He'd been hit by the redheaded brute and on a ventilator before that. Could he help?

Roberta on the next cot also looked to be asleep.

Newman's eyes were open. He sat on his cot near the far wall, his hands doing their repetitive thing. His mother hovered, standing near him, her dark eyes bright and darting.

The second hand swept through the final seconds. Rizz swallowed the lump in his throat. How he'd love to have strong legs beneath him. He put that out of his mind. He had what he had and could not count on anything more.

He aligned his wheelchair yet again, then clenched and unclenched his hands, looking at the hyena. If they live, we die. No in-between. The final second approached. *Let's roll!*

From beneath the towel on his lap, he raised the foot-stirrup he'd removed from a pelvic table and converted to a slingshot. He fully drew back the elastic tubing, pinching the large metal bolt he'd chosen as his projectile. He took dead aim on the lolling Hyena's temple just above and forward of the ear. Rizz visualized the bolt penetrating the thin bone there and dropping the vile creature like a rock. His aim must be true. He held his breath, focused ...

As his fingers loosened, two gunshots sounded in rapid succession from the corridor.

The bolt launched as the hyena's head turned. The hardware missed the temple, hitting Hyena's mouth with a sound like pool balls colliding. He recoiled but he did not go down. Blood flowed from his flayed lips. He swiped one hand to the wound while scrambling to his feet. "Muthafuh—" He spit out fragments of teeth as he pivoted toward Rizz.

The instant after the release of the steel bolt, Rizz used his arms and shoulders to drive himself upward out of his wheelchair. Adrenaline and upper limbs strengthened by his months in the chair fired him upright. He drove forward on shaky legs that felt as if they were not his own. *Fifteen feet!*

Hyena swung his raised rifle.

Damn! Certain of death, Rizz continued forward as time stretched.

Would he feel the bullet? Would Patti live? Just as the hole of the bore showed like the pupil of an eye, movement flashed on the right. The Captain swung the discharge funnel of the fire extinguisher from under his sheets toward the hyena.

Shusssh! The Captain blasted the terrorist point-blank in the face with the fire-retardant powder.

The hyena rocked backward, raising an arm to his eyes, but he still did not go down.

Rizz powered forward. He grasped the Captain's bedrail, then grabbed the fire extinguisher and lurched forward in a staggering charge, raising the steel cylinder high above his head.

Hyena's eyes showed blood red in his deformed and now powder-coated face. Rizz tried to make his feet catch up as he lurched forward with the steel cylinder gripped in both hands.

The hyena's rifle swung. For the second time in a span of seconds, Rizz sensed his impending death.

Thwack! The bolt from the slingshot Rizz had given Newman hit Hyena in the crotch.

Hyena's rifle fired, the *BOOM* deafening. The killer groaned and doubled over, clutching himself.

Rizz collapsed forward, throwing everything he had into a two-handed, overhead slam. The base of the cylinder impacted the back of the bent hyena's head with a sound like a sledgehammer striking a melon. Rizz's hands returned a sensation like ice giving way under his feet on a frozen slough.

The hyena's face and flesh hit the floor with a sound like a wet towel.

CHAPTER EIGHTY-THREE

Rizz raised his chest and head from the floor as if doing a push-up, his legs unresponsive.

Hyena lay face down, his belly pinning his weapons beneath him. One arm lay bent at an unnatural angle. The back of his head was crushed like a stomped beer can. Blood and brain matter marked the powder-covered hospital floor. The fire extinguisher lay beside him, a scrap of scalp and gore on its edge.

Rizz heard a low keening and turned. Newman sat on the floor, hugging and rocking his mother's body in his arms. The bullet from the hyena's rifle had hit her, leaving brain and blood splattered on Newman and the yellow tile wall behind them. The teen's anguished eyes met Rizz's. "In front of me she stepped. She love me," he said. "Her I love." His anguished moans continued.

Damn these bastards to hell!

In the frantic moments other gunshots had come from the corridor. Rizz dropped to his elbows and clawed forward toward the hyena's weapons. There were multiple battles in this war.

The doorway shadowed. Rizz raised his head. The long-bearded crazy stood with a pistol aimed at Rizz's face.

The psycho-terrorist looked at the crushed skull, the blood, and the brain-exposed corpse of the hyena. He showed no more expression than if he'd spied a discarded candy wrapper.

Roberta cried out wide-eyed. "Oh, no!" She put her face in her hands.

The bearded crazy looked toward Roberta and the Captain in the cot next to her. He froze like a hunting cat spying a nearby bird. He held a large plastic bottle in his non-gun hand.

"They're the ones who want to hurt me," he said, keeping his pistol trained on Rizz. He swung the bottle, splashing Roberta, the Captain, and the sheets and blankets surrounding them on their guardrail-protected cots. The volatile lighter-fluid smell of acetone flooded the room.

Roberta sputtered and coughed. The Captain stared as if observing a species unseen in his intergalactic travels.

"The Voice warned me about you two." The bearded man flipped the bottle onto Roberta's bed, reached into his pocket and pulled out a lighter. "I know you can hear him. I won't let you hurt me."

"God no! Please!" Rizz struggled to free a weapon from under the hyena's mass.

"Don't worry. I know what needs to be done." The bearded man snapped the lighter and the flame danced.

He bent and the flame approached the linens swaddling Captain and Roberta.

～

MINUTES EARLIER

Phoenix sat at Patti's feet on one of the blankets they'd loaded into the minor trauma bathroom with the other materials.

Rizz had put her and Phoenix here as a last-ditch backup plan. If the group's first efforts to take down the terrorists failed, Patti and Phoenix would be alive for a final try.

Patti understood the all-or-nothing importance of taking out all the terrorists to assure their survival and prevent the deaths of others throughout the city.

If it came down to sacrificing her life to stop Tolman Freid, would she have the courage?

Phoenix had interacted less and less as the ordeal continued. Her reaction was perhaps understandable—but definitely cowardly and annoying.

Cowardly wouldn't help keep her or others alive.

"Are you ready to fight for your life?" Patti asked softly. "Take one of the weapons."

"You need to listen," the younger woman said. "It's critically important that I survive. Protect me as best you can. It's in everyone's interest. Perhaps someday you'll be able to understand."

"Good God, get over yourself, girl." Patti's empathy tank had run dry. "Pull your 'critically important' head out of your ass and get ready to fight. For yourself, for the rest of us, and for thousands of people in our city. If you can't do that, make sure you keep the hell out of my way."

No clock in the bathroom, but Patti knew it had to be "go-time" for the others any second.

Her heart raced like a scared rabbit's. Her mouth was dust dry and her chest tight.

Muffled gunshots came through the door, then a shout, a groan, a sound like jetting air, then a very loud gunshot followed by a metallic thump. More muffled gunshots. Then silence.

Seconds were eternity. *What is happening?* She heard a low wail like that of an injured animal. She'd held herself back for what seemed an eternity. Waiting required every ounce of her restraint.

Murmuring voices, Roberta cried out, and seconds later Rizz yelled, "God no! Please!"

Patti could hold back no longer. She exploded out the door with her weapon fully drawn.

RIZZ TRIED to free the rifle lodged beneath the bulk of the hyena but couldn't budge it without the use of his legs. He tried to get to his knees. *No time!*

He glanced toward the Captain and Roberta. The lighter's flame neared the drooping tail of their bedding, an instant away from turning them into human torches. *Please, no!*

The air pressure in the room shifted and the lighter's flame jumped with the sound of a door opening. Rizz and the bearded man turned their heads toward the bathroom. The flame paused.

Patti stood alone at the back of the room with her eyes locked and steady, the bowstring of the bow Antoine had created drawn to her cheek.

The fingers of her draw hand flared open. *Pffft!* A glistening streak flashed through the air.

Thutt! The stainless-steel shaft of the improvised arrow ripped through his throat and its blood-streaked tip extended from the back of his neck. The man's wild eyes went wide, and he froze as if caught in a single frame of a paused video.

He collapsed as if made of melting wax, his eyes blank and lifeless, the lighter still clutched in his hand, its flame dying as it reached the floor.

CHAPTER EIGHTY-FOUR

Two minutes earlier

His breathing slowed and Drake focused on those he needed to kill.

Not just needed, but wanted to kill. No pretense of being forced to take lives but a fierce hunger. A hunger to save his own life, those in the ER, and thousands of innocent men, women, and children who would otherwise be blown apart, incinerated, or poisoned. A hunger to save his own life and care for those he loved. His sinew and muscles gathered like a fully-drawn hunter's bow desperate for release.

The light changed as Bart shifted his position next to Drake in the Crash Room behind the senator's bed. The surgeon's towering mass, scent, and rapid breathing registered as if he were a bull readying to charge.

Tolman sat twenty-five feet away at the desk behind the counter, while Red leaned just to the right. The two uniquely dangerous brothers were by far the most formidable of the terrorists. Having them side by side for this battle presented the worst case possible.

Drake rested a hand on the senator's chest. He sensed coarse abnormal vibration as air was driven in and out of the good man's devastated lungs. The foul tinge of the destroyed tissues hung.

Drake eyed the Life Clock—24 seconds.

Drake and Bart gripped their dart-loaded blowguns. Drake took one last look at the flashing clock. His nerve endings tingled, his vision sharpened. He believed his strength, quickness, and killing instincts were enough to have a chance against any man one-on-one and barehanded. But that was not what he faced. He focused on the terrorist brothers, his vision sharpening and magnifying as if through a zoom lens. His breath came fast, his body flushed with molten heat.

He nodded to Bart. The big man winked.

It was time.

They stepped out from behind the senator together and advanced with blowguns raised to their mouths, taking dead aim. They blew, firing their wicked projectiles at the same time, then launched themselves toward Tolman and his massive brother.

Drake's senses registered everything heightened and razor-edged. Things unfolded as if in slow motion. The flash of Bart's spinal-needle dart streaked forward and buried itself in Red's left eye. The brute winced, but his pistol was already rising.

Drake powered toward the counter, supercharged, everything in crystalline focus.

His dart had buried itself in Tolman's upper chest. It did not slow the terrorist leader down. His .45 came up as Drake launched himself over the counter in a superman dive.

The brothers' two gunshots sounded as one. A lightning bolt of pain penetrated Drake's thigh as his hands closed on Tolman's pistol. The barrel's heat seared Drake's hand as he twisted the weapon, feeling the snap of Tolman's finger as the gun ripped free.

Tolman grunted in pain but struck Drake in the face with his other fist. Drake's vision blurred. His thigh screamed as if a steel rod had been plunged through it. His leg gave way like it were rubber. He clenched Tolman's gun in his right hand but backward and upside down. He swung the gun like a rock and connected with Tolman's jaw. The man went down. Drake shifted the gun into shooting position and angled the barrel toward Tolman's head, his finger tightening on the trigger.

Blam! Something impacted Drake's temple like a thrown brick. His vision erupted in spinning lights. Someone pulled at the pistol. He held on with all he had as the floor rushed at him, his vision going black.

FBI COMMAND TRAILER

Special Agent in Charge Dylan McGinnis held his breath as he listened to the exchange between the young civilian at the last truck-bomb and the bomb squad agent. It didn't sound like the kid could disarm it. If a response team got there they'd—

Damn! The clock hit 9:57.

"Shots fired in the ER! Shots fired!" yelled the headset-wearing tech, jumping to his feet.

Dylan's insides clenched.

"Two different areas," said the tech. "No. Check that. Now three different areas!"

The ER doctor's attack was not being easily put down—and the last truck was still not disarmed. *Son of a bitch!* If Tolman Freid felt threatened— Dylan grabbed the mike linked to the FBI SWAT team.

"Full entry now. Repeat—full entry now. Live fire all terrorists. Repeat live fire all terrorists. Put them down!"

Dylan hadn't prayed at any time during this action but he prayed now. As he did so, he considered that the Saint Paul site was about seven miles away. He would hear the explosion if the terrorists' weapons of mass destruction were triggered.

He hunched his shoulders and grimaced waiting for the sound—each second a forever.

CHAPTER EIGHTY-FIVE

Drake's mind had gone dark for just an instant, the blow to his head titanic. He recovered almost the instant he hit the floor. The gun was gone. His ears rang from the gunshots, his vision was blurred, and his thigh was pierced by a branding iron of pain. His look up from the floor revealed a nightmare.

Bart was on his knees, his jaw shattered, bloody, and gaping. His right arm hung limp, cardinal-red soaking the right shoulder of his white coat. He struggled to get up.

Red stepped into Drake's view in front of Bart, a fire ax in his hand. A trickle of blood marked Red's left cheek, and his left eyelid was pinioned shut by the needle that had penetrated his eye. The dart extended from the now-collapsed eye socket where it was lodged.

Despite his injury, the brute wore a smile as he looked at his titanic opponent's struggle to rise. He raised the fire ax above his head, his massive trunk and muscles stretching.

Bart tried to get to his feet, but his legs failed. He dropped back to his knees. He reeled, too battered to challenge the killing blow. He raised his arm and extended his middle finger toward the face of his executioner.

Red reared back an additional inch, the ax at its apex and his lone eye blazing.

A blur of motion and a woman's scream came from behind Red. The bloodied sharpened silver tip of a metal rod erupted from the brutal enforcer's mouth.

Red's eye went wide, his face blanched, and he hung frozen for a moment.

He pitched forward, revealing Tracy gripping the manufactured spear she'd driven from behind through the back of his neck and out his mouth. His giant body collapsed, his face and head hitting the floor with a wet, watermelon-bursting sound. Tracy went silent. Her hands clenched the stainless-steel IV pole as she leaned her weight on it as if to drive Red's face through the floor.

Drake rolled to all fours. *Tolman? Where?*

He bent and grabbed Red's pistol from the floor. He used the counter to pull himself upright, his leg unable to bear full weight. The sound of a body moving came from behind the desk. *God no!*

Tolman rose, took a step, grabbed Tracy from behind, and ripped her free of her spear. He clenched her in a one-armed chokehold, his nickel-plated .45 against her skull, her body a shield.

He pulled her behind the counter. Other than his arm across her neck, he was shielded. She clawed at his arm but was helpless in the big man's brutal stranglehold.

Footsteps sounded in the corridor as Dr. Trist burst into the central ER area with a pistol in hand. He spotted Tolman with the gun and hurled himself back into the hallway.

"Nice try, Drake Cody. I should've known you'd try something heroic but hopeless," Tolman said. The dart in his chest bobbed with his challenged breathing. "I'm getting short of breath—looks like you punctured my lung—but no matter. I'll still accomplish my goal. And if I let you live, I know you'll save me." He chuckled. "And you, Dr. Trist," Tolman raised his voice to reach the corridor, "I know you are desperate to live. I have no such constraint. Those who accomplish great things are winners—we live forever. History will recognize me— that means more than any amount of money."

Drake raised the pistol and tried to target the madman.

"There is no shot, Dr. Cody," Tolman said. "You'll have to kill the nurse to get to me. Take it easy. It will all be over soon." The red cellphone was in the hand of the arm that throttled Tracy. Her color was poor and she no longer struggled.

"If any of you survive, you'll be able to tell everyone you were there when Tolman Freid changed the course of history."

"Stop! I'll shoot," Drake said. There was no shot. *Please, God!*

"Don't do it," Tolman said. "Believe me, doctor, the death of one person close to you hurts more than countless strangers. Failing one you love will haunt you forever. I said good-bye to the only one I care about some time ago when the government took her from me. No one else matters." The terrorist's thumb moved onto the keyboard of the cellphone.

Drake thought of his brother Kevin's accident—the death that haunted him.

He had no shot at Tolman unless he shot Tracy first. The fate of innocent thousands was gripped in his hands. How many people would the terrorist's explosions kill?

Sacrifice Tracy or let untold others die?

He had no choice. He had to... *Oh God.* His mind pinwheeled.

Bart called out from the floor, his words slurred by his broken jaw. "Shoot, ER!"

In Drake's head, the ventilator and ECMO machines silenced. The beeps of the cardiac monitor stilled. Only the pistol mattered, its grip solid in his hand, Tolman's finger taut against the trigger as his thumb moved on the cellphone's keys.

Do it!

"Too late, ER. It's done. I've changed the course of history." Tolman released Tracy and she dropped to the floor, gasping, her hands at her throat. He raised the red phone like a trophy then let it fall to the floor.

Drake's stomach plunged in an unending freefall. Shrieks filled his head. Thoughts of the suffering of exploded, burned, and acid-destroyed men, women, and children overwhelmed him. *Oh, God, please no!*

He moaned, leaning on the counter to keep himself upright. *What did I let happen?*

"I knew you were not strong enough," Tolman said. "Your heart overruled your mind. You did not act fast enough. You're a good man, but you could never be the man history chooses to right great wrongs." He seemed to swell as he straightened and squared his shoulders. "I just triggered three devices. Twelve-thousand-gallon tankers loaded with hydrofluoric acid, jet fuel, and ammonium nitrate. Each at least double the power of my earlier display. Freedom is never free, and the price is always paid in lives. This day will never be forgotten." The mad man smiled as he raised his chin like a Roman emperor overlooking the masses. "And neither will I."

He put his pistol on the countertop and slid it toward Drake. The terrorist's posture changed. He bent, his breathing increasingly labored, the pink cotton tail of the impaled syringe bobbing with each heave of his chest.

He then raised his hands like a pastor addressing his congregation, his color waning. "I've accomplished my mission. Now save me, Drake Cody."

"I hope there's a special place in hell for terrorists," Drake said. He could save the man easily. The thought of the mass murderer preaching his righteousness at trial and beyond was an obscenity. As his finger tightened on the trigger something deep nagged at Drake—a question. How had—

Boom! Boom! Boom!

Drake flinched, his ears ringing.

Tolman jerked as three bursts of crimson appeared in a cluster centered over his heart.

Drake turned.

Trist stood at the mouth of the corridor, a massive pistol steady in his two-handed shooter's stance, the brief ringing sound of the ejected cartridge casings rolling on the ER's floor.

Tolman Freid fell backward, his smug smile Drake's last live image of him.

Drake's mind was on the truck bombs. *Where did they go off? How many dead?*

Drake had failed. Tolman Freid had succeeded in his inhuman mission of hate and depravity.

An explosion from down the hall rocked Drake. A crash followed and loud but muffled voices sounded from the corridor. An acrid stink reached his nose and froze his heart.

Hydrofluoric acid. *God, no!* He'd heard shots earlier as he and Tolman battled. Rizz? Patti? The others? He could only hope.

"Tracy, can you do it?" Drake yelled as he dragged his bleeding leg forward. Despite what she'd suffered, Tracy was already moving toward the Crash Room.

Drake grabbed Bart's arm and tried to pull the huge man to his feet.

"Trist, help me!" Drake yelled. "Into the Crash Room. Now!"

White mist billowed from the corridor, its deadly tendrils reaching for them.

CHAPTER EIGHTY-SIX

"Faster!" Drake yelled at Trist as they half-carried, half-dragged Bart toward the Crash Room. Each step hammered a chisel of pain into Drake's thigh. His feet slipped in blood pooled on the floor. It took all his strength to help Bart's staggering lurch into the Crash Room.

The advancing acid cloud snaked toward them, its bitter scent strengthening. No time!

Drake's contingency plan had seemed sound in theory, but the chaos of battle, critical injuries, and the fast-approaching poison challenged everything. "Light it up, Tracy!"

Tracy had already climbed up onto the bed in Crash Room bay four. Kneeling, she held a trash bin with papers overflowing its top. She extended her hand into the crumpled papers, then stood.

"Get under the counter, Bart." Drake shoved the big man toward the wall. Bart groaned as he went down but dragged himself under the counter. "Trist, help me swing the senator's bed alongside the counter. Watch the equipment and lines."

Orange flames climbed from the trash bin. Tracy raised it from the bed and held it near the ceiling. Trist helped Drake pivot the senator's bed and machines to create a protected space around Bart in the corner. The senator remained motionless, only the racing beeps of the heart monitor confirming life.

The smell of burning paper joined the acrid scent of the approaching hydrofluoric acid.

Drake grabbed the rolled sections of four-foot-wide polypropylene he'd collected from the decontamination room. He unfurled and draped them over the senator, Bart, and the counters, forming a tent-like space under and behind the senator's bed and the counter. He quickly anchored the wall edge of the protective plastic on the countertop with oxygen tanks and allowed the other end to drape over the senator and beyond onto the floor.

"Trist, control Bart's bleeding," Drake said as he secured his plastic tent, wincing with each attempt to bear weight with his gunshot thigh. Blood squelched in his shoe with each step. He anchored the base of the roll of heavy-gauge plastic under two additional oxygen tanks, draping the plastic around them so their outlets and trailing hoses remained within the tent.

"Tracy, you need help?"

A shrieking alarm sounded in response.

Two seconds later, water pelted Drake's face as if in a rainstorm as the fire-suppression sprinkler system kicked in, dousing him and the remainder of the Crash Room. Tracy set the trash can down and climbed off the bed.

"Hurry!" Drake yelled, holding the last flap of the plastic lean-to raised. She dove in as the bitter stink strengthened and the acid cloud surrounded the main ER desk and its leading edge advanced into the Crash Room. Drake collapsed into their refuge and adjusted the plastic under the tank.

"Masks on, cover yourselves with the sheets." They must not breathe any of the devilish acid. "Crank the oxygen wide open."

Tracy opened one tank as Trist opened the other. The hiss of oxygen blended with the sound of the machines and the drumming of the sprinkler system droplets raining down on their tent.

If they could flood their refuge with enough jetting oxygen while the sprinkler did what he hoped... Drake clenched his fists. If he'd reasoned wrong, they'd all suffer the same fate as the senator. Dread knifed his chest. *Please make it work!*

The hydrofluoric acid cloud billowing into the Crash Room met the fire suppression sprinkler's rainstorm output. Drake's studies and chemist background predicted that water should neutralize the hydrofluoric acid and precipitate it from the air.

The wall of mist entering the Crash Room appeared to pause. The tendrils that had entered began to thin and drop. The denser cloud outside the Crash Room near the main desk also thinned in the sprinkler output there.

"It works, ER," Bart said, his words slurred from the deformity of his deformed and obviously broken jaw. "It effing works!" The big man looked pale, propped against the wall as Trist pressed a torn sheet against his shoulder wound. Bart had lost a lot of blood.

"Oh my God!" Tracy screamed, pointing through the water-streaked clear plastic.

No! Impossible. Inhuman.

The man-monster Red was on his feet!

The bloodied stainless-steel shaft protruded from his mouth, his head's position fixed by the penetrating rod. He took staggering steps toward them, dragging his semi-automatic rifle in one hand.

The ravaged brute leaned against the glass wall at the Crash Room's entry, his chest heaving like a great bellows in the acid mist. He raised the weapon in wavering arms and with his remaining eye he aimed its massive firepower their way. The weapon swung. His face twisted in a macabre grin. The gun steadied.

BOOM!

A burst of scarlet exploded in the center of Red's face. He staggered back. His legs gave way as if kicked from beneath him. He dropped, ending propped in a sitting position. The steel rod supported his trunk like the leg of a tripod, with his head mounted at its point as if on a spike.

Drake turned, his left ear ringing.

Bart held the nickel-plated .45 in his non-injured hand, the barrel less than an inch from a small hole in the water-streaked plastic.

Bart shrugged a bloodied shoulder. "Told you I had dibs on that freak." His arm dropped. "Blew him away left-handed with one arm as good as tied behind my back." His voice faded. He looked toward the grotesquely situated corpse. "Kiss my ass, loser." He stared silent for a moment, then spoke so quietly Drake had to strain to hear. "Damn, I'm good." He closed his eyes. "Tired though."

Tracy had an IV and meds in a bag with her and went to work starting fluids and treating the bleeding big man.

Trist turned to Drake and started to wrap a sheet around Drake's thigh above his wound. "We need a tourniquet on that. You've lost a lot of blood, too."

Drake was water- and sweat-soaked, his leg ablaze with pain that somehow felt far away. In the frantic scramble he'd had little chance to think about Rizz or the others. The gunshots that had sounded from the minor trauma area while Drake fought Red and Tolman were not a good sign. Were Rizz, Patti and the others alive? Had they been able to execute his plan to protect against the acid?

No more gunshots from the hallway. The sounds of the sprinkler drops on plastic, the ventilator, hissing oxygen, and the steady beeps of the senator's heart monitor continued. The metallic-sulfur bite of the spent round Bart had fired and the coppery, raw meat smell of blood and injured flesh met Drake's nose.

Muffled voices came from the corridor outside the Crash Room and grew louder.

Hazmat-suited bodies showed on the other side of the glass wall of the Crash Room through the rivulets of water streaming down the plastic wall of their sanctuary.

Their rescuers had come.

He would live.

Apprehension pressed down on him like a two-ton weight.

The immensity of all that had happened in the last few minutes continued to register. He worried for Rizz, Patti and the others—and so many more.

His throat clenched and a hollowness cratered his chest as if his heart had been ripped from it. Tolman had triggered his instruments of death.

Countless innocent men, women, and children had been killed or were at this moment enduring burns, catastrophic injury, or the agony of the deadly acid.

Drake lay injured, unable to help as people suffered, their Life Clocks ticking away the seconds.

His failure had allowed Tolman to accomplish the horror that was his twisted dream of glory.

The terrorist had won.

CHAPTER EIGHTY-SEVEN

Aki's inhalations and exhalations sounded Darth Vader-like in the hazmat suit with its self-contained breathing apparatus. His stomach rose, then dropped, as the flight elevator stopped at the ER level. The doors dinged open. The tactical team's entry through the shaft into the ER had triggered one of the terrorist's rigged explosive and acid release devices but not rendered the elevator inoperable.

Aki stepped into the ER corridor with three others garbed as he was. Through the droplets and thinning mist, he spied one downed body near the counter of the main ER desk. The sprinklers caused rivulets to run down his mask.

The first tactical operations wave had confirmed that all known terrorists were dead. The status and care of the ER staff, the senator, and other patient captives was the focus of the second wave's action.

Residual hydrofluoric acid continued to be purged. The sprinkler systems remained in operation, and exhaust venting had been initiated. SWAT had used a single entry point, so only one of the terrorist's ER-access rigged explosive and acid devices had been triggered. The remainder were being disarmed.

A fully geared SWAT member stepped out of the nearest doorway and waved an arm Aki's way. "In here," he said.

Aki's breathing rate increased. His faceplate fogged and cleared with each breath as he entered what he knew to be the minor trauma area. Three bodies were sprawled in the room among the patient beds. A hazmat-garbed figure with MEDIC printed across the back stood in the rain-like downpour near a closed door at the back of the minor trauma area. Aki approached.

"I'm Detective Yamada. What've we got?" He had to speak up to hear over the sounds of his air delivery.

"I'm Russell. I'm a Memorial Hospital paramedic and member of the regional FBI technical support team. I just established contact with some patients and staff." He leaned close to the door and spoke loudly. "I'm a paramedic. You're safe now. Is anyone in immediate distress? Are you all breathing okay?"

"Russell, it's me, Patti, charge nurse. Minor injuries. No distress. Breathing good. Have oxygen tank and have kept the doorway sealed with linens."

"Strong work," Russell said. "How many of you? FBI team is in control. We're clearing the department of hazardous substances and preparing to get you out."

A male voice answered, "There's five of us. We're packed in here like clowns in a circus car. Damn glad to hear your voice." It was Rizz. Dr. Michael Rizzini.

"Glad you're all okay," Russell said. "Just sit tight. We're doing what needs to be done to get you all out safely."

As they had been speaking, three other hazmat-garbed individuals had entered the room and were setting up rescue equipment.

"Can you stay here?" Russell asked Aki. "I need to check for others."

It was not until that moment that Aki put together who he was with. He knew of Russell by reputation. And had been reminded by the grim news shared among law enforcement since the Maple Grove policewoman's execution at the side of the highway.

"Russell, I'm so very sorry to hear about the death of your lady."

Russell's face was visible through the mask. He stared toward Aki, though he did not seem to see him. Pain etched his eyes.

He hurried off to care for others.

CHAPTER EIGHTY-EIGHT

Drake lay on an ambulance gurney with IV fluids running, as did Bart, nearby. The big surgeon's legs extended well beyond the gurney's edge. He looked pale and his eyes were closed.

Drake clasped the phone in his wet hand as he spoke. "...everything else is as I said. ECMO is keeping him alive, but he's failing." Tracy was bent over the senator, her brow creased. "Do you accept the senator in transfer? Can you mobilize a team as I suggested if we get lucky? I can't see any other chance for him." Drake paused, pain and a profound heaviness making holding the phone to his ear a chore. "Yes, I can hold." *Hurry!*

The Memorial ER waiting room had become the care and triage zone for Drake and the other injured survivors. Rescue workers in full hazmat gear moved in and out of the tent-tunnel set up at the entry to the core of the ER. It had only been a minutes since paramedic Russell had reached them. Drake had received no report on the death and destruction the terrorist's madness had wrought. He'd grabbed a phone from a rescue worker the moment he'd been rolled out through the protective tent-like tunnel and called University Hospital and shared his desperate plan.

Drake imagined University Hospital and all other metro hospitals were overwhelmed with casualties from Tolman's weapons of destruction. *Please say you can help him!*

The University doctor returned to the phone. "No assurances on your plan, but we accept the patient."

"I know you'll do your best. He'll be heading your way as soon as possible. His nurse will accompany him." So many things would have to fall into place, and the senator did not have much time, but he had a chance.

Drake let the phone drop, shocked at how drained he felt. He, and most urgently Bart, needed to get to a functioning hospital.

The refinery and oil pipeline executives had been evacuated from the telemetry area within their safety shrouded gurneys. Trist had covered them earlier, and with their oxygen masks and the overhead sprinklers' protection, they'd remained safe.

Paramedic Russell was on the radio. "Will be heading your way from Memorial Hospital with two male patients with gunshot wounds and blood loss. A shoulder wound for one and thigh for the other. Can't receive care here. We're loading now and coming with lights and siren."

Trist sat on a waiting room chair. He was staring off and smiling. *Smiling?* Maybe he was simply happy to be alive. Perhaps understandable, but something about the bitter emergency doctor increasingly rubbed Drake wrong.

Drake held his breath, waiting to see Rizz, Patti, and the others. He knew the assault he'd headed up had a high likelihood of resulting in release of the acid-loaded explosives. His plan to activate the sprinkler system made sense in theory but if wrong, he'd sentenced his friends to a horrendous death. Russell had reported they were alive. Laying eyes on them would confirm that Drake hadn't failed his friends.

But he'd failed countless others. His leg burned like fire, but the pain faded as his mind went to the edge of a cliff. His gut fell away, and his mind stopped short. He neared a vortex of dread, regret, and despair so black that if he entered it, he would not survive. The darkness loomed ever closer. Drake had allowed Tolman to detonate his weapons of mass destruction. *God, no!*

Victims of explosions, fire, and deadly acid—Hundreds? Thousands? In his mind he could see, smell, and taste the agony of each of those blown up, acid-ravaged, or burned—men, women, and children. *Oh God, the children!*

Russell's voice brought him back from the edge of the abyss. "Dr. Cody, Deb is getting our rig ready, and we'll be loading you and Dr. Rainey right away. How are you doing? You've lost a lot of blood." The paramedic turned to Trist. "Doctor, can you help with loading and transporting Dr. Cody and Dr. Rainey? We can use you."

"Use me, huh?" Trist sighed. "Okay, I'll help." He got to his feet.

Shrouded figures filed out from the ER's tent-tunnel, dripping with water. Two gurneys, a wheelchair, and three upright figures exited under protective barriers, guided by rescuers in full hazmat gear.

Rescue personnel pulled back the protecting drapes.

Miss Roberta sat wide-eyed.

The Captain was on his feet and stopped when he saw Drake. "What these people did is pure evil—even for your backward species." He frowned. "I'm most gratified to see you alive, Bones, but I sense your spirit is drowning. Do not despair. For one of your planet, your efforts are most admirable."

Drake's heart lifted at seeing that the Captain had survived yet again. But the mentally ill, chemically dependent, and mysteriously wise man was on target—Drake was drowning.

Next was Newman. The boy looking sunken-eyed and disengaged. His mother was not at his side. *Oh no!* The Captain moved next to him and wrapped an arm around the boy. The boy leaned into the grizzled street person and looked a little less lost.

Phoenix followed, looking inexplicably bright-eyed. She walked with head up and shoulders back. "Someone needs to get me a phone," she called out. "Right away."

Next came Patti, pushing Rizz's wheelchair with one hand, the other on his shoulder and with his hand over hers.

Drake's chest eased. *I didn't lose them.*

Rizz met Drake's eyes. Drake nodded, gave a thumbs-up, and then placed his hand over his heart. For once Rizz had no joke.

The rescuer at the end removed his hood and breathing apparatus —Detective Aki Yamada.

"We need to move," Russell started rolling Drake's gurney toward the ambulance bay.

Aki hurried over and grasped Drake's shoulder. "Good God, Drake! You did it again—a miracle in the midst of tragedy."

"No miracle." Drake's voice broke. How could the detective be smiling? "Tragedy is right. I failed, Aki. I didn't stop Tolman from triggering his weapons of mass destruction." How would he carry on? *Some wounds are beyond healing.*

"You're wrong." Aki vibrated as he moved alongside the gurney, the detective's positive emotion as puzzling as Trist's. "I just got the report from the FBI. All devices found. All devices disarmed. None of the remaining weapons were triggered. No one else was hurt."

"What?" Had Drake's ears played tricks on him?

"No explosions, no chemicals released. None of the remaining devices were detonated. They've all been found and disarmed, the last one within seconds of it being triggered." Drake's stretcher accelerated toward the waiting ambulance, and Aki in his bulky gear stopped. He called out final words, "A miracle!"

The meaning of Aki's words took hold—*all disarmed, a miracle*. It was true! Drake's body rocketed towards the surface—his pain gone. His mind catapulted from the darkness. Relief filled him like a first desperate breath after edge-of-death minutes under water and drowning.

He was saved. *Hallelujah!*

CHAPTER EIGHTY-NINE

The siren's wail died as the ambulance swerved. Drake's thigh spiked with the movement. His injuries and blood loss had made the fifteen-minute transfer from Memorial Hospital a fog. He was in no shape to direct his or others' medical care.

Bart did not react to the ambulance movement. He looked bad. Russell held pressure on the surgeon's gunshot shoulder. Dr. Trist had the tourniquet tight above Drake's thigh wound. Drake's leg and shoe were saturated. The ambulance smelled like a slaughterhouse.

"Worse than I thought," Paramedic Russell said. "It's a zoo."

From his spot on the gurney, Drake could see that the ambulance bays and driveway outside Sister Kenny Hospital's ER were overrun. Ambulances, private cars, and police cars had flooded the entry circle and were backed up around the corner. Medics, techs, and orderlies were moving patients on carts and wheelchairs, while a stream of battered, bleeding, and walking-wounded patients approached on foot. This hospital, the emergency medical system, and all other metro hospitals were overrun due to the Golden Valley detonation and Memorial's level one trauma ER being out of action.

"We can't get within a half-block," Russell said. "We're going to have to hoof it. How about right there, Deb?" He pointed.

"As good as we're going to get." She ripped the wheel over, came to a quick stop, double-parked, and was out the door in a flash. The ambulance's rear door opened. "What are you thinking, partner?" she said.

"Doctor Rainey first," Russell said. "He's more unstable. Help me, Deb and Dr. Trist. We'll get his gurney on the street, then wheel him all the way down the block to check him in. The tourniquet has Dr. Cody's bleeding under control." Cars honked and more wounded people streamed toward the ER. "He'll definitely need blood. Dr. Cody will be the same. They both need the OR."

Bart was not speaking, his eyes were closed, and his normal dark complexion was now sickly pale. The three-hundred-pound giant's body extended over both ends of the litter. Russell, Deb, and Trist strained as they wrestled the gurney and its load out of the rig. The support wheels extended and locked.

"Deb, you help me transport Dr. Rainey while Dr. Trist stays and keeps control of the bleeding from Dr. Cody's leg. Give me your radio." Russell set it on the linens near Trist and alongside Drake. "We'll be back as quick as we can, but it could take some time to get Dr. Rainey checked in," he said to Dr. Trist. "Radio me if his status changes." They muscled the gurney and its giant load toward the entry.

Trist climbed in the ambulance and closed the rear door.

"Who does General Patton think he's ordering around?" Trist said. "Bossy dude for an Uber driver with a first aid merit badge, isn't he?" Trist removed a heavily blood-soaked dressings from Drake's thigh and reached for a fresh pack.

"You're not funny." The more Drake was around Trist, the more disturbing he found him. Something was seriously wrong with the guy. "The man you're bad-mouthing helped save our lives when just hours ago, his girlfriend was killed by Tolman Freid."

"No shit. She must've been the cop Tolman dropped on the highway. Talk about being in the wrong place at the wrong time."

Drake's anger sloshed like boiling water in a jostled pan. He was weakened and in pain, but the surging hostility he felt was due to more than his discomfort. *There's something seriously messed up about this guy.*

"Well, at least she didn't inhale a cloud of hydrofluoric acid from exploding polyethylene balloons and end up getting barbecued from the inside-out like Mr. Fat Cat senator. Amazing you kept him alive. As they rolled him out, he looked like a roasted husk of corn that somehow had vital signs. A nice science project for you, but hopeless. No way he makes it."

Drake's last ER act had been to initiate transfer of the senator to the University Hospital. Drake had not given up. Trist and his 'hopeless' could kiss Drake's ass. *Polyethylene balloons?*

Thoughts flashed among the clouds in Drake's head like dry lightning.

The moment before Trist shot Tolman, the terrorist had said to him, "You plan to live, but money is not what it's about." The terrorists' takeover and other actions showed a deep knowledge and familiarity with the ER and its security setup. They'd infiltrated the ER's inadequate but not insignificant defenses with ridiculous ease. The claims of possible carbon monoxide exposure had gotten five of the terrorists into the ER as patients—the medically perfect phony complaint to guarantee admission to the ER.

The unease that had gnawed at Drake in his interactions with Tolman had not died with the terrorist killer. There were so many things that no trucking operation and farmer-militia leader from central Minnesota would or could know on his own.

Oh my God! It felt as if the gurney had disappeared from under Drake and he was in freefall—his stomach lurched like the ending of the flight elevator's high speed descent. *Damn. It all fit!*

Trist was not just a jerk and a bitter, burnt-out emergency doc but something unimaginably worse.

As Drake moved, he knew was in no position to do so, but his fury slipped loose. He gripped the thin doctor's arm and clenched.

"Ouch! God damn."

Drake used the last of his strength and pulled so they were face-to-face. "You're going to pay, you bastard."

"Damn, man! First, you assault me because of some homeless, drunken, psycho loser, and now you flip out because of a fucking minimum-wage medic. Back off, you sanctimonious prick!" He slammed Drake's wrist down on the guardrail, easily causing Drake's grip to break. His strength had bled away far more than he'd recognized.

He'd been battered, head-smashed, and shot. In his reeling state, it had come together, and he finally recognized kind of animal he was dealing with.

Drake's head rolled back. His vision blurred. Flashes of light like swarming fireflies lit his periphery. He kept speaking as if his answer to the puzzle might otherwise slip away from him. He couldn't let the asshole get away with it. He needed to communicate the ugly truth.

"I knew something was wrong about you," Drake said. "It just all came together for me. You were part of it with Tolman."

"Huh? What the hell are you saying?"

Drake saw Trist's pupils widen. He heard the phony inflection in the man's voice as he asked a question for which he already knew the answer.

Drake felt his head loll. He recognized with a chill that Trist no longer held pressure on his thigh and the tourniquet had been released. The meaty, metallic smell of his own blood flooded. The warm flow of his uncontrolled bleeding pulsed down his thigh. "Stop the bleeding. Hurry!" Drake called out as loud as he was able. "You're one of them. You're a terrorist!"

"Quiet down. I hear you fine." Trist opened the ambulance medical tray. "And don't worry about the bleeding. As the old joke says, 'All bleeding stops—eventually.' Ha!" He took out a 10 ml syringe. "Oh, I forgot. You're too virtuous to have a sense of humor."

"You helped Freid and his gang set up the takeover," Drake said, the exertion of speaking causing him to pant. "Insider information. Someone who knew hospitals and the type of security ERs have. Knew my ER. I know it was you."

"You're delirious from blood loss and pain." He removed a med vial and filled the syringe.

"Polyethylene balloons—that's what you said. Hydrofluoric acid eats through metal and must be stored in plastic containers."

"So what?"

"You weren't at the refinery event. You were busy in the ER. You said the acid was in polyethylene balloons. But I never mentioned the balloons. I didn't know that was where the acid was released from, but it fits. You couldn't know about the balloons at the refinery explosion unless you knew beforehand. You knew. You're as guilty as Tolman Freid."

"Kiss my ass, Dr. Sanctimonious Prick. And you're wrong. I'm no terrorist. I'm a businessman. I'm finally collecting on what's owed me. I helped Tolman with his delusionary bullshit. I was working in the ER where his wife was brought in when the government parasites ripped him off and destroyed their home. We were both victims of a system that sucks. We hooked up. He wanted justice. I wanted money. He was the only one who knew of my involvement. Whatever demons possessed him, one thing was undeniably true, and I sensed it from the start—the poor son of a bitch truly was a man of his word. I trusted him, but in the end I made sure he remained quiet."

Drake felt himself sliding toward darkness. Everything was shutting down. "You'll be executed or put away forever." His words had slurred.

"Dead wrong, hotshot. And how dumb are you to say this to me now? I have your life in my hands. I'll never even be charged because it's over for you. I now have fifteen million dollars free and clear, so you can kiss my ass as you die, boy. I'll finally be living the life I deserve."

Trist fit the syringe onto the remote port leading into Drake's vein.

"I did mess up with the balloon comment," Trist said. "You're a self-righteous son of a bitch, but you are smart. But your detective gig is over. As you die, why don't you give some thought to who the real smart one is?" He chuckled. "I'm going to inject a mega-dose of a paralytic drug, and rather than intubate and breathe for you, I'm going to watch you die. You might bleed to death first, as blood is pumping out of you like an oil well, but one way or the other you'll be a carcass long before your first-aid merit badge medic friends get back."

Trist depressed the plunger and a burning sensation flared in Drake's veins. He'd suffer the same horrific death he'd imagined in the past.

Rachelle and the kids filled his mind. So many plans. *Was I heard? Please, God!*

Air shifted and light brightened as the door to the ambulance swung open. Russell dove in, launching himself at Trist.

Trist pulled a pistol out of his white coat. Drake used his last flicker of strength to swing the radio he'd clenched with the transmit button pressed for the last few minutes. He hit Trist in the temple, allowing Russell to grab Trist's wrist and bend it back. The pistol dropped. Russell swung to a rear choke on Trist's head and neck. Russell's jaw was clenched, his eyes far away as his muscles strained.

A *snap* like the cracking of a giant knuckle sounded as ligaments sheared and the vertebra of Trist's neck gave way. Russell released and Trist's body slumped.

Trist's head hung twisted at an impossible angle. His eyes were open. As Drake stared into those eyes, his own vision fluttered. An uncontrollable wave of muscle trembling ran through him.

He could see, hear, think, and feel, but he could not move. He could not breathe. His gaze aligned with Trist's eyes. Drake witnessed the man's dread, knowing panic as the certainty of the paralysis and death his broken neck registered.

Drake sensed what was happening as a breathing mask came over his mouth and air was forced in his lungs. Some seconds later he felt a flush in his vein and a wave of calm washed through him.

He could not breathe but it did not matter. The hate that had threatened to cause him to burst into flames slipped, along with everything else, into a place of nothingness.

He was gone.

CHAPTER NINETY

Drake's eyes opened, his thoughts slow and fuzzy, as if his head were filled with cotton. He was flat on his back, head propped on a pillow. A discomfort registered deep in his throat and a swallow caused a twinge. His thigh ached. He smelled disinfectant. Jumbled images and sensations, flashes of recall—a nurse talking with him post-op. He'd been in the "I love everybody" fog of the OR's narcotic drugs, then he'd slipped back to numbness until awakening now.

His thoughts sped up. The back of the bed was partially raised. He looked around. He was in Sister Kenny Hospital. He'd scored a private room with carpet, stuffed chairs, a TV mounted on the wall, and a window view from one of the upper floors. The rooftops of nearby buildings and, farther on, lower apartment buildings and private homes stretched all the way to Lake Calhoun. The city's numerous trees glowed in their autumn technicolor and the morning sunshine.

His gauzy focus sharpened as everything that had happened came back to him.

"You've got an 11 p.m. to 7 a.m. shift to cover in the ER tonight, Drake." Rizz was in his wheelchair at the bedside, smiling. "Are you going to make it or are you going to wimp out?"

Drake reached out a hand and Rizz grasped it in a brother clasp.

"We made it, amigo. Holy shit, we took those bastards down."

"How's Bart? He wasn't looking good."

"I just visited him. Even with just getting out of the OR with the gunshot wound repaired and his broken jaw wired, he's somehow already giving the nurses mega-crap. Can you imagine having to care for him?"

"He's a warrior, Rizz. Wouldn't have made it without him. Glad he's okay. Was worried." His thoughts of the big man were mixed, but he'd learned that underneath his personality issues, the surgeon's heart was as oversized as he was.

Rizz grimaced. "The kid Newman got a real bad deal. His mother was killed. She stepped in front of him and took a bullet from the hyena. The boy is going to need a lot of help." Rizz shook his head. "Amazing kid. He saved my life."

"Murdering bastards." Drake said. Tolman Freid thought nothing of killing thousands of innocent people. The terrorist had truly seemed to care about his wife. If someone that messed-up could love, that's what it seemed he'd felt for her. But could someone so pathological truly love anyone? Mental health professionals would be analyzing the terrorist leader's pathological makeup for years. Drake had no idea how Tolman had become the monster he was, but one thing was certain—he was glad the mass murderer was dead. The thought of him arrested and given a stage at trial to spread his egomaniacal madness made Drake's lip curl. Tolman had been complex and even winning in some ways, but his soul was as ugly as those who'd joined him in his brutal quest. Red and the others were vicious, heartless animals whose hate-based tattoos and bigotry readily signaled their evil.

But as events had showed, Tolman, despite his normal outward appearance, was the infinitely greater threat. He was a fanatic, and his delusional egomaniacal notions had blackened his soul. He'd convinced himself he killed for a cause, and like all terrorists, he believed there was no limit on the deaths his cause justified. Terrorism—the intentional murder and brutalizing of innocent men, women, and children—was mankind's most abhorrent form of evil.

"Everyone else made it through the attack okay," Rizz said. "I was shocked about Trist—but then I wasn't. Bitter and burnt out, a gun and electronics freak, money-hungry, hated the IRS, and enraged about being screwed over by malpractice and divorce law. Plus, the terrorists knew too damn much about the weaknesses of our ER security system and how things worked—someone helped them. Looking back, it all fits. It makes me want to puke. How could a guy with DNA that twisted ever get to be an emergency medicine physician in the first place?"

"Tolman and Trist—other people didn't matter to either of them," Drake said. "It was all about money for Trist. He betrayed everything good he'd ever done for money. Sick." Wherever Trist's and Tolman Freid's minds had gone was a place Drake didn't want to imagine.

"Rizz, do you know where Rachelle and the kids are?"

"Why? You want to see them?"

"Hell yes, what do you—"

"Ha! Jerking with you, amigo. They'll be here any minute."

Drake's IV pump started beeping. Rizz turned his wheelchair, looked at the control panel, entered a few keystrokes, and the beeping stopped. "You and I are getting too much experience with medical care for ourselves. "

"Thank God for it. Without it, we'd both be long gone."

"A couple of negative things I need to share with you," Rizz said. "Annoying, not serious."

"Okay." What was Rizz's definition of annoying, after what they'd survived?

"First is Stuart Kline. The hospital's walking, talking turd of a CEO has been in the news. Check this out." Rizz handed Drake a cellphone. "I copied a small part from the newsfeed from this morning. A representative quote from our fearless leader. And there are TV interviews that are even more ridiculous."

Drake read from the screen. *The following is from Memorial Hospital CEO Stuart Kline after his harrowing experience as a hostage of the terrorists: "Someone asked about how I remained calm throughout the horrific events. I'll simply say I was able to continue in my usual leadership role throughout the terrorists' life-threatening actions. I'm widely being called a hero, but I'm too modest to accept those multiple accolades. I'm just a humble man lucky to be the CEO of a top-notch healthcare institution serving wonderful customers. My actions, call them heroic if you must, were nothing more than a reflection of my character and my hospital's ongoing commitment to our customers."*

"Oh, my God," Drake shook his head. "It would be funny if it weren't so twisted."

"Speaking of twisted, that's the other thing I wanted to give you a head's up on."

"What's that?"

"More like *who's* that," Rizz said. "Phoenix Halvorsen. Turns out she's a reporter for the Star Tribune. She's reporting accounts that have her as a combination Joan of Arc and Ruth Bader Ginsberg, with a touch of Che Guevara. Heroine and social warrior. She's co-opting Tolman's revolutionary spiel and spinning it her way. There's a sizable segment of the population who are lauding Tolman as the patriot and martyr he believed he was. She's using his illicit soapbox to spew some borderline anarchist shit. The usual 'US is evil and corrupt' bullshit. She's making shit up, Drake. It's sick."

"Damn her self-centered, entitled ass. We're going to have to set the record straight. I knew she had an agenda. Couldn't figure it out."

"Her 'you need to protect me' was bizarre. Incredibly conceited and condescending, but I figured she was just a spoiled little rich girl. They say the two biggest career draws for narcissists and power-seekers are politics and media. Tolman and Phoenix support that theory. She's all over the national news—a media hero."

"She has no conscience." Drake felt sick. Her warped accounting was to be the media record of what had happened? He let it go for now, but it was not right. "Unethical, self-serving journalists are a plague."

"Speaking of damage, I self-administered another dose of D-44. My spinal cord recovery is continuing. Thank you for that, brother."

"I'm glad, Rizz. You stepped in front of a bullet for me and mine like Newman's mom did for him. Your full recovery will make me one very happy guy."

"Not as happy as me." Rizz bounced his eyebrows.

"Did I see you and Patti looking kind of close as you came out of the ER? It seemed intense."

Rizz waved a hand. "Don't say any more, Drake. Let's not go there right now. It scares me, and I have to get my head around it. What else do you want to know?"

"How were Tolman's weapons of mass destruction found and disarmed? That's the greatest miracle of all."

"It was trucks. Four of them. Tolman had a trucking operation, and his weapons of mass destruction were converted massive tanker trailers. The first was the Golden Valley explosion we heard and felt. His kid Sigurd told Aki about the others, and the FBI tracked GPS transponders to the other three. FBI explosives ninjas talked first responders through disarming the first two. The story of the third one is incredible and being repeated about every two minutes on the news. Let's see if we can find it." Rizz took the TV controller in hand.

The screen lit up and Rizz hopped through several cable news channels.

"Here, this is it." He turned it up.

The anchorwoman spoke, "... and once again here is the remarkable footage that captured the heroic actions of a young Minnesota man. Eighteen-year-old Juanito Morales is a resident of Saint Paul. He learned of the last remaining terrorist device when warned by his uncle, a metro police officer. Rather than run, after getting his mother and three siblings on their way to safety, Juanito took his pickup truck and went off-road to the site shown here."

The image shifted to an overhead shot. "This helicopter view shows the major highway bridge and power plant adjacent to the Mississippi River. The massive tanker trailer was positioned at the base of the bridge, and young Mr. Morales drove his work truck up to the destructive device and dialed 911. FBI explosives experts over the phone identified that the triggering device was within a heavy metal box welded to the frame of the truck and secured with an impregnable lock. First responders had used Jaws of Life and other equipment to open and disarm the first two devices, but the young man had no such tools. With seconds remaining and the experts without a solution, the following footage shows what Mr. Morales did."

The image switched, still a helicopter view but infrared. A pickup truck adjacent to the tanker could be seen, as well as the heat signature of a body moving back and forth from the tail of the pickup to the tanker.

"Mr. Morales is the infrared image you see taking action here."

They saw the man identified as Juanito jumping into his truck. It accelerated briefly, then visibly jerked before continuing its sprint. As the truck advanced, less than a trailer length away from the tanker the screen ignited in a blinding flash originating from the space between the tanker and the pickup. As the screen cleared, the pickup veered to the side and stopped. The driver got out and collapsed on all fours.

The anchorwoman again filled the screen. "Truly amazing. The FBI, first responders everywhere, and now the entire country are applauding the courage and ingenuity of this young man. His work earlier in the day involved tree removal and pulling a stump out. He attached his thirty-foot work chain to the welded box that containing the weapon of mass destruction's triggering device and connected the other end to his truck's trailer hitch. He jumped in the truck and as he accelerated, the chain ripped the box free of the terrorist's massive destructive payload and dragged behind him. The triggering explosive was detonated by the terrorists only seconds after it was ripped free, but it did not succeed in igniting the trailer contents. His pickup was damaged, but thankfully Mr. Morales was unharmed. The weapon of mass destruction has been removed and rendered harmless by FBI specialists. Authorities identify that if it had been triggered, the death and destruction would have been incalculable."

Rizz turned down the volume. Drake was open-mouthed. It had been a miracle.

"By preventing those deaths and injuries, he saved me too, Rizz. I failed to stop Tolman and I couldn't have handled what that bomb would have done."

"You didn't fail, Drake. It was you, brother." Rizz's voice choked. "Our Flight 93 didn't crash and burn. You led the charge. Can't imagine anyone else ever who could have. We stopped the fucking bastards. Your idea also protected us from the acid. You saved our lives. Nothing of the badness that happened was your fault. Anything but."

Drake revisited the badness. It had started with a beautiful fall day ripped apart by the refinery explosion and the start of the senator's acid agony. Then Tolman's roadside execution of Russell's policewoman longtime partner and the killing of Marcus, the senator's friend and protector. Red gunned down the highway patrolman in the first seconds of the ER takeover, then later, Hyena stabbed Cecil, the well-intentioned protester. Newman lost his loving mother, and the honorable and courageous Antoine was horrifically killed. *Semper Fi, sir!*

A nightmare, but it could have been oh so much worse.

Senator Hayden Duren—where was he in his desperate struggle? Drake hoped and prayed he was still battling. Was there any chance that Drake's idea might—"

"Hey, check this out," Rizz said, turning up the TV.

"We have breaking news related to the remarkable events of the terrorist takeover and tragedy of the past twenty-four hours. University Hospital has released a report that Senator Hayden Duren, the initial victim of the terrorists' explosion and chemical attack, has undergone a heart-lung transplant. The donor was a teenage boy found barely alive near the epicenter of the Golden Valley terrorist explosion. Young Jeff Berglund suffered severe burns and blast injuries and had certified himself an organ donor on his driver's license. Jeff passed away in the late hours last evening and his tissue was a match for Senator Duren.

Jeff's parents say he was a beautiful and very special boy who especially loved nature and wildlife. Hospital representatives say the senator is in critical condition, but early reports are the procedure was a success."

Drake hung his head, joy and sadness whirling. His longshot hope for the senator had come to be. The cost was the life of a boy whose gift would demand the senator give his best every day in order to be worthy.

The flood of emotions flooding Drake could not be stronger.

"Drake!" Rachelle flew in the door with Shane and little Kristin at her side. Rachelle's warm and tender body, soft hair, and magical scent engulfed him. The kids grasped his arms.

The flood crested higher yet.

ACKNOWLEDGMENTS

The exchange, friendships, and fascinating info I learn from all those who contribute to the creation of each book make the process fascinating.

Special thanks to Jodie Renner who, once again, went far beyond the call of duty in helping me get this book to press — an outstanding editor and friend. Thank you to friend and author Douglas Dorow for his technical knowledge and key support in getting the book to print. It is an honor to be a member of a profession that includes such first-class people.

FBI Special Agents Thomas O'Connor and Christopher Langert shared graciously of their hard-earned experience battling terrorism and are heroes in all respects. I feel as if these protectors of us all offered friendship in addition to their incredible knowledge and experience. Any inaccuracies related to authentic FBI practice are mine — altered for story purposes or the result of my error. Please see this book's dedication for more detailed recognition of these agents.

Much appreciation to Taija Morgan for her first-pass editing and story support.

Thanks to Michael (Sears) Stanley, author of the award-winning

Detective Kubu Mystery series, for his detailed reading and on-target writing suggestions.

I also want to acknowledge those who provided technical expertise and feedback on *Insurrection* (any and all technical/factual errors are mine). I apologize in advance for overlooking contributors. Thanks to:

Cory Kissling (Paramedic, dignitary protection for four US presidents, story inspiration), US Senator Dave Durenberger, Mark Contrerato (Emergency MD, ECMO researcher, Medical Director – ambulance services), Rada Jones (MD, author), Tim Combs (25-year Police Veteran, Homicide/Major Crimes), Donna Hirschman, RN (ER, critical care nursing), Tom Wright, MD (anesthesiologist), Tom Peltola, MD (General/Interventional Radiology), Randy Istre ("eagle-eye" proof and beta reader – errors are mine), and Jan Coultas (beta reader).

Thank you to my family for their support.

My special gratitude to the nurses, doctors, and many others at North Memorial Medical Center and the Mayo Clinic who have been there for me when I needed them most.

At times, I compromise medical, law enforcement, and EMS procedure or protocol for the sake of drama and readability. I appreciate readers' indulgence.

Top acknowledgement is to you, the reader! I hope you found the book as engaging to read as I found it to write. I greatly appreciate any who share reviews and recommendations.

Thank you! Please keep on the lookout for the next book (www.tom-combs.com)

ABOUT THE AUTHOR

The people and experiences of twenty-five years as an emergency physician in busy, inner-city, level-one trauma center ERs provide the foundation for Tom Combs' unforgettable characters and riveting plots. Blessed with multiple friends and contacts on the frontlines of law, business, law enforcement, government, media, and business, he's well-positioned to write authentic stories of intrigue, suspense, and thrills involving people and forces that affect us all.

Tom lives with his artist wife near family and friends in a suburb of Minneapolis/St. Paul. Visit his website at www.tom-combs.com or contact him via email at tcombsauthor@gmail.com. He attempts to respond to all communications.

Reader reviews and recommendations are much appreciated. Having more readers enjoy the Drake Cody series is Tom Combs' fondest wish. *Nerve Damage*, *Hard to Breathe*, and *Wrongful Deaths* are internationally bestselling books one, two, and three of the Drake Cody series.

Tom is currently working on Book #5.